Clare Morrall

Clare Morrall was born in Exeter and now lives in Birmingham, where she works as a music teacher. Her first novel, *Astonishing Splashes of Colour*, was shortlisted for the Man Booker Prize of 2003. Since then she has published six novels: *Natural Flights of the Human Mind*, *The Language of Others*, *The Man Who Disappeared*, which was a TV Book Club Summer read in 2010, *The Roundabout Men*, *After the Bombing* and *When the Floods Came*.

The
Last
of the
Greenwoods

CLARE MORRALL

SCEPTRE

First published in Great Britain in 2018 by Sceptre
An imprint of Hodder & Stoughton
An Hachette UK company

This paperback edition published in 2018

1

A CIP catalogue record for this title is available from the British Library

Paperback ISBN 978 1 4736 4918 7

Typeset in Sabon MT by Hewer Text UK Ltd, Edinburgh

Printed and bound by CPI Group (UK) Ltd, Croydon, CR0 4YY

Hodder & Stoughton policy is to use papers that are natural, renewable
and recyclable products and made from wood grown in sustainable
forests. The logging and manufacturing processes are expected to
conform to the environmental regulations of the country of origin.

Hodder & Stoughton Ltd
Carmelite House
50 Victoria Embankment
London EC4Y 0DZ

www.sceptrebooks.co.uk

To Alex and Heather

I

Zohra Dasgupta emerges from the narrow pathway into a field of scrubby, stunted grass and stops abruptly, staring at the two railway carriages parked (is that the right word?) at the far end. She glances down at the envelope in her hand: Mr J. and Mr N. Greenwood. 'Well,' she says out loud. 'The name is appropriate.'

The carriages, linked end to end on an old rusty track, are almost submerged by trees. Clearly, no one here is familiar with the concept of pruning: the trees are spreading wildly – up, out, down – embracing the carriages with passion, wrapping them in vigorous greenery. Branches tumble on to the roofs, lean over the sides and take advantage of the light breeze to make their presence felt, tapping against the windows with a mischievous glee.

Zohra can't identify the trees. Her parents, who arrived in England from northern India before she was born, have little knowledge of English nature. When she was growing up, their expectations were that she would become a doctor, which wouldn't have required a familiarity with the distinguishing features of oaks, birches or horse chestnuts. Their infrequent talk of trees has been limited to mangos, banyans and the babools that dominated the tropical, thorny forests of their childhood, and any information that could be interesting or useful to Zohra is tainted with nostalgia: laments for the sun; sighs for the parents who died in their absence; memories of the fruit and spices that they can now buy in England, but are somehow never quite as good as they were in the old country.

Zohra crosses the neglected field and approaches the railway carriages, astonished by their existence barely a mile from the

Wychington estate. In all the years she's been going up there to help with the restoration of the old railway line, these carriages have been sitting here, unknown, unseen, rotting quietly away. If only Nathan and Crispin could see them.

Zohra has always been interested in trains. It's the one topic of her parents' reminiscences that she can tolerate. She's absorbed their conversations, trying to sift fact from sentimentality, not wanting them to know that she sometimes finds them worth listening to. They talk of a land where railways drove the economy, where no one would contemplate closing a line. 'All people pour on trains in India, Zohra,' says her mother. 'Like hot bean sauce over shredded lamb. Not possible for English girls to understand. They climb on roofs, hold on outside of doors, hang from sides. They would never do such a thing here.'

'Too cold,' says her father.

'Not permitted,' says her mother.

Her father had arrived in Bromsgrove in the late seventies, a young man full of aspirations, joining his uncle and aunt who had been building up Dasgupta's Corner Shop for the previous seven years. But when all three returned to Lucknow for his wedding five years later, his uncle and aunt, defeated by the cold, wet weather of the Midlands, decided to remain in India and the newly married couple came back to take over the business.

As with all her parents' discussions about their almost mythical home, Zohra can never be certain if the situation remains the same as it was when they lived there, or if Uttar Pradesh has moved into the twenty-first century. She would like to investigate further, but it would involve the Internet, and she can't even think about that without the familiar panic rising up inside her. She can no longer see a keyboard without a hiatus in her breathing. The sound of her father clicking away in the corner fills her with nausea.

She studies the carriages in front of her. They're clearly old, but not quite falling apart. The paint, dark maroon at the bottom, cream at the top, around the windows, is blistered and peeling, dappled green by moss, grey by mould, orange by streaks of rust that are bleeding down from the roof. In the centre of each carriage there's a nameplate, painted in large white letters, still decipherable. The left-hand one is Demeter, the right-hand one Aphrodite.

She can almost hear Crispin behind her, dancing with delight. She knows exactly what he would say: 'What's a bit of moss between friends? We can rebuild – no problem.'

And Nathan, unable to control his excitement: 'We've got to have them, we've got to have them, we've got to have them . . .'

The buffers between the two carriages are coupled with a chain and the corridors connected by an enclosed gangway. The door of the left carriage, next to the link, has been given the role of front door. There's a knocker – a large brass scroll, once grand, now dark and tarnished – screwed on just below the shuttered window, and an old railway lamp – the kind that signalmen would have once used – hanging from a nail beside the door, its glass almost completely obscured by cobwebs. There's no letterbox; no indication anywhere that either Mr J. or Mr N. Greenwood might be anticipating communication from the outside world.

All the windows along the side of the right carriage, Aphrodite, have blinds – horizontal, not all straight, and partially closed, so that someone could look out, but no one can see in. Demeter has closed curtains along its entire stretch. Zohra's mother would not approve. She spends a great deal of time and energy on curtains – perfect drape is very important to her, the only attainable Nirvana here in the middle of England, where the unreliability of British suppliers reduces curtain buying to a lottery of nail-biting uncertainty. These curtains have no drape. They're almost flat and a uniform cream, stained with grime and neglect, an exquisite match with the exterior of the carriage.

For the last twelve months, ever since she finished her training, Zohra has been driving along Long Meadow Road, often more than once a day, entirely unaware of the existence of the railway carriages. Long Meadow Road is exactly what it claims to be. Long. How would anyone know about this place? Maybe it was known to Zohra's predecessor, Ted, who kept the round for forty years until he had a heart attack and fell off his bike into the path of a milk float, but nothing else has ever turned up for a Mr Greenwood since Zohra took over the round. Not even junk mail – no local election manifestos, no catalogues of stair-lifts, no leaflets offering pizzas (although these tend to be hand delivered, so she doesn't actually know this), no adverts for cotton shirts. If nobody sends anything to a particular address in the country, if the house is hidden behind trees and at the end of a secret pathway, it seems that knowledge of its whereabouts will die out.

When the letter turned up yesterday at the sorting office – no postcode – she couldn't believe it was a genuine address. 'It must be a mistake,' she said, showing it to Bill, the manager. 'There aren't any railway carriages on Long Meadow Road.'

'You'd be surprised at what's hidden away round these parts,' said Bill, a large solid man with a bald head and eyes that crease easily into a smile. Now that the sorting office has to be open to the public for several hours every day to accommodate the ever-increasing number of parcels that can't be delivered and the resulting volume of complaints, he makes a good front man. Always unhurried, skilled at looking perplexed, he spends a great deal of time hunting for parcels that have gone missing, picking up anything visible on the shelves, even when it's clearly the wrong shape; opening and shutting drawers; eventually discovering them on the PO Box shelf when they should have been with the signed-for, or filed under C instead of Y. When people get angry, he just smiles. 'Might take some time,' he says. 'But I'd take it up with the senders anyway if I was you. Get a claim form from the Post Office.' For no obvious reason, he hates the staff at the Post Office and loves to complicate their lives. He's not as amiable as he looks.

'But nothing else has ever turned up for this address,' said Zohra.

'Loads of people don't do post any more,' said Rohit, the failed student who is always running half an hour late, looking up briefly from his frenetic sorting. 'Cheaper online.'

'But what about bills?' asked Zohra. 'Gas, electric, poll tax.'

'Council tax,' said Matt from the other side of the room. 'It's called council tax now. Poll tax brought down Thatcher. Same thing, but names matter.' He likes to think he knows things. He does pub quizzes.

'Online,' said Rohit. 'Like I said.'

'Long Meadow Road's definitely your round,' said Bill accusingly, as if she was trying to avoid delivering it.

'I never said it wasn't,' said Zohra. 'But I've never seen any railway carriages.'

'Check with Dougie,' said Matt. 'He knows everyone round these parts.'

Bill turned to glare at him. 'Are you implying I don't?'

'Come on, Dougie,' called Rohit. 'Wake up. Rise and shine. Zohra wants to know about the railway carriages.'

'On Long Meadow Road?' asked Dougie, finally taking an interest in the conversation. He's an elderly man, due for retirement, who takes too long to sort and starts out on his round later than everyone else. I'm thorough, he says when challenged. (Lazy, says Bill, who doesn't do empathy. Too confident of your impending pension.) 'That's the Greenwoods' place. Last time I went there . . .' He stopped working, sighed and scratched his head. 'Thirty, forty years ago when I had to do Ted's round for a while. Not like him to be off sick, but he broke his leg. Normally healthier than a marathon runner, he was. Till he dropped down dead. Never was much post for the Greenwoods – just the usual, circulars mainly. There's two of them, brothers. One's an accountant, works at Miller and Brownlee in town. I see him around, pass the time of day, that kind of thing. The other one, Johnny, he's a bit of a recluse.'

5

'Which side of Long Meadow?' asked Zohra. 'Which end?' She drove up the road in her mind. There was hardly anything there: hedgerows; ditches; gates leading to converted barns or directly on to fields; enormous farmhouses with generous block-paving drives and huge gardens. She knew them all. It couldn't be one of them. She'd spent enough time outside their security gates, struggling to squeeze large packages into their neat little post-boxes, to be thoroughly familiar with every house. Sometimes she had to ring the bell and wait, knowing perfectly well there'd be no one there except the occasional nanny if she was lucky, so there was time to examine the signed-for and speculate on the people behind the names. No Mr Greenwood ever featured in any of these scenarios. Could The Railway Carriages be the previous name of one of these houses, a name that no one used any more? Would she have to ring every bell, attempt to speak to every occupant (an exercise with little prospect of success) to ask if it was them? But she knew the answer already. Mr Greenwood, J. or N., didn't live at any of these addresses.

'Tennis players they were,' said Dougie. 'Not bad for a while, won a few matches. Me and my mates, we got it all worked out – we was going to book a box at Wimbledon, come the day, champagne, strawberries. But Nick and Johnny, they was like . . . well, they never really stuck at things. Got it from their old man – good-for-nothing, he was, couldn't earn a decent penny to save his life. What he had he threw away on the ponies, dogs, anything that moved, as long as he could place a bet. If there was anything left over after that, he was down the pub. Don't remember much about him, really. Died when we was kids. Bet the week's housekeeping on a horse called First Class in the Cheltenham Gold Cup. Reckoned the link was too good to miss – trains, see – then watched him tumble at the second fence. He knew he couldn't go home and face the missus, so he went and got drunk with his mates, usual thing. Fell into the canal. Not found till the next morning—'

'But where exactly is it?' interrupted Zohra. Dougie would go on forever if she didn't stop him. It was already nearly six a.m. If she didn't start soon, she wouldn't get home in time for a decent nap before helping her dad in the shop.

'Between Four Winds and The Woodpeckers.'

Zohra traced the lane again, walking rather than driving in her imagination, but still couldn't work it out.

Dougie resumed his sorting. 'You'll see it if you look. Best to park up in the lay-by, mind, and walk. You can't stop in the lane, nobody'd get past. Make sure the stream's at your back, then it's on your left, gap in the hedge, opposite side. Not far. Used to go there a lot once, but they stopped having us round after—'

'Okay, I'll give it a go,' said Zohra. She wasn't convinced, but she needed to get going.

'Might as well take that pile of Greenwood post in the corner,' said Bill. 'If you're going. Over by wrong addresses. Just circulars, adverts, that kind of thing.'

Zohra stared at him, exasperated.

'We gave up taking them ages ago,' said Bill. 'No letterbox. Nobody ever opened the door. We left cards, notices to collect, but they never came. Don't know how that one got through to you.' He glanced at it again. 'Proper letter, I suppose. Got to do something about that, don't you?'

'So you knew where the railway carriages were all along,' said Zohra. 'Thanks a lot.'

'No,' said Bill. 'Knew the address, not the location.'

'A logical response would be nice occasionally,' said Zohra.

'I'm the most logical person I know,' said Bill. 'It's everybody else what's got the problem.'

'Well I'm not taking the junk,' said Zohra. 'You can recycle that.'

To the right of the carriages, a metal bridge crosses the tracks and disappears into dense bushes at the bottom of a steep hill that overshadows the field. Beyond the bridge, the rusty, weed-smothered track curves round a bend and out of sight, heading for a railway system from the past. Could it be connected to the

7

Wychington line? She tries to create a map in her mind, link them up, but her sense of direction isn't good enough.

The track on the left of the carriages stops after a few yards, with an ancient metal barrier that looks too insubstantial to stop anything, backed up by some splitting sandbags. The sand has spilled out on to the surrounding ground, creating a bed for a mass of little white flowers with fleshy leaves and pink stems. Clumps of plants with clusters of yellow daisies are scattered elsewhere through the grass, as if someone has thrown a packet of seeds to the wind and allowed them to settle wherever they fall. A few overgrown bushes bend and crack with the weight of neglect, supporting a handful of desiccated flowers and sad leaves.

Zohra studies the letter in her hand again. The address is handwritten, postmarked Toronto, Canada. The writing is elaborate, with curious sweeping marks cutting through each half of the *B* of Bromsgrove and an ornate treatment of the capital *G*, full of curls and swirly strokes. A bit of colour and it would resemble the opening of an ancient manuscript. This is a real letter from a real individual, not a faceless organisation. She climbs the wooden steps and reaches up. The knocker is stiff and difficult to move, so she has to use both hands to pull it up, then pushes it down hard. She can hear it echoing inside.

There's a long silence.

Dougie's got it wrong. Nobody lives here any more. Should she knock again? Maybe once more, just in case. She raises her hands, prepared for another go, when she hears something. A shuffle. The clearing of a throat? She listens intently. She hears herself breathing.

More shuffling. Some clicks, a grunt, and the door slowly starts to open outwards. Zohra jumps hurriedly down to the ground, realising that she'll be sent flying if she stays where she is. The door swings out and right back against the side of the carriage, which it hits with a bang. It rocks gently and settles. A man is standing inside, swaying slightly, peering down at Zohra with a combination of irritation and fear on his face. He's tall, broad, perhaps a little older than Zohra's father. His wavy hair – greasy, unwashed – is a mix of grey and light brown, receding at the front, but creeping well past the collar of his red and black lumberjack shirt at the back, and his brown cords are held up over the widest part of his substantial waist by a narrow leather belt. He has a beard – shaggy and long – giving him the aura of a Maharishi or an ancient prospector for gold. His face is pale, the rims of his eyes red and the sockets dark and hollowed, as if he hasn't slept for days. He doesn't look like a tennis player – or even an ex-tennis player. But his eyes, staring at Zohra with an unnerving intensity below over-abundant eyebrows, are keen, blue and strong.

He frowns. 'Who are you?' His words are unexpectedly well-formed, clearly articulated.

Zohra holds out the letter without climbing the steps. 'Mr J. Greenwood? Or Mr N. Greenwood?' She feels she should check. She can't hand over a letter – a letter addressed by someone who cares about presentation, who has spent time crafting a miniature work of art – to an unknown person who might be a squatter.

The man grunts, but doesn't exactly acknowledge that he is a Mr Greenwood. He prepares to take the letter, looks down to examine it, then stops just before he takes it out of Zohra's hand. He freezes. An instant transformation, his whole body setting. Every part of him becomes motionless, as if he's just died and hasn't yet had time to fall over.

Zohra's arm is starting to ache. 'So are you Mr Greenwood?' she asks again, uncertain how to proceed.

The man finally moves – rigidly, like a puppet, dependent on someone else to manipulate his strings. He drops his hand. It returns to his side, still bent at the elbow, not loosening as it falls. 'Next door,' he says, in a dry, low voice.

'No,' says Zohra. 'The houses next door are Four Winds and The Woodpeckers. There are no Mr Greenwoods living in either of them.'

9

'My brother,' says the man. His voice sounds as if it lacks practice. He jerks a clumsy thumb towards the carriage on his left, Zohra's right, the one with the blinds.

Zohra looks towards the carriage, Aphrodite, but it appears to be deserted. There's something fascinating about the whole situation. An abandoned train, two elderly brothers living almost invisibly in separate carriages, one reclusive, the other absent, a mysterious letter from overseas – it's hard to believe they've been able to live here as long as Dougie said.

'So could you give it . . .' she begins.

The man doesn't reply. He leans out to pull the door back.

'Wait,' says Zohra. 'How do I—?'

The door slams into place and Zohra is left alone outside. She stares at the right carriage, wondering if she could try knocking on its door, but there's no knocker, no steps, no indication that it's still in use. What now? She can't spend much longer here. She'll be late for the rest of her round. People complain if you're not regular.

But a stubborn streak refuses to let her leave. She wants to know what's going on, she wants to deliver the letter, so she reaches up and knocks again. 'Mr Greenwood!' she calls. Maybe they take it in turns to answer the door. Maybe the other one will come.

Silence descends. A quick breeze rustles through the uncut grass, stirring the yellow daisies into a delicate dance. After another couple of minutes, it becomes clear that nothing is going to happen. She steps back reluctantly and surveys both carriages. She doesn't like to give up, but what else can she do? She can't wait forever.

She could mark the letter, 'Addressee unknown', and return it to the sender. But nothing is returned if it comes from abroad, so it'll just end up in a recycling bin. She wonders if she could slip the letter under the door – at least she's established that someone actually lives here – but a moment's investigation makes it clear that it's too well sealed. Maybe she could leave it outside, on the top step where it would be seen. Or propped behind the railway light. She knows there's someone in, so she can't be accused of leaving it unattended. There's not much shelter, but it's not raining.

'Well, a postman. I haven't seen an example of your species in I don't know how long. Do you have something for me?'

Zohra swings round to confront a man approaching from the direction of the road. He's better presented than the first man, considerably slimmer, but still almost identical – the same fierce blue eyes. For a brief moment, she thinks it's the same person; that he's gone indoors and changed into this more respectable version of himself, then somehow dodged round the back to confuse her. But this edition has a shorter, neatly trimmed beard, smarter clothes and hair that's clearly been attended to by a professional. He's wearing a dark grey suit and a sober navy tie. This is unmistakably the brother.

'Ah,' he says. 'Postwoman. Should have realised that from the hair.' He sounds exactly like the other one.

'Are you Mr Greenwood?' asks Zohra.

'There are two of us,' says the man. 'I live in Aphrodite.' He points over Zohra's shoulder. 'And he lives in Demeter. Right, left.'

Zohra nods, wanting to appear in control of the situation. 'I've just met your brother,' she says.

'Really?' says the man. 'Well, good for you. Don't suppose he said much.' He almost smiles.

'He didn't stay,' says Zohra, wondering if she should smile with him. 'Out and back in a couple of seconds.'

This time the man roars with laughter. He's overreacting now, as if he's performing for an audience. Zohra holds out the letter. 'So I can leave you this?'

But the man doesn't respond and Zohra once again finds herself with her hand outstretched, unable to let go without the letter falling to the ground.

'I'm Nick, he's Johnny. Is it for me or him?'

'It's addressed to both of you. You could just sort it out between you.'

Nick Greenwood shakes his head. 'I think not. We can't sort anything out between us. We don't talk to each other.'

'Please take it,' says Zohra. 'I have to get on with my round.'

'I suppose I'll have to,' says Nick after a pause, and finally removes the letter from her hand. He glances down at it, then reacts in the same way as his brother. Every trace of humour vanishes and he becomes still and rigid. A statue, alive but immobile.

Zohra waits for another few seconds in silence, embarrassed to leave him in this state, but eventually loses patience. 'Well,' she says. 'Good.' She starts to back away.

This Mr Greenwood recovers more quickly than his brother, moving slightly less awkwardly. 'Thank you,' he says in a voice barely above a whisper. He turns back to the carriages, still clutching the letter, climbs up the steps, yanks open the door and disappears inside. The door shuts with a bang.

Zohra stares at the closed door, worried that she could have managed the exchange better.

But her mission has been accomplished. She heads back towards the road.

2

Nick Greenwood peers through a gap in his blinds and watches the postwoman walk back across the field to the road. It's easier to watch her than to think. She stops for a moment and looks back, examining the railway carriages again. She's short and slim, almost childlike from this distance, with a cloud of black hair that reaches halfway down her back. It's tied into a pony-tail, although not entirely successfully. Her head is surrounded by rebellious wisps that shift and sway as she walks, producing an impression of changeableness and unpredictability, like drift-ing shadows. When they were closer, he'd considered her face unremarkable, with flat cheekbones and pale scars from healed acne scattered randomly across the brown skin, but after a while he'd found his attention drawn to her large, very dark eyes. Her gaze was steady and earnest, as if she was compelling him to like her.

She turns and eases her way through the narrow, overgrown pathway back to the road, pushing away low-hanging branches with her hands, ducking to avoid an out-of-control hawthorn. He's embarrassed by her struggle, aware that it's his responsibil-ity to clear the access properly. For decades, nature has been running riot, romping around like an unchecked child, deliri-ously asserting its right to roam, and he's barely noticed.

He must do something about it . . . tomorrow.

An image of his dad flashes into his memory. He's standing on a stepladder, chopping away at a towering cotoneaster, getting down occasionally to push his fork into the soil, jiggling it back-wards and forwards between the tangled roots, forcing them loose, severing the smaller shoots with his secateurs and the thicker ones with his saw, worrying away at the system until it gives in and surrenders to his will.

How ever did Ma persuade his dad to do it? He wasn't exactly a man who got on with things. It must have been important – maybe the bushes were in the path of their planned plumbing. Maybe Ma's nagging had overwhelmed him. And why think about this now? His dad's death happened long before Debs's.

The letter is burning in his hand.

He tries to be rational, to go through all possible explanations for the existence of the letter, but the speed of his thoughts is frightening.

Johnny is close by but hidden, his presence a silent blockage somewhere in the opposite corridor, interfering with the flow of air. Nick swivels hurriedly to the side, opens the door into his own corridor, just past their shared bathroom, and lets the door slide shut behind him. He can hear Johnny now, coming out of Demeter, motionless in the central section, breathing, existing. Nick stands still, pretends he's not there and waits, his pulse pounding in his head, trying to order his thoughts.

There's a long pause, as if Johnny is thinking (unlikely – as far as Nick can tell, his brother rarely produces evidence of serious thought) then a grunt, *sotto voce*, a creak of clothing as he turns in the confined space and shuffles off in the opposite direction, the sound of his existence fading gradually into nothing.

Nick takes a deep breath without moving, still listening intently before padding carefully towards his living room. Unexpectedly, another memory jumps into his mind. The fun they all had when he and Johnny helped his father knock down a partition wall to turn two compartments into one, creating a larger room where they could all watch the new television together. A lounge, according to his father, who was yearning for the thick, companionable atmosphere of a pub. A parlour, said Ma. She had aspirations, but didn't realise – until she'd watched more television – that her terminology was rooted in the past.

Why does he keep slipping backwards? Why can't he concentrate on the letter?

It had been a glorious day; swinging on the bars of the luggage racks to loosen them from their fixings; hooking a crowbar down the side of the wood panelling that divided the compartments and yanking it away from the walls; running a Stanley knife across the centre of the seats, whooping with pleasure and satisfaction as the stuffing burst out like the innards of a dead animal, expanding into its new freedom. They pulled it out in handfuls and chucked it at each other, filling the air with fluff and breathing in the intoxicating fumes of wreckage, barely able to believe that they were allowed to indulge in such uncontrolled destruction.

Johnny spoiled it, of course, as always, suddenly bending over and starting to cough aggressively. 'I can't breathe. Stop it, stop it!'

'Okay,' said their dad. 'Time's up. Let's do the tidying now.'

Nick was infuriated by the way his brother always managed to turn everything into his own personal drama. Why should he be the one to decide when they'd had enough? He grabbed a clump of the stuffing and thrust it into Johnny's face. 'You don't fool me,' he hissed into his ear. 'I know you're just after hot chocolate.'

'Aargh!' gurgled Johnny, trying to push him aside. 'Dad, he's trying to kill me!'

'Cut it out now, lads,' said their dad, pulling Nick away. 'Your ma'll not be best pleased with this mess.' He was a calm, easygoing man who rarely asserted himself. He had brown, leathery skin and narrowed eyes that always seemed to be looking into the distance. He'd spent his early years on a fishing boat out in the North Sea, off the Suffolk coast, before the demise of the herring industry, and he still preferred to be outdoors, unable to relax if he couldn't feel the warmth of the sun on his face or hear the wind in his ears.

'Too right.' Ma's voice travels down through the decades and vibrates in Nick's ears, still crisp and affectionate, still sufficiently authoritative to freeze him into instant obedience.

The creation of a kitchen from the two compartments clos-est to the main door in the left carriage and a bathroom in the equivalent position in the other one had been a more subdued affair, more urgent, more workmanlike and involving a great deal of digging. A mate of their dad's, a railway guard, had come every day for a fortnight to help install proper plumbing. He had to finish by early evening and get back for his late shift, so there was no time to waste. Everyone knew what was required of them and they got on with it, all of them desperate to make the connection with the mains water supply. No one wanted to continue the misery of trips to the standpipe in a neighbouring field, wading through mud, dodging between thirsty Hereford cattle on their way to the water trough. And the existing sani-tary arrangements were unsuitable – the whole place was start-ing to smell.

Nick and Johnny still share the kitchen and bathroom. Nick rises early, Johnny doesn't. Nick can use the bathroom, shave, shower, make his breakfast and wash up before there are any sounds of life from next door. If he senses Johnny is on the move, he withdraws. There has been an occasional close encounter in the middle of the night, but they've both become practised at strategic retreats, prepared to hover further down their corridors until the coast is clear.

He avoids looking at the letter. He can't look at it. The writing is as familiar as it was forty-eight years ago.

But it's impossible.

Johnny knows the writing too. He recognised it immediately.

When the postwoman stood in front of him, holding out the letter, there was nothing to indicate the significance of the moment. Johnny stared at her, surprised by the fact that she was a woman, surprised she was there at all.

'Mr J. Greenwood? Or Mr N. Greenwood?'

His eyes were drawn to the letter, the names, the address . . .

An arrow, venomously sharp, flew through the air at

enormous speed and pierced him in the heart. The pain was instantly crippling.

He knew it wasn't a heart attack. This missile had hit him once before, a long time ago. The aftermath was prolonged then. It went on for months and months, its intensity waxing and waning until it eventually became a dull ache that has never entirely left him.

On that occasion, it had been a policeman, PC Banner, who came to the door, his voice deep and growling but oddly formal. 'Can I come in, Mrs Greenwood?'

And Ma, flustered, her face suddenly scarlet, the colour then fading abruptly and disappearing, until her skin became pale as paper, shiny like a pearl. 'Yes, yes, of course,' she said, holding out a hand as if she were a practised hostess, ushering her guest into her parlour.

As PC Banner passed through, bending awkwardly under the low ceiling and squeezing past Nick and Johnny, who were hovering in the corridor, equally panic-stricken by his presence, Ma went back to the outside door, leaned out, grabbed the handle and slammed it shut. They were locked into an interior silence now, an awkward group in the small living room. PC Banner took off his helmet and held it in his hand, but he was still much taller than the rest of them, his chest broad, his uniform dark, his buttons shining. They all knew him well. He had a knack of appearing out of nowhere, his large hands unexpectedly grabbing the boys by the back of the neck as they climbed over forbidden walls with their pockets full of half-ripe apples, or tried to sneak into the cinema without paying, or hovered round the station, hoping for a free ride.

'Please sit down,' said Ma, gesturing at the bench-seat that was part of the original railway carriage. 'Can I offer you a cup of tea?' She knew. They all knew the news was going to be bad. It was the way PC Banner stood there, his head leaning forward slightly, his shoulders stooped and his mouth sagging at the corners, dragged downwards by the moustache, and the way he kept clearing his throat. Not a cough, not quite, but a manifestation of impending disaster, a harbinger of bad news.

'A glass of water, then? Or some orange squash?' Ma didn't want to hear what he had come to tell her. She was stalling, as if a delay would change the outcome.

PC Banner cleared his throat more loudly. 'Perhaps we should all sit down.'

'No,' said Ma.

PC Banner, unaccustomed to outright disobedience, looked confused. He turned to the two boys, his eyes uncertain, searching their faces to see if they would be sensible enough to take responsibility.

Johnny, used to seeing Ma as a furious, fighting, protective force, stared at her, bewildered, not recognising her indecisiveness and threatened by the lack of normality. He was conscious of tears gathering in the corners of his eyes. He couldn't speak.

'Ma,' said Nick, younger than Johnny, but always willing to take charge. 'Just sit down. PC Banner wants to talk to you.'

'Oh,' she said. And she dropped down almost immediately, as if she knew the seat was right behind her all the time; as if she believed the boys were there to tell her what to do. The message to Johnny was that the situation had become out of hand. He could feel his legs trembling uncontrollably, with a jarring lack of rhythm, while a dingy gloom seemed to be closing in around them. In their family, she was the headmistress, the sergeant major, the pirate king. The idea that her offspring would one day usurp her position and give her instructions had never occurred to any of them.

The boys sat down on either side of her. PC Banner perched on the opposite bench, uncomfortable, too big for the seat, and fiddled with his helmet. 'Mrs Greenwood – Doris . . .' he said. There was an intake of breath from everyone at the use of her first name, which hardly anyone used. It was audible, it boomed around the compartment, echoing backwards and forwards. Johnny felt an urgent desire to say something, to change the subject, to pretend everything was exactly the same as it was three weeks ago. He opened his mouth and tried to speak, but nothing came out.

'They've found a body.'

The silence was so absolute it hurt Johnny's ears.

'Up in the woods – Bournheath.'

'Oh?' said Ma, her tone curiously loud.

A body? thought Johnny. The only dead person he knew was his father, who'd been fished out of the canal six years ago, and he hadn't been allowed to see his body, not even at the funeral. The coffin had been nailed down.

'We think it could be your girl, your Debs.'

And that was the moment: the loosing of the arrow; the instantaneous contact; the silent shriek of pain.

He could hear his ma's voice from a vast distance. 'Will we have to identify her?'

There was a long silence, then PC Banner cleared his throat. 'Unlikely,' he said. 'The weather – it's not been good – you won't be wanting to see the body like that—'

'It'll be a mistake then,' said Ma, her voice suddenly firm. 'It's not her.'

PC Banner's words were slurring, running into each other, confused in Johnny's ears. '. . . post mortem – clothes – personal effects . . .'

Decades later, with a postwoman in front of him instead of a policeman, Johnny experienced a shocked familiarity as the arrow pierced him for a second time, the point of entry identical to the first.

Why was there no arrow when his dad died? Did they only fly if you were old enough to recognise them? Or when Ma died? When any sensation would have been welcome.

It's not possible, he thinks, after shutting the door on the postwoman. He bends over, crippled by the intensity of the pain. He was fifteen when the body was found, and sixty-three now. The floor is vibrating under his feet, there's a sensation of motion, as if the train has started to move. What's happening? Is he slipping backwards, losing his place in the present and tumbling back to the past? How can this be?

He can hear the postwoman knocking again, her voice calling, and eventually silence. She's gone. Now he can move. But then he hears his brother's voice outside, his exchange with the post-woman. The corridor is darkening, although it's only the middle of the morning.

He hears his brother's hand on the handle, the turning of the latch, the gradual opening of the door. He has to do something. He can't meet him now. He steps into his own compartment as his brother comes inside. He knows Nick is standing there with the letter in his hand, hears his uneven breathing. He was right. Something momentous is taking place.

His brother slams the outside door. Johnny can hear his foot-steps as he goes past the kitchen into his own corridor.

Johnny doesn't know what to do. How can he speak to Nick, break a silence that has lasted for at least seven years? But he has to know. He should have taken the letter, he realises that now, but the arrow, the confusion, the disbelief – he wasn't thinking rationally. No one could make good decisions with that kind of pain pinching so tightly inside. He listens. He can't hear anything. He waits, a long time. There's nothing but silence.

Best to get on. Best to ignore it all.

He stops, uncertain, then makes a decision. He slides open his door and realises, almost straight away, that Nick is doing the same thing. They're both standing there, their eyes making contact.

Nick examines Johnny. It's a long, long time since they've been face to face like this. He's older, he thinks, and deteriorating. His beard is untidy, out of control, and he clearly hasn't washed his hair for some time. Or his clothes – there are food stains on his shirt. He really should make more effort. He looks like a tramp.

Johnny clears his throat. 'The letter—' he says.

'I haven't opened it,' says Nick.

'It looks just like—'

'I know.'

'It can't be.'

'I know.'

Nick lifts the letter in his hand and examines it more carefully. The elaborate *R*, the blue-black ink, the firm, strong downstroke of the *J* with a swirl on top, the way the line across the middle of every *e* doesn't quite meet the curve on the left. It's a coincidence, it must be. But on the back of the envelope, on the sealed flap, there's a doodle. A tiny squirrel.

His head is spinning. A cloud seems to have found its way into the railway carriage and settled over them both, making it difficult to see clearly.

Johnny shuffles closer and Nick edges backwards. Johnny stops moving, as if he can sense Nick's discomfort. As if he cares about it. 'Open it,' he says.

'It's addressed to you as well,' says Nick.

'Give it to me then,' says Johnny. 'If you can't open it, I will.'

'No,' says Nick. 'I'll do it.' He puts a finger under the edge of the flap and tries to ease it up, maybe hoping to avoid tearing the squirrel. But it's sealed too strongly and rips. Slowly, slowly, he pulls out the letter. A single sheet, folded, the writing on one side only.

They both study the sheet of paper, unwilling to believe in it, to accept its existence.

'Oh come on,' says Johnny, trying to snatch it out of Nick's hand. 'What does it say?'

Nick swings it away from Johnny and nearly drops it. 'Wait,' he says. 'Give me a second.' He swallows, opens the letter and starts to read out loud. He tries very hard not to look ahead, not to assume anything until he's read it properly. 'The address is somewhere in Canada. Hamilton. Never heard of it. Oh, Toronto. The house is called Satisfaction.' He looks up and meets Johnny's eyes. He knows he must be thinking the same as him. 'I Can't Get No Satisfaction'. The Rolling Stones. Debs's music.

He looks down again and starts to read.

Dear Johnny and Nick,
Where do I start?

I'm not dead. That seems to be the most important thing to say. It wasn't me.

I realise this will come as a shock to you both, but I've only recently discovered that everyone thought it was me. I came across a site online called Bromsgrove Memories. And there it all was. Nobody knew about DNA then, did they? There wasn't a way of checking.

I've been in Canada for the last forty-five years. I couldn't come back, but now I need to see you both and explain. I'm imagining you still there, in the railway carriages, but I realise that's unlikely, so I don't even know if this letter will find you. You're probably both married with children, grandchildren, miles away from where we grew up, although neither of you seems to have an online footprint.

I'm dying. Lymphoma, too advanced when they found it, nothing to be done, and I want to tell you what really happened while I've still got time. So I'm setting off as soon as possible. By the time you get this, it will probably be too late to contact me and I'll be on my way. If you're not there, I'll ask around, see if I can find you. We have to talk.

No precedence intended by the order of your names – it's alphabetical. I haven't forgotten how you were.

Debs

Johnny snatches the letter out of Nick's hand and studies it. Nick watches him reading, unable to sort out the confusion of his own thoughts. When Johnny's finished he looks up, straight at Nick, his eyes sharp and challenging, as if he's trying to say something, but can't find the words. Eventually, he throws the letter on the floor and turns away. He slides open the door, goes through. The door shuts behind him.

3

Zohra parks her van at the bottom of the hill. It leans alarmingly towards the hedge, unbalanced by the steep camber of the lane, but remains steady. She opens the door, careful to prevent it from swinging out too violently, grabs the handful of letters (does a smart white envelope, personally addressed, really persuade anyone to buy life insurance or vitamin supplements?) and climbs out, placing her feet strategically on the tops of the ridges where the mud has dried and hardened. She slams the door, locks it and heads for the row of small terraced cottages further up the hill on the left.

They're nailers' cottages, built centuries ago when Bromsgrove was the nail capital of the world. The workshops were placed at the front where all the business was conducted, while friends and family approached from a parallel street at the back through the long, narrow vegetable gardens. Now the only access is through these gardens. The backs have become the fronts.

Zohra can see Mr Albert Troth, the old man in number 1, watching from a distance as she negotiates the stepping stones over his narrow lawn. They're placed slightly too far apart, though it wouldn't matter at all if she missed and stepped occasionally on to the grass, but she sees it as a matter of pride not to. Or a return to childhood, where boundaries are well-marked and decisions are clear-cut.

'Got time for a quick drink, bab?' he calls, as he does every day. 'Cola, water, a coffee?' He wants to have it ready before she reaches his front door, so he doesn't waste the face-to-face time. She occasionally stops for a quick glass of water – not because she wants it, but because she feels sorry for him. She once tried his cola, but it was disgusting – a cheap supermarket imitation that he must have bought specially for her. Not worth the price of the bottle.

She worries about Mr Troth. He's lonely, desperate for a glimpse of a human being, too easily pleased by a human presence, the sound of a voice, the bestowal of a casual smile. Zohra has been alerted to the dangers by *Midlands Today*. There are vultures out there, hovering, watching for prey: salesmen; conmen; anyone with a hunger for profit, feeding on the old and vulnerable.

She was tempted to accept a cup of coffee once or twice last winter, only a few months after she'd started the job, when an icy wind from Wales whipped across the open countryside towards Bromsgrove, potent enough to drown the ever-present noise from the motorway. It was hard to think straight when it was blowing so mercilessly, cutting through her beanie and hood as if they weren't there, ignoring the fingerless gloves, treating her red, all-weather coat and waterproof leggings as a challenge, searching for weaknesses, gaps, an entrance. On the worst days, the thought of a warm drink was almost irresistible. But she knew that coffee would take too long. It would delay her entire round. There would be complaints.

'Not today, thank you, Mr Troth,' she always says, smiling, wanting to stay and talk longer because she likes him, but knowing she must resist.

He's tiny, little more than skin and bone, shrunk down to essentials. He appears to be bald (although she can't be sure since his head is always protected by a neat trilby) and his face bulges with bones that seem too large for their context, covered by a thin wrapping of leathery skin. He looks like a man who has climbed out of his grave, a zombie who's ready to fall back into it at the touch of a finger. But his eyes are alive and he's still active, against all the odds. His garden proves that. Clumps of brilliant blue irises – 'old irises, bab,' he says, 'you won't get a scent like that from modern ones' – are dotted gloriously

25

throughout the garden during May and June. Now, in mid-September, they're dying off after a second flowering. 'Two for the price of one,' he says. 'There's not many plants give such good value.'

'Do you do next door's garden as well?' asked Zohra when they started to bloom on both sides of the hedge.

He nodded gleefully. 'Used to, when me legs was in better nick. Since I get to look at it every time I go out, I reckoned I might as well make something of it.'

'But don't they mind?' Zohra was thinking of her mother, her delight in the tiny garden at the back of the shop, the preciseness of her instructions to Zohra's dad. She wouldn't be prepared to accept anyone else's advice, let alone allow them to take over.

He chuckled. 'Not many round these parts who'd turn down a free gardener. Them next door are just young things, out to work, never there. No time for gardening.' He accepts all humanity without judgement and probably doesn't even notice his neighbours' lack of communication. He finds ways to make contact with people, complaining about his phone line, gas supply or television reception, in order to summon repairmen. He sends for a steady supply of brochures so that Zohra can deliver regularly.

'Late today,' he says, coming out of his front door, beaming at her.

'Sorry,' she says. 'I had to find an address I've never been to before, some old railway carriages off Long Meadow Road where two brothers live. It's the first time I've ever had post for them, although I'm told they've been there forever.' They're really old, she's about to say, but realises just in time that Mr Troth must be older.

He's immediately excited. 'I know them. The Greenwoods – they used to play with my lads. Tennis players – for a while, anyway. Could have been good, but didn't stick at it. Nice family, though.' His smile fades. 'Till they lost their big sister. In her twenties, she was, like a mother to them. Never solved.'

Zohra can't walk away from such interesting information. 'What do you mean, lost?'

His eyes drift past her towards next door's garden, unfocused as he searches through his memory for details. 'There was two lassies went missing, but only the Greenwood girl was found – dead in the woods. Nasty business . . .' He pauses to take a breath. 'Nobody took much notice when they first disappeared – took a while for the police to take it seriously. Then smart-alec coppers from Birmingham rolled up and started to throw their weight around – fancied they was on *Z Cars*, didn't they? – and got us locals to volunteer for searches. We all went – set off from the Nailer's Arms – checking the fields, woods, barns, outhouses. Found the Greenwood lassie in the end, half in and half out of a pond, under some bushes, so you couldn't see her unless you went right up close. Roy, only a young kid he was, worked in the new Wimpy Bar, he stepped on her – put his foot right into her stomach . . .' He stops and shudders. 'You wouldn't wish it on your worst enemy. But it was July, see, one minute sweltering hot, the next it's tipping down. Bodies don't last long in weather like that. Shame about Roy – never recovered. Drank himself to death . . .' Mr Troth's voice fades away, as if he's forgotten he's talking out loud.

'What about the other girl? Did they find her too?'

'No, but they found her things – the coat turned up weeks later, after the searches was called off, washed downstream, and her bag was found miles away, on the side of a road, nothing left in the purse. They reckoned it was the same killer, even though they never found her body, no trace. Her mum kicked up a right old rumpus, blamed the fuzz – she were a one, I can tell you, addled as a jar of pickles, couldn't stay upright most of the time. Right upsetting, it was. People talked and talked and talked, held meetings, wanted to know what the police was doing, why they wasn't keeping us safe.'

Zohra shivers, imagining how it must have felt to believe there was a murderer around, maybe living next door. 'It must have been terrifying.'

Mr Troth nods solemnly. 'All them fancy police methods, never did no good. We thought he was still out there, waiting to kill again and we was all scared. It got everyone watching everyone else, wondering who done it.'

Didn't they know this in the sorting office? It's not exactly the kind of thing you forget. But nobody said anything. Was that what Dougie was trying to tell her? But how was she to know he had something meaningful to say? Everyone stops listening once he starts rambling on. 'Didn't they have any suspects?' she asks Mr Troth.

'They arrested a few people, but then let them all go, so we knew they didn't have a clue. In the end, the talking just stopped. Nothing more to say, see, you run out of words. And there wasn't no more murders. Me and the missus, we always reckoned it was one of those serial killers passing through – a travelling salesman, delivery man, something like that, someone who travelled round for his job. No computers in them days to link all the killings together. Someone'll come along some day soon, mark my words, and start putting two and two together. Cold cases, that's what they call it, isn't it? Like on the TV. They could probably sort it now, if they had a mind to.'

Zohra is struggling to take this in. First she discovers the existence of the two men living in train carriages, then she delivers a letter that makes them both behave very oddly, and now – a murder mystery without Miss Marple.

'Wondered if you was going to come today,' says Mr Troth.

Zohra is offended. 'I always come, Mr Troth. You know that. I'm reliable.'

'I know,' he says, nodding, his bony head bobbing up and down as if it'll never stop.

Zohra leaves him on his doorstep, still nodding, happy with his brief encounter, and heads back to the gate, following the artificial stream that runs the length of the garden. Mr Troth has told her how he installed it in his younger and fitter days, when he could still dig trenches and when he had a wife to please.

Underground cables lead to a series of switches in the house – Zohra's seen them, just inside the front door – from where he can start the flow of water, turn on lights, activate the fountain and shut everything down at night. But it's been there a long time. Is it still safe? Recent torrential storms have expanded the volume of water, brought the overflow area dangerously close to the house.

Zohra stands in the middle of the little oriental bridge for a second to examine the water before leaving. You can't pass a bridge without crossing it – even if you're in a hurry.

She continues up the row of nailers' cottages, pushing circulars and official letters through the letterbox of Mr Troth's neighbour, Mr Terence Clarke, knowing he won't be in, grateful for the demanding jobs which keep him and his wife away from home. Mrs T. Clarke, it says on her post, without ever giving her first name. Theresa, Tanya, Tiffany?

Mr Troth was right about them being out all the time, but not about their youth. They have a continual stream of packages, which Zohra usually has to leave with Mr Troth. She's never seen the wife, but she's met the husband once. He's in his forties, very tall, fleshy, already losing his hair, and he lacks manners. He took the parcel – from Amazon – out of her hand, grunted and shut the door before she had time to step away. No smile, no thanks, no warmth. She'd hesitated for a few seconds, hearing him inside, talking to the invisible wife. 'What are you playing at? It's your job to answer the door. Not mine.'

Not a nice man.

But nothing is as simple as it seems. Zohra could hear the wife's voice in the background. Strident, aggressive, the response of a woman who cannot allow a challenge to go unanswered. 'Since when have I been the maid? Are you incapable of dealing with a postman?'

The relationship can't possibly have a future.

Zohra hurries on. Most of the time she loves her round. She has a van, but there's still a considerable amount of walking

– many of the big farmhouses only allow pedestrian access and some of them are a long way from the road. As she tramps up muddy, pot-holed paths to distant houses, she breathes in the freshness of the air and takes pleasure in her growing fitness. But walking takes time, and she sometimes envies Dougie's town territory, where new-builds huddle up to elderly cottages and it's possible to race round in half the time.

Most of the gardens of the nailers' cottages are neglected, perhaps deliberately wild. Signs of activity are limited: a path of trampled grass leading to a dilapidated shed under dangerously overhanging trees; bowls of cat food on a doorstep, some licked clean, others left for too long, once the remnants of an entire roast dinner including vegetables and gravy, the contents hard and darkened, ignored by local strays; rows of flower pots cluttering the approach to a front door, recently acquired pelargoniums, vibrant and shocking, mingling with dried-up purchases from the past.

Number 7, renovated in the last few months, is the exception. A giant glass block juts out into the garden, fronted by a generous porch. Inside, the internal dividing walls have been knocked down so you can see the entire ground floor, including the spiral staircase and the granite kitchen, all the way to the window on the opposite side. Pale wood parquet flooring, cream sofas, white walls and small elegant sculptures, their shapes fluid and undefined. Soft muslin curtains hang on either side of the floor-to-ceiling windows, draped so beautifully that even Zohra's mother would approve. It's hard to believe anyone can actually move through the space without disturbing the ambience, but Miss Poppy Stevenson does seem to exist – unless someone else is picking up her mail. The glass door gives a view of the long, empty floor beyond, and yesterday's post has always been removed by the time Zohra returns.

Zohra likes to spend a few moments looking in, admiring, wondering. Is Poppy Stevenson an architect who designed the house to suit herself, or did she pay someone? Is she as sophisticated, as ultra-modern, as her name and home suggest? Why would she choose to live in Bromsgrove?

Zohra used to think she'd like to be an architect.

Number 8 haven't been here long. A married couple, Mr Freddie and Mrs Amelia Bakewell (their names have a young, breezy sound to them), who've been giving most of their attention to the garden. The front door remains cracked and peeling, the window frames rotting, but they cleared the soil as soon as they moved in, marking out furrows and planting a huge variety of vegetables in neat rows. Many of them have now been harvested, but there are plenty more still flourishing – cabbages, lettuces, brussel sprouts. Zohra has a signed-for letter. It's annoying to have to wait for a signature, but unavoidable. She considers putting the letter with the rest of the mail, pretending she hasn't noticed, but it's a risk. If, against all the odds, Mr or Mrs Bakewell are in and they're the sort of people who know their rights, the consequences could be serious. Rohit, the failed student, has confessed to her in an unguarded moment that he sometimes has the missed-occupant card ready to put through the letterbox before he leaves the sorting office, with all the correct boxes ticked. No one at home. Date, time, no safe place to leave it. Please allow twenty-four hours before collecting from the local office.

'How can you put the time on?' asked Zohra. 'You won't know till you get there.'

'I smudge the writing,' said Rohit. 'So you can't read it properly. Then they can't pretend they were in.'

'But they might be in. Wouldn't it be easier to check first?'

'Oh, come on. Half these people don't hear the bell, and if they do, they can't be bothered to open the door. Too busy talking on their phones. I can't stand on doorsteps all day. What do they want from me? Blood?'

But it's his job. He's meant to stand on doorsteps. 'Time isn't blood,' said Zohra. 'It's not like you're lying fatally wounded on the side of the road. You get to go home in the end.'

The mystery is that he's kept going as long as he has. He'll lose his job if he gets found out, then he'll have all the time in the world. Blood and time. Perhaps that's what he really wants. He doesn't seem very keen on working.

She couldn't break the rules like that. A respect for truth has been instilled in her since birth. 'The one thing you will always have, that no one can take away from you,' says her father, 'is your integrity.'

She presses the doorbell and reaches up to knock as well, in case the bell isn't working, but drops her hand when she hears a long ring echoing through the house.

There's a noise inside, something dropping on to a hard surface, a muffled female exclamation of irritation. Sharp clicks, high heels crossing the floor authoritatively.

The door is flung open. Zohra lifts her hand with the signed-for . . .

There's a brief silence as they stare at each other.

Amelia Bakewell, wrapped in a rose-coloured silk garment – more negligee than dressing gown – and wearing matching shoes with substantial heels (not the gardener then), recovers first. 'Zorry!'

Zohra tries to hide her dismay. 'Mimi . . .' she says eventually, her voice dry. 'I'm – I'm . . .'

Mimi throws her head back and roars with laughter, the sound echoing out across the gardens of the nailers' cottages. It's eight years since Zohra last saw her – sixth form, the A-level exams – but she doesn't seem to have changed much. She's been to uni, found a profession, married Mr Freddie Bakewell and bought a house – all the things Zohra has failed to do.

'You're the postman!' says Mimi with genuine pleasure. 'How . . . unexpected. Sorry about . . .' She indicates her dressing gown. 'It's all a little early. The shoes don't quite go, do they?' She laughs again. 'First thing I could find – you can't walk barefoot on these floors . . . Come in.' She turns back into the house, expecting Zohra to follow.

'No,' calls Zohra, remaining on the doorstep. 'I haven't time. Can you sign—?'

'Nonsense,' says Mimi without turning her head, her voice strong and clear even when she's facing the wrong way. 'You've got a couple of minutes for an old friend. Nothing's that urgent.'

Zohra struggles with herself. How many disruptions can you reasonably expect in one day? But she has to get the signature. Reluctantly, she steps in, pulls the door behind her without shutting it completely – she needs the safety of an emergency exit – and follows Mimi through the narrow hallway into the back room.

It's a tiny dark room, the only light coming from an ungenerous window that looks out on to the lane where purchasers of nails used to come. This would be where the forge was situated in the past, where the world-famous nailers worked, usually a whole family round the kitchen table. There's a small two-seater sofa on elegant legs, a one-person desk from Ikea with an open laptop on it, a tall plant in a pot in the corner and a television screen on the wall (large, but not as large as the one owned by Zohra's parents, whose screen size seems to be based on their perception of the distance from home – growing steadily over the years).

Mimi lowers herself on to the desk chair, shuts the laptop and indicates the sofa. 'Sit,' she says. 'I can't believe it's you, Zorry, after all this time. How wonderful.'

No, thinks Zohra, it's not wonderful. 'I don't really have time to stop,' she says. 'I need you to sign this.' She gets out her mobile device, scrolls down the screen to the right place and hands it to Mimi. 'Just there, in the space.' The signing stick dangles on a spiral wire.

Mimi examines the screen, but doesn't sign. She looks at Zohra thoughtfully. 'Fancy you being the postman,' she says. *How odd*, she means. 'I always thought you were destined for great things.'

You can't possibly have forgotten, thinks Zohra. 'I love the job,' she says. 'Fresh air, exercise, social interaction. Much better than being stuck in an office.'

'I suppose it's hardly surprising that we'd bump into each other eventually. It's a small world.'

Actually, it is surprising. Zohra's routes and pathways are carefully controlled. She constantly checks – questions people who wouldn't know anything about her background, but know people who know people, makes vague enquiries that won't give the impression she's interested. She's learnt to listen and wait, discovered that time and patience almost always produce information. She knows which universities the girls went to when they left school, and which subjects they studied. It's just luck, of course, that none of her previous friends has decided to come back to live in the area – you can't pick and choose your round – but it's always been a possibility. She's rehearsed what to say if they suddenly appear, if she should ever meet them in town. She's been ready for years.

'You must come round,' says Mimi. 'Meet my husband. He's a GP.' She smiles and Zohra notes a hint of pride. Look at me, she's saying. I'm living a successful life.

'How nice,' says Zohra, relieved to see something in Mimi that she doesn't like. It was harder when she was nice. She holds out her hand. 'Have you signed?'

'Oh – yes,' says Mimi vaguely. She scribbles briefly. 'They don't work well, these things, do they? It doesn't look much like my signature.'

'They never do,' says Zohra. 'It's just to prove I was here. And someone has taken the delivery.'

'Red tape, I suppose,' says Mimi. 'To match your T-shirt.'

Is she mocking? Zohra takes the device from Mimi's hand and turns towards the front door. 'I have to get on,' she says.

'Of course,' says Mimi immediately, following her.

Zohra hesitates on the doorstep and forces herself to look back. She can't just walk away.

34

'Do you ever come across anyone else from school?' asks Mimi.

Their eyes meet.

'No,' says Zohra. She turns away.

'Lovely to see you,' calls Mimi, recovering her poise. 'I'm sure we'll meet again.'

'I'm sure we will,' says Zohra over her shoulder, forcing herself not to run.

4

Nick sits at the desk in his office, Johnny's old bedroom, lays the letter out in front of him, forces himself to look at it, and tries to focus on the words. Is someone pretending to be Debs? Is it a scam, the lead-up to extortion? But it would be pointless. She'd never be able to keep it up. Nobody could pretend to be someone else for any length of time.

Is it remotely plausible that the letter is authentic, that the body wasn't Debs?

But that's ridiculous. There was a post mortem. The forensic experts knew what they were doing – it wasn't the dark ages.

He turns on his computer and types: 'how to identify bodies without DNA' in the Google search bar.

Plenty of hits. He skims through, skipping the case studies. It turns out that everyone's been watching too much television, and it's much harder to identify a body than is generally thought. He reads a little about the progress of putrefaction (it starts almost immediately, quicker than he'd realised), finding a lot of unpleasant detail about bloating, maggots, bacteria consuming the body from inside. Water and unusually hot weather speed up the process, so facial recognition and fingerprint identification can become impossible within a few days. Then there are foxes, badgers, rats . . .

Nick stops reading, feeling sick, his heart pounding. Conditions had been almost tropical – hot, wet and steamy. He can remember the oppressive nights, the struggle to draw breath in the thick, heavy air, but also the rain, torrential for several days on end. And she was found in a pond. This would have caused her to decompose even more quickly. No wonder they weren't asked to identify her – she would have been unrecognisable.

Could the experts have got it wrong? Was everything he thought to be true not true? He stands up with an overpowering desire to run away from it all, to physically remove himself from the situation.

But the letter will still exist, wherever he goes. He can't just throw it away.

He sits down again and continues to read.

Height, weight, they'd all have been checked. Dental records, evidence of earlier illnesses, bone injuries.

Debs was healthy – he can't remember a single occasion when she was seriously ill. She'd had occasional colds – like everyone else – but she never went to the doctor's. 'You won't catch me down at that surgery,' she said if Ma suggested she might need antibiotics. 'Not where all the germs hang out.' So no injuries – except the blow to her head that killed her. And she didn't bother with dentists, none of them did in those days. No need. They had Ma's teeth, tough as steel; they could bite buttons off cardigans, rip plastic tops off squash bottles with their teeth – never a suggestion of toothache as long as he can remember.

A growing darkness is rolling towards Nick, seeping through his skin. This cannot be possible. Everyone said it was Debs – the police, the coroner, Ma, everyone.

He forces himself to continue reading. To help with identification, the police talk to people who last saw the victim, people who knew them well, find out what they were wearing, where they would expect them to be. They ask family to identify clothing, jewellery, any personal effects.

This is more concrete. Nick can remember being taken down to the police station with Ma and Johnny and shown the clothes in sealed plastic bags, asked if they recognised them. Of course they did: the short green dress with its neat white collar and big black buttons down the front; those knee-length boots that she was so proud of, white plastic, which she continued to wear during the extreme heat because she was more interested in the look than the practicality. They were Debs's clothes. He can remember the shock of seeing the mud-covered boots, the ripped dress, everything stained with brown, faded blood, her blood. They were unmistakable, part of their Debs, his Debs: they'd made her who she was. And the contents of her bag, which was found close to the body: her purse; her house keys; lipstick, mascara; a powder compact with the transfer of a squirrel, peeling slightly, on the silver lid; a letter from a boyfriend they'd never heard of, who lived in Italy, who spoke to the police over the phone, but had no information to add, who had an alibi anyway. He was in Rome at the time, teaching a classful of ten year olds how to interpret maps.

What about Bev Newton, Debs's friend, the other girl who disappeared? She looked a bit like Debs. Was there any possibility it was her body they found and not Debs at all?

Nick takes a deep breath. Surely forensic scientists would have been able to tell the difference – wouldn't they? But what if both girls were wearing the same clothes? They did that sometimes. And if the face had rotted away . . .

No, this is not possible. Experts would have been able to tell the difference.

The police said Bev had died somewhere else, although they never found her body. It wouldn't have been easy to get her personal possessions identified. It was unlikely her mother had ever seen them before.

Bev's mother drank. All the time. And there was no father to help – nobody knew anything about him. Bev had spent a great deal of her childhood sitting outside the pub, waiting to go home, coaxing her mum up off the pavement or trying to prevent her from singing too loudly when everyone else was in bed. She often used to come back to the railway carriages with Debs after school because it meant she could talk to someone who would acknowledge her existence.

Bev probably never went to the dentist either, so they wouldn't have been able to check her dental records. If Debs didn't go, it wouldn't have occurred to her to go. She didn't have initiative. She was a follower.

Nick's thoughts return to the body itself, the search for identifying marks. There must have been something more that led the coroner to his final, definitive judgement. Something that removed all doubt.

They found the squirrel, the tattoo.

Not straight away, because the skin was rotting away. He types in 'tattoos on decomposing bodies'. This is more helpful. The ink goes through to the dermis, the second layer of skin, and endures longer than fingerprints. Tattoos can be traced. It was the final part of the puzzle. The squirrel on her arm confirmed it was Debs.

So that's it, then. All this going round in circles, all this frantic research hasn't taken him anywhere except back to the beginning. He wants to be reassured, relieved that Debs is really dead and nothing has changed after all. But something is still stirring inside him, a strange, unfamiliar excitement that planted itself when the letter arrived and has continued to grow steadily ever since.

He reaches out for one of his spiral notebooks – A5, lined, plain blue covers – that are piled neatly on the side of the desk, waiting their turn in an orderly queue, and picks up a pen. It starts to shake as it approaches the paper, so he puts it down and holds his right hand out in front of him. There's an almost imperceptible tremor, exaggerated when he holds the pen.

He frowns, annoyed with himself. He would like to believe he has enough control to prevent a visible reaction. He sits up straight, stretches his neck, regulates his breathing and opens and closes the hand, observing it closely. After a few seconds of this, he's pleased to see that it has become completely still. Mind over matter.

He draws a line down the middle of his page and writes a heading at the top of each column. Yes. No. Yes, the letter is from Debs. No it isn't.

He's diverted by the concept of dividing the world in half. Debs or not Debs. Aphrodite or Demeter. Nick or Johnny. Before or after.

His pen hovers over the Yes column:

1. The handwriting is authentic, the swirls of the *G*, the *J*, the *B* the *es*, each of them exaggerated, ridiculously ornate – he knows every stroke. Calligraphy was one of her obsessions – she spent hours with a pen and ink, experimenting.
2. The squirrel on the envelope – her trademark, evidence of her presence: a signature in the sand when they were on holiday; a notice stuck on her bedroom door (KEEP OUT DO NOT ENTER ON PAIN OF DEATH); a cheery signing-off on a note to tell Ma she'd be late home; the tattoo that caused the row with Ma, shortly before she died.
3. Her desire for drama. *I'm dying. It's too late to contact me.* The old Debs would have thrived on this. (She'd have loved the mystery when she disappeared, the search parties, the hysteria when her body was discovered. Nick can still remember wishing she'd been with them at the time, able to delight in the excitement.)
4. Her reference to the rivalry between him and Johnny. She always knew how much it mattered.

In the No column:

1. She was twenty-two when she was writing in this style. If she hadn't actually died, but gone elsewhere, her handwriting would not be the same after forty-eight years.
2. The body had to be Debs, not Bev. Bev didn't have a tattoo.
3. Mistakes have been made – he's just read about some of them – but it's not that common. Everything was examined meticulously by experts, who were trained to question every detail. They gathered all the evidence, considered it, came to the only possible conclusion.
4. Debs wouldn't have left them for forty-eight years without a word, a message. She was never cruel.

Debs had ambitions. She and Bev were in the same class all the way through school, leaving at fifteen, taking the same secretarial course and continuing to work together in a typing pool. They regularly went out in the evenings, wearing skirts so short they disappeared under their coats, tight pointed shoes, pale lipstick and luxuriant mascara, and came back late, both of them squeezing into Debs's bedroom for the rest of the night. Nick never found out where they went but, judging by their good humour the next day, they always had a good time.

They spent their weekends dressmaking, taking the bus to the Birmingham rag market and getting excited about materials, patterns in magazines, bright colours. They made dresses, designed accessories and dreamed about setting up their own business, opening a shop in Carnaby Street, hitting the big time.

Nick's bedroom was in the same place then as it is now, at the end of the right carriage, as far away from their parents' room in the other carriage as possible. He, Johnny and Debs had a compartment each for their bedrooms, side by side, Debs in the middle. Nick's room was next to the original WC at the end of the carriage. When they were finally connected to the water mains and sewer system, with a bathroom and kitchen on either side of the gangway between the carriages, the dead WCs at either end were left for storage: tennis racquets in the waterless toilet, handles down, heads poking out, encased in presses; footballs in the basin, boots hanging from the taps by their tied laces; piles of textbooks and school exercise books tottering in the corners; and coats flung in over the top of everything else. Debs's bedroom was crammed with her possessions, but immaculately organised. She somehow managed to fit in her bed, a small wardrobe and a dressing table with a mirror, but there was barely room to stand up. She refused to contemplate sharing the WC. 'Your footwear is in there,' she said with contempt when Nick offered her storage space, her large round eyes peering out from under her fringe. 'It's thick with stink.'

One Sunday night, two years before Debs died, when Nick was twelve and revising in his room – History: Charles I and the causes of the Civil War – he could hear Debs and Bev laughing next door, louder than usual, clearly enjoying themselves. Sound travelled too easily through the walls of the railway carriages. They were built for commuting, never intended as sleepers – Bromsgrove to Birmingham, day trips to Weston-super-Mare or holidays to the southwest. Nick was hot, bored, in need of a diversion. He came out of his room and paused, longing to join in with the girls' laughter. Maybe he could offer to bring them cups of tea. He knew what they were doing: trying on half-sewn clothes; pinning up hems; easing out armholes – but, right now, he would tolerate anything.

They'd all painted the windows that looked into their rooms from the corridor – privacy had to be protected in such a small space – but Debs's door wasn't completely closed, so when he put his eye to the crack, he could see in. Bev was just in front of him, facing away from the door as she fiddled with her skirt, trying to do up a safety pin on the side, wriggling her hips as she smoothed it down. She wasn't wearing a blouse, and he could see the back of her bra: silky nylon, green with purple roses, dotted with snagged threads. It was intended to be glamorous, he could tell, but somehow didn't quite manage it. The torn lace on the edges would have been white once, but now it was just tired, old and sad. It was too small for her, had perhaps shrunk in the wash, and was digging in, creating a welt of reddened skin on her left side as it disappeared under her armpit. She was skinny, like Debs, but the flesh bulged slightly under the pressure.

Nick was moved by her vulnerability, her flawed appearance, and he wanted her to cover up. At the same time, he had an overwhelming desire to put out his hand and place it on that naked, goose-pimpled back, feel the bony knobs of her spine, rub the colour back into her pasty skin. He could feel his arm rising, driven by a compulsion in his fingertips to touch her, feel her.

She turned and saw him. She shrieked.

He froze, knowing he should run, but unable to make his legs work.

Debs came into view. She stormed over, slid the door open and grabbed him. 'What exactly do you think you're doing, Nicholas Greenwood?' she demanded, her nails digging into his arm, brutally erasing his vision of contact with naked skin.

'Nothing,' he said.

'Don't you give me that,' she said. She leaned towards him in the confined space, stood on tiptoe – she was small and he was already heading for six foot – and placed her face as close to his as she could manage. 'If I ever catch you spying again,' she said in a low voice, 'I'll be in your bedroom, sorting through your stuff, finding out what you're hoarding in that box under your bed, and cross my heart, hope to die, if I find anything incriminating, I'll be taking it directly to Ma.'

Then she pushed him hard, stepped back into her room and slid the door across sharply. He could hear her drawing the bolt across.

'If you go anywhere near my stuff,' he shouted, rubbing his back where he'd crashed into the rim of the window, 'you'll be sorry. I've got mates, you know, who can duff you up any time you want. Just say the word.' He returned to his own room unsatisfied, aware that his threat lacked sophistication.

He wasn't at all sure what she expected to find in the box under his bed. It didn't contain much: school certificates; a small shield, the Progress Prize from his first year at senior school, an honour never to be repeated; the photo of his last class at primary school, with Mrs Pringle, the headmistress, pleasingly large and soft, sitting bang in the middle of the front row; a Valentine's card from an admirer who he'd never managed to identify, despite a rigorous investigation. There were some old clothes, shirts he'd always liked but grown out of, emergency underwear he could still squeeze into if he had to, and Lenny the Lion – so old the fur had smoothed away and turned to a soft, well-handled grey. His tennis trophies, not really his responsibility, weren't part of this collection. They were displayed in a cabinet in the living room with Johnny's, regularly dusted and rearranged by Ma.

He was pretty sure his brother had been through the box several times already, on the off-chance of finding something to use against him. Johnny operated in his own personal underworld: sneaking around, finding things out, denying everything when challenged. He got away with it because he had panic attacks if he was confronted – visibly shaking, producing a tuneless, high-pitched wail, flapping his arms – and nobody was quite sure how to deal with him. If he'd found anything, the information would have somehow, mysteriously, found its way to Ma's ear, and it never did, so Nick knew there was nothing incriminating. But he liked the idea of his sister believing he had secrets. It made him feel important.

Johnny paces up and down, rocking the corridor as he gets faster, whirling round each time he reaches the end of the carriage, outside what used to be his parents' double bedroom, now his living room, and heading back for the kitchen at the other end before the previous vibrations settle. Is it the corridor that shudders, the doors that rattle as he passes, the air that swirls in the corridor, or is the movement in his mind? Is he here at all, or is everything happening in his imagination?

He needs to remember what Debs looks like; he needs to be able to know it's not her if she turns up like she says she will in the letter.

Debs can't turn up. She's dead.

It's the Internet. Someone has been searching, finding out, plotting. They won't come here – it's some kind of practical joke.

But it's not funny.

What do they want? Money, a false identity?

Johnny needs a picture of Debs in his mind, just in case, so he can place her firmly, reject the impostor. But he can't seem to put a face on her, give her a shape, and this blank spot in his memory is filling him with frustration.

She was always a blur to him. A whirlwind of surplus energy, rushing past on her way to somewhere, anywhere as long as it

44

wasn't here, reaching up and ruffling his hair as she passed. It was infuriating. At the age of fifteen, in the year that she died, he was struggling to deal with a defiant tuft of hair that insisted on bouncing up from the centre of his head. Brylcreem, applied generously and extravagantly, could tame it for about an hour. The casual way in which Debs messed it up, somehow asserting her authority over him, would send him into a fury that he couldn't articulate.

He can't do this. The pain in his chest is still there. He has a sense that his hearing is going, his eyesight, his brain. He needs to find a safe place, a way of bringing himself back to the present. He drags himself to his desk, sits in front of the computer screen and touches a key. *The 39 Steps* starts playing at the point where he paused last night. Old black-and-white films have soothed him for years – an escape from chaotic thoughts during sleepless nights. It's much easier to accompany Richard Hannay on to the *Flying Scotsman* as he tries to evade the police search, watch him enter a compartment where a woman is the sole occupant and lean over to kiss her . . .

But it doesn't work. The familiarity refuses to distract him. He can hear himself humming – a loud, tuneless drone – and doesn't know how to turn it off.

Could it be her?

Funny how he can remember Ma so well, and Dad too, even though he died so much earlier, but not Debs.

He stands up, unable to stay in one place any longer.

If it really was Debs, how could she dare to show her face here? After all the trouble she's caused.

Of course it's not her.

But what if it is?

The hum in his head, which is also buzzing in his ears, is getting louder.

He needs to pace again, to free some of the frustrated tension in his legs. Should he go outside? Would he be able to move more freely?

But what if Nick's out there? Two encounters in one day – it's already been too much . . .

He manages his life online. He books a time slot with Tesco once a fortnight and waits at the side of the road for the van to arrive, so that the delivery man won't have to come up to the railway carriages. He buys all his computer equipment, the upgrades, new devices, from one firm, from people who know him well in the virtual world, and the courier rings him when he's on his way. While Johnny waits, he paces, unsafe outside, panicked by the occasional passing car, aware of the enormous sky above him, its potential to descend and crush him.

It's only inside Demeter, with his computer, that he feels safe.

He and Nick communicate online, and only about bills, which Johnny sorts out. He would have liked separate accounts for everything, but it's too complicated and would involve engineers coming to install separate meters. So Nick transfers his share into a joint account and Johnny manages the standing orders, the direct debits. If the amount changes, he emails Nick, who alters his contributions. It works well enough. They can maintain their separate worlds.

When Nick leaves for work every day, the space opens up and silence circulates more freely.

Johnny acquired his first computer twenty years ago, at the age of forty-three and finally discovered that he could be good at something. Nobody taught him. He just worked it out, bit by bit. In the early days, he was so enthralled that he forgot to eat, but not for long. It gradually dawned on him that he and his computer could earn a living together. He no longer had to stack shelves, unload lorries or sit at a till and try to communicate with people. The more he could order online, the less he went out, until he reached his personal paradise – a world of space and silence.

He calls himself Mr Digital and fixes other people's computers remotely. His customers are sad, unknowledgeable people, who need guidance on very basic procedures. The first lesson is all about managing an online bank account, so they can pay him. He doesn't understand why (although most are now directed to him by existing customers, which may have something to do with it), but they trust him. With a keyboard under his fingers and a screen in front of him, he's a different person, powerful, in charge.

In the years since he and Nick have stopped talking, it's become even more important to Johnny that nobody shares his space. Demeter is uncontaminated by the outside world, and the invasion of the postwoman was unexpected, alarming.

But that was overshadowed by the letter.

All of this is Nick's fault. It must be. He's almost certainly written to someone, prodded a sleeping snake, undermined the foundations of their security. He never could leave things alone.

Nick replaces the pen on the desk, dissatisfied with his list, which somehow fails to address the issue, and tries to organise his thoughts. He doesn't want to think about Debs – it's always been too painful, the knowledge that he was powerless to stop anything, that he couldn't save her, that they never found out who did it. The moment she enters his thoughts, everything starts to slip out of control again.

Once he'd completed his college course and qualified as an accountant, he'd intended to leave and never come back. But something has held him here, tied him to the place where his life was interrupted. It's as if the bodies of Dad, Ma and Debs are buried in the field and he can't abandon them, as if they still have something to say to him. So, now, beyond all logical reasoning, even though he knows that the letter can't be from Debs, he can't shake off this inexplicable sense of hope. It shouldn't be there, but it is: a thin seam of precious metal which vindicates his decision to stay put, a faint glitter that draws him, even though it doesn't exist.

This is nonsense. The sister he knew would never have just disappeared, gone off somewhere else, without letting them know where she was. And even if she had, which, of course, she hadn't, why make contact now?

Because she's dying. That's what she says in the letter.

47

How dare this stranger do this, pretend to be someone else, appeal to his sympathy? It's something to do with money, it must be. Why else would anyone take the time and trouble? Is it remotely possible that it could be Bev, not dead at all, expecting to appeal to their charity?

He remembers another occasion – the timing uncertain, but after the time he'd seen Bev half-undressed – when Debs and Bev were there again, but talking softly and more urgently. There was something unusually intense about this conversation, with the volume rising occasionally, then long silences before they started again. It sounded like an argument. He hadn't heard friction between them before, so he pushed his door open a little further, wanting to hear the details. But train doors can't be opened quietly, however carefully you try, so he wasn't particularly surprised when Debs suddenly appeared in his doorway.

'If it's safety pins you're after,' she said, 'to pin back those flapping ears, you only have to ask.' She was flushed and annoyed, but Nick understood that her animosity wasn't directed at him.

He grinned, embarrassed to be discovered trying to eavesdrop, but at the same time perversely pleased to have her attention for a moment, even if it was hostile. 'Oh, sorry,' he said, pretending to be surprised. 'I didn't know you were in.'

'Hmm,' she said, raising an eyebrow cynically, as if she could relieve some hidden pressure with humour. 'That's my boy.' But she didn't smile.

She was wearing a bright purple miniskirt that barely covered the top of her thighs. It had started off longer, but she'd recently adjusted the hem, hoping to be spotted by someone with influence, to be snapped up by a roving talent spotter and invited to be the next Twiggy. Her legs were swathed in light tan tights and when she moved too quickly, her mauve knickers, edged with two pale rows of lace, could just be glimpsed. Ma had forbidden her to go out in this skirt, but she just put another one over the top and removed it as soon as she was down the road, out of sight. Nick had seen her do it, let her know that he'd seen it, but not told Ma. He reasoned that the information might come in handy for future negotiations. On top, she wore the white knitted polo-neck jumper that she'd only just completed. It had been created painfully, over several weeks, during *The Avengers*.

'Oh no! I was only supposed to increase every four rows—'

'Shhh!' from Johnny. 'I can't hear.'

Ma patiently unravelling the knitting, winding the kinked wool into a small ball, reinserting the needle and picking up the lost stitches. Working her way through it carefully and meticu-lously, untwisting each stitch individually, knitting up the next row to set it all back on course.

Debs's hair was light brown, shoulder-length, endlessly brushed, but never sleek or flat enough. Her fringe rested just below the eyebrows and her large hazel eyes, so round that she looked permanently surprised, glared at him from beneath it. 'Get lost, Nick,' she said, her voice tighter than usual, as if she was struggling to sound normal. She tapped her nose. 'Little boys need to keep their ears shut, their eyes shut and their doors shut.'

Nick could feel heat rising in his cheeks. Little boy indeed! 'I wasn't—' he said.

'No,' she said. 'You weren't and you aren't. If you don't learn to mind your own beeswax, you'll wish you hadn't been born.'

But he could still hear their voices from his room. He liked the fact that they were arguing, even though he couldn't pick out the words. It added tension, the threat of conflict to his predictable world.

Now, forty-eight years later, he starts to give Bev more atten-tion. Her hair was flatter than Debs's, more willing to stay in place. She had knitted herself an identical jumper to Debs's because she liked it so much, but without the mistakes, sitting with them on Sunday nights, not interfering with *The Avengers*, getting on with it. An almost invisible girl who slotted easily enough into their home, even under the exacting scrutiny of Ma, because she was no trouble. Prepared to efface herself because it was easier to be there than at her own home. Nick experiences a

49

sudden sadness about her death – and realises that he's never addressed this properly before. At the time, everything was dominated by the loss of Debs. But Bev spent so much time with them, always quietly there in the background (although she was more present when Ma was out) and she's remained silent ever since. Lost, never found. A girl who never really got started.

Who would pretend to be Debs? Why? Who would know enough about her to get away with it?

Bev is standing behind him, in her well-knitted jumper, tapping on his shoulder.

Johnny has no problem remembering Ma. He can reproduce her, conjure her up with a snap of his fingers. She's in the room with him now, a small bundle of energy with huge reserves of determination, all of it packed in tightly, permanently ready for action, a tigress programmed to defend her children at a moment's notice. Her own parents, Johnny's grandparents, moved away when she was sixteen, leaving her on her own, and she hadn't seen them for years. She wasn't going to abandon her family in the same way. Even their headmaster was scared of her. If she threatened to go in and tackle a teacher, he would try to head her off before she got there, writing conciliatory letters, taking every action possible to avoid confrontation. But Ma, wiry, not an ounce of spare fat on her, her muscles powerful from cleaning, washing, rinsing, hanging everything out on the line and racing back out at the first hint of rain, waded in without fear on more than one occasion. She probably never realised that it was Johnny who would be most scared. Her tactics were almost always successful, whether anyone agreed with her or not.

Johnny can't remember now what any of her complaints were about. He and Nick were well-behaved pupils as long as they were kept apart. They did their homework, spoke politely to their teachers – Ma would never have tolerated rudeness, bad grammar, sloppy accents – and usually only scrapped with each other at home. The more serious trouble came later, after Debs had gone.

When Nick was six and Johnny seven, only ten months apart in age, she used to go out early in the morning, dressed in a yellow overall, ready to clean houses all over Bromsgrove, leaving the boys in the care of the fourteen-year-old Debs. Someone had to supplement the meagre amount their dad produced as an occasional builder's mate. It was rumoured amongst the children's friends that she lived on spinach, had muscles like Popeye and once she'd agreed to clean a house, dust mites packed their bags and left of their own accord. Prospective clients queued up for her services, knowing how good she was. She was a woman with so much energy she should have been a marathon runner. She would have conquered the world if she'd been born into a more privileged life.

Her sense of rightness was as strong as her arms. She would defend Debs and the boys to outsiders, then lay into them without restraint when she'd got them back home. Words weren't always necessary. She could slay them with a look.

Oddly, Johnny can remember Bev more clearly than his sister. Small like Debs, but not so pretty, he thinks, with straighter hair. Or has he muddled them? Was Bev the more attractive one? So if he can see her, why can't he just change the focus a little, summon up Debs? Unlike Bev, she was so much more than a physical presence.

If he met her now, how would he know it was her?

But why would anyone pretend to be Debs? And who except Bev would know enough about her to get away with it?

Johnny stops pacing. His mind starts to slow down and Ma retreats. She's no longer standing next to him.

The letter wasn't sent by a stranger.

It was Debs or Bev. Bev or Debs.

5

Zohra wakes with a jump, her mind quivering with over-activity, and resists the urge to leap to her feet and run. Her pulse thumps relentlessly in her ears, overwhelming, disorienting. It's the guilt, even more crushing than usual, running wild at the edge of her consciousness, attacking while she's at her most vulnerable. It bounces, thick and suffocating, on her chest. She pushes her way through the tangled layers of dreams and struggles to identify the trigger.

Mimi.

She's in the room, hovering in the air above the sofa, smiling as if nothing had ever happened, as if they're still great pals. Katy and Carys lean in around her.

And behind them the shadow of Fiona Chung. Her thick, shiny hair, cut into a sharp bob, shivers with healthy vitality as she leans forward, a sleek cascade of black shimmering against her smooth cheek.

Ignore them all, postpone the analysis of the consequences of meeting Mimi; concentrate on today. Relax. But as soon as Zohra's mind becomes active, anxiety starts to pour in again, wild and uncontrolled.

She should give up these afternoon naps. Daytime sleep undermines her defences, erodes the carefully constructed fortifications, leaves her wide open. Her father's advice, probably driven by guilt about his own wasted youth, but once her only source of knowledge, echoes around her. 'Remember, Zohra, the world rewards hard work. Punctuality, industriousness, eagerness – these are the things that earn you respect, wherever you are in your life.' He never sleeps during the day, despite his long working hours.

He doesn't say this any more. Despite the inclusivity of that phrase, 'wherever you are in your life,' delivering letters wasn't really what he had in mind. He hadn't envisaged her driving a red van round Bromsgrove or trudging up muddy pathways to remote cottages with a large bag on her shoulder – this was never part of the future he'd mapped out for her.

The original plan, when her father first came to England, was for him to become a solicitor – this is what his parents were expecting when they released him into the care of his uncle and aunt – but he was needed in the shop and whenever he had spare time, he chose to explore his surroundings. He bought a bike and visited all the small towns and villages within cycling distance, enjoying the contrasts between his old life and the new. 'I thought there was plenty of time,' he has told Zohra, sadly – often. 'Next year didn't seem too far away. I thought I could apply for a course once I was settled.'

When he returned with his new wife, his intentions were for them both to study. He would qualify first, he told her, and then she could train as a nurse if she wanted to. She did want to, but without his uncle and aunt, the corner shop consumed more of their time than they'd foreseen. They couldn't afford to employ an assistant. Their school certificates, so proudly attained in Lucknow – still on the wall in their sitting room, framed, regularly polished, but beginning to go yellow round the edges – offered nothing more than unfulfilled possibilities. Time dripped away and their aspirations gently faded. So Zohra, who turned out to be their only child, whose conception took so much longer than they'd expected, was meant to make up for the lost opportunities and her father's foolishness. Her scholarship to Finstall High School for Girls was just the first step in the right direction.

Everything they did, every sacrifice they made, was for her. They made a decision to speak only English at home, abandoning their native Hindi. Zohra's father quickly became fluent (as her mother frequently pointed out, he'd had five years head start and spent far too much of his time chatting with customers when he should have been getting on with his work), while her mother struggled. But she persevered, determined to do the right thing. 'My daughter is true English girl,' she would say, prepared to give up her own ability to express herself easily for the sake of her daughter's future. 'Enormous privilege.'

'With true English prospects,' said her father. 'You must never forget that.'

In the difficult time after she'd left school, they clung stubbornly to the belief that she would recover and go to university. If it meant waiting a little longer, with Zohra going as a mature student, then that's what they would do.

'Oxford, Cambridge,' her mother still says every now and again, although less frequently as the years pass and nothing changes, 'never too late. Your father and I are prepared to tighten belts, give you opportunity.' Zohra has always tried to explain the significance of grades which her mother knows perfectly well, but pretends she doesn't – but in the end it's easier to nod and smile.

When they insisted she go to a doctor, take anti-depressants, then see a therapist, Zohra responded obediently (she didn't have enough energy to resist), going once a week to sit quietly with a variety of highly qualified, kindly individuals who did their best to make her talk. She worked with an occupational therapist – painted pictures, read poetry, decorated pots that emerged pleasingly intact from the kiln – did whatever they asked. She was prepared to co-operate, as long as she never had to explain what had happened. After a year, to her relief, everyone gave up. Since then, her mother has come up with various solutions to help her gain further qualifications. Go to nearby university, Worcester, live at home. Part-time. I come with you every day on bus. Always have me for support.'

'Accountant. Work a little, study a little. No stress. All slow.'

'Open University. Perfect solution. You heard of this?'

'Yes, I've heard of it,' said Zohra.

'So you know this and you not tell me? Study still possible.'

But Zohra has no intention of studying ever again.

Her father, perhaps conscious of his own failings in this area, has made fewer attempts to persuade her. After a while, he asked her if she would like to help in the shop, and she agreed. At first she was content to stock the shelves but eventually she began to engage with the customers. It felt safe there – not the kind of shop her ex-school friends were likely to frequent. Then Crispin, the only friend she kept after school, invited her up to Wychington Hall to help him and his father Perry in the war against the neglected wilderness of their estate. It was like painting the Forth Bridge. As soon as they'd cleared one section, they'd move on, not looking back, only too aware that weeds were creeping up behind them, new life exploding, armies of seedlings nestling down nicely in the freshly turned soil, ready and willing to start again. But Zohra found she was enjoying it more and more as time went on. Working outside was satisfying, healing.

The idea of being a postman came gradually. Occasionally, she would see the postman drive up to the hall, get out of his van and breathe deeply. He would leave the post in the entrance, then stand and admire the view for a while before climbing back into his van.

'Nice up here,' he remarked once, catching sight of her. But most of the time, he said nothing.

It was the way he took his time that she liked, his unhurried contentment. What a nice job, she thought. You can be on your own, enjoy the countryside and do something useful.

Her father was surprisingly supportive when she made the suggestion about eighteen months ago. 'If you want to do it,' he said, 'then of course you must do it.'

'You wouldn't mind?' she said doubtfully, aware of how much she had disappointed him.

'Mind? Why would I mind if my daughter finds something that pleases her?'

'Well – it's not exactly a glittering career.'

He looked at her thoughtfully. He was never going to sweep her up in his arms and shower her with fatherly kisses – it wasn't his way and even strong emotion can't change the habits of a lifetime – but his expression was tender. 'Gold glitters but it's heavy. Air has no obvious weight, as if it's worth nothing, but it gives us life. Is it necessary to have debates about which matters most? All I want, all I've ever wanted, is your happiness.'

You can't rush these things. The recovery has been long and slow, measured in months and years rather than days and weeks. Time creeps painfully, on tiptoe, but it does move inexorably forward. The daily chore of getting up, breathing and existing without drama, has become bearable. Zohra knows you can't ever eradicate the memory of pain, but you can rub in the ointment that is offered by people who genuinely care. If it's applied carefully, as part of a manageable routine, it can at least soothe, even if the restoration can only ever be partial.

School eight years ago, the sixth-form common room, a friendly talk from Mrs Girling, the headmistress.

Fiona whispering into her left ear, like a bee mooching between the petals of a flower, searching for pollen. 'Why weren't you on Facebook last night?'

'Too much to do,' said Zohra, wanting to shake her head, flap her away. She was aware of Mimi on her right and Katy and Carys behind her, straining to hear.

Mrs Girling was droning on in the background. 'We take our charity work very seriously here at Finstall High. The governors and I would like to encourage you to use the wealth of knowledge that you've acquired here at Finstall High, your privileged position, to benefit the rest of society. We are introducing you to voluntary work now in the hope that it will lead to a lifetime of willingness to help others . . .'

Fiona had joined the school at the beginning of the sixth form, when her family moved into the area. Almost immediately, she insinuated herself into Zohra's group of friends with casual ease, opening her hand and inviting them to land, capturing them with barely a word, just assuming they would be drawn to her. She offered privileges, unexpected bonuses, rewards.

'We will be dividing you into small groups,' said Mrs Girling, 'and each group will be allocated . . .'

'We're having a barbecue, this evening, at my house,' Fiona had announced earlier in the sixth-form common room, her invitation rushing past Zohra to Katy, Mimi and Carys. 'My brothers are just back from uni.'

A frisson of excitement. The enormous house just outside Bromsgrove – heated swimming pool, stables, horses, an indoor cinema and a track round the perimeter of their grounds, where they could try out the collection of classic cars. Tristan and Sebastian, the brothers: fit, ultra-clever Chinese boys, studying medicine at Imperial, poised to dazzle the world.

'I'm sorry, evenings are difficult for me,' said Zohra. 'Too much homework.' And she would be needed to help in the shop.

'Oh come on,' said Mimi. 'Just this once.'

But it wasn't that easy and Fiona somehow knew this. Until she turned up, they had been four: Katy, Mimi, Carys and Zohra, united in a friendship that reached back to Year 7. Then they'd allowed Fiona to join them, to make them five ('points of a star,' said Carys; 'a full hand,' said Mimi). But this wasn't exactly what was happening. While Fiona became more established, Zohra started to slip out of sight and the others carried on as if there were still only four of them.

Fiona was academically clever. Very. But King Edward High in Birmingham, the most obvious school for her, had already allocated its places when she moved into the area, so she'd had to settle for Finstall High School for Girls. She recognised almost immediately that Zohra, studying the same subjects as her, would be her most serious rival.

She turned to Zohra again, leaned over and breathed into her ear. 'But you go online,' she said. 'I've seen you.' Her soft breath was an arrow of dry rot, worming its way in, heading for the point of no return.

'Only for research,' whispered Zohra. She was trying not to think about last night.

She'd recently gone with a small team from her school to an engineering workshop in Cardiff. They'd all had a really good day, building bridges, inventing spaceships and helping to design a small vehicle that would run on dandelion juice, so when she later found friend requests on Facebook from some of the people she'd just met, she was pleased. She was a little uncertain who was who. The photos helped, but not with everyone – if you've only met people when they're wearing jeans and T-shirts, it's a little startling to see them in party clothes, lip-sticked and spar-kling. But when she'd checked their contacts and found they had plenty of friends in common, she accepted them all. Her friends list was finally starting to look as healthy as everyone else's.

It was exciting to go online and find messages, interesting comments, plenty of 'likes', people who wanted to talk to her:

Michelle Carson wrote 'hi hun, you looked fabulous at Cardiff, loved that top where's it from'

'Thanks. It was Miss Selfridge.' Which one was Michelle? 'You looked great too.'

She felt she was being offered a passport into a foreign coun-try, a way in to a previously unreachable culture where she could create a new identity and not worry about the loss of Katy, Mimi and Carys. She recovered a sense of belonging, the knowledge that she was appreciated.

Lucy Manning wrote 'I'm soooo jealous of your hair. Mine's just thin and wispy.'

But last night something changed. Michelle posted a message on her wall, where everyone could read it – 'youve told the others haven't you, the one time i ask you not to blab and you have to go and do it anyway'.

Zohra was confused, not sure what she was talking about – she would have apologised if she'd known what she'd done

– but Michelle wouldn't focus on anything specific. After a while, she went uncharacteristically quiet, then came back with strange unconnected comments – 'you should have told me you dyed your hair', 'did you actually pay for that top?' – then disappeared again. It was the unpredictability that made it so alarming.

'just because you go to a posh school you think you can treat the likes of us like we're something disgusting under your shoe'

'No, it's not like that at all—'

Other people came to her rescue. 'Don't worry, sweetie. She's lovely really. She doesn't hold on to things for long. She'll be fine in no time, you'll see.'

'She'll get over it. She always does.'

'I know you don't feel as if you're in the wrong, but there are always two sides to an argument. It's probably easier to just agree with her. Then at least she'll calm down.'

What argument? What sides? But Zohra wanted to keep her friends, so she pretended she knew what was going on, apologised and after a brief silence, Michelle came back as if nothing had happened. 'You're gorgeous, hun. Did I tell you that?'

But what was it all about? It was hard not to worry. Where were Mimi, Carys, Katy? Why didn't they offer some support? Were they even interested? She wondered if she should block Michelle. But people didn't like being blocked and it might alienate everyone else. She didn't want it to turn nasty.

Fiona was still hovering by her ear, almost silent, but not quite. 'Are you trying to avoid me?' The words hung in the air, for Zohra's ears only.

'No!' said Zohra indignantly. 'Of course not.'

'If you feel you have something to contribute, Zohra,' asked Mrs Girling, 'you're welcome to come to the front and tell us what you would like to say.'

'No, Mrs Girling,' said Zohra. 'Sorry.' It's hard to contribute anything when you feel as if you're disappearing.

*　　*　　*

59

Zohra lies still, her heart pounding after her nap, breathing in, breathing out. It will pass if she waits. She's learnt how to let it be there, how to manage it, but that's all. Once the agitation has started to ease, she gets up and makes herself a cup of coffee, checking the time on the clock above the mantelpiece. Her mother will come upstairs to prepare supper in about half an hour and Zohra will have to take her place in the shop. It's the busiest time of the day, when the schools come out. Her father is usually exhausted by now, having already worked for nearly twelve hours, but he only takes breaks for meals, even when Chrissie, their new assistant, is there. To be a newsagent is to accept a lifetime of curtailed sleep. Work starts before dawn (except for the few bright weeks around the summer solstice), when the newspapers are dropped off.

Her father doesn't trust anyone else to sort them. 'I have to be sure,' he says. 'I can't allow the wrong supplements to get into the wrong papers. This is how newsagents fail.'

It's important to him to be the provider. He wants to prove to Zohra and her mother (and himself) that he's done everything possible to make up for his own foolishness. He can provide the lifestyle he always intended, despite his squandered youth. 'As good as a solicitor,' he says. 'No difference.'

Zohra has pointed out that they'd never experienced the alternative and therefore couldn't possibly know if they were matching it or not. And that if he'd been a solicitor, she wouldn't be doing shop-work. 'Why pretend?'

'Makes him feel better,' said her mother.

'It's not necessary to humour me, Mother,' said her father. 'I can take criticism.'

'You work too hard,' said her mother. 'One day you wake up and find you're no longer alive. And what will you do then – eh?'

Zohra's phone rings and she picks it up, checking first to see who it is. 'Hi, Nathan.'

'Zohra . . .' He sounds agitated. 'We've found a – found a . . .'

He's too excited. She lowers her voice, slows the words. 'What have you found, Nathan?'

'Carriages,' he says. 'Two carriages – 1965. British Railways Mark One.'

'Where?' How can he have found out about the Greenwood brothers when she's only just discovered them?

'A s-scrapyard in Devon. Just s-sitting there, abandoned like a s-starship that nobody wants, adrift in s-space.'

'You mean they're floating?' This must be a fantasy. He's seen a picture and forgotten where he saw it.

He sighs. 'They're on the ground. Obviously. But abandoned. Like a s-space hulk.'

Star Trek again, presumably – although it could be *Star Wars*. 'Are you sure you haven't just seen it in a film?'

There isn't an answer and she suspects he's shaking his head. 'In words, Nathan. Tell me in words.'

'No,' he says. 'They're in good condition, s-structurally s-sound. That's what Crispin says.'

This sounds more promising than she expected. 'What do they want for them?'

'I don't know. Crispin says he's going down on S-Sunday to have a look and I can go with him. Do you want to come?'

Zohra hesitates. 'I'm not sure, Nathan. Does Crispin want us all to go?'

Silence again.

'Are you nodding, Nathan?'

'Yes.'

'Okay,' she says. 'I'll check with Crispin.'

'Bye, Zohra,' he says. 'Don't forget you're going to marry me.'

He always says this. She worries that he might mean it. 'Nathan—' she says, but he cuts her off.

She stands for a while with the phone in her hand, making calculations. A trip to Devon with Crispin and Nathan. They could go to the beach. She could forget all about Mimi.

Crispin was the only one who came to find her when she walked out of school after her last exam and never went back. She'd gone home, taken some pliers and a hammer from her father's toolbox and smashed up her hard drive, wrenching it apart, breaking it into small pieces. She'd thrown everything into the skip at the back of the store, where it sank into a pile of cherry Bakewells that were past their sell-by date. She switched off her phone. No one knew because nobody cared. Except Crispin.

He turned up at the shop after a week and her parents, bewildered by her silent withdrawal, abandoned their principles and sent him upstairs to her bedroom. He sat down next to her, on the floor, back to the wall, for three hours without speaking. Then he got up, stretched, and left. But he came back the next day and the next. She learnt that friendship doesn't necessarily require words.

'Put your phone back on,' he said eventually. 'So I can check you're all right.'

'No,' she said.

'Switch off all the settings except for incoming and outgoing calls. Block every number except mine.'

'You do it,' she said, because he was the gadget man.

When her A-level results arrived, she threw away the envelope without opening it.

Crispin threw his away too, because he knew his results would be rubbish, although Zohra thought he should have looked at them first. 'I ought to have done some work,' he said. 'But it was boring. My dad won't mind. He's always insisted I was wasting my time in school.'

Zohra ignored letters from Birmingham University, not even knowing if they'd rejected her or if they were holding the place open. Eventually, all correspondence stopped. The school secretary phoned the landline at the beginning of the autumn term, to find out why no one had replied to the invitation to Awards Night, but Zohra wiped the message before her parents could hear it. She never went back; never spoke to anyone from Finstall High again.

She can hear the murmur of the shop below: the ping of the door as a customer comes in; a greeting from her father, always gentle, always courteous; the song of her mother's voice, rising and falling, with or without an audience. Everything okay. Nothing to puncture the pattern of her life. She picks up her phone to ring Crispin, but it rings before she has the chance.

'Hi Zohra,' says Crispin. 'Just woken up?'

'Don't know what you mean,' she says. 'Nathan phoned. He says you're going to Devon on Sunday. Something to do with some carriages?'

'Yeah, just mooching online and bingo, there they were, in a scrapyard! Eat your heart out, Severn Valley. But we have to keep it quiet. Can't risk an auction with the big guys. Good condition, as far as I can tell. Want to come?'

'If it's okay with my father. Are you seriously going to take Nathan?'

'Think I can't take five hours of coupling rods, bogies, and starships?'

'You're a far, far better man than I,' says Zohra.

'Self-evident,' he says. 'It has to be done. Don't forget I wasn't the one who reckoned there'd be spare carriages all over the place. Ten a penny, I seem to remember was the expression.'

'Actually . . .' she says, and pauses, wondering if it would be unprofessional to reveal the whereabouts of Mr J. and Mr N. Greenwood.

'Zohra? Are you still there?'

She makes a decision. 'Well – you might be interested to know that I was right.'

'What's that supposed to mean?'

'I've just found out that there are two carriages not a million miles from here. Long Meadow, hidden away on an old railway track, invisible from the road. I delivered to them for the first time today. Two brothers, old, beards.'

'How cool is that?' says Crispin, sounding like Nathan. 'Living in a railway carriage.'

'That's not all. They have a really interesting history. Their sister was murdered when they were teenagers.'

'Seriously? In the carriages?'

'No, but it was somewhere in Bromsgrove. Older people will remember it. Ask your dad. I bet he'll know what happened.' She's already asked her father, but he was no use at all since he hadn't arrived in Bromsgrove until almost a decade later. He thought his aunt might have mentioned it – she'd have heard something from customers – but he couldn't recall the details.

There's a pause. 'This is encouraging,' says Crispin. 'People tend to move when bad things happen.'

She sighs. 'We're talking nearly fifty years ago. No one takes that long to make a decision.'

'Hmm, good point. So what do you reckon? Would they be interested in selling anyway?'

'How would I know? It's not the kind of thing you ask when you first meet someone: "I like your home. Can I buy it?" Anyway, we didn't exactly have a conversation. There was some issue about the letter. They reacted rather oddly when I gave it to them.'

'I wonder if it could be a siding connected to the Wychington line. I'll have to look at the map, check the records.'

Zohra suddenly remembers the rest of her morning and the carriages lose their significance. 'Do you remember Mimi?' she asks.

'Amelia?' he says. 'Amelia Whalley? Scantily clad, purple toenails, went out with Dan Arminton?'

'That's the one.' She hesitates again. 'She's moved into a house on my round.'

'Ah,' he says. He hadn't had a great deal to do with Mimi – he wasn't into parties – but he would remember her as part of Zohra's old set, the friends who stopped being friends a long time ago. 'Have you spoken to her?' he asks eventually.

She nods. 'She hasn't changed. Came to the door in a silk negligee and five-inch heels. I could have been anyone.'

He laughs. 'That sounds like her.'

'She's living in one of the nailers' cottages on Wildmoor Hill. Some of them are considered to be quite upmarket these days.'

'She's probably renting,' he says. 'Or got a rich husband. She didn't seem the type to go for high-powered jobs, did she? Too frivolous.'

This is what Zohra likes about Crispin. Without really saying anything, he always manages to make it clear he's on her side. But this makes her worry that he spends too much time with her. She's suggested that he should get out more, that hanging around with her is cramping his style, but he just laughs and changes the subject.

'So are you coming with me and Nathan to the seaside?' he asks.

'I'll have to check that my father can manage without me in the shop.'

'And if the scrapyard carriages don't work out, there's now an alternative. We can buy your railway carriages instead.'

'They're not my carriages. And I want to go to the seaside.'

Zohra first met Crispin on a literature course. It was part of a long-standing arrangement between Finstall High and Finstall Comp, whose playing fields backed on to each other. Every Friday afternoon, the sixth forms met up for extra-curricular activities.

Mrs Girling addressed the Lower Sixth before the first encounter. 'We expect you to act with good manners at all times,' she said. 'When your sessions are at the comprehensive, remember that you are our ambassadors.'

'Finstall Comp won't know what's hit them,' whispered Mimi, widening her eyes with excitement. Her blonde hair was expensively cut into deliberate disarray, and she was wearing her most recently acquired Oasis top and skirt. Dressed to impress.

'They're not doing it to benefit us,' said Carys. 'It's all to do with VAT.'

'Meaning?' asked Zohra.

'If we don't share our facilities with state schools, we lose our status as a charity and have to pay VAT.'

'And you know what would happen then,' said Katy. 'Higher fees, more defaults, fewer pupils, the end of Finstall High.'

'No bad thing, then,' said Zohra, experimenting with a chuckle. But no one laughed. Wrong timing.

Zohra found herself separated from the others, allocated to Twentieth-Century Literature. There were only eight pupils in the group and the small number immediately made them feel special. They read a book a week – John Steinbeck, Margaret Atwood, Ian McEwan, Julian Barnes – and debated passionately, often finishing late. Why aren't there more women on standard lists of great writers? Has slavery altered the consciousness of Americans? Does humour strengthen or weaken a book? Can only black writers write about black issues?

When Crispin first came into the classroom, Zohra immediately liked the look of him. He moved more self-consciously then, folding his long, skinny limbs carefully when he sat down, as if he was afraid they would tangle. He'd made an attempt to look smart for that first meeting – an open-necked shirt and white chinos, but it sent out an immediate message that if there was anyone at home who knew how to iron, they weren't bothering to do it. He soon reverted to his customary jeans and T-shirt and a dark, army-style jacket that went everywhere with him. His hair – long, abundant and blond in the summer, thriving in the sun like an exotic flower; shorter and darker in the winter – was nearly always messy. But despite the impression he gave of casual indifference towards the rest of the world, he would always give Zohra his undivided attention. Whenever she spoke to him, he would fix his green, brown-flecked eyes on her unblinkingly and nod earnestly, letting her believe that her opinions mattered.

For some reason that she never understood, the other girls showed no interest in him whatsoever.

Sometimes Crispin and Zohra would walk home in the same direction after the class, still debating, feeling their way towards friendship. Crispin never intended to go to uni – 'too expensive, I'm anti-debt' – and he now drifts between temporary local jobs, refusing to consider commitment and preferring to work with his father on their grounds at Wychington Hall.

His father, who considers education to be beyond contempt, likes to have him around and can't see why anyone would want to do anything else except work on the land. 'All that money for what? Nothing worthwhile ever came from sitting indoors with a load of pretentious so-called thinkers. You have to do things, smell the soil, breathe the air.'

'Not his idea for you to do A-levels, then?' said Zohra to Crispin.

'My choice. I like knowledge. Just hate the exams.'

Perry has no qualms about messing about with machinery, though, contaminating that same air with fumes from a large variety of gadgets, including a tractor, a hedge-cutter and a motor-cycle.

Crispin doesn't talk about school. He lives in the now, refusing to plan ahead or analyse what's gone before, as if nothing ever happened. It's refreshing, liberating, safe. And her parents approve of the friendship, even if they can't understand why it remains platonic. How could they not approve of the son of a man with a title?

'Your father is Lord Hillswood?' said her father when he first met Crispin, carefully low-key, anxious to appear not even slightly impressed. 'So . . . you will inherit Wychington Hall?'

'Well, yes,' said Crispin, uncomfortably. 'But there's nothing there. Most of the land was sold off years ago. And the house is a wreck. We only live in the east wing – the rest is falling down.'

'The east wing,' repeated her father, grinning with delight.

'You stay for supper?' said her mother. 'Nothing much, natu-rally. You might not like our Indian food.'

'I will,' said Crispin, who was always up for a free meal. 'But not if it's any trouble.'

'Trouble?' said her mother. 'Cooking for me is never trouble.' And she disappeared into the kitchen, mixing spices, marinating chicken, baking sweetmeats, thrilled to be cooking for an appreciative audience.

Crispin's mother died when he was two years old – he has no memory of her – so he lives with his dad, Peregrine, in casual squalor, existing on McDonald's and Morrison's ready meals. Zohra finds this no-fuss approach, the refusal to cook, the lack of interest in healthy options, dizzyingly exciting.

It was Peregrine – 'call me Perry, my dear, everyone else does' – who rediscovered the old branch line running along the boundary of the remaining part of his estate. He fell off his quad bike one day in a patch of neglected woodland. He was roaring round, having fun, pretending to work, when he collided with a fallen tree trunk. The bike tipped over and Perry kept going, flying through the air, miraculously missing the upright trees, falling headlong into a long gulley on the far side, where he found himself staring at a rusty piece of metal.

Zohra and Crispin were attempting to clear out the lily pond, lifting streaks of blanket weed and cutting through the tangled roots of the lilies, when Perry came limping out of the trees towards them, his grey ponytail yanked to one side, strands of hair hanging loosely down the side of his face.

Zohra saw him first. 'Crispin!' she said urgently. 'Your dad!'

But there was nothing wrong with Perry, apart from his appearance. In fact, he was more cheerful that she'd ever seen him. 'The railway!' he yelled as they approached him. 'I've found the railway track!'

Neither Crispin nor Zohra knew what he was talking about. 'Always knew it was there, just not certain where exactly. It's the Wychington line!' He was almost dancing, waving his arms, lifting one leg at a time – he had arthritis, he wasn't up to actual jumping – and revealing his uneven teeth (which he usually kept discreetly hidden) in an enormous grin.

An investigation online revealed that there had once been a spur, joining the line that went through Stoke Prior Works, edging the Wychington estate, then heading out towards Tardebigge, but doubling back in a giant circle before it got there (as if no one really wanted to go to Tardebigge) and rejoining the main line at Stoke Prior. It wasn't clear what it was for – possibly a siding for maintenance on engines or carriages, or a way of transporting produce from the estate to the main line, or taking workers to and from a slate quarry (long-since abandoned) on the far side.

'I expect it was for the Wychington family,' said Zohra. 'Whenever they wanted to go into Bromsgrove.' The idea of having a train as your own personal transport appealed to her.

They searched through old maps and discovered that the estate still owned the entire track. Most of the land on either side had been sold off ages ago, but the sales hadn't included the railway line. So they followed it in both directions and found a station not far from the hall, hidden by dense undergrowth. They climbed up the rusty steps, their footsteps echoing into the surrounding silence, and emerged on to a long metal platform. There had once been a roof over one end, but it had collapsed at some point, the spikes still visible amongst the fallen remains, wrapped and protected by the benign touch of buddleia and rosebay willowherb. At the other end of the platform, the shape of a wooden bench rose up through a mound of ivy, almost intact.

'It can't have been for maintenance, then,' said Crispin. 'No point in having a station if you just want somewhere to put the trains to bed.'

'And you'd need a shed for that,' said Perry. 'A gigantic one.'

Zohra peered over the side at the bright orange track. It was surrounded by oil-stained stones and smothered with daisies and dandelions. 'It's a bit rusty,' she said.

Crispin had suddenly come alive, pacing up and down, pulling at the ivy and revealing the bench, jumping down on to the track. 'We could restore it,' he said. 'Like the Severn Valley Railway, the Bluebell line. People love heritage railways.'

'But wouldn't you need a train?' said Zohra.

When an article was written about the railway in the *Bromsgrove Messenger*, people started to contact them, emerging from their specialist lairs, experts who had been ticking away quietly like death-watch beetles, waiting for the opportunity to reveal themselves. These were people who spent their holidays at steam rallies, whose attics were landscaped with miniature tracks and Hornby trains, who would be willing to empty their entire bank accounts for a trip on the *Flying Scotsman*. They knew the history and the timetables, the position of the branch lines before they were closed by Dr Beeching in the sixties and abandoned.

'They've got one-track minds,' said Crispin.

'Appropriately,' said Perry.

They arranged a meeting. It was about five years ago, in an old barn at Wychington. There was a buzz of activity on Facebook and Twitter, but they didn't believe people would actually turn up in real time.

'Should we offer refreshments?' asked Zohra, as they arranged a few chairs in the barn.

Perry stared at her in amazement. 'Are you serious? Do you have any idea how much it would cost?'

'If we can't afford refreshments,' said Zohra, 'how can we afford to renovate a railway line?'

She underestimated the situation dramatically and was shocked when at least a hundred people turned up. She positioned herself at the back, in a corner, terrified that someone might recognise her. But they came from all over the country, experts in local history and railway restoration – there were no familiar faces. Several of them had already researched the area before they got there, tramping around the local countryside, ignoring boundaries and claiming ignorance if they were challenged. They'd mapped out the entire track and found it overgrown and forgotten, fenced off in gulleys backing on to housing estates, behind derelict factories, on the edge of fields. Amazingly, it had never been dug up, the trenches never filled in. There had been two other stations between Wychington and Stoke Prior. Legal investigation into ownership of the property was confirmed by a retired solicitor and it was decided that the railway could reasonably be reactivated.

In the end, a core of about twenty people formed a management committee. Enthusiasts from further away were prepared to offer technical knowledge, legal expertise and guidance on online fund-raising. Crispin set up a website to record their progress.

Three teams of volunteers were established. One set was restoring the station, a second set clearing the track, heading towards the newly discovered station at Hunter's Farm, and the third set, with real experts, was renovating an engine (class 0-6-0, 1936, GWR). This was located early on in the project, along with the shed; the engine had been semi-restored by another heritage railway site, but abandoned after a legal dispute. With the help of a generous donation from a Bromsgrove businessman, everything was shipped up to Wychington and positioned just outside the station.

Money came in from donors across the country, even the world – astonishingly, there were contributors from as far away as Australia, people who'd grown up in Bromsgrove, who still remembered the pre-Beeching railways and wanted to believe everything could go backwards again. Internet campaigns were started, standing orders set up, and somehow they have managed to keep on top of expenses.

Crispin was happier than Zohra had ever seen him.

On Friday, the day after her delivery to the railway carriages, Zohra completes her round more quickly than usual and goes straight to Bromsgrove Station, where she has arranged to meet

Crispin and Perry. They're expecting Trevor, an expert on couplings, who's coming down from York for a final inspection. She arrives just in time, as the train approaches the platform. It's early afternoon, not busy, and only five people alight. They spot Trevor and head towards him, but Zohra is diverted by a hand on her arm.

'Excuse me.'

She turns to confront a woman, short, elderly, wearing a red coat. Two suitcases stand on the platform next to her. She looks exhausted, her face pale and shining with sweat.

'I'm sorry to bother you,' says the woman. 'I've booked a taxi, but I can't seem to see the driver anywhere – I was hoping he'd meet me on the platform – and there aren't any trolleys for my cases. Do you know where I could find one?' She has a slight American accent, mixed with something more familiar. 'You're a mail carrier, aren't you?'

Zohra smiles, pleased with the terminology. 'I don't think we're sophisticated enough in Bromsgrove to have trolleys. But I can help.'

The woman relaxes a little. 'Thank you, thank you, that's so kind. I'd have managed it easily once, but when you get older . . .'

The cases are on wheels, but they're clearly very heavy. 'How did you get them on and off the train?' asks Zohra as they head out through the exit.

'Oh, people are surprisingly responsive if you look helpless.' She stops abruptly as they emerge from the exit and looks around in bewilderment. 'I don't recognise this at all.'

'The station's recently been rebuilt,' says Zohra. 'Although it's not far from the old one. Are you from round here?'

'Once,' she says after a pause.

They locate the taxi – there's only one, so it must be waiting for her. 'Actually,' says the woman, 'you could probably help me. I've come all the way from Canada – such a long journey – and I'm hoping to stay for a while. There used to be some railway carriages near here. I should remember the way, but—'

72

'The Wychington Steam Railway?' asks Zohra. She doesn't look like a steam-train enthusiast, but you never can tell. There isn't really a type.

The woman looks even more confused. 'No,' she says. 'People used to live in these carriages. The Greenwood family.'

'Oh,' says Zohra, surprised. 'I made a delivery to them yesterday – it was the first time I'd been there. The taxi driver should be able to take you. Tell him Long Meadow Road, about halfway up.'

'They're still there, then, the Greenwoods?' says the woman.

'Oh, yes,' says Zohra. She helps her into the taxi and returns to Crispin and Perry, who are chatting to Trevor while they wait for her.

'What was that all about?' asks Crispin.

'She's here to see the Greenwoods,' says Zohra, as she watches the taxi drive away. 'She needed some help.'

'The brothers?' Crispin looks alarmed. 'In the railway carriages?'

Zohra nods. 'She's from Canada. Like the letter.'

Perry turns to watch the taxi drive off. 'She's something to do with the Greenwoods?' he asks.

'Yes,' says Zohra. 'Do you know them?'

'You couldn't not know them once,' he says. 'Their sister was murdered. No idea what happened to them, though.'

'See,' says Zohra. 'I knew your father would know something.'

'So do you think she's come to buy the carriages?' says Crispin. 'Before I've even had a chance to see them?'

6

Nick is sitting in his living room, quite motionless, his hands spread out over his knees, examining the sky through the window. He's observed the gathering of clouds, become aware of the gradual withdrawal of sunshine, the imminent arrival of rain and an encroaching chill, but another part of his mind, the significant part, has been travelling on a different journey. He checks his watch and realises with a shock that time has been ticking away without him noticing and he's lost a good half-hour. This is distinctly alarming. He's spent the day at work, concentrating without thinking, but now he's back home, he can't think clearly about anything.

The truth is, he doesn't know what to do. He wants to compile another list – it would help him think – but at the same time, he knows that a list would be inadequate. You can't be logical about something that makes no sense.

'Less writing, more doing.' One of Ma's expressions, regularly resurrected by Johnny after her death, employed every time he wanted to needle Nick. It might have made Johnny feel better, but it had the opposite effect on Nick.

The list forms in his head:

It's not Debs. She's dead.

It's not Bev. She's dead too.

It must be someone else.

But who?

Not an impressive list. Hardly worth writing down.

How would a stranger know about Debs's handwriting, the squirrel?

It's odd that the writer of the letter has given an address. Why would she make herself traceable? He could write a letter to her

74

(or him – if it's some kind of confidence trick, it's just as likely to be a man), demanding proof. When there's no reply he and Johnny will have their answer.

The address is almost certainly fictional.

If he writes a letter, he'll have to add Johnny's name to it – he can't give the impression that he's making decisions without him – but he can't reasonably do that without his brother's permission. If a strange woman turns up waving a letter that's apparently from both of them, and Johnny knows nothing about it, there'll be trouble. The thought of a face-to-face confrontation adds to his sense of impending disaster.

He could compose a letter, then email it to Johnny for approval. But Johnny won't agree to anything he's written. It would be a matter of principle to him.

He reads through the letter again, for the thousandth time, and then notices the date. It was written over a week ago. Could this person actually be making her way here now, believing she can pass herself off as Debs? If she is, replying is no longer an option. She and the letter would simply pass each other somewhere over the Atlantic.

Maybe the body was a different, unknown girl. But there's never been any suggestion of another missing person. Why would she be wearing Debs's clothes? And there'd still be no explanation for Debs's sudden disappearance.

It's not possible to become another person. If anyone tried, she'd give herself away within five minutes. This has to be Debs or Bev. No one else could reproduce the handwriting on the letter so convincingly.

Could Debs have decided to go to London on her own and set up the business she'd always talked about?

But she'd hardly have left behind her bag containing her purse and personal possessions.

Round and round. Backwards and forwards. The muscles are tightening at the back of Nick's legs, the pain working its way up to his stomach, clamping, squeezing, tearing. He's felt it before.

That day with Johnny and Ma on the bench in their living room, silently watching the BBC report, staring at the photograph on the screen that they'd never seen before: Debs and Bev caught by a colleague's camera, queuing outside a coach in sleeveless summer dresses, grinning into the sun, on their way to the previous year's office outing.

The Americans landed on the moon the day after her body was found. The newspapers were no longer interested in anything else. So if either Debs or Bev were still out there somewhere, they might never have known that everyone thought they were both dead. That's what it said in the letter. It said she didn't know.

What if Bev was still alive? If Debs had died and she hadn't, she wouldn't have stayed in Bromsgrove. It would have been too difficult without her only friend. So maybe she was the one who went to London.

But why would she have gone so suddenly, without telling anyone?

Nick stands up, restless, needing to move, light-headed with the complexity of it all.

Do nothing. Wait. The situation will resolve itself. Time reveals things, alters perspectives.

Debs gave him this advice years ago when he was attempting to analyse his performance after losing disastrously in the early rounds of a local tennis tournament. 'Let it rest for a while,' she said. 'Put space round it, frame it, stand back and take time to think. When you come back tomorrow, you'll see different things, things you can't see today.'

Nick is moved by this memory, by the clarity of her voice in his ear, by her common sense. He's back at her bedroom door (he seems to have wasted far too much time spying on them), watching her and Bev applying lipstick, backcombing their hair, admiring themselves in the mirror.

In the absence of a suspect (apart from three confessors, dismissed with contempt by PC Banner), there wasn't a trial, so police enquiries were never made public. It would be interesting to find out how carefully they investigated, what conclusions they came to. Can you just walk into a police station and request to see their records? Nick's knowledge of police procedures is hazy, based only on *Traffic Cops* (speeding offences, motorway pile-ups) and box-sets of *Hill Street Blues* (American, out of date). If the investigation hadn't been thorough enough, could they decide to reopen the case? Digging it all up again might cause more harm than good.

But the letter changes everything.

He knows Johnny is pacing next door, the vibration spreading from Demeter to Aphrodite, stronger than usual, more menacing. It reminds him of how Johnny used to sit on a bench next to Nick just before a match, his legs jumping and jiggling, as if he was plugged in. But he's over sixty now and needs to show some dignity. Can't he find a better way to channel his anxiety?

Nick turns on his computer. He might be able to find out something online. He stretches out his hands and examines them again. Solid. Still. He can cope. He's not like Johnny, who reacted so badly to their first major family crisis and was never the same again. It derailed him in some way, undermined his resilience.

It was the day when the landlord, Mr Cromwell, lost his patience. Their last experience of a normal, tiled roof over their heads, flat ceilings and walls constructed out of bricks and mortar, plastered, painted.

Nick was seven, Johnny was eight. They were playing tennis in the garden. Debs was around somewhere, not interested in what they were doing any more than they were interested in her. Dad was lounging on the sofa in the living room, compiling lists from library books – deep-sea fishing was his enthusiasm at the time. The month before it had been butterflies. Ma was out cleaning. Nick had taken down the washing line and re-tied it between two trees on either side of the lawn, waist height, dividing the garden in half. The intention was to put everything back to normal before Ma got home, so she'd never know. Johnny had marked out the edges with stones, guessing at the dimensions, and they were playing in their vests and underpants – the closest they could get to white tennis gear.

'Set point. Greenwood to serve.'

'And another ace! First set to Greenwood.'

'New balls, please.'

'Deuce.'

'What a shot! Advantage Greenwood.'

Johnny, who was nearer the house, suddenly stopped. Nick whacked the ball, watched it whizz past Johnny and grunted with satisfaction, only to realise that Johnny had let it go deliberately. He stopped, infuriated that his brilliant shot had gone uncontested.

'What?' he said, his hands on his hips.

Johnny put up his hand. 'Shh,' he said.

There appeared to be an argument going on between Dad and Mr Cromwell, who always came on Tuesday to collect the rent. Mr Cromwell was doing all the shouting, while Dad wasn't saying much. Nick and Johnny looked at each other nervously. Ma needed to be here. She knew how to deal with difficult people.

Nick shrugged and started bouncing a ball up and down on his racquet. 'It's only Mr Cromwell,' he said. 'He likes shouting.' It was probably about money. It was always about money. 'Come on, new balls.'

But Johnny wouldn't continue. He stood in the middle of his side of the court, frozen.

'Get out the way,' said Nick, deciding he would practise his serve. He threw the ball up in the air, circled his arm above his head, threw the racquet forward – and missed. 'Kapow!' he shouted, almost losing his balance. He hadn't quite got the hang of it yet.

But Johnny came over and grabbed his arm. 'Something's wrong,' he whispered. 'More wrong than usual.'

Some of his fear crept into Nick. He stood still and strained his ears, not knowing what he was listening for. When he could eventually hear his father's voice, it was harsh, angrier than he'd ever heard it. 'Come on, man. What about the children?' Silence, then they could hear Mr Cromwell's footsteps on the gravel out at the front. Their father's voice again, calling after him: 'Wait till my wife gets home. She'll have something to say about this.'

There was no reply. Just an emptiness that seemed to go on and on.

'Let's play,' said Nick at last. He knew things weren't right, but didn't know what to do about it.

And suddenly, Johnny was leaping on top of him. 'You daft ha'p'orth,' he hissed in his ear, his voice tight and urgent. 'You don't know anything.'

Nick was taken by surprise. He couldn't understand what was going on. He tipped over with Johnny on top of him and they rolled across the grass in a tight embrace. Nick struggled to get hold of Johnny's hair so that he could pull hard enough to make him squeal, but Johnny grabbed his head and started to bang it up and down on the ground. Nick went limp for a second, hoping he'd ease off, planning to force himself back up again and surprise him.

He was suddenly lifted by an arm round his stomach and found himself dangling in mid-air, his legs running nowhere and his hands scrabbling to grab hold of something. 'Aargh!' he yelled. 'Let go.'

It wasn't Johnny who was holding him – obviously – it was his dad, who, astonishingly, was shouting too. 'Stop it! Stop fighting, you scurvy pair of mutineers.'

Nick relaxed and waited, assuming he'd be lowered to the ground sooner if he was passive, preparing to embark on a new onslaught on Johnny as soon as he was back on his feet, but nothing happened for some time. When he managed to crane his neck round, he could see Johnny lying on the ground a few yards away, flat on his face, with Debs sitting on top of him.

'Now listen up,' said his dad.

'Help!' shouted Johnny from his prone position on the ground. 'She's killing me. I'm dying!'

'Shut up, toad-face,' said Debs, poking him. 'Don't you two ever stop fighting?'

'No,' said Johnny. 'Let me get up or I'll—'

'You'll what?' she said.

'Enough of that!' said their dad. 'The situation's too desperate for arguments. We have to stick together.' He lowered Nick so that his feet finally came into contact with the ground and Debs let Johnny sit up. All three of them stared at their dad.

'What do you mean?' said Debs, her voice oddly shaky.

'We're going to have to start packing,' he said, his voice calm. 'That man . . .' He took a breath. 'He wants us out.'

'You haven't paid the rent, have you?' said Nick, shaking his head with disbelief.

Dad stared at him, but didn't offer an alternative explanation. Instead, he sighed heavily and seemed to shrink a little.

'Clever clogs,' said Debs. 'What do you know about anything?'

Nick shook his head. He didn't want to be right. He just knew he was.

'Come on,' said Dad, recovering some of his energy. 'There's a lot to do.'

'You mean he's right?' said Debs, her voice shrill with disbelief. 'We're going to do a moonlight flit?'

'Call it what you want. But Mr Cromwell will be back tomorrow with bailiffs and, if we're still here, they'll confiscate our stuff.'

'He can't do that,' said Debs.

'Oh yes, he can. They'll chuck us out and he'll have the locks changed. So if we don't get out now, we lose everything. It's a salvage job, chaps, I'm afraid. If you want to keep something, make sure you grab it now and keep hold of it.'

'But where will we go?' asked Debs.

Dad sighed. 'I don't know, sweetheart. I really don't know.'

Nick looked up at the darkening sky. It was nearly bedtime. The air was chilly, unfriendly. How do you empty a house in the middle of the night? 'When's Ma coming home?' he said. She would know what to do.

'In a bit,' said Dad. 'Come on lads, action stations.' He started running towards the house. Debs stood and stared at his disappearing back, her face hard and closed. Nick and Johnny eyed each other nervously.

Johnny started swinging his arms, flapping his bent elbows backwards and forwards against his sides.

'It's all right,' said Nick, his voice coming out awkwardly as he struggled not to cry. 'Ma'll be home soon.'

Johnny sits down in front of his computer screen, trying to ignore the trembling in his fingers. He has two mice plugged in, one on each side, ready for use with the left or right hand. He worries about repetitive strain injury and he's been training the left hand to share the burden. Without the computer he would be paralysed, no longer able to communicate with the outside world.

He's spent all day emailing clients, not allowing himself to think about Debs. Now he takes a breath, opens Google Chrome and types in DEBS GREENWOOD. Over 91,000 hits, although not many people actually called Debs Greenwood. The murder was discussed a few years ago on Bromsgrove Memories, the site mentioned in the letter, but it didn't last long, and there were a few mentions in personal blogs, but not much. He hovers over the few Deb Greenwoods with Facebook profiles, but they're the wrong age. There are plenty of Greenwood Streets round the country and a place called Greenwood in Indiana with a large number of Deborahs, Debbies or Debs – most of them shops: Deb's Posies, Greenwood; Deb's Night Out, Greenwood. Most of the photos include local residents, only of interest to the people themselves, and some artistic shots of the lake. He stops to read a report about mysterious lights appearing over the city and watches a video in which experts offer explanations: a research programme; a secret government experiment to manipulate the weather; a UFO.

The videos temporarily divert him. His preferred explanation would be a UFO but he still manages to indulge in an outburst of contempt at other people's gullibility.

He ignores another ping from an email. Whoever it is, they can wait. But when he glances at the name of the sender, he sees it's from Nick.

No, surely not. Nick doesn't communicate with him unless it's absolutely essential. Johnny hesitates. Is he interested in what Nick wants to say to him?

He opens the email. A one-word message. Bev?

He stares at this for a while. Bev? Is he looking for the wrong person? But how can he search for Bev when he can't even remember her surname? How easily he forgot her after Debs's body was discovered. He googles: BEV, BROMSGROVE.

Very few hits – it must be decades since anyone called their daughter Bev – the same ones as he found in the search for Debs. A few theories emerged: it was the art teacher – he'd been briefly arrested; the man who owned Ronnie's Records (bearded, crooked teeth, sandals), whose chat-up lines were not as clever as he thought; two men with Irish accents who worked at the secretarial college, who everyone thought belonged to the IRA. There was no reference to anyone living in Canada.

But at least Johnny finds out Bev's name. Beverley Newton.

Why is his memory of her so hazy? They must have talked about her after Debs was found, expected her body to turn up next, tried to communicate with her mother. Then he remembers how they'd gone round to her house at the beginning, when the girls were first missed, how her mother had refused to open the door. Instead, she turned up at the railway carriages later that night, spectacularly drunk, shouting and throwing clods of mud, as if it was all their fault. She wouldn't talk – far more interested in perfecting her aim – and, in the end, they had had to send for the police. The woman constable who came was firm but kind, and escorted her away surprisingly quickly, as if they met up every night for a quiet chat.

It wasn't me, said the letter.

But who is me?

What would be the point of impersonating someone? In the end, you've still got to live with yourself. A different name doesn't change who you are.

She's lying, says a voice in his ear, so real that he spins round.

There's no one there. How can Debs speak to him when she's not even alive? Or is it Bev?

He clicks *Reply* on Nick's message and types in 'yes'. It's too definite. He deletes it and types 'maybe'. He's still not sure. He doesn't want to start a debate. He retypes 'yes' and presses *Send*. Immediately, he knows it's the wrong answer. How can they possibly know? Nick shouldn't be asking him. The motor inside him starts to accelerate, vibrating painfully in his chest.

He returns to his inbox, careful not to think about it. There are more emails now: Mrs Knowles (mrsknowlesatsecretaries-rus@hotmail.co.uk), who has learnt how to send emails, but is getting aggressive again about her inability to open her inbox – he'll have to ring her; Littlebird2000@gmail.com, who can't get rid of a screen that keeps popping up out of nowhere inviting her to invest in a goldmine in Australia; Kenthechippy@aol.com, who's convinced someone is scanning his computer and stealing his secret recipe for the ideal chip; sorrybutnot@gmail.net who wants help with setting up an online dating service.

He gets up to stretch his legs before starting to work on it all, scattering a pile of redundant keyboards on to the floor. He slides open the door into the corridor; a gap in his blinds reveals Nick walking away from the railway carriages. He dodges back into his office, not wanting to be seen. Where's he going? What's he up to? Is he going to want to discuss this letter with him again?

'What do you think?' he might say. No – unlikely. He won't be interested in Johnny's opinion. 'Could it be her?'

Johnny can't answer, even in his imagination.

'But why would she come back after all this time?'

Why indeed?

'Is it some plot, a conspiracy? Is someone hoping to take advantage of us, get our confidence, then clean us out?'

It must be Bev, Johnny wants to say, not a stranger. Except that would be acknowledging that Nick was right

Nick was sitting on the front wall, swinging his legs, when Ma came round the corner with the two Co-op bags that she always carried, one in each hand, stuffed with cleaning materials. Johnny was huddled at the base of the wall, inside the garden, biting his nails, humming to himself. It was an irritating sound, tuneless and unidentifiable, but Nick was too tired to care any more. They'd been carrying furniture out of the house for hours and he was aching from head to foot. Now I know what it's like being bombed by the Germans, he was thinking. Like you've been picked up in the air by the blast and dropped, hard, on the ground. Whoosh! Splat! Their dad had gone off ages ago. 'Need to find my mate at the pub,' he said. 'He's got a truck.'

Five mattresses were piled up on the front lawn with sheets and pillows tied up in bedspreads like giant toffee apples, along with heaps of blankets and towels. Boxes of crockery and bags of clothes were scattered across the garden, the first ones neatly packed, but most of them carelessly thrown together as it got later and later and the boys started to get worn out.

'Why aren't you in bed?' called Ma as she got closer and saw Nick. Before he could answer, she caught sight of everything on the front lawn. She stopped at the gate, dropped her bag, placed her arms on her hips and stared. 'What's going on?' she said very quietly. They could all hear her. Even the wind died down when she spoke.

Johnny leapt up and ran towards her. 'Ma!' he wailed. 'Dad says we've got to go.'

Nick tried to explain. 'It's Mr Cromwell,' he said. 'He was cross. He kept shouting.'

Debs came out of the front door. She took Ma's arm and they moved away from the boys for a long, urgent conversation.

'He can't do it,' said Ma angrily. 'We've got rights.'

'That's what Dad said. But Mr Cromwell wouldn't listen.'

'So he'd just have us all out on the streets? Even the babbies?'

'He doesn't care,' said Debs.

A large open-topped truck, dusty with mud and concrete, came jerking along the road and squealed to a halt. The driver's door rattled, shook, and eventually swung open. Dad got out, grinning. 'Not bad, eh? I've never driven a truck before.'

'You're not insured,' said Ma.

He shrugged. 'No one'll know. Things can't get any worse than they are already.'

'I'm going to sort that man out,' said Ma. 'Right now.'

'You can't, Doris,' said their dad. 'It's nearly half past ten. He'll be going to bed.'

'I don't care if he's sitting naked in his bath,' she said. 'Drive me there, now.'

After a brief argument, Dad gave in and they climbed into the truck, banging both doors, and drove off.

'I want to go to bed,' said Johnny, who would normally do anything to avoid sleep. He was sucking his thumb.

Baby, thought Nick. But he didn't say it out loud. He was worried that his own thumb would slip into his mouth when he wasn't thinking about it.

'Come on,' said Debs, picking up some blankets and coming to sit on the grass between them, her back against the wall. 'Lie down here.'

They stretched out on either side of her, their heads on her lap. She put her hand between their heads so they wouldn't bump into each other, and Nick could feel the warmth of her skin on his hair, moving almost imperceptibly, gently tingling and soothing. She draped a blanket round them, tucking in the edges to

85

keep out the cold. The streetlights cast a shadow over them, separating them from the rest of the garden, making them private and secret. Nick could see the lights going on upstairs in neighbouring houses as people went up to bed, and imagined them looking out over their garden before drawing the curtains. What were they thinking? Would they feel sorry for them? Would Mrs Bennett rush downstairs in her nightie and dressing gown, her great bosom wobbling with indignation at the way they were being treated? He wondered if she'd come out of her front door and invite them into the warmth of her house, offer them hot chocolate, show them into her spare bedroom. But nothing happened. Nobody came.

He was finally growing heavy, beginning to doze, when the rumble of the returning truck woke him up. It trundled awkwardly up the road, gears clashing, and halted outside their house. Ma got out with a grim face.

Debs stood up. 'What happened?'

'That man should be strung up on the nearest tree,' said Ma.

'Hanging's too good for him,' said Dad.

They didn't need any further explanation. They staggered to their feet, trembling with the cold, bleary and confused. 'What do we do now?' asked Nick, frightened that he might cry.

Ma crouched down and put her arms round both of them. 'Nothing to worry about, my little soldiers,' she said.

But there was something to worry about.

'Where are we going to go?' asked Debs, and even her voice lacked its normal strength.

Dad came round from the other side of the truck. 'Let's load up,' he said.

'I'm not going to do anything until you tell me where we're going,' said Debs, her hands on her hips, looking and sounding exactly like Ma.

Johnny started crying and Nick could feel an earthquake rising through his stomach, a hard lump in his throat, a trembling in his legs. He swallowed hard.

'Don't you worry, lass,' said Dad. 'One thing at a time.'

Ma smiled at all of them. 'We'll think of something,' she said. 'You'll see. We'll end up much better off in the end. Oh yes, Mr High and Mighty Cromwell can stuff his rat-bagging, overpriced dump up his backside. We don't need him.'

They loaded the truck. By the time they'd finished, it was the middle of the night.

A window was pulled up in a house opposite. 'Keep the noise down,' shouted a man. It was Mr Roberts, who was usually really nice. If he passed the boys playing on the pavement, he sometimes gave them a penny, or a stick of chewing gum out of his pocket. Why's he different now? 'Some of us have to go to work tomorrow.'

They drove for about fifteen minutes, then pulled over in a layby. Ma put two of the mattresses down flat in the back of the truck, and they all squeezed up close, with blankets over them. The light from the moon was silvery and mysterious, as if they'd slipped into a different world where normal rules no longer applied. 'We'll have to pray it doesn't rain,' she said, which struck Nick as very odd. She never prayed about anything. He dropped off to sleep eventually, huddled up next to Johnny, who seemed to snivel all night, his feet resting against Debs's soft stomach, with her feet tucked up by his right ear. It was cosy. Maybe it's not so bad if we don't have a house, was his last conscious thought.

When he woke, Dad and Ma were talking quietly.

'Walter says we can have his bottom field. The one where he kept the horses last year.'

'What's the use of that? We need a roof over our heads. You're going straight to the council in the morning, first thing. And you can stay there till they give us something.'

'They'll split us up, put us in hostels, take the children away. I'm not having that.'

Nick stifled a gasp of panic. Go somewhere without Ma and Dad? Could the council do that? A whole dark world seemed to be opening up in front of him, a giant hole with no bottom. They were already tumbling down it, head first, with no way back, on and on into nothingness. His heart was beating too fast – it was pounding in his head now. Perhaps he was going to die. Maybe that's what happened if you got too scared.

'There are those carriages – you know, the old trains that no one wants any more. Walter says he doesn't mind if we use them.'

'And have you given a thought to why no one wants them? They'll be filthy.'

'We can clean, can't we? It's only dirt. You're good at that.'

Ma snorted quietly. 'Oh, I see,' she said. 'Get the skivvy on to it.'

'Of course,' said Dad. 'That's what women are for, isn't it?'

There was a brief scuffle, some squealing, and then, unbelievably, they were both laughing softly.

'Walter'll be wanting rent,' said Ma after a while, just as Nick was slipping back into sleep.

'Nothing like what that crook Cromwell's been taking off us. It'll be peanuts. Walter's not fussed. It'll give us the chance to sort ourselves out.'

'You'll not be getting your hands on the housekeeping money again, you know that, don't you?' Her voice was sharp and earnest again, more like the Ma that Nick knew. 'I earn good money and it's going straight into my pocket. And from now on, you'll be keeping away from those mates of yours in the pub. Buying them rounds, letting it all slip through your fingers. No more trips to the dog tracks, either, I'm telling you now.'

'Stop whining, woman. I've found us somewhere, haven't I? My mates in the pub got us the truck and the field. What more do you want? A pound of flesh?'

When they woke in the morning, Ma had fetched a loaf of bread and some milk, which they devoured with enthusiasm. Then they drove a short distance and stopped in a deserted lane with fields on one side and trees on the other.

'Our new home,' announced Dad, indicating a muddy pathway between the trees.

'Where's the house?' asked Johnny, puzzled.

'I know,' said Nick. He jumped down and ran up the pathway, with Johnny and Debs close behind him. They stopped on the edge of the field and stared at the two abandoned railway carriages in front of them.

'We're going to live in a train,' said Johnny. 'Hurrah!'

'Is that the best you can do?' asked Debs with disbelief. 'You expect me to live here?'

'Beggars can't be choosers,' said Ma.

Several years later, when they were settled, shortly before Dad died, Ma paid Walter a lump sum for the field. He wasn't interested in being paid for the carriages, just the land. He wanted cash in hand, so he could expand his herd of Herefords without declaring it to the tax man, but Ma went and found a solicitor. She wanted a piece of paper.

'Nobody ever chucks me out again,' she said.

Walter wasn't happy about signing a contract, but she didn't give him a choice. He signed, she signed, and the field and the carriages became theirs.

Halfway through his correspondence with kenthechippy, Johnny remembers the photos. There used to be so many of them, on display in their living room and in albums in the bookcase. Black-and-white snaps carefully slotted in by Dad, a few in colour in the later years. When they knew it was Debs, when it was confirmed that it was her body, Ma systematically removed everything that reminded her of Debs. He remembers her sweeping through their home, collecting up anything that was even remotely connected to her.

It was unsettling. 'Ma, stop it. You don't need to do this.'

'Do stop mithering, Johnny. I'm just cleaning.'

'Are you throwing it all away?'

She was whirling through the carriages like a tornado, lifting, demolishing, removing, leaving almost nothing in her wake.

'Don't fret, it's only rubbish.'

But that wasn't true. The furniture remained – the television, the table and chairs, essential crockery – but everything personal was being erased, swallowed up into huge black bags.

Johnny had even enlisted Nick's help, bursting into his bedroom in a panic.

'Hey!' shouted Nick, who was listening to the Bee Gees, twitching his head in time, pretending to be with-it. 'You're supposed to knock.'

Johnny leaned over and took the needle off the record. 'She's chucking it all away,' he whispered.

'I was listening to that,' said Nick.

'Everything, absolutely everything. There'll be nothing left if we don't stop her.'

Nick followed him out and nearly fell over the piles of black bags that she'd already placed in the corridor. She'd reached Debs's room. Every cupboard door, every drawer, was open. Ma was gathering up the contents and shovelling them into bags.

Nick stepped in. 'Maybe that's enough for now, Ma,' he said, taking her arm. Between them, they managed to lead her to the living room. She cooperated, unexpectedly meek, and sat down where they put her. 'Let's have a cup of tea,' said Nick.

But as soon as he left the room she was up again, grabbing the pictures and ornaments displayed on the shelves in the living room, and Johnny didn't have the authority to persuade her to stop. She paused when Nick came back with a cup of tea, but even as she took a few sips, her eyes were straying round the room restlessly. In the end, she wouldn't respond to either of them, so they let her burn herself out. By the time she'd finished, in the middle of the night, there was no trace of Debs left; no indication that she'd ever existed. The bedroom was bare, stripped of sheets, curtains, pictures, even light fittings. Ma hauled the black bags to the roadside, creating an enormous pile that was in danger of toppling over and causing an obstacle to passing traffic.

'We'll have to get a special collection,' she said. 'Phone the council. They'll come and fetch them. You can do that for me, can't you Nick?'

'No problem,' said Nick.

He and Johnny eased her to bed and then huddled together in the living room, staring at each other nervously.

'She'll start looking for some of it later,' said Nick. 'When she wants to remember Debs, she'll regret getting rid of everything.'

Johnny nodded. 'We could hide the bags.'

'Where?'

'The dead WC in Demeter. We could get them in if we pile them up.'

They worked through the night, cramming the bags in and forcing the door shut. They told Ma the next day that the council had taken them away.

She didn't question the speed of the collection. She just nodded. 'Good,' she said.

Now Johnny opens the door to the dead WC and contemplates the bags in front of him. They've stayed where he and Nick left them, nearly fifty years ago, never examined, almost forgotten. When Ma died, they did something similar, bagging up her clothes and the few personal possessions that remained and depositing them in Debs's old bedroom. Their entire history was stuffed into black bags, unexplored for decades.

He shuts the door again and leans against it, breathing heavily. He feels sick.

Nick and Johnny nursed their mother in the final stages of her cancer, working together in a way they never had, before or since. She'd refused to go to the hospital, refused to have treatment, and only allowed a doctor near her in the last few weeks, when she'd needed pain relief. She couldn't walk by then, and they'd done everything for her, negotiating with the hospital for a wheelchair, pushing her to the toilet, washing and dressing her in the morning, brushing out her white, brittle hair, preparing meals and helping her eat. Later, Johnny had rigged up a bell from her bedroom to the corridor outside their rooms and they took it in turns to help her during the night. If she needed the commode, they both had to come, gently lifting her rapidly diminishing body, making sure she was balanced securely, placing her feet on the footplate, then settling her back down in bed again and tucking her in. They took it in turns to empty the commode.

They'd both been there when she died. She'd shrunk so much that she was barely recognisable, her fury and resilience long faded, and she was unable to talk above a whisper. They had to lean close to hear what she had to say. None of it made sense by then, and the strain of trying to listen, struggling to find a vocabulary of comfort from their own limited experience, with their lack of expertise in emotional language, was exhausting. Johnny was twenty, Nick was nineteen, and neither of them had suitable words.

In the end, she just stopped breathing. They went on sitting there for a long time in the silence, waiting for something to happen, aware that she had died, but uncertain what to do. It was raining outside and wind was blowing against the windows, the real world untouched by their personal tragedy. It felt as if they'd been abandoned, left behind while everything else raged past them. They were trapped into a still, parallel vacuum, where things had just stopped.

Once or twice, in a disloyal moment, it has occurred to Johnny that she hadn't treated them kindly. She just gave up when Debs died. Perhaps she should have remembered that she still had her boys, her sons. Were they less important than Debs? They'd already lost their father. Why hadn't she considered that they were struggling too, that they might have needed her guidance?

7

At 8.25 on Sunday morning, Zohra is waiting for Crispin, standing just inside the shop door, watching through the glass. They're going to Devon today. Stacks of the *Mail on Sunday* and *The Sunday Times* fill the space beside her and beyond them, swaying alarmingly whenever anyone passes, are bags of potatoes: Maris Piper – on special offer because, annoyingly, tomorrow's date is stamped on the front. On the other side of the door, against the counter, there's a pyramid of individually wrapped brownies (a hundred calories a bite) in a cardboard display stand: 'A Little Something to Keep You Going', it says in big orange letters. She moves every time a customer comes in, but it's not busy. Most of them linger, passing the time of day with her father, grateful for a conversation with a real person rather than on the Internet.

Zohra waited outside to start with, despite her mother's disapproval: 'Girls hanging round, hanging on, hanging up, whatever. It gives wrong impression.' She likes to pretend her grasp of English is tenuous if she suspects Zohra is going to argue.

'I'm not a girl,' said Zohra. 'I'm an adult. If people want to draw the wrong conclusion, that's their problem.' It's not as simple as that, as she well knows, but her mother attaches too much significance to other people's opinions.

Part of the problem is that her mother is still influenced by the village where she grew up, outside Lucknow, where she was suffocated by tradition. 'Couldn't even take a breath,' she says, 'without someone telling you off for doing it wrong.' That's one of the reasons why she left for the city as soon as she finished school and never went back to live there (the other reason was that she married Zohra's father and came to England). When she worries about Zohra, she forgets her own bid for freedom and reverts to a way of thinking that she never actually had.

But Zohra has been forced back indoors to keep warm. The sky is an effortless blue, prophesying intense, all-day sunshine, exactly right for a trip to the sea, but there's an autumnal chill in the air. The leaves of the plane trees opposite the shop glitter in the sunlight, still wet with dew, and they dance like over-excited children every time the air is disturbed by cars pulling into the small bay in front of the shop.

She finds herself thinking about the mysterious woman at the station. There are so many coincidences. The visitor was from Canada, the letter to the Greenwoods was from Canada. She knew about the railway carriages. How strange that she could turn up the day after the arrival of the letter. A week earlier, and Zohra wouldn't have known the Greenwoods existed.

Crispin pulls up at eight thirty precisely in his silver Astra (Y reg, alloy wheels, two blue stripes over the roof, from the front of the bonnet to the back of the boot). Did he wait round the corner so that he could turn up exactly on time? Zohra dashes out to meet him. 'Bye Dad,' she calls.

There are no customers in the shop at this point, so her father follows her out. 'Good morning, Crispin,' he says through the open window of the Astra. 'I trust Peregrine is well.'

'Ready when you are,' says Zohra.

But Crispin gets out to talk to her father. They shake hands, always formal, even though they've known each other for years. 'Hi, Mr Dasgupta. Dad's great, thanks. You're coming for the big event, aren't you, the engine's first run?'

'Of course,' says Zohra's father. 'The date is already in my diary. Let us hope the engine performs as well as expected.'

'You sound exactly like my dad. He wanted to keep it small, just in case something went wrong, but he was overruled. Susie – you know, the PR advisor from that posh firm – she says it's the right time to make a splash. She's pretty good, actually – we're advertising all over the place and it looks like we're going to get a big turn-out. Tell the world, she says. Get ahead of the game.'

'Quite right. If you don't take risks, you don't find success.'

'Dad and I had a bit of a barney about it actually – he thought I should side with him – but he gave in. He didn't really have a choice.'

Mr Dasgupta purses his lips. 'You're arguing with your father, Crispin? Come now, where is your respect for age, experience?'

The two men have an easy relationship, which Zohra has never really understood. It's not clear how serious her father is when he lectures Crispin. If he was talking to her like that, she would be itching with resentment, determined to do the opposite of what he says, but Crispin seems to like it. As if being admonished makes him feel part of something he never had. Running wild has its drawbacks, he says. It's all very well growing up with a half-mad father who's more interested in tractors than meals, doing whatever you want to do whenever you feel like it, no schedules, no curfews, but you don't exactly feel cared for.

'Way to go, Mr Dasgupta. Anyway, you have to be there. It's going to be brilliant.'

'My wife and I will be honoured to attend,' says Zohra's father. He nods gravely, but his eyes are smiling with genuine pleasure. 'We will arrange for cover in the shop.'

The door of the passenger seat suddenly opens and Nathan bursts out. 'Hi, Mr Dasgupta,' he says breathlessly, rocking slightly as he struggles to find his balance. He's even taller than Crispin, his arms and legs so thin they resemble pieces of rope, but he's much stronger than he looks. His pale eyes are watery and unfocused, giving the impression that he's just woken up, and his wispy hair, uncombed, frames his face in an unruly halo. They've known him for five years, since he was sixteen, when he turned up to their first railway meeting in Perry's barn after a three-mile walk. He's been there ever since – weekends, school holidays – digging, working on the heavy machinery, running errands, willing to do whatever anyone wants, first to arrive, last to leave.

'Good morning, Nathan,' says Zohra's dad, without offering to shake hands, aware that Nathan is uncomfortable with physical contact. Mr Dasgupta is frequently confused by Nathan, but he has understood that he's different, that you can't have any expectations about how he will react, and he continues to treat him with the same respect that he pays to everyone else. Zohra has never detected the slightest hint of impatience or contempt in him.

'You know I'm going to marry Zohra, don't you?'

Zohra's dad raises an eyebrow and looks at Zohra.

'It's all right,' she says. 'He doesn't mean it.'

'Yes I do,' says Nathan.

'We have to get off,' she says impatiently. 'The sea awaits.'

'We're checking out railway carriages,' says Nathan, frowning. 'Not the s-sea.'

'I know,' she says. 'But you can't drive all the way to the coast without going to the seaside.'

Nathan's right leg starts to jiggle. 'But we can't rush,' he says. 'It's important.'

Crispin pats his shoulder twice – the longest he can tolerate. 'Be cool,' he says. 'There'll be time for both.'

The tension in Nathan's face eases slightly. 'Okay, Crisp,' he says, and turns back to the car.

'In the back, Nathan,' says Crispin.

'I want to sit on the flight deck.'

'Sorry. Zohra's got that position.'

Zohra is about to suggest that they take it in turns when she realises that Crispin probably wants some sensible conversation. 'You've got much more space in the back,' she says. 'You can stretch out.'

'No I can't. Not if I'm wearing a s-seat belt. And I have to. It's the law.'

'It's still more roomy. And you can eat sweets without asking.'

'I'm not allowed food with additives.'

'I need you in the back,' says Crispin. 'To keep an eye on the speed cameras when we pass them, check they haven't flashed.'

'You're not planning to break the speed limit?' asks Mr Dasgupta.

'No, of course not,' says Crispin.

A voice from above makes them look up. 'Have a lovely time, all of you.' It's Zohra's mother, in the yellow and silver sari that she always wears on a Sunday, leaning through an upstairs window and waving. She wants Zohra to go out, have friends, be happy – find someone to marry.

'No worries,' says Crispin. 'We will.'

Mr Dasgupta hands Zohra a large bag. 'Some goodies for the journey.'

'Yeah!' shouts Nathan.

'What about the additives?' asks Zohra.

'It's okay,' says Crispin. 'There's chocolate. Thank you, Mr Dasgupta.'

Crispin starts the engine. 'And we're off,' he says. They wave as they pull away.

The scrapyard is located on the edge of Dartmoor, hidden in a valley that's not visible from the main road. They come off the A38 at Ivybridge and turn on to a B-road, which narrows into a single-lane carriageway. As they round a sharp corner, Crispin brakes abruptly. 'Oh my goodness!' he says.

Rows and rows of railway carriages soar up into the sky in front of them, giant pieces of Lego, cunningly slotted together in neat stacks, five high, ten deep. There's a sprinkling of colours – brown and cream, silver, red and cream – but the vast majority are blue and white, deeply scratched, rippled with dents. Every window has been shattered, revealing black, sinister interiors, and most of the doors are swinging loose. They're like blocks of flats from the 1960s, thinks Zohra, those awful soulless maison-ettes built in the cheapest way possible, as if nobody had bothered to consult an architect. And they're balanced so delicately, as if they're waiting for the last straw, ready to topple at the slightest threat – vibrations from a collision on a nearby road, perhaps, the quiver of thunder through the air, or a mild earth tremor.

Crispin pulls up along the side of the road and puts on his hazards. 'It's British Rail,' he says. 'The blue and white. Eighties.'

'There's a housing crisis,' says Zohra. 'Why has nobody thought of putting these to use?'

'Access could be a problem,' says Crispin.

'If they can get them up there, they can bring them down again. They could put them in a field. In rows, like caravans.'

In the back of the car, Nathan is radiating awe, speechless.

A footpath, littered with sweet papers, Diet Coke cans and crisp bags, runs parallel with the scrapyard. It's separated by a tall metal fence and continues on, overshadowed by the heaps of carriages, past the entrance to the scrapyard towards a Premier Inn beyond.

'A hotel?' says Zohra. 'Seriously?' The logo, a crescent moon with a cluster of stars against a dark purple-blue background, has been placed on the side as a welcome, and there's a road leading round to the far side. This is clearly the back of the hotel – there's no sign of an entrance – and rows of wide, generous windows, presumably bedroom windows, overlook the scrapyard. 'Whoever would want to stay there?'

'Railway enthusiasts,' says Crispin. 'As we all know, there are lots of them around.'

Zohra laughs. 'Come to sunny Devon. Walks on Dartmoor, trips to the sea, a view of dead trains from your hotel window.'

'Cool,' says Nathan. 'I'd s-stay there.'

'We'd better move,' says Zohra, as a lorry roars past them. 'We're in the way.'

Crispin pulls away and they swing into the scrapyard, through rusty gates propped open with large oil drums. Heaps of mangled carriages become visible, concealed from the road in what looks like an abandoned quarry, all broken and twisted, crumpled by a giant mechanical hand and discarded, thrown aside like unwanted toys. They're crammed together, forced into artificial waves, rising and falling, like the cars of a fairground ride. The front of each carriage seems to be pushing upwards towards the sky, as if they're all gasping for breath. Four cranes lean gracefully over them like guardian angels, keeping an eye on everything. Smoke from scattered bonfires rises up in thin spirals.

They park in a space next to an old, very dusty Mercedes and climb out of the car. Zohra wonders how safe they are, overshadowed by precarious piles of trains. Nathan spins round slowly, gazing up at the cranes, the stacked carriages, as if he's in a dream.

'Over here,' says Crispin, heading towards a small wooden hut with a handwritten notice on the door: RECEPTION. *All visitors must report here.* He knocks. When there's no reply, he turns the handle and goes in. It's warm and cosy inside, but unoccupied. Gaps in the walls have been stuffed with scraps of material – maroon moquette, textured, heavy duty – that look as if they've been torn from old train seats. There's a small desk, a heater that isn't switched on, although the atmosphere is thick with the smell of charred dust, piles of papers on every available surface, and an ancient armchair with the stuffing coming out, dangerously close to the heater. A red landline is balanced on one of the arms and a plastic container full of sandwiches on the other. Wholemeal bread, hand-cut, bursting with chunks of chicken and lettuce.

'Who are you?' asks a loud voice, and a short, stocky man comes through the door, smelling powerfully of bonfires. His legs, thick and muscled, bow outwards at the knees. 'What are you doing in my office?' He studies them, radiating suspicion, his face tight with hostility.

Zohra exchanges a look of bafflement with Crispin. 'The notice says this is Reception,' she says.

'I emailed,' says Crispin. 'About the two carriages you've got advertised on your website – the ones in good condition.'

'I don't read emails.'

'But you replied.'

'That'll be the wife.'

'Okay, we'll talk to her,' says Nathan, finally finding his voice. He looks around. 'Where is she?'

The man narrows his eyes and examines Nathan, who immediately looks away and starts to shuffle his foot over the floor, rubbing and scraping, as if he's trying to erase a chalk marking. There's a sudden shift in the man's face, almost recognition of something, and the muscles round his mouth loosen. He turns back to Crispin. 'Alberto,' he says. 'Alberto Gaglioni.' He holds out his hand and Crispin introduces everyone. Alberto seems to understand that Nathan won't shake hands and doesn't attempt to make any contact. He doesn't look or sound Italian. 'Saw the car,' he says. 'Thought it might be the police.' He almost smiles, as if he's revealing secrets, as if he now considers them to be on his side.

'So where have you hidden the dead bodies, then?' asks Zohra.

'Under the bogies, I'll bet,' says Crispin.

Nathan frowns. 'What bodies?' he asks. 'How would you get them under bogies?'

Alberto Gaglioni abandons the last of his suspicions and laughs. 'Good point,' he says. 'My son's just like you. Gets straight to the point.'

Nathan looks pleased.

'Can we see the carriages?' asks Crispin.

Alberto pauses for a moment, thinking. 'Good condition – she must mean the ones on the west bank. I'll drive you out there. There are rules, though.' He pauses to pick up some yellow hard hats, and hands them out. 'Health and safety. No wandering off.'

Nathan plonks the hat straight on his head. 'Take a photo, Crisp,' he says. 'With the trains behind me.' Zohra examines hers. It's filthy, coated with oil and grease, very different from the one she uses at Wychington.

'Just bung it on,' says Alberto.

It feels inadequate. On their railway, Frank from Worcester, who teaches French in real life, operates the crane. He's been on courses and knows all about safety. It's impossible to know how reliable these cranes are as they manoeuvre unimaginable weights backwards and forwards over their heads. How could something so insubstantial as a yellow hat protect them from such powerful forces?

Alberto leads them to his car.

'What are you burning?' asks Zohra, pointing to a column of smoke rising behind the hut.

'Just old paperwork,' says Alberto vaguely. 'Can't keep everything forever.'

They climb into his car – which smells of cigarettes and chips – and he drives them past the piles of carriages, round the trains in the quarry, to a less cluttered area, further away from the road and surrounded by gorse-covered hills. There are several railway tracks laid out here, side by side, each one stopping abruptly where the ground starts to rise, and on them are five carriages, blue and grey, two to a track. They have a business-like appearance, as if they're waiting for passengers, expecting the railwaymen to come and connect them up to the engine, so they can be pulled away from this dismal place and back into active service.

'They're 1965,' says Alberto. 'British Railways Mark 2 basic. All in good nick. It's a job lot, though. Can't let them go separately.'

'Oh,' says Crispin. 'You didn't mention that in the email.'

'I don't email,' says Alberto.

'Can we see inside?' asks Zohra.

Alberto smiles at her, then rolls his eyes at Crispin. 'Obviously,' he says. He pulls open one of the doors, then stands back to let them climb up.

'There's no corridor,' says Zohra, instantly disappointed.

'Doesn't matter,' says Crispin, 'we can still make it comfortable.'

The accumulation of moss on the windows means that everything inside is tinged with green, and there's a strong smell of damp, rotting wood. Beetles, ants and woodlice are swarming in and out of holes in the seats, black, busy specks, unconcerned by the presence of humans. There's little left of the original fabric.

Zohra shudders. 'It's a bit . . . it'll need work.'

'You've got decades of life there,' says Alberto from the doorway. 'Steel frames.'

'Come on,' says Zohra to Crispin, anxious to leave. 'We've seen all we need to.'

Crispin lingers. 'Try to imagine it in its heyday,' he says softly. 'New upholstery, fresh wood veneers, full of people, families, buzzing with life.'

Zohra is having trouble with this vision. The smell's too strong, the insects too invasive. She leads the way back out and takes several deep breaths of fresh, sunny air.

'Can we have all of them?' asks Nathan. He's staring around him, quivering with excitement, uncertain which instinct to follow. 'I want to work here.'

'You can't,' says Crispin. 'You live in Bromsgrove. It's too far away.' He turns to Alberto. 'We can't take all five. We don't have the space and they'd cost too much to transport.'

'Got your own lorry?'

'No, we'd have to hire one.'

'I'll throw in half-price transport. Can't say fairer than that.'

'Yess!' says Nathan.

'How much?' says Crispin.

'Make me an offer.'

'Dodgy condition,' says Crispin thoughtfully. 'Three grand for two?'

Alberto stares at him, scratches his head and steps back towards the car. 'Are you having a laugh?' he says. He's expecting them to haggle, make a higher offer.

'They'll need major restoration,' says Crispin.

'We've got to have them,' says Nathan, pulling at Crispin's sleeve.

'We need to think about it,' says Zohra hastily, worried that Crispin might be preparing to make a rash decision.

'I'll have to discuss it with our financial backers,' says Crispin. This is good – suggesting he can't make the final decision. 'But we definitely won't be able to take all five.'

Alberto turns on his engine. 'No deal then,' he says. 'It's all or nothing. Best not to leave it too long, though. Plenty of others interested.'

'We'll be back later,' says Zohra, suddenly anxious to get away as quickly as possible.

'Please yourself,' says Alberto. 'Your decision.'

They drive to Bigbury-on-Sea, buy ice creams and sit on the beach, close to the water. Nathan eats his rapidly and crunches the last of the cornet, leaving a rim of white round his mouth.

'Dogs eat like that,' says Crispin, licking his own ice cream neatly, catching each drip, smoothing the surface with his tongue. 'Just wolfing it down. Can't possibly taste it.'

'How would you know?' says Zohra. 'You haven't got a dog.'

'True,' says Crispin. 'But I had a friend who did.'

Nathan's mind is on the trains. 'Can we go back now?' he says.

'There's no hurry,' says Zohra. 'They're not going away.'

'But he might have s-sold them. He said other people were interested.'

'There were hundreds of railway carriages. Thousands.'

'No, most of them weren't any good.'

'It's just a sales tactic,' says Crispin. 'There's nobody else. He just wants to scare us, get the highest price he can.'

Zohra lets the sand run through her fingers and examines the tiny grains. So many colours, so many shapes, all merging into yellow. The sound of the waves is soothing. 'Have we got three thousand?' she asks.

Crispin smiles. 'Don't worry about the money,' he says. 'I have the exact figures in my head. I know how far we can go. The most important thing is, we can't let him push us into taking more than two carriages.'

'Right,' says Zohra, not convinced he knows what he's doing. She points towards Burgh Island. 'Shall we go out to the island?'

'It's not an island,' says Nathan. 'You can walk to it.'

'It becomes an island at high tide. See the sea tractor up there? That's to take people across when it's cut off.'

Nathan studies the island, the causeway and the tractor. 'Cool,' he says after a while. 'Can we wait for high tide and give it a go?'

'I don't think so,' says Crispin. 'We'll be heading back home by then.'

'Let's not think about that yet,' says Zohra, folding up her coat and leaning her head back on it. 'We've got plenty of time.' She closes her eyes. The sun is warm and comfortable on her face.

'I'm hungry,' says Nathan. 'Can we get something to eat?'

'In a bit,' says Crispin.

'You've just had an ice cream,' says Zohra. She can sense Crispin stretching out next to her and feels oddly pleased that he's decided to follow her example. She turns towards him and opens her eyes, squinting against the brightness. His head is not far from her own, propped up on his backpack, and he's facing in her direction. He's watching her, strangely still, his eyes serious. As soon as he realises she can see him, he winks and they both smile at the same time. Curious how a smile can create such a sense of well-being, a promise of security.

'So who murdered the sister?' he asks her.

'No idea,' she says drowsily. 'I can't help thinking the letter's something to do with it – and the Canadian woman off the train.'

'The plot thickens, then.'

'Mmm . . .' She can feel herself drifting towards sleep, caressed by the heat, suspended in a half-conscious world as if she's being rocked, waves lapping in the background of her thoughts. This feeling of complete relaxation, this release from anxiety, is rare. She lets her mind wander.

And she's worrying again. About her parents, the future of the shop. They like to believe that they do more than supply goods, that they're part of the community and people depend on them for support, human contact. But things change. There's a Tesco Express just down the road now. The customers have strong opinions about powerful big business, but bargains alter people's perspective. In the end, if Tesco's is cheaper, Tesco's will win.

'They're bullies,' says her father over dinner.

'It's market forces,' says her mother.

'They're trying to push us out, the small shop owners who believe in hard work, integrity, determination.' Asians, he means, but doesn't like to say so.

'You have to have business plans nowadays,' says Zohra, 'projections, a relationship with the bank. Nothing remains static any more.'

Her father is incensed. 'So hard work not good enough,' he says, raising his voice slightly (he can't allow himself to speak too loudly, having spent his entire life declaring that shouting is the mark of an uncivilised man), and waving his shaami kabab wildly in front of him. Splashes of chilli garlic sauce fly through the air.

'My tablecloth!' says her mother indignantly. 'Only just washed.'

Her father's anger dissipates as quickly as it came. 'I could have been solicitor by now,' he says sadly, mopping up the juice with a paper napkin provided by his wife. 'Instead I work all hours of day and night – to no avail.'

They've talked about returning to India one day, going back to Lucknow and their nephews and nieces, of whom there are a great many, and living out the rest of their lives in the shade of the banyan trees, which would undoubtedly be superior to the scrubby plane trees opposite the shop. But they've been here for so long. They've never even gone back for a holiday, never been willing to close the shop for a fortnight or entrust it to anyone else. Zohra's mother complains about the summer heat, here in Bromsgrove. How would she manage in India? Do they really want to check their wardrobes for cobras every morning?

Zohra contemplates the possibility of going with them, but the prospect of starting a new life fills her with fear.

'Where's he gone?' says Crispin suddenly, bringing her back to the present with a jump.

She sits up, dazzled by the brightness, confused by the babble of voices coming from a large family which has set up camp in front of them and blocked their view of the sea. Crispin is standing up and peering round. There's no sign of Nathan.

'Oh dear,' says Zohra, pulling herself upright. It's easy to forget that Nathan is a child in a twenty-one-year-old body. He might know all about trains, but he needs constant attention. She shades her eyes with a hand as she searches for him. 'Could he have gone over to the island?' she asks, shaking out her coat.

They walk towards the sandy walkway and study the people coming and going.

'We'll never find him,' says Crispin, 'the island's too big.' He turns round to scan the beach and lets out a sigh of relief. 'It's okay. He's been diverted by the machinery.'

Nathan is examining the sea tractor with great interest, apparently measuring the wheels, talking to an elderly man with a large stomach and a long scar on his right arm. 'Interesting use of hydraulics,' he's saying loudly as they walk up. 'Not much use if the weather's bad, though.'

'That's the drawback,' says the man. 'You have to sit it out and wait if there's a storm. Shame for the visitors who've paid a fortune and can't get to their posh bedrooms.'

'How often do they s-service it?' asks Nathan.

'Nathan!' calls Crispin. 'Fish and chips.'

'Got to go,' says Nathan. He grins at the man and bounds towards Crispin and Zohra.

'See,' says Crispin. 'Just like a dog.'

Crispin explains his plan. 'I'd like to get two carriages for four grand. We can go up to five at a pinch, but that's the absolute limit. The cost of transport is going to be crippling. More than two is out of the question. No negotiation on that.'

'But he didn't sound as if he was going to give in,' says Zohra.

'He's bluffing. He's desperate to make the sale.'

'How can you know that?' Zohra is baffled by his confidence. As far as she knows, he's never done anything like this before.

'Trust me,' says Crispin. 'By this evening we'll be the proud owners of two railway carriages.'

'I think we should take all five,' says Nathan.

'We know you think that,' says Crispin. 'But it's not going to happen. If you so much as squeak while I'm negotiating, we won't stop at a service station on the way home.' He turns to reassure him. 'But if all goes well, you can have a Big Mac.'

They're parked in the scrapyard, outside the hut. It's hard not to feel overwhelmed by the hugeness of the place, intimidated by the equipment required to move everything, by the sense of the past.

'How sad it feels,' said Zohra. 'These trains were once the centre of everything, the only way for most people to meet up before everyone had cars, and now look at them.'

'I keep thinking about all the work that's gone into them over the years,' says Crispin. 'All that energy, the cleaning, the maintenance, just to keep them moving.'

'And they end up here,' says Zohra. 'Abandoned in this sad graveyard, watched over by a man who's only interested in money.'

'You have to be interested in money,' says Nathan. 'Otherwise you die.'

It's not like a human graveyard, where every gravestone represents an individual. It's a mass grave. The trains have lost their identity and become part of a giant, composite memorial – rusted, twisted, suffused with a desolate beauty that reflects their place in history.

'So where's Alberto?' says Zohra. 'He knew we were coming back.' They go into the office, but it's deserted. Everything remains as it was earlier in the day, except that the sandwiches have been eaten.

'Listen!' says Nathan. 'Here come the other buyers.'

They can hear several vehicles approaching.

'I wonder why he doesn't lock the door,' says Crispin. 'You'd think he'd be worried about security.'

'They'll be here any minute,' says Nathan, a note of panic in his voice. 'He s-said we weren't the only ones interested in the carriages. They're going to beat us to it.'

'That's okay,' says Crispin. 'They can have the other three.'

'It's probably just someone driving past,' says Zohra as they go outside again. 'Heading for the Premier Inn.'

But two police cars swing through the scrapyard entrance and pull up next to each other in front of the hut. Several policemen in uniform get out, slamming the doors, and head for the hut, while the two in plain clothes stay by the cars, scanning the surrounding area, section by section, with intense concentration. 'Game's up, Alberto!' shouts one of them after a few seconds. 'We've got the paperwork!'

Alberto emerges from behind a pile of rusty carriages and walks slowly towards them. 'Okay, guv,' he says tiredly. 'It's a fair cop.'

Nobody laughs.

'What's going on?' asks Zohra.

'Who are you?' One of the policemen has finally noticed Zohra, Crispin and Nathan.

'We came to buy some carriages,' says Crispin.

'Right,' he says. 'Like you do.'

Alberto is being led to the car, but before getting in, he turns back. 'You've got it all wrong, Sergeant Lucas,' he says. 'You can't do this.'

'Actually, Alberto,' says Sergeant Lucas mildly, 'we can.'

The car crunches away. The entire episode has taken less than five minutes.

The remaining policemen are now removing papers from the hut in plastic bags and placing them into the boot of their car. One of them is talking on his phone. 'We're going to need some help,' he's saying. 'More paper here than you'd find in a branch of Staples. Turns out he's a bit of a dinosaur – doesn't use computers.'

'Does this mean we can't have the carriages?' asks Nathan.

'Do you think that's why there were so many bonfires?' says Zohra to Crispin.

Sergeant Lucas gets a notebook out of his pocket. 'I need names and addresses,' he says to Crispin. 'And the nature of your business with Mr Gaglioni.'

'Like we said,' says Crispin. 'We were hoping to buy some carriages.'

He studies them, slightly puzzled. 'For what purpose exactly?'

'We're renovating a railway,' says Zohra.

'On Crispin's estate,' adds Nathan.

Sergeant Lucas reacts slowly. He's clearly been trained to take his time, to calm things down, to allow everyone space to come to their senses if they are contemplating violence or resisting arrest. 'Crispin's estate?' he says, raising an eyebrow.

'It's a charity,' says Crispin. 'We have backers, it's all official. You can look it up – Wychington Railway.'

'What's Mr Gaglioni done?' asks Zohra.

'Is he Mafia?' asks Crispin.

Sergeant Lucas turns unexpectedly away from them, temporarily diverted. 'What're you up to, sunshine?' he says sharply.

Nathan has wandered over to one of the police cars, where he's peering through the side window, examining the dashboard.

'Ford Focus,' he says amiably. 'Nice. Not up to warp s-speed, but good for a hot pursuit up the M5. That's where the villains go, I'll bet. Birmingham.'

'Don't mind him,' says Zohra. 'He's . . .' She stops, realising she can't say what she wants to say. 'He's interested in cars, that's all.'

'And presumably trains,' says another policeman, coming up behind them.

'Yes,' she says.

'Does this mean we can't buy our carriages?' asks Crispin. 'We've come all the way down from the Midlands for this.'

'Nobody's going to be doing business with Alberto Gaglioni for some time,' says Sergeant Lucas as he climbs back into his car.

'Why not?' asks Zohra.

He shuts the door and talks to them through the open window. 'He'll be going down for a while, guaranteed. Your best bet is to head back home before you find yourself implicated in money laundering.' The car pulls away before anyone can reply and crunches over the rubble towards the gates.

The journey back to Bromsgrove is depressing, and no one says much until they're well past the M4 exit. Then Crispin sits back in his seat, keeping his hands on the steering wheel, and straightens his arms. 'I really wanted those carriages,' he says.

'You just wanted the glory,' says Zohra. 'To come back and tell everyone what a wonderful deal you'd made. But you should know by now that things never go as you expect them to. Just be grateful we've had such a nice day.'

'When are we stopping, Crisp?' says Nathan. 'You said we could have a Big Mac.'

'That's true,' says Zohra, 'you did.'

'We'll have to look at alternatives,' says Crispin. 'Let's check out the Greenwoods' carriages some time, have a look at their condition.'

'But nobody's suggested they'd be interested in selling.' She pauses. 'I suppose it would be a good way of finding out if the woman off the train's living there.'

'I've never known you be so nosy before.'

'No – it's just . . . I suppose I felt sorry for her. It was the way she looked around so eagerly when we got out of the station, as if she expected everything to be familiar. She seemed so disappointed when she couldn't recognise anything.'

'She's probably a long-lost lover.'

'No – it was more than that.'

Crispin sighs. 'Well, I just want a plan. We can't go back to Wychington empty-handed.'

'We didn't,' says Nathan. He starts whistling strangely, in short, high-pitched blasts. The sound is loud and irritating in the confined space.

'Stop it, Nathan!' says Zohra. She turns, trying to see why he's doing it.

He's waving around a metal tube, about 40 centimetres long, hollow and with a curved handle on the side. 'Nathan,' she says slowly. 'Did you take that from the scrapyard?'

'Yes,' he says, sounding pleased with himself.

'What is it?'

'A whistle.'

'That's stealing,' she says sternly.

'No it isn't. If Alberto's in prison, he won't need it. No one will ever know it's gone.'

'He's got a point,' says Crispin quietly. 'And, let's face it, there's no way I'm going to turn round and take it back.'

'We needed a whistle for the engine,' says Nathan. 'So I got us one.'

8

The following Friday, after a week of sleepless nights and uncertainty, Nick leaves the office early. He nods goodbye to Madeleine, the German receptionist, who's already shutting windows, switching off lights, setting the alarm. It's usually his job to be the last out. Handing over the responsibility to someone else makes him nervous.

He heads up the emptying High Street, past Poundland, Lloyds Bank, Argos, to the library. He hasn't stepped inside a library for a very long time, and he's disconcerted by the presence of so many computers. He feels better once he's located the bookshelves, grateful for their familiarity, and spends a little time walking up and down between the shelves, studying the headings, approving of their neatly notated reference numbers. He occasionally stops to move books around and put them in the correct order.

But he hasn't come for the books.

Eventually, he approaches the desk, where two librarians sit silently, studying computer screens. Neither of them seems aware of his presence. He clears his throat. The young man – a slick centre parting, the hair on either side arranged precisely over his forehead in two limp, jagged-edged waves, which are mystifyingly motionless – looks up. 'Half a sec,' he says. He's wearing a lanyard round his neck, identifying him as Charles Crawford.

The other librarian, a gaunt, severe-faced woman with two pairs of glasses hanging on chains round her neck, but none on her nose, ignores him. What can be so urgent that they can't speak to him?

'How can I help?' asks Charles, finally turning away from his screen.

'Where would I find copies of old local newspapers?' asks Nick.

Charles doesn't seem surprised by the request. 'Are you researching family history?'

Nick stares at him. How can he possibly know that? 'Sort of,' he says.

Charlie nods approvingly. 'You'll be needing the microfilm,' he says. He leads the way to a row of machines set out on tables along a back wall. 'The *Bromsgrove Messenger* goes all the way back to 1860 and the *Bromsgrove Standard* starts from 1996. Do you have a particular year in mind?'

'Nineteen sixty-nine,' says Nick, but then adds – not sure why, but anxious to disguise his real interest – 'and 1970.'

'Right,' says Charlie. 'Some of the *Messenger*'s online, but only up to 1937 so far, I'm afraid.'

Nick already knows this. He spent most of yesterday evening trawling through online records, hoping to avoid this trip, until it became clear he wasn't going to find the information he wanted.

Charlie fetches the relevant scrolls and demonstrates how to use them.

'Is there a search facility?' asks Nick.

'I'm afraid not. The only practical way is to go through them – much as you would with hard copies.'

Nick settles down and waits until Charlie has returned to his desk. This shouldn't be too difficult. He knows the dates: the first visit to the police to report Debs missing; the searches; the discovery of the body three weeks later. But as he scrolls through, he finds himself stopping to read articles, diverted by accounts of local events. A fire in the fish-and-chip shop – he can still remember the smell – thick, sickly, fishy; six-year-old Danny Wheelock falling off a flower-garlanded carnival float and ending up in hospital with a broken leg – Nick and Johnny went to visit him, reluctantly handing over the bar of Cadbury's Dairy Milk that they'd hoped to keep for themselves; the owner of the news-agent prosecuted for indecent exposure – goodness, he didn't know about that, although he can picture the man: surly, bearded, rumoured to be an axe-murderer. Nick would have gone there for his sweets because it was closest to school, but Johnny was too scared of him, so they had to trek all the way to the newsagent at the other end of town for their sherbet dabs and gobstoppers, where the girl who served them didn't hate children. He recognises a girl called Beatrice – two years ahead of him at primary school, ugly then with a crooked ponytail and sticking-out teeth – unexpectedly glowing in a swimsuit, with clouds of dark, corkscrew hair, the winner in the first round of a beauty contest.

He stops at another picture, scrolls back, enlarges the image until it blurs, shrinks it back to its original size.

Two boys of about thirteen or fourteen, tall, but neat and contained, their arms and legs lean with toned muscle. They look like twins, exactly the same height, with their arms round each other's shoulders, beaming with triumph, angling their tennis racquets over their heads in an upside-down V, an arch to frame them. You can see the latent energy in their easily arranged limbs, the determination behind their grins. LOCAL CHAMPIONS HIT ABOVE THEIR WEIGHT, says the caption. Even Johnny looks good. How did the photographer get him to stare directly at the camera? The article goes on to explain that they had both reached the finals of a tournament in Worcester.

Nick puzzles over it for a while, not sure why he can't remember the occasion, not recognising the background. There's no mention of a murdered sister in the article and it's unlikely that a journalist would have ignored the connection, so it must have been before Debs disappeared. They give the impression that they're pals, but this was just a pose for the camera. There wasn't ever a time when their relationship wasn't corrupted by rivalry. Somehow they'd managed to stand close to each other and say 'cheese' without gritting their teeth. How did they manage to fool the journalist?

So who won? The article, written before the match, couldn't predict the result. It could have been either of them – they were equally capable.

They're not pretending to be friends to please Ma; she wouldn't have been there. He can't remember ever seeing her at a match or even checking they had the right kit before they set off for the bus stop. The assumption was always that they'd get on with it. She was proud of them, but not really interested in details. She took charge of any trophies or shields, put them in the cabinet, cut photos out of the paper and put them in folders if she knew about them. But she resented the cost of it all and dragged them out of bed in the middle of the night to do news-paper rounds so they could buy their own kit, insisted on them doing chores round the house for bus money. 'Nothing comes free. No work, no money, no food,' she'd tell them. 'And if you can't eat, you won't have the strength for tennis.'

Then the washing: 'Whose daft idea was it to play tennis in whites? Didn't anyone give a thought to the laundry?' She wasn't impressed by the organisations that made the rules. 'If you've got enough spare cash to swan around the world playing games, you're not going to be interested in who looks after the clothing – no chance of that lot putting their soft precious hands into hot water, they'll all have dailies. It wouldn't amaze me if they've missed the invention of washing machines – why would they care when they can get people like muggins here to do everything for them? The laundry's collected, they hand out the dosh, and hey presto, it turns up clean and ironed the next day! I'd be willing to bet they've never even noticed grass stains. If money's no object . . .?'

Ma had been invincible then, full of righteous indignation, never too distracted to catch him and Johnny out. She just seemed to sense what they were up to, appearing unexpectedly in the middle of a fight, superwoman, yanking them apart, shrill with fury.

'What's the matter with the pair of you?' she would yell, barely out of breath, holding one at each end of her outstretched arms. 'Numbskulls! Pea brains! Couldn't you give me a break for once in your tiny little lives – just every now and again?'

After Debs she'd had a permanent break. Never mended.

He forces himself to breathe and carries on to 22 June 1969. A small article, page 5. LOCAL GIRLS MISSING. Deborah Greenwood and Beverley Newton, not seen for three days. Police would like to speak to anyone with knowledge of their whereabouts.

Nobody seemed too worried at this point – the story, by a clearly sceptical reporter, wasn't given much prominence – and even he suggested that they'd run off to London for the bright lights. They'd had ambitions, everyone knew that.

'They should have given proper notice,' said a spokesman from their place of work. 'It's not acceptable to just walk out like this.'

Something shifted over the next few days. Why hadn't they told anyone what they were doing? There'd been no sightings on trains or buses, no messages to anyone. An inexplicable silence. The story worked its way to the front page, speculation became heated, searches were organised, and two weeks later, the body turned up. It reached the national newspapers. Now there was a good reason for headlines to be hysterical – there was a murderer in their midst.

Nick reads the reports carefully, trying to find more information about Bev. They knew she'd been there – her necklace was discovered near Debs's body, although most of her other belongings were much further away. If she'd ended up in a stream, and everything was swollen with rain by then, she could have been swept away, maybe into the river Severn and eventually all the way out to sea. It's not clear when or why they stopped searching for her, but the reports gradually became shorter, less frequent, until they faded away altogether. Bromsgrove took a breath, shrugged off its tainted past and moved on.

But the Greenwoods didn't move on. Nick can remember the bleakness at home, the lying-awake-at-night, the dark, cold realisation that Debs wasn't ever coming back, that Ma was barely functioning and might collapse altogether, that he and Johnny might end up on their own. Bev didn't feature much in their thoughts.

Could she have survived? Did she leave for some other reason, wanting to pretend she was dead when she wasn't? Could she be the one who wrote the letter?

But why make contact now? What would she gain from attempting to impersonate Debs all these years later?

Bev's mum hadn't accepted the post mortem. She'd decided it was a conspiracy, a plot to push her aside and appease Ma, who had far more respect in the community than she did. She apparently started to create trouble at the police station regularly, blurred with alcohol, screaming with fury, demanding to see the body, long after Debs had been cremated, insisting they'd just invented the tattoo. She came a second time to the railway carriages, a few months later, long after the funeral. She'd shouted and screamed at first, and Nick and Johnny had attempted to appease her, anxious to keep her away from Ma. But when they stepped out of the door, she switched unexpectedly into a heap of tear-stained bereavement, leaking guilt and grief. 'We should have had a funeral for my Bev. It wasn't fair – pushed away, forgotten – she was worth twice your tarty girl . . .' They'd had to ring the police again in the end, unable to deal with her.

Could she possibly have been right?

But other voices, neighbours, people in the shops: 'She's enjoying the attention, the chance to get noticed, so she can scrounge off the rest of us.'

'If she'd given a bit more attention to that poor girl a bit earlier, you could understand it . . .'

'She's after money, that's what it's all about. If she got it, she'd only drink it away with her dodgy mates.'

'Wouldn't surprise me if one of that lot turns out to be the murderer.'

Guiltily, Nick remembers that his voice joined in with the chorus, blaming Bev's mum, forgetting that she was a victim too.

Another voice from the past, soft, silky. Paula: 'It was obviously Bev, wasn't it? She killed Debs. Everyone knew how jealous she was.'

He shakes his head, trying to dislodge the buzz in his ear. Paula couldn't possibly have known that unless it came from him. She wasn't even in Bromsgrove at the time.

Why has she decided to come crawling into his head now?

Johnny is working his way through the contents of the black plastic bags looking for photos. It's taken him all week to summon the courage to open the door again, pull out the bags and start sorting. He rejects most of it immediately, flinging it all behind him as if he's digging his way through a rock fall, growing increasingly angry. It's been shut away for forty-eight years, sweating through the summers, freezing during the winters, rotting in the darkness of the plastic. Why didn't he and Nick follow Ma's instructions and arrange for a council collection?

In the background, on the computer screen, *Brief Encounter* is loudly reaching its climax, steam from the train engulfing the platform.

There's bedding in the first few bags: once-pink woollen blankets; yellowed, crumbling sheets; a mauve candlewick bedspread. Then clothes, the contents of Debs's drawers and wardrobe: nylon, polyester, Crimplene, unfaded with time but giving out the pungent odour of neglect, the whiff of old sweat. Debs and Bev are on the move in the air around him, jiggling their feet, their heads, their fingers; the Rolling Stones – 'Jumping Jack Flash', '19th Nervous Breakdown'; smooth, bare arms, frenetic energy, imagination, youth. Life.

He swings round with a snarl, incensed by the smell, the distraction of the music from the film, the way Debs and Bev are dancing on his nerve ends, and realises that he's trapped himself in the entrance of the WC. He drags everything back into the bags, stuffing it in, stamping down to make room. He pulls the edges together and ties them fiercely, determined to prevent the contents ever escaping again. He'll put them out with the rubbish, one or two every week in the wheelie bin, buried amongst the general waste.

The fourth bag is the one he's been looking for, the one holding the contents of the living room. Their shell collection, brought back from Weston-super-Mare on the train; tennis trophies and shields (odd that Ma associated them with Debs, who never played tennis); the china shepherdesses with swirling skirts, once Ma's pride and joy (inherited from an affluent great-grandmother, worth a pretty penny, she said). He finds a framed certificate from his primary school. Second prize, flat race. John Greenwood. He holds it for a while, taken back to a more gentle past that he'd almost forgotten, a time when days stretched out, long and easy. Some of the anger inside him subsides a little.

There are photographs, some framed and others in albums, a folder of cuttings, all neatly snipped from newspapers, blurred and fading.

He takes his time, leafing through the pages, examining each one carefully. He and Nick are pictured in most of them, posing with their racquets, always together, as if they couldn't exist apart. The snapshots in albums are mostly black and white, taken by Dad, Ma, Debs, or, presumably, when the whole family is in the picture, a passing stranger. He remembers very few of the occasions. There's one of him and Nick, toddlers with well-fed baby faces, on their father's knee. Dad is grinning, soft and proud. Johnny stares at the photograph, entranced by their childishness, struggling to spot anything that signposts their later development, and realises that he doesn't know which boy is which.

They're almost identical, with the same earnest eyes, staring outwards with an air of bewildered curiosity; thick, abundant hair, combed, plonked over their heads like a Roman helmet; flappy ears, sticking out like semi-transparent wings, the source of much trauma over the years. It must be possible to recognise himself. But it's not.

Why did Ma remove all the photos, even the ones that didn't include Debs? Why did she make the assumption that everything ended with Debs?

Debs used to prepare supper when Ma was out working, sort the washing, do the ironing. She and Ma would stay up late, long after the boys had gone to bed, watching old horror films. Johnny can remember lying in bed, hearing the music, the screams, wondering how they could find such pleasure in fear. They didn't talk a great deal, but there were occasional epic arguments that went on for days: Debs's skirts were too short; decent girls shouldn't be out after midnight; why couldn't she just be grateful for what she'd got instead of always hankering for more?

Why did they stay out after midnight? It only happened once, but nobody ever found out what they were doing. The police showed considerable interest in their social life, but no dark secrets ever emerged. Debs wasn't secretive by nature, she was just a girl who knew how to enjoy herself.

Maybe Ma's desire to erase Debs after her death reflected guilt, a realisation that she shouldn't have been so demanding, that she shouldn't have been so angry about the tattoo, that the failure might have been hers.

A picture of Ma and Dad when they first got married, looking like children. For a moment, he thinks it's not Ma, but Debs, a reluctant bride, forced into a secret marriage that he didn't know about. Perhaps there wasn't a body at all. Could it have been just a cover so that Debs could marry some unsuitable man and Ma, uncontrollably furious, hid the truth from everyone else?

But this is Dad, of course, in his National Service uniform, as amiable as Johnny remembers, gazing into the distance as if he's still at sea, his face glowing and weathered, delighted by the way things have turned out, blissfully unaware of the responsibilities ahead that he would never be able to fulfil. Ma, barely seventeen, clutching a makeshift bunch of lilies, holding them awkwardly so they don't stain her dress, slightly startled, as if she's got herself into an unexpected situation and doesn't know how to get out of it. There were no relatives present, no adults available for help or guidance. Dad's parents were both drowned at sea, which is why he headed inland, and Ma's had gone south in search of work. A short, brief letter – weather fine, hope you are well – would come from them once a year if they were lucky, an occasional pound note slipping out of an envelope, and then, eventually, silence. They faded out of existence long before Debs died – Ma took a rare day off work to take the train down for her mum's funeral, but she only knew that her dad had gone when a neighbour sent her some odds and ends in the post – so they were spared the trauma of recognising their grand-daughter in the papers.

He finds a picture of Debs and Bev together and spends some time examining Debs, surprised to discover that her face is familiar after all. How could he have forgotten her? He's slightly annoyed by Bev's presence next to Debs. Although she was regularly around, including her in the photo seems like an acknowledgement that she'd reached the centre of the family. The two girls look alike. Almost the same height; their hair cut – by each other – into the same style; their clothes, sewn together on Debs's Singer, made from identical materials, using the same patterns. But there's a difference in their faces if you look for it, if you know it's there. The shape of the nose, the roundness of the cheeks, the height of the forehead. You can tell Debs is the one in charge – it's in the upward thrust of her chin, the defiance that's implied by her narrowed eyes. Don't mess with me, she's saying. There's a look of Ma about her, determination, authority.

Bev has copied everything; she even has tiny bows stuck on the front of her scuffed shoes in exactly the same place as Debs. She's worked to create the right impression, but not entirely succeeded. There are little giveaway signs: a mark on the collar of her blouse, the hem hanging down on the left side of her skirt. She's not capable of reflecting Debs exactly. She's tried to construct the same image, but the reproduction has distorted, lost its sharp edges, developed an uneven surface.

The more Johnny studies the photo – he thinks it must have been taken about a year before they disappeared – the more he begins to wonder if there was something not right between them. When they were younger, they giggled all the time, separated themselves out for secret conversations, wanted to be together all the time, but there's a distance between them here. They're not touching, and although Bev is leaning towards Debs, Debs is not reciprocating. She's looking away, past the camera, almost as if Bev isn't there, as if she's irrelevant. Was she growing out of her, irritated by her?

Opportunity Knocks on the telly, Debs and Bev, Nick and Johnny squashed on to the old train seat in the living room, Ma out cleaning.

Debs suddenly leapt to her feet, grabbed a glass from the table, tipped the last of the orange squash into her mouth, then turned the glass upside down, leaned towards it as if it was a microphone and started to belt out 'Boom Bang-a-Bang' at top volume, moving around the room, a bundle of fierce energy, just like Lulu.

'Yeah!' cheered Johnny, who loved it when she started behaving badly, especially when Ma wasn't there to stop it.

'Knock it off,' said Nick, who was interested in the ventriloquist with the Harold Wilson puppet and a miniature sweet shop.

Bev jumped up and grabbed another glass, but it was still half full and she forgot to drink the squash first, so it tipped out all over the mat. She shrieked and stood staring at the liquid on the floor. The fun drained out of Johnny as quickly as the squash drained out of the glass.

'Now look what you've done,' said Debs, stopping abruptly. 'Johnny, run and get a cloth, there's a love. Before it stains.'

Johnny leapt up, all jitters, terrified that Ma would suddenly come home and discover the mess. He hated it when she was angry. A sleepless night lay ahead, with guilt hovering above him, telling him that everything was his fault, unformed terrors leaping out at him the moment he closed his eyes.

Nick roared with laughter as the ventriloquist tried to shove liquorice allsorts down Harold Wilson's throat and the mouth mechanism jammed. 'He's calling him Harry,' he yelled with delight.

Bev pretended to examine the damage to the mat. 'It's not that bad,' she said nervously.

'Yes it is,' said Debs, glancing out of the window, as if Ma was due home at any moment. It had to be dealt with – they all knew that. 'Bring a bowl of water, Johnny.'

Johnny filled the washing-up bowl under the kitchen tap and came back through, water slopping dangerously over the edges. Bev started to scrub, but she was spreading the stain outwards, making it more noticeable.

Johnny had an idea. He grabbed a handful of old newspapers from the pile next to the telly and placed them over the damp patch. 'We need to soak it up,' he said, stamping his feet up and down over.

'Yes, good idea,' said Debs, pulling each wad of paper out of the way when it became saturated and replacing it with fresh sheets.

Opportunity Knocks was still blasting out on the television, half the audience cheering and the other half booing. Nick was hooting with hysterical laughter. Debs glanced across at Johnny and rolled her eyes with exasperation. He grinned back, thrilled to be on her side. Him and her against the world. It was a good feeling.

Bev tried to mop up with the cloth, but Debs pushed her to the side. 'Get out of the way,' she said. 'You're just making everything worse.'

Bev stared at Debs, tears forming in her eyes. 'There's no need to be nasty,' she said in a small voice, and sank on to the bench next to Nick, refusing to look at anyone.

'Try being more helpful then,' muttered Debs, her voice softening.

Johnny puts the black bag aside for a while, angry again, not wanting to remember Debs as unkind. It was Bev's fault. She was so irritating.

None of these photos is going to tell him anything he doesn't already know. He places the picture of Debs and Bev face down on the desk and leans back in his chair, glancing at his inbox. There are several emails from customers, the ones who fuss, the ones he deals with daily. A few formal words of thanks (from people who haven't quite captured the correct breeziness of emails), further requests for assistance, one or two urgent situations that he deals with immediately with careful explanations and links to relevant websites.

There's a knocking sound, a banging.

He sits up in surprise. Has something come loose on the outside of the carriage? But it's not windy. It takes him a few seconds to realise it's the doorknocker.

The postwoman? Again? Surely not. She's taking advantage. He can't decide what kind of advantage, but she's clearly up to something.

He remains stationary. Nick can deal with it. It's nearly evening, he must be back from work by now. He's probably in the kitchen, chopping, frying, stirring, creating smells to taunt Johnny when he goes in to put his ready meal into the microwave.

The banging continues, but there's no responding vibration from Aphrodite. No one walking to the door, opening it, dealing with the postwoman.

Does post come this late in the day? Don't they have shifts, specific times for deliveries?

He could just ignore it. She can leave the delivery on the door-step and go.

What if it's another letter, one that needs a signature? What if it tells them when Debs/Bev is going to turn up?

He heaves himself out of his chair, opens the door to the corridor and stands for a moment, listening. The knocking starts again. He moves slowly, reluctantly, shuffling his feet, his heart beating too fast, attempting to banish the sensation that he's a child about to find himself in trouble. He doesn't want to open the door. He tries to peer through a window, attempting to lift the edge of a curtain without making it obvious, but he can't see anything. It's bleak out there, a gathering grey mist, damp accumulating on the grass, the branches of the trees near the road drooping miserably.

He yanks the handle and pushes the carriage door outwards, aware that if he moves too slowly, he'll change his mind.

It's not the postwoman retreating to the bottom of the steps as the door swings open. It's an unknown woman in black trousers and a red coat. She stares up at him, moving her mouth as if she wants to say something, but can't produce the sound. It's hard to see her properly from this angle, get any sense of what she looks like. The haze over her face begins to clear, her features form themselves into a pattern, and he sees that she's elderly, maybe in her seventies. A flood of relief seeps through him as he realises he's never seen her before in his life.

'Nick!' says the woman at last. 'Johnny?' Her voice is weak, old.

Could this be the letter-writer, the impostor? She's pretending to know him! He refuses to descend the steps, to get any nearer to her.

At this point, Nick appears in the small pathway from the road, carrying two Asda bags. When he sees the woman by the steps, he hesitates and slows down, as if he's preparing for a quick getaway. He stops a few yards away, peering closely at the woman.

Seeing Johnny's eyes slipping past her, the woman turns and follows the line of his gaze. 'Nick?' she says again. 'Johnny?' But her voice is fading with uncertainty.

Nick puts down his bags. 'Do I know you?' he asks, not sounding like himself.

Johnny is grimly pleased by his inability to take control.

'I should hope so,' says the woman.

All three of them contemplate each other in silence.

Nick can't think clearly. When he first saw the woman, just for a brief moment, he thought – he thought it was Ma. Then it wasn't her at all. It must have been wishful thinking after reading the letter, the sense of returning to earlier times, old memories of standing here with Debs, with Bev, with Ma. He clears his throat. 'Sorry?' he says and attempts to smile. 'And you are?'

The woman's face softens with apparent confusion. 'Actually,' she says, 'I'm having trouble – Nick? Johnny? Which is which?' Her accent is softly American, or Canadian – how do you tell the difference?

He approaches her with his hand out. 'Nick,' he says.

Her arms briefly rise, and for one horrifying moment he thinks she's going to embrace him, but she hesitates, lets them drop, then takes his hand instead. She smiles, almost shyly. 'Hi, Nick,' she says. They squeeze each other's hand for no more than a second and then break contact. 'Did you get my letter?'

'Well . . .' says Nick. 'But we didn't . . .' The three of them examine each other, no one prepared to take the initiative. For the first time in years, Nick feels as if he and Johnny are on the same side. Doubles. A return to form.

'You've given the carriages names,' she says, standing back and studying them. 'Nothing stays the same. It's so—'

'We weren't expecting . . .' says Johnny.

They stop.

'Let's start again,' she says. 'I'm Debs, but you've already worked that out.'

No, thinks Nick. Of course not. 'Maybe,' he says, not prepared to acknowledge anything. Johnny looks past him, towards the road, not making eye contact with anyone.

He can feel her eyes on his face. 'Yes,' she says eventually. 'Johnny and Nick. I've got it now. Alike, but not alike. I reckon I could have worked out who was who, once I'd had time to think about it.'

'But you're not Debs, are you?' says Johnny, and his voice is rough, jagged, unfriendly. 'Debs is dead.'

There's another pause. 'Well,' she says quietly. 'I guess that's what we have to sort out.'

9

Zohra slots letters into racks as quickly as possible. Nothing for the Greenwoods, of course. She's spent all week hoping for another letter, a circular, anything that would give her the opportunity to go back to the carriages.

Crispin has been getting carried away. 'We could do murder-mystery days. The Bromsgrove murder re-examined, that kind of thing.'

He's starting to be irritating. 'You can't possibly do that. Not when people still remember it and there are relatives still alive.'

'Why not? They reconstruct unsolved murders on television all the time. And if we had the original carriages—'

'I told you, it didn't happen there.'

'Nobody's going to care about details. It's the spirit that counts.'

Bill has strolled past three times so far, without urgency, and the lightness of his step indicates a good mood. 'That's it,' he says. 'Good to see smoothness and efficiency.' His eyes are scrunched and amiable, his mouth almost stretched into a smile, but she knows the cheerfulness can't last. Things never proceed smoothly. So the next time he comes close, she stops him. 'Bill, do you remember that letter – the one that was addressed to the railway carriages on Long Meadow Road?'

'Mmm?'

'Did you ever meet them, the Greenwoods?'

He stops and stares past her into the distance, his mind elsewhere.

She tries a different approach. 'How long have you lived in Bromsgrove?'

He focuses on her now, clearly shocked that she has to ask. 'Born and bred, girl, breathing Bromsgrove air from the moment I opened my eyes and saw my dad's great ugly phizog grinning down at me. And the longer I stay, the more I like it. If I ever have to go anywhere, I do what I have to do, quick as possible, and come scooting home as fast as my legs will carry me. It's a dangerous world out there.'

'What about holidays?' says Rohit from the next bay, 'trips to the seaside?'

Bill rolls his eyes. 'Got everything I need right here. Country walks, streams, bluebell woods, farmland, all on your doorstep. David Attenborough'd save a penny or two if he started looking in front of his nose instead of swanning off to the other side of the world. You just got to know where to look, that's all.'

'You're having us on,' says Rohit. 'Everyone goes on holiday.'

'Nope,' says Bill with satisfaction.

'You must have known the Greenwoods when you were younger, though,' says Zohra. 'There can't have been that many people living in railway carriages.'

Bill frowns. 'How long ago are we talking?'

'Not sure exactly. Sixties, seventies, maybe.'

'How old do you think I am?'

This places Zohra in a difficult position. He looks about the same age as her father, but it's impossible to be sure. Would he want to be seen as older (wiser) or younger (still up there with the kids)? 'You tell me,' she says eventually.

'As if,' he says.

'What about the murder? You must remember that.'

He nods slowly, finally interested. 'Ah – I'm with you now. You're talking about that girl – what was her name?'

'Deborah. Deborah Greenwood.'

There's a long silence while Zohra waits for him to comment. She knows he will. He has an opinion on everything. 'It's not like I remember it exactly – wasn't more than a babby at the time. Got the story later on though, from my older brothers. My dad went out in the first search – the whole town turned out, you couldn't not go. But he got back really late, ages after dark, and my mom was hopping mad. She laid into him something awful. He'd ended up in the pub, hadn't he, downing his wages. She wouldn't let him out the next day, and he had to stay at home with us while she went on the search instead. Served him right. Nasty piece of work, my old man.' He chuckles, then lapses into thought.

Zohra waits a while. 'So did they ever find out – you know, who did it?'

Bill doesn't reply immediately, as if there's a solution he hasn't quite worked out and he needs time to untangle it. 'Not so far as I know,' he says.

The bell pings in the outside office as someone comes in to collect a parcel. He heads off to the counter.

'Don't know why you don't just wait for Dougie,' says Matt, who's about to set out on his round. 'He knows everything about everyone.'

Dougie walks through the door at that precise moment. 'Did someone mention my name?'

'Zohra's asking about a girl that was murdered,' says Rohit. 'Ages ago, long before the likes of us were born—'

'Debs Greenwood,' says Zohra.

'Wondered when we was going to get round to that,' says Dougie, heading for his sorting area. 'Nasty business. Never solved.'

'Did no one have suspicions?' asks Zohra.

'There was plenty of gossip – but that was all. She was a good girl, Debs, she didn't deserve what happened to her. Nick and Johnny turned a bit wild after. We stuck around with them for a while, me and my mates, but they got too out of hand for us, and in the end, they went and blew it anyway. We all drifted off then. Last time I seen Johnny was his ma's funeral – must be at least thirty, forty years.'

'Did they find the second girl?' says Zohra. 'What happened to her?'

'No, but there was loads of theories about her. My mom and dad had plenty, mainly to do with the mother. I remember her right enough. Drunk out of her eyeballs most of the time, out on the streets, shouting her mouth off, accusing everyone of kidnapping her girl. Most people reckoned she'd got something to do with it herself – all those weirdos she hung around with – but nothing was ever proved, far as I know.'

There's a danger Dougie won't stop. Zohra picks up her mailbag, but can't resist asking. 'How did Nick and Johnny blow it?'

'The accident,' says Dougie solemnly. He checks his watch. 'Look, sweetheart, you and me, we don't have time for this. I'm late and you will be too in a jiffy. You want to know more about them, why don't you talk to my Lil? She remembers things better than me. Fancied one of the brothers for a while – Nick or Johnny, not sure now. Never could remember which one did what. It was their party trick, blaming each other for everything.'

'I'd like that,' says Zohra.

Dougie starts sorting. He's neat and methodical, but slow. His bald head is dark and leathery from exposure to the elements, and he's started to shrink, she suddenly realises, in the twelve months since she first met him. He doesn't smile a great deal, but when he does it devours his entire face. He smiles now. 'Why don't you come round this afternoon? Lil would be thrilled to meet you. She never sees no one. It's all boys in our family, see, not a girl between them. You come and see her and you'd make her happy as Larry.'

'Does he ever stop talking?' mutters Rohit.

'Could we make it evening?' says Zohra. 'I have to help in the shop this afternoon.'

'Moonlighting, eh?' says Bill, coming back in.

'Don't be daft,' says Zohra. 'It's my dad's shop. I'm just helping out.'

*   *   *

Later, after she's finished her round, she leaves the van in the secure car park at the back of the sorting office and walks home across the park. She used to avoid this route when she first started working at the Post Office, but it's the quickest way home, so she's forced herself to use it. At first, she couldn't even see the park in the distance without the sharp taste of acid rushing into her throat and half choking her, but the agitation has finally begun to dull, and she now finds, after eight years, she can manage it with relative composure. But she still holds her breath when she passes the school entrance, waiting for a shout, a challenge, even though it's unlikely anyone would recognise her. It's a different generation of girls now. And teachers move on.

She once came across Fiona here in the park, several months after she'd last lingered by the gate with her friends before heading home. When she thinks of those times, it's like dipping into a comfortable book of children's poetry, a world where all four of them squeezed together under one umbrella, passed round Haribo Tangfastics and Starmixes that she'd brought from the shop, giggled helplessly, flourished in the embrace of long-lasting friendship.

Which turned out to be not so long-lasting.

In that last summer of school, with A-levels looming, when everything was starting to fall apart, she used to leap out of her seat as soon as the last bell sounded, dash out, and leg it to the exit as fast as possible. Two members of staff were placed there as sentinels, watchers, a safeguard against bullying, but how could they possibly make a difference? Things can appear to be transparent when sunshine is flooding into the dark corners, when windows are left open until late, when arms are bare and feet aired in open-toed sandals. But what happens when the temperature drops and the snow falls and everyone huddles into themselves, hiding away in coats, hats, scarves, gloves? It's the secret world that counts, the one that you don't even know about unless someone leads you there and gives you the password.

Teachers posted outside in the open could never penetrate that icy world.

On the day Zohra met Fiona, she ran out with her head down and kept going, up the pathway, round the boating lake, past the cluster of trees where she would be out of sight. Once she felt she was safe, she slowed down, took a few deep breaths, to remind herself that the air was still breathable, and went over maths formulae in her head. The repetition was soothing and calmed her chaotic thoughts.

'Hi.'

She stopped, recognising the voice immediately, but didn't turn round.

'You're out early,' said Fiona from behind her. She sounded breathless, insecure without her supporting chorus.

Zohra could feel the impulse for flight pulsing through her (it's an illusion, don't trust her, don't let the barriers slip), but at the same time a paralysis in her legs prevented her from moving, so she could only stand and listen, straining her ears, willing herself to disappear.

Fiona came round the side and placed herself in front of her. She seemed less polished than usual, oddly unsure of herself, not so achingly cool. Her black hair was as immaculate as ever, sharply cut, shiny and fluid, and the bow of her lips tinted, with enormous care, to appear casual. But she seemed to just miss the mark, as if she was a photograph of herself, not the real thing. She didn't speak.

This was difficult. If neither of them was going to say anything, how would they ever be able to break contact? 'What are you doing here?' asked Zohra eventually. She was aware that she sounded blunt, that her words might be reported back to the others and analysed, but it was the best she could do.

Fiona swallowed before answering, as if she was making an enormous effort to appear normal. 'Just on my way home. The Physics coursework wasn't as bad as I was expecting, so I finished early.' The words were rushed, unnatural.

It didn't explain why she was in the park. How would she get home from here? Someone from her family always came to pick her up in the car.

'Got to rush,' said Zohra. 'Too much to do.' She flexed her right leg and found that it would now move. Cautiously, she started to edge away.

She was dismayed to find that Fiona fell in alongside her, as if they were going for a stroll. What now? 'Don't you go the other way?' she said.

'Oh, I'm just pottering,' said Fiona vaguely.

There was more to it than that. She wasn't showing any animosity, more an inexplicable friendliness, apparently pleased to see Zohra, but without any reasonable explanation for being there. Her face was flushed, as if she'd been running.

There were shouts in the distance, behind them.

'Oh no,' said Fiona, suddenly agitated. She grabbed Zohra's arm. 'Keep walking,' she said. 'Pretend you haven't heard.'

'Who is it?' asked Zohra.

'Too late,' said Fiona and stopped, pulling Zohra to a halt next to her. 'They've seen us.'

They turned out to be her two brothers, Tristan and Sebastian. The hot Chinese boys, the medical students home for the summer, only eighteen months apart in age, studying in the same year – the older one had delayed entry so they could go together. They were difficult to tell apart with their olive skin, their dark, intelligent eyes, their neatly cut black hair. They weren't boys at all, but men, with neat, carefully trimmed moustaches and goatee beards, sophisticated and worldly. Zohra had only ever seen them from a distance, never spoken to them.

'What on earth are you doing out here?' one of them said to Fiona after they'd sprinted over to the girls.

'I was early, there was time for a walk in the park,' said Fiona, surprisingly defensive. 'What's wrong with that?'

'What's wrong with that,' said the other one, 'is that we've been waiting in the car park. We have things to do, you know.'

'So what made you come out here, then?' asks Fiona.

'Your friend said she saw you heading this way – what's her name? Mimi.'

It was clear that they weren't pleased with her, but they weren't just irritated, they were menacing. In a quiet, unspoken manner. And Fiona's response to them was curious – defiant, but also anxious.

'Who's your friend?' said the taller one, eyeing Zohra.

'Zohra,' said Fiona, without offering any further detail.

'Hi Zohra,' he said. 'I'm Sebastian. This is Tristan.'

'Hello,' said Zohra, unable to look directly into their faces, studying a crack in the tarmac of the path where dust was emerging and ants were swarming. She allowed herself a quick glance up, then down again, finding the ants more reassuring. The brothers had assumed the aura of celebrities, remote, overwhelming.

'What do you do after school, then?' asked Tristan, leaning towards her, so she was forced to look at him.

'Work,' she mumbled. She wanted to step aside, but she felt trapped by his proximity, unable to move away.

'Leave it off, Tris,' said Fiona, her voice very slightly uneven.

'What?' he said, spreading his hands with deliberate innocence and turning to face her.

'You know,' she said.

'I have to go,' said Zohra, seeing her opportunity. 'My father will wonder where I am.' She managed to slip to the side, dodge out of the shadow of their presence, and started walking rapidly away.

'We can give you a lift!' shouted Fiona.

'It's okay,' she called over her shoulder. She sped up, wanting to run. But she didn't want to appear too obvious, too cowardly.

She turned back once, just before passing the tennis courts. They were still standing there, watching her, a curious little group, close to each other, but oddly separate. She felt reasonably safe, far enough away to lift a hand and wave, but none of

134

them responded. There was something unnerving about the way they interacted, not at all as she would have imagined. They were supposed to be a really close family, but that wasn't how it seemed. Fiona seemed somehow diminished in the presence of her brothers.

A few hours later, new messages appeared on her Facebook wall from Michelle. 'Scum. You're just out to get me, aren't you?'

This time Katy, Mimi and Carys sent private messages. 'What's it all about?' So they hadn't completely forgotten her.

'I don't know. She just says these things out of the blue. I never know what's going on.'

'Ignore her then.'

'Block her, she's not worth it.'

Nothing from Fiona.

'Come in, come in,' says Dougie as he opens the door to Zohra, clearly delighted to see her. 'This is Lil, my wife. She's been looking forward to meeting you.' He ushers her through the front door, into their tiny living room, and settles her on the dark brown brocade sofa. On the coffee table a tray is laid out – cups and saucers, milk jug, sugar bowl, a plate of chocolate biscuits. There's a smell of stale cigarettes, an empty ashtray on the table.

Lil is in a wheelchair, but she seems well organised and manoeuvres with practised ease. 'Dougie loves having you in the sorting office,' she says. 'A civilised presence, he says. Keeps Bill in his place.'

'Really?' says Zohra, pleased with the compliment, but worried that it's not justified. 'What would Bill be doing if I wasn't there, then?'

'He's got a real temper on him, has Bill,' says Dougie. 'Not a pretty sight when he's firing on all cylinders.'

'I've seen him get annoyed,' says Zohra. 'It didn't seem that bad.'

Dougie chuckles gently. 'Give him time,' he says. 'You haven't seen the half of it.'

Lil goes out to make tea. 'Dougie!' she calls after a couple of minutes. 'Teapot!'

He leaves the room, wordlessly obedient, and comes back with the teapot, followed by Lil. He starts pouring and Lil offers the plate of biscuits to Zohra. She takes a chocolate finger. 'It's really nice of you to spare me the time,' she says.

'Lil's been dying to meet you anyway,' says Dougie.

'He talks about you all the time,' says Lil.

'Really?' says Zohra, surprised.

'Take no notice,' says Dougie. 'She's exaggerating – same as always.'

'Thought I'd better check you out, though,' says Lil. 'Always best to meet the competition.'

Zohra flushes. 'So how many children do you have?' She needs to change the subject. 'And grandchildren?'

'Two sons, four grandsons,' says Dougie. 'Not close, though.'

'They live miles away – far side of London,' says Lil. 'We hardly ever see them. They work so hard, they just don't have time . . .'

Dougie leans over and puts a comforting hand on hers.

They suddenly remind Zohra of her own parents. A couple who've lived together for so long they can anticipate each other's reactions, know what the other is going to say, but need occasional contact with an outsider to help them appreciate the warmth of their own relationship. 'You must miss them.'

'It's jobs, isn't it? You have to go where the work is,' says Lil. Her hands tremble constantly. Her cup rattles on the saucer, a gentle accompaniment to their conversation. She smiles suddenly. 'So. You want to know about the Greenwoods?'

Will they think she's just being nosy? 'I've started to take an interest in local history. Walking around, doing the post, it makes you notice things . . . Then when I discovered the railway carriages, all hidden away like that, it was such a surprise. I've been helping with the Wychington Railway – you know, up at the hall?'

136

Lil nods. 'Perry's place. It was in the paper – week tomorrow isn't it, the big do? Dougie's hoping to go.'

'So we're restoring the railway line, searching for the right equipment, and the Greenwoods' railway carriages have been sitting there, all this time, for decades, just kind of left behind, like a museum that no one ever visits. It seemed such a coincidence.'

There's a pause while Lil and Dougie consider this.

'The family go back a long way,' says Lil. 'Their ma, Doris – one of five, the brothers and sisters all left, wanted the city life – she got married early and stayed put. Their dad wasn't from round here, though. Came from the coast. Never quite got used to being inland, couldn't fit in right. Doris was tough as old boots, especially once he'd passed and she had to do it all on her own. She had a tongue on her, sharper than acid. She could reduce grown men to jelly just by looking at them, seen it with my own eyes, and when she really got going, she'd strip the flesh off them, lick them clean. All their swagger – it didn't count for nothing with her. They became blathering babbies. There wasn't nobody, not man, not woman, willing or able to take her on.'

'She neglected those kids, though,' says Dougie.

Lil shakes her head. 'Only later. After her girl got murdered. But you couldn't say nothing to her. Wouldn't take help from nobody.'

'You can't blame her, can you? With all the local men under suspicion.'

'Really?' says Zohra.

'Stands to reason,' says Dougie. 'Not knowing who done it. Could of been any of us.'

'There was a search, wasn't there?'

'It's when me and Lil got together,' says Dougie. 'Proper, like. We knew each other already, but not like that. She fancied Nick first—'

'Johnny,' says Lil.

'Hmm,' he says. 'Married six months later, just after my seventeenth birthday.'

They both gaze into the distance, their eyes slightly misty, apparently unconcerned that their early romance would always be associated with a murder.

'You had to grow up a lot quicker in them days, earn a wage, settle down,' says Dougie. 'Now it's like you can go on being children forever if you want.'

'Give it a rest, Dougie. Our Josh and Charlie are good lads. It wasn't like you was mature then, not really.'

'And did you know Albert Troth?' asks Zohra. 'He says his sons were friendly with the Greenwood boys.'

'Oh yes, the Troth lads,' says Dougie. 'Long gone now, got jobs in London, years ago. They was a bit younger than us, but we was all mates.'

'And the Greenwoods were good at tennis?' asks Zohra.

'Could of been,' says Dougie. 'Some hot-shot coach turned up to watch them and thought they'd got talent, offered to take them on. They travelled up to Birmingham twice a week for a bit.'

'Everyone reckoned tennis would be their way out, their ticket to a better life,' says Lil. 'What with their dad being such a waste of space, and their ma out working all hours of the day and night, slaving away to put food on the table. But then all that with their sister – it finished them off.'

'Nobody never recovers from something like that,' says Dougie.

'They didn't have it easy,' says Lil. 'People staring at them all the time, talking behind their backs; nobody was interested in the tennis any more – just their dead sister.'

'They started messing around,' says Dougie. 'They should of known better, the pair of them, but there wasn't no one to tell them.'

'That Paula did,' says Lil. 'She didn't have no time for that kind of nonsense. But they was old enough to work it out for themselves. Seventeen, at least – not much younger than you, Dougie, and we was married by then.'

'They was just lads,' says Dougie.

'Out of control,' says Lil. 'I know their ma was suffering, but even so – she could've seen what they were up to if she took the time to look.'

'They started this craze, see,' says Dougie. 'Climbing buildings. All the local lads was joining in. They had charts, everybody was clocking up scores—'

'You too, Dougie,' says Lil. 'Own up. Me at home with a new babby and you out there with your mates, not taking your responsibilities seriously—'

'All right, all right,' says Dougie. 'I was a kid too. Shouldn't of got married so early, should I?'

'Like I said,' says Lil. 'Not so different from Josh and Charlie.'

They half smile at each other, clearly familiar with the argument, both retreating into an amicable truce.

'There was seven of us altogether,' says Dougie. 'Paula wasn't there—'

'She didn't never come to the climbings. Didn't like it.'

'Smarty pants, she was. Too clever for the likes of us. The Troth kids were there. We didn't let them join in, not properly – too young, and their old man would have killed them if he'd got wind of it – but they came along anyway, totted up scores, knew who'd done what. Some of us wasn't sure, didn't like going where we shouldn't, but most of us stuck with the Greenwoods because we felt sorry for them. We was working our way round all the Bromsgrove buildings that had more than two levels, climbing on to the roofs. It wasn't a big deal, not really, and it was okay once you were up. You could see for miles. But just climbing wasn't enough for them Greenwoods. One of them always had to walk along the ridge, didn't they? – you know, along the top—'

'No fear,' says Lil. 'They'd do anything for a dare. Anything.'

'So the one day,' says Dougie, 'we got into Bromsgrove School – it was holiday time, nobody much there – and climbed up one of their posh buildings. Made us feel good, like we deserved to be there because we was just as good as they was. We got up easily enough – I forget how many floors, but quite a few – and sat looking out; Johnny, Nick, Kevin Baggott, Trevor Sanders, and me, the Troth lads down below. You could see all the way to the motorway. I shouldn't of been there, really. You'd sent me out for a bottle of milk, and I met the lads on the way. I remember it was a nice warm day – reckoned you wouldn't miss me for half an hour—'

'It ended up a lot longer than half an hour,' says Lil. 'I decided you'd been run over by a bus. Had you dead and buried.'

Dougie smiles. 'I was scared to go home, thought you'd never have me back. Anyway, once we was up there, we lay back and sunbathed. The heat gets into the roof tiles, soaks into the skin. We liked to drop sweet wrappings on people below, then lie down flat so they couldn't see us. We'd laugh ourselves silly, nearly wet myself once or twice, listening to them trying to work out what was going on.'

'You'd have got caught in the end,' says Lil. 'You thought you was getting away with it, but they knew.'

'But there wasn't nobody in the school, only a couple of cars parked below us. Workers, maybe, don't know. So we didn't bother to chuck things down.'

'You'd have been in big trouble if you'd been caught,' says Lil. 'If it wasn't for the accident, I reckon you'd have been arrested.'

'So we're up there, on top of the world,' says Dougie. 'Drinking too – had a few beers before we went up – and Johnny's had more than the rest of us – he often did then, after Debs. He's getting louder and louder and Nick's getting more and more annoyed with him, thinks we'll get caught. So he tries to hurry it all up. "You first, Johnny," he says, "along the ridge." He's always the one that pulls the shots, the one in charge. Johnny stands up, looks down, sees how far it is. When he starts to sway, Trev and me pull him down. "Not today, son," says Trev. Johnny looks at Nick. "After you," he says. But Nick's not having it. "I dared you first," he says. They stares at each other. "You're on," says Johnny. So up he gets again. He's swaying a bit. Even he can see it's stupid. We're too high, the ridge is too long, he's not steady on his feet. "No," he says, "the deal's off unless you do it too." "No way," says Nick. "It's your turn." Johnny thinks for a bit, swaying backwards and forwards like the wind's rocking him. Sun's gone in by then, clouds coming over. "Scared, then?" "Not in a million years," says Nick, getting to his feet like a shot. They was always after each other, slogging it out, killing themselves to be top dog. It was the only thing that mattered to them two. So Nick's on his feet now, and they're standing at the end, clinging on to each other, not wanting to, and the wind's getting up. "Leave it," says Trev. "You don't have to do it," says Kev. "Time us, Dan," shouts Nick, who always makes sure it's done proper, like. "I'm on it," shouts Dan Troth, who's watching from below. So in the end, Nick goes first.'

Dougie stops talking.

'They didn't make it, then?' says Zohra after a while.

'Oh, they did, both of them got to the other end. Johnny first, Nick straight after. But when Dan gave them the times, that's when it got nasty. Same as always, see. No outright winner. So they had to do it again. It was starting to get cold. The rest of us was getting cheesed off and wanted to go home. But they wasn't having it. We slithered down the drainpipe – the wind was whipping up a treat by then – but they didn't come. We could see them up there – fighting, can you believe it? Like little kids, scrapping around like they was on flat ground. "Cut it out," shouts Les Troth. "Someone's going to get hurt." But they didn't take no notice. It was like they'd been waiting for this for ever.'

He stops again, gazing into space.

'They fell?' asks Zohra.

He nods. 'Yup. Johnny said it was Nick tipped them over. Nick said it was Johnny. Who knows? Either way, they came flying through the air together and landed on a car, just by where we was standing.'

'How come they survived?' asks Zohra. 'It must have been a long way down.'

'The car broke their fall. Triumph Herald. Saloon. Someone's pride and joy. Never found out who it belonged to. Massive dent in the roof. Trev dashed off to find a phone box and dialled 999 and they was carted away to hospital.'

'They were badly hurt, then?'

'One was worse than the other,' says Dougie. 'Couldn't walk for quite a while.'

'Nick,' says Lil.

'No, Johnny,' says Dougie.

They stare at each other but can't agree.

'Anyways,' he says solemnly. 'The moment they set foot on that roof, they was doomed. It was the end of the tennis. The one that broke his leg in several places – Johnny – when he stopped, Nick stopped too. It was like they couldn't do it on their own, like they needed each other, only they never knew it.'

'Guilt,' says Lil, nodding solemnly. 'Nick couldn't live with it. Or Johnny.'

'So whose fault was it, would you say?' asks Zohra.

They speak at the same time. 'Nick,' says Lil. 'Johnny,' says Dougie. Their eyes meet. 'Not as if it matters,' says Lil. 'Same result.'

IO

Johnny wakes on Saturday morning and opens his eyes, startled to find himself bathed in sunshine. Light is pouring through the window, ignoring the thin, inadequate curtains, wrapping his bed in a benign glow. He turns his head to see the clock and discovers that it's half past twelve. How could that have happened? The last time he checked, aching from hours of thrashing round the bed in the dark, restless grip of memory, it was quarter past five.

Debs has pushed her way into every dream, standing over him, laughing, ('Can't catch me, can't catch me'); irritated, ('I've been waiting for you two for hours. What do you think you're playing at?'); angry, ('Don't you dare let anyone pretend to be me! Just don't dare, you hear me now?').

He hears all right.

Who does this woman think she is, coming here, pretending to be Debs, taking advantage? Whatever she says, however convincing she sounds, she's lying. Debs is dead. There's no way she would have turned up like this (hey presto! I'm alive). She would never have just disappeared, gone off somewhere else, and not let them know.

The woman is short, like Debs, or Bev, but that's the only thing that connects her with them. Lots of people are short. Otherwise, she's nothing like either of the tiny, neat figures in his memory. She probably doesn't even have cancer. Anyone can pretend. Especially if they want sympathy.

Last night, Nick led them into his living room, once the family living room, where they used to watch television, and offered to make a drink. Johnny sat down opposite her and stared out of the window in silence. When Nick returned with the mugs, he positioned himself on the same side as Johnny, keeping as much space between them as possible.

'So you're from Toronto?' said Nick, eventually.

She nodded. 'I arrived here last Friday.'

'Last Friday?' said Johnny loudly, unable to bring his voice down to a sensible level. It's not possible that she's been here all this time, breathing the same air as them, without their knowledge.

'The travelling knocked me back a bit – I needed time to recover. I'm at a hotel, the one on the A38, heading out of town towards Birmingham.' Her voice was disconcertingly weak. Not at all like Debs, who was always so firm, so decisive. She sipped her cup of tea. 'Nice,' she said with appreciation, sounding stronger. 'Tea never tastes this good back in Toronto.'

'Nostalgia,' said Nick. 'Or imagination.'

'How many sugars do you have?' asked Johnny.

She stared at him, then slowly smiled. 'Good question,' she said, 'but hardly anyone has sugar now, do they?'

He persisted. 'All right. How many did you used to have? When you were younger?'

'Well – it's hard to be absolutely certain, since I must have gradually cut down, but I guess the time you're thinking of, it was three. And lots of milk.'

Johnny didn't want to admit that this is how Debs used to drink her tea. It was probably just a good guess. They needed more questions, definitive questions that nobody else would know the answer to, that would only apply to Debs. It was so hard to think clearly. There must be something . . .

'I felt quite unwell when I first arrived,' she said.

'Jet-lag,' said Nick. 'And if you're ill anyway . . .' He didn't sound convinced.

'Oh, I really do have cancer,' she said. 'I can see you might not believe me – it's easy to say, I know – but I don't need your permission to recognise my own illness.'

This sounded too much like the Debs Johnny used to know: convinced of her own rightness, undaunted by cynicism, not interested in their approval.

Nick reacted as if he'd recognised this too. 'Are you still having treatment?' he asked in a more conciliatory voice.

She shook her head. 'Just painkillers now. You reach a point when you've had enough of it – all those tests, scans, needles – and one day I just thought, that's it. No more. That's when I made the decision to come here, find you, tidy up things I should have dealt with years ago.'

'So how did you get travel insurance?' asked Nick.

She gave a little closed smile. 'I didn't,' she said.

Nick stares at her, clearly shocked. 'What happens if you need emergency treatment?'

'Oh, I have no intention of going anywhere near another hospital,' she said. She was too smug, almost superior, as if she knew so much more than they did, and wasn't going to tell them. For a few moments, she was unlikeable. Then she seemed to reconsider, and offered more information. 'Don't worry. If circumstances take over, it won't be a problem. I have money.'

'Do you have any idea how much the NHS charges overseas visitors?' asked Nick.

She looked at him calmly. 'I'm not poor,' she said. 'Mack, my husband – he died a year ago – left me more than adequately provided for. I could easily afford private care if I needed it.' She paused. 'Don't forget I'm still a British citizen.'

But which British citizen? Debs, Bev, someone completely different?

'Can we see your passport?' said Nick.

Without a word, she picked up her large bag, rummaged through it, and pulled out a blue passport.

'Canadian then? Not British?'

'I could have renewed my British one,' she said calmly, 'but it didn't seem necessary at this stage.'

Johnny grabbed it and fumbled through the opening pages with trembling fingers. The photograph was clearly the woman sitting in front of them. The name in the passport was Deborah Goodchild. He stared at it, aware of a hopeless, sinking sensation, as if everything was slipping out of his grasp.

The woman leaned over and patted his knee gently. 'My married name,' she said. 'What you really need to see is my birth certificate, but I've left that in the safe in my hotel room. I can bring it tomorrow, if you like.'

Now Johnny lies in bed, staring up at a large, expanding patch of mould on the ceiling, wrestling with the available information. It's a Sudoku puzzle, where you pencil in possibilities, rub them out again, keep moving alternatives around until everything fits. But there is no solution to this one.

The passport said Deborah, not Beverley.

It doesn't prove a thing. Lots of people are called Deborah. It will be more interesting to see if she can produce a birth certificate.

A thin, hard needle is drilling its way into the back of Johnny's mind, refusing to be diverted. It's fear. Was Debs capable of deceiving them for nearly half a century?

It should have been obvious once she was there in front of them, talking to them. But it wasn't.

She's old, she's spent years in a different country, she's not going to resemble a young woman who died in July 1969 at the age of twenty-two. Ma was only forty-six when she died, so there isn't even an image of an aging mother in his memory to give some clues.

They need to ask her questions. Lots and lots of questions.

In 1969, Johnny was fifteen, tall, strong and fit, but he wasn't observant. All his life, he's been consumed by an inexplicable anxiety that's prevented him from looking the world in the eye. That's why tennis was so satisfying, with its focus on physical movement, on rhythm, on calculation, without a need for personal interaction. He could ignore onlookers, concentrate without distraction, and if he won – especially if Nick was his opponent – the adrenalin would provide a temporary surge of elation that helped him through the aftermath.

So his memories can't be trusted. He'd have recognised her if she'd come back as a twenty-two-year-old, instantly, without a thought, but he struggles now to pinpoint anything specific about her physical appearance. And his knowledge of Bev is even vaguer, almost second-hand. Debs was the reality and Bev the mirror image.

So, in theory, if they recognise Debs, they'd recognise Bev too, but only as Debs, not Bev. Which is no help at all.

They'd struggled to maintain a conversation last night. 'You know Ma died shortly after . . .' Nick stopped.

'I heard,' she said quietly.

'What do you mean you heard?' said Johnny loudly, with a sudden flash of anger. 'Who told you? Someone in Bromsgrove who knew where you were? Why didn't you write – we didn't know anything – we thought, we thought . . .' He found himself choking on his words, suddenly unable to organise all the accusations that were rolling around inside his head.

'Nobody told me,' she said. 'It's all there on the Internet, but I've only recently looked. I know this is hard to believe, but I'd somehow managed to hide it all away, even from myself – you, Ma, what happened. It was as if my mind had built a wall, and I could only concentrate on one side at a time. I knew the other half was there, but I couldn't give it any attention. Then, after Mack died and there was no one to talk to, I was sitting at the table in my breakfast room, staring at the empty place opposite me, wondering how I was going to fill the time before I died too, when I realised that the wall had gone – crumbled away. Everything was there, at the front of my thoughts, demanding my attention. So I went online and started to search. I found it all eventually, although it was annoying that the local newspapers for that period weren't online. Like I said in my letter, Bromsgrove Memories, and a few blogs. Funny, isn't it? Something as big as that and people just forget, move on. It's taken me a while . . .'

The way she did that, faded into nothing, as if she was running out of steam, reminded Johnny of Ma in her last years. The way she'd abdicated, relinquished her authority bit by bit – and eventually dissolved. Suddenly it all felt too much. 'It might be easy for you to find out about us,' he said, 'but how are we supposed to know who you really are?'

'I'm sorry,' she said, putting her cup down and wiping her forehead with a trembling hand. She stood up, slightly unsteady, paler than when she arrived. 'I can't . . . I thought I was prepared – but it's been more exhausting than I was expecting. I should have given myself longer . . .'

Johnny pulled himself to his feet, distressed and confused, embarrassed by his anger. 'No,' he said. 'You can't go now.' She had to offer them something more concrete before leaving.

'Could you possibly drop me off?'

Johnny looked at Nick, baffled. 'It's too far . . .' he said. 'You'd never—'

'We don't have a car,' said Nick.

'So how do you get to work?' she asked. 'Helicopter?'

'There are buses,' said Nick abruptly. 'At the bottom of the road. And I can walk.'

'All the way into Bromsgrove?'

'Yes.' He sounded defensive, as if she'd discovered an inadequacy in him. 'I like it. It keeps me fit.' He took out his mobile. 'I'll call a taxi.'

'No,' she said. 'It's okay, I'll get the driver who brought me here.' She spoke briefly into her phone and rang off. 'He's just round the corner. Says he'll be here in three minutes.'

'Best to wait on the road then,' said Nick.

They went out into the corridor towards the main door. The floor of Aphrodite creaked, as if the train was on the move, destabilised by the unfamiliar presence of three people.

'Oh!' she said, animated again once she'd descended the outside steps and looked back. 'You've still got the railway lamp. I didn't notice it before.' She reached out and wiped away some of the cobwebs with her hand, fluttering her fingers to release them into the air. 'Do you remember . . .' She stopped, as if she wasn't sure what she remembered, as if she was wondering what was real and what wasn't.

They walked silently out to the road, and the taxi drew up almost immediately.

'Are you coming back?' asked Johnny, suddenly terrified that they'd never find out what they needed to know.

'I'm hardly going to come all this way and ignore you,' she said. 'Shall I ring or text when I'm ready?'

'We can come to the hotel,' said Nick.

'No,' she said. 'I want to come here, to the railway carriages. I'll get a taxi.'

'It's Saturday, so I'll be here all day,' said Nick. 'I'll give you my mobile number in case you can't make it.' As if she will have so many things to do in Bromsgrove.

The taxi pulled away. They stood and watched it fade into the distance, waiting for a few seconds after it was gone, just in case she changed her mind and came back. Then they turned without a word and walked back to the carriages.

Nick gets up early the next morning, exhausted from a long and sleepless night. He shaves, dresses, makes some breakfast. He's annoyed with himself for offering such an open invitation. Now they have no idea when to expect her.

He'll have to go to Asda for food – lunch, presumably, and possibly supper as well. It's important that he appears competent, domesticated, a man who strides decisively through life without stress, not someone who fell apart when his sister was murdered. Whoever this woman is, she shouldn't be allowed to think she can walk into his life and take advantage. He's not going to allow this stranger, this impostor, an easy ride.

She's so adamant that she's Debs.

She's had plenty of time to practise.

Could they all have been wrong: the coroner, Ma, everyone?

The sister he remembers wouldn't have disappeared like that, without telling them, without ever contacting them again, she just wouldn't. There was no reason for her to fake her own death, no scandals that came to light afterwards, nothing she would have wanted to run away from.

Is it possible to have a wall in your mind? Can you know something but not know it?

You could make up a lot, or guess, on the basis of observation. It's back to Bev again, the most likely possibility. No body, no absolute proof of her death. But why come back after all this time? What does she want?

The woman who came yesterday knew things about them, the way they think, and once or twice even sounded like Debs. But Nick doesn't want her to be Debs. Does he? What acceptable explanation would make that all right?

At eight o'clock, he sets off for Asda. It's an exhilarating morning, the air sharp and crisp, yellow leaves starting to appear in the trees. The exercise relaxes him a little, stops his thoughts clattering so loudly.

Does she look like Debs? Ma? Bev?

Yes . . . No . . . Maybe . . .

He walks up and down the busy aisles, realising with irritation that he'll have to feed Johnny too.

What makes a person who they are? Appearance does matter. It's the initial, most powerful identifier. But everything changes with age. Body shape, elasticity of the skin, ease of movement. Even the voice alters, as vocal chords weaken. He's fairly sure he wouldn't identify his own teenage self if he met him in the street. It would be unrealistic to expect her to be recognisable.

It's more complicated than that, of course. Whatever's happened to the exterior, the inside of a person will connect with the past. But how do you see through the outer layers, penetrate to the parts that matter? What if everything's been altered by later experience? Memory is unreliable – even genuine memories won't always match up exactly with anyone else's. It would take so long to be sure.

But a trace . . . A fleeting expression, an unconscious movement, a mannerism that reminds them of Debs or even Ma. That's how you identify families, how you recognise the action of the genes, the laws of inheritance. Is that what he saw yesterday, when he first saw her and thought immediately that he knew her? It wasn't there when he looked again, and afterwards he couldn't understand why he'd made such a mistake.

He bumps into a young woman with his trolley. 'Sorry,' he says.

She scowls at him. 'That really hurt,' she says, rubbing her ankle. She's thin, muscled, well toned, in tight black leggings. There's a red weal at the back of the ankle where he hit her.

'I'm so sorry.' He feels guilty, but can't think of a reasonable way to help.

'You should be more careful,' she says, turning away.

Young people are so vocal, so unafraid. He doesn't think he could have talked like that to an older man – or woman – when he was her age. You did as you were told, or you ignored them, depending on the level of your confidence.

He selects cold meats, fruit, salad, bread, potatoes, vegetables, biscuits. He's never put so much in his trolley before and when the total is rung up on the till, he's shocked. 'Goodness,' he says to the girl. 'I wasn't expecting that.'

'Tell me about it,' she says. 'Are you having a dinner party?'

'No,' he says. 'Not exactly. Just a long-lost . . .' He stops. Why is he telling her this?

She smiles. 'Ooh, sounds exciting. Like that programme. The one where they trace their ancestors.'

Nick smiles back and wills himself to say nothing. His cheeks ache with the effort.

He walks home, puts the food away and settles down in his sitting room with paper and pencil, preparing to compile a list. Questions: How old were you when you left school? (too obvious); who won the match between Nick and Johnny in June 1968? (even he's unsure who won which one when); what was your favourite pudding? (too much like the one about sugar in your tea – it depends on the time period); what year did we move into the railway carriages? (not personal enough – something she could find out).

It's not as easy as it seems.

Time drags on. At two o'clock, it's clear she's not going to turn up for lunch. This is not considerate of her. She should have phoned. He hasn't heard anything from Johnny. Usually there are muffled sounds, the loo flushing, activity in the kitchen (the pricking of plastic on ready meals, the ping of the microwave), but there's been nothing today. He must be up to something, but it's hard to know what. He's not a man who goes out.

Three o'clock. He can hear Johnny now, the creaks as he moves around, the rocking of the adjacent corridor. The passing traffic, which is never busy, dies away. Three thirty. Is she going to come at all? Four o'clock . . .

There's a knock on the door.

Nick jumps to his feet, then slows himself down. Be measured, thoughtful, don't give an impression of eagerness.

Johnny opens his sliding door at exactly the same time as Nick. They stare at each other.

'Aphrodite?' asks Johnny.

Nick nods. The last time he saw Johnny's living room – a very long time ago – it was almost impenetrable, overflowing with computer magazines, manuals, obsolete equipment, unemptied carrier bags. No spare seats, no facilities for entertaining.

Johnny opens the outside door slowly, uncharacteristically considerate, careful not to knock her over. She's standing at the bottom of the steps with a box in her hand. 'Cakes,' she says, handing the box to Nick. 'I thought we could all do with something nice.'

He takes the box, leads her into his living room, then goes to the kitchen to make tea. When he returns with a tray, she's sitting opposite Johnny and they're both staring out of the window again, exactly as they were yesterday.

There's a long silence, as a curious shyness descends on them. None of them seems certain how to proceed.

'The birth certificate?' asks Nick quietly.

She half smiles, takes a piece of paper out of her bag and hands it to him. 'I didn't forget,' she says.

Deborah Greenwood, it says. Father – Peter Greenwood: occupation – bricklayer. Mother – Doris: occupation – cleaner.

How do you know if it's genuine? He hands it to Johnny, who studies it intently, as if it will release hidden information if he stares at it long enough. Their eyes meet. A silent uncertainty passes between them.

Johnny tries to analyse her appearance for clues. The recognition of something physical would solve everything – the shape of her nose, perhaps, or a familiar mole on her cheek. There's the squirrel tattoo, of course, but she's wearing long sleeves. But even to think this means that he believes she is Debs. And he doesn't.

Did he ever know the shape of her nose? He should have examined the photos more carefully. He can only summon a vague perception of Debs's presence: a voice that read to him in a motherly way (but is he confusing Debs with Ma?) when he was little, and occasionally sang 'Puff the Magic Dragon' or 'Jake the Peg'; a sister who lost her warmth when he entered puberty; who challenged him about everything that mattered – although it might have been him doing the arguing rather than her; who nagged him about body odour, the need for showers and aftershave; who accused him of having jeans that were so encrusted with dirt they could stand up on their own (he's slightly concerned that none of this has changed). His only vivid memory of her physical presence is the time when he beat Philip Dorchester, the reigning champ, in the semi-finals at Exeter. She grabbed him when he came out of the changing room (where was Nick, who had just won the other semi-final? Perhaps she was really waiting for him) and gave him a soft, crushing embrace. He caught a whiff of her deodorant, the fleeting smell of a powdered cheek, smooth and artificial against his face.

Were there any birthmarks? He conjures up a misty image of her dancing around at the seaside in a blue swimming costume, covered in plump yellow cartoon fish, throwing a Frisbee, playing cricket, organising a city of castles in the sand. There must have been something.

All they really need to see is the tattoo. It appeared shortly before Debs disappeared. They were squeezed round the kitchen table eating supper – heart stew, thick and comforting – when she lifted up an arm to brush hair out of her eyes. Her sleeve fell loosely back, and on the top part of her arm, just above the elbow, they could see a large plaster. Ma grabbed the arm immediately, before Debs could pull away. 'What's this? You didn't tell me you'd hurt yourself.'

Debs was oddly reluctant to discuss it. 'It's nothing,' she murmured, twisting her head away from Ma's gaze, trying to fork up a piece of potato with the other hand.

Immediately, everyone knew it was something. Ma didn't waste any time. She ripped off the dressing, and Debs gave a little cry of pain, which she hurriedly suppressed.

It was a tiny squirrel, bright and oily, gleaming with defiance.

Johnny remembers his audible gasp, the moment of absolute silence that followed.

'You're hanging around with that filthy, greasy motorcycle gang,' shrieked Ma, standing up so suddenly that her chair tipped over and clattered against the cupboard behind her.

'Don't be daft,' shouted Debs, kicking her own chair back. 'What would I be doing with them? I just wanted a tattoo. It's what people do.'

'It most certainly isn't, young lady. In my book, tattoos are not for nice girls – it's sailors that have them, or criminals. I've given the best years of my life making sure you grow up to be a decent person, to give you opportunities I never had, and this is how you reward me?'

Debs picked up her plate. 'Can't you just leave me to get on with my own life?' she raged. 'All I wanted was a tattoo! Why does that have to turn me into a monster?' And somehow the plate fell to the floor, splintering into fragments, drops of stew flying through the air and decorating every surface.

'Get out of my sight!' yelled Ma. 'I can't bear to look at you.'

'It's a pleasure!' screamed Debs. They could hear the outside door slamming furiously as she flung herself out into the dark – although this wasn't necessarily intentional. It was the only way the door would shut properly.

The argument continued for three days. Johnny went out, played tennis with anyone available down at the park, wandered up and down the High Street long after the shops were closed, placed himself as far away as possible. He couldn't stay indoors. The violence of their voices penetrated deep inside him, creating a tight pain in his chest, and when they stopped shouting, the hard, accusing silences sucked away his ability to think.

Nobody ever found out why Debs had the tattoo done. Curiosity, perhaps, or the desire to be different, to set a new trend. Two weeks later, she was gone, and all that passion was replaced by silence.

But the tattoo identified her. It was the deciding factor.

Now, Johnny examines the woman in front of him, her arms discreetly covered, and wonders how to ask her to show them the tattoo.

'I'm amazed you're still here,' she says in her Canadian accent, sounding even less like Debs or Bev. 'It was freezing in winter then. I can't imagine it's improved much.'

'It's not ideal,' says Nick. 'I have thought about moving—'

'Since when?' says Johnny. Shouldn't he have mentioned this before? But then Nick hasn't said anything to him for over seven years.

'No wives, partners, children?'

Neither of them replies. Johnny experiences the familiar sense of shame, the belief in his own failure, that used to accompany him everywhere. He hasn't experienced it for a while – since he no longer goes anywhere or encounters anyone. In the end, he just shakes his head.

'You're not a chatty pair, are you?' She moves awkwardly, trying to make herself more comfortable. She's well dressed today. Smart black trousers; a floaty kind of cream blouse over a black cotton T-shirt with a low neck (but long sleeves); a necklace that nestles comfortably in the crease of her just-visible cleavage – large ceramic flowers, maroon, smooth and shiny against the crumpled texture of her skin; a hip-length black cardigan that looks expensive; black shiny shoes with square heels.

'The thing is,' says Nick, 'anyone could claim to be Debs.'

'I realise that,' she says. 'I'd hoped – crazy really – that you might just recognise me. I wasn't thinking clearly, I can see that now, but it's kind of disappointing. I know who I am, obviously, and you don't. And not only that, you don't want to—'

'You can't reasonably expect us to,' says Nick.

'No, of course not,' she says. 'Well – I'm here to tell you what really happened, so I'd better get on with it.'

'That's what we're waiting for,' says Johnny.

'Yes . . .' She pauses. 'But I'm finding it hard to know where—'

'For a start,' says Nick, 'you could tell us who we cremated. Because someone went up in smoke. One of the guys on the search found a body, the police saw it, the forensic people identified it – and we had a funeral. We were all under the impression it was Debs.'

'It was Bev,' she says.

There's a confused moment. Johnny has to let this play through his mind for a few moments. She was obviously going to offer this explanation. If you want to impersonate someone who's dead, you'd have to find a good explanation for them being alive. 'So why did everyone think it was Debs?' he asks.

'It *was* her,' says Nick. 'We knew because of the tattoo.'

Yes, thinks Johnny. That's right.

Slowly, Debs releases the button on the cuff on her right wrist and rolls up the sleeve to just above the elbow. A small, neat squirrel nestles amongst soft rolls of tanned, wrinkled skin. It's faded, but very distinct.

There's a long silence while they all stare at it.

'But . . .' Nick is struggling to sound coherent. 'But . . . the forensic people told us . . . it was on the body . . .' His face suddenly clears. 'You've had it done recently, that's it, isn't it? So you could pretend you were Debs.'

It hasn't been done recently. You can see that from the way it threads through the wrinkles.

'I'm not that devious,' she says. 'But Bev was. As soon as she saw mine, she went off and had an identical one done, in exactly the same place. By the same man as me. Then he went off on his travels – he was only passing through anyway – and nobody was any the wiser. I couldn't believe it when she showed me.'

'Why would she do that?' asks Nick.

'Ah,' she says. 'Now we're coming to the point.'

There's a silence while she pulls the sleeve back down and buttons it. Everything seems even more precarious than before.

'If you're Debs,' says Nick slowly, 'where have you been all this time? And don't just say Canada. That's not good enough. Why would you make yourself disappear?'

'I didn't have a choice,' she says.

'Everyone has a choice,' says Nick, sounding angry.

She stares at them and takes a deep breath. 'Because I thought I'd just killed Bev.'

Johnny finds himself blinking wildly, trying to focus on her face as it starts to disintegrate in front of him. 'What do you mean, you thought?' he says. 'How can you not know something like that?'

'Just tell us what happened,' says Nick, his voice tight and unnatural.

'Okay,' she says. 'But you'll need to understand a few things about me and Bev. You knew her, right? What do you remember about her?'

Nothing, thinks Johnny. Absolutely nothing.

But Nick is a little more forthcoming. 'She was here all the time, almost as if she'd moved in, become part of the family.'

She was here when Ma discovered the tattoo. After the argument, Bev remained sitting at the table while Nick and Johnny cleared up the mess of Debs's broken plate. She finished her stew and wiped the table before finally following Debs out into the night.

She nods encouragingly. 'And do you know why?'

'Something to do with her mother, presumably,' says Nick. 'She was an alcoholic – very scary.'

'She's dead now, isn't she?' she says.

Nick nods. 'Not long after. More or less the same time as Ma.'

She's silent for a while at the mention of Ma. 'Go on then,' she says. 'What else do you remember?'

What does she have in mind? Johnny can now place Bev in the railway carriages, sleeping on a lilo in Debs's tiny, cramped room, occupying precious inches, sharing their meals (why didn't Ma ever complain about the cost?). But he still can't produce any real sense of her. She was just there, breathing their air, eating their food, occupying Debs's attention.

'She wanted to be like you, didn't she?' says Nick.

'Yes!' she says with satisfaction, as if he's finally said something significant. 'That's it. That's exactly what she wanted. She copied everything – my actions, my clothes, my language – everything that made me Debs, the person I knew myself to be.'

'Like a shadow?' offered Johnny.

'More than a shadow,' she says. 'Much, much more. In the end, she didn't want to just be like me, she wanted to be me. She was a giant photocopier with a mind of its own, determined to produce a copy that was so perfect you couldn't tell which was which – and then destroy the original. She wanted my life. But she didn't want me to be there too.'

'What are you saying?' asks Nick. 'She wanted to take your place somehow?'

'Yes,' she says.

'But that's ridiculous.'

'That's what I thought,' she says.

It's becoming complicated, difficult to comprehend.

'Imagine what you would do,' she says. 'Supposing it was you two instead of me and Bev. Nick, think of how you were when you were twenty-two. You knew who you were, what you wanted, you had ideas about your own future, career, girlfriend, wife, children, home, all those things you dream of when you're young . . .'

Johnny can't remember ever making plans like that. Debs was dead by then, and life had ceased to follow predictable pathways. 'I'm not sure it was quite—'

'Okay,' says Nick. 'Carry on.'

'And then Johnny decides your life is better than his.'

'In your dreams,' says Johnny.

She smiles. 'Whatever. I just want you to imagine it. So Johnny decides that if he could be Nick instead of himself, everyone would treat him differently, believe in him more. And because they have higher expectations, Johnny would become Nick, no longer second best. He'd be the one with the future.'

'Are you suggesting Nick's future was more promising than mine?' says Johnny.

'I'm illustrating,' she says. 'You're not supposed to take it literally.'

'But I'd still be there,' says Nick. 'He couldn't be me.'

'Exactly,' she says. 'So what would Johnny have to do?'

Nick hesitates. 'Get rid of me?'

'Yes,' she says, and gazes round at them triumphantly.

Johnny takes a bite of lemon tart to allow time for thought. 'But,' he says slowly, then stops for a moment as the tartness of the lemon trickles down his throat and forces him to swallow, 'if Bev wanted to get rid of Debs, and if only one of you is dead, then that must mean you're Bev . . .'

She doesn't reply immediately. 'Things never quite work out the way they're meant to, though, do they? I'll have to go back a bit. Do you remember that she used to dress like me?'

'I've seen it in a photo,' says Johnny. 'Bev and Debs are wearing the same clothes – but it's easy enough to work out who's who. Bev's stuff is usually more makeshift, more pretend.'

'Not always,' says Nick. 'Sometimes she was the one getting it right.'

She looks annoyed. 'No she wasn't. That's rubbish.'

'Her knitting was better,' he says. 'Debs was always dropping stitches, needing help from Ma.'

She gives a dismissive snort. 'That was just cosmetic. She didn't have any real vision, no creativity; she could only copy. She was just a reproduction of me. We started having arguments—'

'I remember,' says Nick. 'There was one once – not long before – that went on and on . . .'

Why don't I remember this? thinks Johnny. Why didn't I notice?

'At first it was flattering – like a compliment – then it became irritating, but then it became more than that – upsetting. If I went to the rag market and bought material, she bought the same thing. If I designed a pattern, she managed to copy it – at first I just thought she was doodling, pretending to do her own design – but then she'd turn up in it – sometimes even before I'd finished putting mine together. So it looked as if we were working as a team, or even as if I was copying her, when really all the ideas were coming from me. She wasn't being supportive, she was draining me, stealing my personality. If I bought some shoes, a bag, a coat, she'd stand there in the shop next to me, wait until I'd paid, then go back and buy the same thing. I'd reached the point when I'd had enough and I wanted her to go away, leave me alone. But of course she wouldn't – or, more likely, couldn't. She had too much invested in my life. Without me, she was nothing. Unless she actually became me.'

The implication is still that Bev killed Debs.

'I couldn't turn round without finding her just behind me, or move without stepping on her toes. I couldn't look in the mirror and be certain I was seeing myself and not her.'

'Actually,' says Nick to Johnny. 'You were like that. Trying to wear the same things as me.'

'Don't flatter yourself,' says Johnny. 'Everyone dressed the same. It was the fashion. Why would I have wanted to be like you?'

'I was better than you at tennis. You were jealous.'

'You've got that the wrong way round,' says Johnny. 'I kept beating you, remember?'

They glare at each other. And they've slipped backwards, become teenagers again, lost any perspective they've gained over the last decades.

But what perspective have they gained – ever? It seems as if they've always been teenagers with each other, never able to move beyond the rivalry, the jealousy, the desire to win. Is that why they both seem to have decided in the last few years that it's easier to stop trying, easier to pretend the other one doesn't exist?

'Believe me,' she says. 'Neither of you were like Bev. She was sinister, suffocating, terrifying. I started to believe that she really did intend to do away with me.'

'Except you're claiming it was the other way round,' says Nick.

She sighs, takes a deep drink from her mug of tea, and sits back. 'Goodness,' she says, leaning forward again. 'It's like trying to relax on a slab of concrete. I can't believe that in all these years you've never considered replacing it with something more comfortable.'

Nick watches her, aware that things are shifting, that the certainties he's lived with for so long are being challenged. He's known about the inadequacy of the seats for years, registered that there's something intrinsically unsatisfactory about the whole way he lives his life, but he's never been able to summon enough energy to do anything about it. The invisible ties, the obligations to people who are no longer there, the nonexistent bodies buried in the field – they've taken away his ability to make the decision.

There's a financial advantage to living here, of course, but he's not penniless. He could afford to go elsewhere, abandon this absurd tiptoeing around Johnny, this pretence that he doesn't exist. Why doesn't he just move, put some distance between them? Johnny could probably afford to move as well, if he wanted to. He must be earning some money with his online business and he doesn't give the impression he's spending much of it.

'You still haven't given us any real explanations,' he says, annoyed that his attention has been diverted.

'I had a plan. I'd been putting money aside, hoping to head off on my own, soon as I'd had enough. I wanted a new life that didn't involve Bev.'

So, according to her, while Nick and Johnny were going to school, collecting trophies in tournaments, fancying Alison Wilcox, Brenda Taylor, Judith Carter, all this was going on in the background. In a parallel, unseen world. She's making it all up. 'Debs would have told us,' he says.

'Or Ma,' says Johnny. 'Ma would have known.'

'I couldn't tell anyone,' she says softly. 'In case you let something slip to Bev. Ma would have talked me out of it, insisted I stay for your sakes – both of you. But you didn't need me with you, not any more. You were off doing your own thing by then – you probably wouldn't even have noticed I'd gone.'

She's got that wrong. They did need Debs, although neither of them realised until it was too late.

'The Debs I knew,' persists Johnny, 'wouldn't have left without saying anything.'

She hesitates. 'Well – it would have been hard. I'd have done it, though, and let you know later – sent a note, told you not to worry, that kind of thing . . .'

'The police said Bev and Debs could leave home if they wanted to – they were both adults,' says Nick. 'We told them Debs would never do that, but they weren't interested. It took two whole weeks before they took the disappearance seriously, and another week to find the body.' A coldness is creeping into him, a sense of dread. She's telling them they were wrong, that they didn't know her as well as they thought they did.

She doesn't meet his eyes. 'I'm sorry,' she says, and waits for a while before continuing. 'I started applying for jobs in London. I sent drawings, designs to show what I could do. Most of them didn't get back to me, of course – I didn't really expect them to. But then one did. A shop in Kensington, a boutique, who said they liked my ideas – I'd sent some drawings, designs – and asked me to come and see them. They were only small, but they were looking for someone different, individual. You can't imagine how exciting that was. Just the thought of them knowing my name gave me goose pimples.'

'It wasn't a job offer, though?' says Nick. 'Just an interview?'

She smiles. 'Well, obviously. But I was twenty-two years old, a Bromsgrove girl who believed London was the only place in the world – the King's Road – bursting with glamour – Twiggy, the Rolling Stones, Jean Shrimpton – and I really thought everyone was just waiting for me. You don't contemplate failure at that age. I was all set. But then everything went wrong.'

'Bev found out?' says Johnny.

She nods. 'There was a works party. They'd hired the hall at Bournheath for a summer dance – a big deal in those days. Everyone was trying so hard – it makes you weep to think of it. Bromsgrove was finally getting there, learning to be groovy. We ironed our hair between sheets of brown paper to make it straight, backcombed it on top. Pale lipstick, huge false eyelashes with black eyeliner, you remember all that? I was determined Bev wouldn't wear the same clothes as me, so I lent her a dress, one I knew she wanted.'

'I thought all Bev's dresses were the same as Debs's,' says Nick.

She smiles. 'Well – I managed to keep one step ahead of her for as long as I could.' She stops.

'And?' prompted Nick eventually.

She starts to speak again, slowly, looking inwards, the words no longer flowing. 'I can't remember a lot of it. When I started to work it all out again, some of the detail just wasn't there. I can go so far, and then it just whooshes away. There's a big blank hole in the middle.'

'Useful,' says Nick, but then decides he sounds too harsh. 'Understandable, though, I suppose.'

'We walked to Bournheath because we walked everywhere then – everyone did. It was starting to drizzle, but we had macs, and we wanted to save our money so we could get a taxi home. We were both really excited. There were going to be lots of guys there, drink, dancing. Bev had her eye on this boy – Stuart. He was more interested in me, I knew, but I was feeling generous and I'd got this chap in Italy – gorgeous, we wrote all the time – and I wasn't going to let on. We were out in the country, no houses nearby, just farms, no one around.'

Nick can picture them, Debs in the pale green polyester mini-dress with the round collar she was wearing when she was found, big black buttons down the front; a silk scarf tied under her chin to protect her hair from the rain; her legs sleek in new tights; white, knee-high plastic boots; the short mac with huge lapels and wide belt. And Bev next to her in her mac and boots, nearly the same but not quite, wearing a different dress underneath.

'It felt good, like we'd gone back to the way we used to be – good friends again. Because I knew that Bev was wearing something different for once, I had this crazy sense of freedom, like opening the doors of a prison, letting in the fresh air. Only then I thought of how she'd have to make her own way once I'd left, how she wouldn't have anyone to walk home with any more, or to copy, and I started to feel mean.'

'You told her,' says Nick.

She nods. 'We'd both had one of those little bottles of whisky before we left – you know, the sort you get in hotels. We'd bought them from the outdoor the night before, so we'd be able to go straight into the action, ready to roll. The truth was, neither of us was very confident about partying; we were all talk, no real experience. I wasn't used to alcohol, and I guess it went to my head.'

'No,' says Johnny, 'that's not right. Debs was living it up all the time.'

She smiles. 'You were easy to impress.'

That was probably true, thinks Nick. He'd assumed she was having sex too, all the time. Everyone else seemed to be, so why wouldn't his glamorous, worldly-wise sister? He can still remember the desperate ache as he watched them going out, longing to be part of their sophisticated, fun-loving world.

'It was stupid to tell Bev, I must have known that, and as soon as I'd opened my mouth, I regretted it. But I felt sorry for her. It wasn't her fault she was like she was. She had so many awful things in her life – people picked on her at work, she didn't really get on with anyone; her mum was a nightmare.'

'We thought Bev's mother was terrifying,' says Johnny.

'But – and this really shocked me – Bev already knew. Everything: the interview, my preparations to leave. She said I'd left the letter out, from the boutique, but I knew I hadn't. I was really careful with it. I didn't even keep it in my bag in case she saw it there. I kept it in a pocket in my coat – that's where it was that evening. I'd underestimated her. She'd gone through my things, she probably did it regularly – and it was as if she could see into me, right through to my centre and out the other side. You think her mother was scary, but you didn't know Bev.' She takes a breath. 'I can still see us there, standing in the middle of the road, facing each other as she started to unbutton her mac. Even then I knew what was going to happen, but I couldn't quite accept it, didn't really believe—'

Nick has guessed. 'She was wearing the same dress as you underneath?'

She nods. 'When I realised – it was like that prison door had slammed shut in my face. I don't think I've ever been so angry – there was a terrible pain in my chest – I can remember thinking, I'm having a heart attack . . .'

There's a long pause. 'So what happened?' asks Johnny after a while, his voice barely above a whisper.

'I think – I'm not entirely certain – it's all very muddled in my mind – but I can only think that once she'd taken her mac off, once she knew that I knew she looked exactly the same as me, I must have lost it . . .' She stops again, her breathing heavy and laboured. Her face has gone very pale and sweat has started to drip down from her forehead. She rummages in her bag for a tissue and wipes it roughly over her cheeks. 'I've never told this to anyone – not even Mack. I couldn't have. It wasn't even in my memory then. I'm trusting you – not sure if I should after all these years, but we are family, even if you don't believe that yet. Anyway, if you turn me in, I'll be dead long before it comes to trial.'

'But what was Bev hoping to achieve?' asks Nick, trying to be rational. 'She can't seriously have believed she could become Debs.'

'I've thought about this a lot recently,' says Debs slowly, 'and I know it's hard to get your head round, but I genuinely believe she was intending to get rid of me. It was the job, wasn't it? Her great opportunity. She knew all about it and she wanted it. She could have gone off to London, pretended to be me, and nobody would have been any the wiser.'

'That's absurd!' says Johnny. 'Supposing one of us came across her at some time in the future? Didn't it occur to her that we might have noticed?'

'And what would be the point?' says Nick. 'If she wanted to be Debs, surely it was her existing life she wanted to copy, not some vague prospect far away.'

'But she would be living my life. I was going to leave, so she could leave too. She would never have believed she could be found out because she was me in her mind, and if she couldn't see the difference, why would you? I was the inconvenience, not her.'

'So which one are you? Debs or Bev?' asks Johnny, impatiently, angrily.

He's right. She has to be one of them, but they still don't know which one.

'I'm getting there, honestly. The trouble is, I genuinely can't remember what happened. There were woods on both sides of the road, a stream – I remember running, running so fast I couldn't breathe – maybe I was chasing her – maybe she was chasing me . . .' She stops.

Nick is running with her in his mind. They were probably about half a mile from Bournheath Hall – he knows the area – stumbling between trees, tripping over tangled undergrowth, abandoned, rusty farm machinery, too far away from people and safety—

'And?' says Johnny harshly. They need the resolution, the definitive answer.

She stares at him for a moment, her eyes blank, as if she's forgotten where she is, then takes a deep breath. 'I don't know.'

A bird is singing in the willows at the back of the field, on a branch above the railway carriages. A car drives past, revving noisily as it accelerates up the hill.

They know what happened. One survived, one didn't. She's here in Aphrodite, telling them the story, and the other one was cremated nearly fifty years ago. There was no serial killer, no one in Bromsgrove with a terrible secret, no stranger passing through. It was this woman sitting in front of them. Bev or Debs.

The clock ticks, electronically, artificially convincing. But time is no longer functioning properly.

'I'd grabbed a bag, thinking it was mine, but it turned out to be Bev's – they were the same, of course. I can remember the terror, the urgency of having to run, to escape, get away as fast as possible, but everything that happened in between . . .'

'It was ages before the body was found,' says Nick. He meets Johnny's eye and sees his own shock reflected back at him. What do they do with this knowledge? How should they react? 'The forensics people said it was Debs.'

'Well, they would, wouldn't they? She was wearing my clothes, she had my bag, and she had my tattoo, which no one else knew about. It seems obvious now that everyone would think it was me. She believed she was me and, in the end, she was right. She took over my life – and then she took over my death. So she won. I've wondered recently if she planned it to happen in that way, so we'd fight it out. Like a lottery, winner takes all, that kind of thing.'

'But why didn't you go to the police?' asks Nick, watching her closely.

'I knew I was guilty, I suppose,' she says. 'I must have killed her, and I was presumably in shock, unable to think straight. I can remember wandering along a road in the dark, crying, not knowing where I was, even who I was. If I was the killer, I thought, I must have been Bev, because Debs wouldn't kill anyone. I was so confused.'

'So where did you go?' asks Nick.

'There was a lot of cash in Bev's purse – all part of her plan, I suppose – so after I'd calmed down a bit, I emptied it and threw the bag away. Then I went to the station, cleaned up as much as I could in the Ladies, and got a train into Birmingham and on to London. It was busy, crowds of people heading for the night clubs – no one really took any notice of me.'

'You'd never get away with that now,' says Johnny.

'No,' she says. 'There are cameras everywhere.'

It's cold in the railway carriage. The atmosphere is heavy, threatening, slowing down Nick's thoughts. We're talking to her as if she's Debs, he thinks. It's not the best place for this conversation – too many connections. This woman in front of them has killed someone, she's a murderer, and they're contemplating the possibility that she's their sister. How can he think about this calmly?

'The job was a con – they just wanted me to make tea all day and work for peanuts, so I didn't take it. I found another one cleaning offices. The hours were antisocial, up at five and home again before most people were up, but it suited me. I rented a room, stayed indoors, and became someone else.'

'You could have let us know – somehow,' says Johnny, his voice rising. 'If you'd just sent us a message, told us it wasn't you who was dead . . .'

She looks down, upset, her eyes watering, and her voice weakens. 'I never thought – I assumed everyone would know it was Bev. I considered coming back, I really did. Several times, I found myself at the station, about to buy a ticket – but I was scared – I couldn't do it . . .'

'But why not? Didn't you ever think what it did to Ma, to us, believing you were dead?' Johnny is visibly shaking, a teenager again, flapping his elbows wildly in and out.

'I couldn't bear for you to think of me as a murderer.' She puts a hand out to comfort him, but withdraws it before she makes contact.

'But you could have said it was self-defence,' says Nick. 'It might have turned out all right . . .' How different everything could have been.

She takes a tissue out of her bag and blows her nose. 'I wasn't thinking straight. I couldn't eat or sleep, and when I did finally manage to think more clearly, it just seemed easier – kinder to everyone – to stay where I was. End it there. The thought of a trial, going through it all again – I just couldn't . . . In the end, I suppose I succeeded in doing what Bev never could. I lost sight of the original Debs and became someone else.'

'When did you go to Canada?' asks Nick.

'That was after a couple of years, when I'd saved a bit.'

'How did you get a passport without any documents?'

'It was shockingly easy,' says Debs. I sent away for a copy of my birth certificate, then all I needed was a photo and someone to vouch for me.'

'But there would have been a death certificate by then.'

'Different departments,' says Johnny. 'They didn't exchange information in those days. No computers.'

Nick looks at him in surprise. 'How do you know that?'

'Everyone knows. It's how people create false identities. Don't you ever watch detective series, the news? They're probably more careful now, though.'

So seeing her birth certificate didn't prove anything.

'I stuck a pin in a map. I told myself I would write to you, once I was settled, but I kept putting it off. I just couldn't find the words and it became more and more impossible as time went on, until it felt too late. Because I hadn't done it earlier, I couldn't do it later. I met Mack, married him, and helped him with the business. Actually, I've almost been happy. But nothing goes on for ever.'

Johnny gets to his feet awkwardly. 'Do you have any idea . . .?' he says, his voice rising, then trailing away.

She bows her head, unable to speak for a few moments. 'I'm sorry,' she says. 'I want to put it right. That's why I've come.'

'But you're too late,' says Johnny. 'Far too late. Ma's dead and gone. Or perhaps you haven't noticed.' He pulls open the door and stalks out, leaving his anger behind him in the room, swirling around Nick and Debs.

Nick sees his list, the questions he'd intended to ask, folded in half on the coffee table, waiting to be consulted. He thought he'd easily prove she couldn't be Debs. Now it feels foolish, trivial. He leans forwards, picks it up and puts it into a drawer. They sit quietly for a while, letting the air settle after Johnny's dramatic departure.

'Do you have children?' he asks.

'No,' she says sadly, studying the space where Johnny had been sitting. 'We wanted to, but – Mack had a medical problem. So it's just the three of us now.'

The last of the Greenwoods. Nick and Johnny, who've remained here in the family home while it disintegrates around them, watching each other, barely communicating, quietly preparing to carry their separate selves into a solitary darkness, and – maybe – Debs, who's returning, not with the promise of distant relatives and new generations, but with illness and the prospect of an imminent end.

The sun has gone down and cold air is beginning to seep in through the cracks under the door. Condensation is dripping down to the bottom of the windows.

She pulls her jacket round her more closely. 'Don't you believe in heating?' she asks.

11

'Come on,' Crispin says to Zohra on Sunday, as they sit on a restored bench on Wychington platform and share samosas prepared for them by Zohra's mother. 'Time for you to introduce me to the Greenwoods. You can do it. You know you can.' From where they're sitting, they can see the engine just inside the shed, gleaming, ready for action. Don, seventy-eight, white-haired, with arthritis in both knees, who retired from his job as an engineer on the railways almost two decades ago, is unusually optimistic. 'Almost there,' he's been saying every day for the last month, as he oils and checks and checks and checks.

'We've been through this,' says Zohra. 'The fact that I know all about their murdered sister doesn't make us friends. I've met them once in a professional capacity and I've directed a mysterious woman to their doorstep. I can hardly turn up, accompanied by someone who wants to deprive them of their home, just to say hello.'

'That's not fair,' says Crispin. 'I only want to talk.'

'For what purpose exactly?'

'Well – I'd like to know what model they are, their condition.'

'The Greenwoods or the carriages?'

'Very funny.'

'But why should their condition concern you if you have no designs on them?'

'Okay, I'm interested in them, but it's all hypothetical. How old did you say they were? The brothers, that is. Any chance of them dying off in the foreseeable future?'

'Crispin!' She's shocked. 'They're people, not commodities.'

He grins. 'I know, I know. But how do we know they don't want to sell if we don't ask? Anyway, we can always invite them to come next Saturday if nothing else. They must be mildly interested in trains.'

She gives in. 'Okay, I'll show you where they are, but I'm not going to speak to them.'

'Fair enough. Best if I see them first.' He gets to his feet, scattering crumbs everywhere. 'Come on, then. Let's do it now, while Nathan's tucking into lamb and roast potatoes with his mum.'

'Nathan doesn't eat meat.'

'No, but he's not here, which is the important thing.' He sets off down the platform steps and strides across the field towards the car. She has to run to keep up with him, and only just manages to jump in before he pulls away.

She directs him to Long Meadow Road and points out the entrance to the carriages, but Crispin drives past several times before parking further up the road. 'Casing the joint,' he says.

'Not entirely sure you're doing the right thing, then?' she says.

They walk back up the road. 'Act cool,' he says. 'We're going for a stroll in the countryside. It's what people do.'

'Keep your voice down.' She tries whispering, but the ever-present sound of the motorway on the wind compels her to speak louder than she intends. 'You mustn't alert them to our presence.'

They stop at the end of the pathway. 'It could be a public right of way, for all we know,' says Crispin.

'Except that I know it isn't.'

'Actually, you don't,' he says. 'They quite often go through people's gardens.' He takes a breath. 'Right, here we go. You can wait here.'

She watches him disappear up the path, aware of her heart beating faster and a tension in her muscles. She doesn't know what she'll do if one of the brothers comes walking up the road right now. A warning yell would just bring Crispin face to face with them.

173

He's gone for several minutes. When he eventually appears, he's moving fast, but grinning. 'Yes!' he says.

She starts heading back up the road towards the car before he reaches her. 'Hurry up,' she says over her shoulder. 'It's bad form to loiter at the scene of a crime.'

'They're perfect. Absolutely perfect.' He puts a hand on her arm, trying to slow her down. 'It's all right, Zohra,' he says. 'We haven't done anything wrong. And anyway, nobody saw me.'

She can't relax until there's enough distance between them and the carriages. When she finally stops, she's surprised to find that Crispin's hand is still on her arm. 'So what did you think about their condition?' she asks, intending to pull away, but postponing the action, soothed by the physical contact. 'They're falling apart, aren't they?'

'Compared to the ones in the scrapyard,' he says, 'these are the height of luxury. Although it would have been better from our point of view if they weren't so good – for bargaining purposes.'

'Crisp, we can't just walk in and offer to take them off their hands. They live there, it's their home. These are not abandoned carriages.'

'I know, I know,' he says, finally dropping his hands. 'But you can't help thinking . . .'

At 5.45 the next morning, not long after Zohra's arrived at the sorting office, her phone vibrates with a low, persistent buzz. She doesn't need to check the screen – who else except Nathan would phone at such an early hour? She answers softly, knowing that he'll keep ringing until she answers. 'Nathan, I can't talk now. I'm at work.'

There's a silence. She's just about to cut him off when he speaks, his voice low and resentful. 'You should have taken me with you.'

So Crispin's told him about the trip to the carriages. 'Nathan, will you please go? I'll talk to you later.'

'It's not fair.' His voice is whining, resentful.

'Later, Nathan, later.'

'I'm out of here,' he says, suddenly sounding normal. His mother must have come into the room. 'Warp Speed Five.' The phone goes dead.

Zohra turns back to her work, but finds Bill standing immediately behind her, so close that her face almost collides with his large chest. She steps back with a gasp of annoyance. 'Haven't you heard of personal space?'

'Boyfriend?' He leans forward, fixing her with a penetrating look.

She's about to deny it, but reconsiders just in time. 'What's it got to do with you?'

He leans back, folds his arms and smiles. 'No personal communication during work-time. Royal Mail aren't paying you to manage your personal life.'

'You're being ridiculous,' she says, pushing past him. 'That call took less than a minute. Now you're in the way. I've got work to do.'

He lets her pass and grins, slipping easily from censorious to companionable. 'Just curious. Why would anyone else be conscious at this hour? Here we are, slaving away for them while they turn over in bed, all nice and cosy, and snore for England, without a thought for us. But, mark my words, we'll be the ones who'll save the world. It'll be us, ready with coffee and ginger nuts when the aliens come. Never mind the politicians, we'll be the peacemakers.' He's given to this kind of rhetoric early in the morning. By the time Zohra gets back from her round, it will all have worn off and he'll be lounging at his desk, tired and irritable with everyone: the public who come for parcels he can't find; the sorters who put everything in the wrong place; the PO Box people who deal with businesses, whose website is far from intuitive, whose customers are forced to come to the sorting office for explanations he can't give.

'What about the train drivers?' asks Rohit from the other end of the room. 'They'd be up to greet the aliens. Or the milkmen?'

'Not only are they up,' says Zohra, 'but they're outside, in the open. We're shut away, far from the light of day. We'd have no more chance of seeing the spaceships landing than anyone else.'

'On the plus side, we've got a good chance of surviving a nuclear explosion,' says Matt. He considers himself to be an expert in science fiction, but his knowledge is rooted in the past: John Wyndham, H. G. Wells, J. G. Ballard. 'We'd miss the flash, avoid the radiation, and still be able to see when everyone else has gone blind.'

'And what about the time zones?' asks Rohit. 'Someone's up and around every hour of the day. Why would they come to the UK? If they're sophisticated enough to navigate their way round the universe, they won't have a problem pinpointing the best climate.'

'Anyway, it won't be for much longer,' says Zohra. 'Milkmen are past their sell-by date – the supermarkets are winning – trains will soon be driverless, and we'll be made redundant by the Internet. Our days are numbered. The end of post as we know it—'

'All right, all right, that's enough,' says Bill turning away. 'Wish I'd never started it. Back to work.'

'Some of us have never stopped,' mutters Matt.

'No more personal calls during work hours,' says Bill.

'I know,' says Zohra, not sure if he's quoting official Royal Mail regulations or making up his own rules. 'I told him to go and he went.'

'Only boyfriends do as they're told,' says Bill with satisfaction.

Zohra sighs with exasperation. She picks up a package and reads the name and delivery address. Mrs Amelia Bakewell, 6 Nailers' Cottages. First Class. Not heavy enough for a parcel delivery, but too big to go through the letterbox. The conversation in the sorting office recedes, and although their voices carry on in the background, she doesn't attempt to listen. She'll have to ring the doorbell again, speak to Mimi.

Is this going to keep happening?

* * *

For several days after Zohra's encounter with Fiona and her brothers, Michelle was absent from Facebook. Was she sulking, or just busy? She rarely gave much away about her own life. Then she popped up again, all friends, as if nothing had happened. 'Hi, hun, what's with brett walker?'

This was bewildering. Michelle was in Cardiff – wasn't she? Or from one of the other schools taking part in the engineering workshop. Not Bromsgrove. What possible connection did she have with Brett Walker? Did she know someone local? 'What do you mean?'

'You've been spotted. outside mcdonalds. with brett walker:)'

Zohra's first instinct was to demand where the information came from. But she hesitated. Brett Walker! He was hot! You'd have to be a corpse to not want to be seen with him. She couldn't bring herself to deny it, even if it wasn't true, so she spent a few seconds trying to work out the best response. She needed to be breezy, casual, but in control. 'So? Jealous?'

Two days later: 'sanders park? lee kirkwood. seriously?'

But Lee was all right too, and Zohra liked the idea of being seen with him. It seemed safest to play along with it rather than admit that this wasn't the kind of thing she would ever do. She didn't want to give the impression she was judging anyone else's behaviour. 'Woohoo!'

She worried that her parents might see this exchange. Her father knew her password – he'd set up the computer. The official school advice was: check who your children are talking to online. Could they be monitoring her Facebook profile? She could imagine the conversation they'd have with her, their disappointment and shock that she wasn't defending their family values. She knew her father so well: 'Some things are more important than popularity,' he would say. 'If we can't defend our personal standards, we fail. It's a matter of integrity, Zohra, integrity.'

She changed her password. Just in case.

'darren morton now? gross.'

'sam harris. michael dale. zain oakham.'

'Seen you. on the train. redditch shopping centre. along the river at evesham. droitwich town centre.'

It turned nasty. 'Can't think what they see in you slag.'

Mimi with a private message: 'She's big trouble. Block her.'

Katy: 'You can't do that. It's bullying.'

Zohra blocked Michelle. She knew that this would be the end of her Facebook community, but didn't know what else to do. She'd stopped sleeping and couldn't concentrate on her work. Immediately everyone else leapt to Michelle's defence.

'Michelles really upset'

'What kind of person blocks someone?'

'Its a really nasty thing to do to someone'

These were people who almost never commented, people she could hardly remember from Cardiff. They must have been sitting there silently, watching, waiting.

'Who do you think you are, making judgements about other people?'

'Not exactly purer than pure yourself, are you?'

These people had pretended to be her friends. Why were they all turning against her? They'd been so nice after the workshop and now they were like different people. Couldn't they see how nasty Michelle had been?

Shortly afterwards, Carys sent Zohra an email. 'You'd better look on the school Facebook page.'

'Check out the Finstall Comp page,' emailed Katy. 'Don't know where it's come from.'

It wasn't just words any more. Photoshopped images had appeared, distorted but recognisable versions of her profile picture and other photos she'd posted on Facebook. Somebody had turned Zohra into a cartoon character, a curvy, sadistic prostitute in high heels and very few clothes, smoking cannabis. People were finding it hilarious. More and more people were sharing the information, sending it to all their contacts.

She tried to talk to Katy, Mimi and Carys, ask if they had any idea who'd started this.

They were sympathetic at first. 'Just ignore them,' said Carys. 'They'll give up in the end.'

'They're losers,' said Mimi. 'It's a way of making themselves feel better.'

'They're just jealous,' said Katy. 'Make the most of it.'

'But none of it's true.'

'Nobody cares. Everyone likes a good laugh. They'll have a go at someone else in a couple of weeks.'

Zohra tried to think like them, but it was impossible. What if her parents found out?

The voices wouldn't go away. 'Spotty, greaseball, grossout . . .'

'tarbaby . . .'

Zohra felt as if she'd walked straight into a trap, a hole in the ground, which she should have seen coming, and she didn't know how to climb out of it. It was her own stupid fault. She should have closed her Facebook account right at the beginning.

It was far too late for that now. She had to keep checking – the computer was the only thing she could control, her only means of knowing what people were saying about her. And she was clinging to the last threads of hope – maybe one day she'd turn it on and find that everything was gone. Maybe everyone would just be nice again.

Was it her fault? Had she done something once, something she'd forgotten about, that deserved this kind of retribution?

Of course not. That was crazy. She'd remember. Wouldn't she?

But, but . . .

The way these people corrupted everything – it was so easy to them, like flicking the controls on a remote. It was hard to be certain about anything.

When it became obvious that everyone at school knew, Zohra waited, silent and miserable in the sixth-form common room, for comfort from Katy, Mimi and Carys, for solidarity. But they seemed to be so busy, distracted by their activities with Fiona. It felt as if they were avoiding her, as if they thought they would be contaminated by the association.

She began to wonder if they could be part of it, maybe even the ones who had started it all. She could imagine them bonding on the huge sofa in Fiona's living room, in the shadow of the David Hockney painting (a portrait of the Chung family, posed in a light-filled room, worth more than anyone could imagine), feeding the computer, giggling as they created the cartoons, enjoying the sense of power.

Later, long after it was all over, Zohra decided it had been Fiona doing it on her own. She must have created an account, called herself Michelle – if she had more than one email address, Facebook wouldn't necessarily pick it up – or maybe she was just feeding information to the real Michelle, putting the final touches to her plan to take Zohra's place. Katy, Carys and Mimi couldn't have been part of it – they'd been friends with Zohra for too long to betray her like that.

But none of them came to help.

Conversations stopped abruptly when she went into a class-room, loud laughs boomed out when she left. Whispers followed her along a corridor, but if she turned round, everyone was looking the other way. She saw the way people exchanged glances whenever she approached. People she hardly knew were suddenly jostling her as they passed; her arm was accidently knocked, coffee spilt, so that she had to walk round with a stained blouse all day ('I didn't do anything. Are you accusing me?'); an apparently random kick from a Lower Fifth ('Oh, I'm *so* sorry, did I get you? Hope you're okay'). Was she inflating every incident, creating a huge balloon out of the tiny puffs of everyday life? Was there anyone in the school who hadn't seen the images?

Lucy on Facebook: 'I don't know how you can live with yourself.'

Don't log in today, she said to herself every morning, lying in bed after a sleepless night, arguing with herself. But what if . . .? Maybe she'd misread something. Maybe it wasn't as bad as she thought. Maybe it had all gone away . . .

What if there's more, what if it's worse? I can't *not* know. A quick click . . .

Turn off the computer . . .

Go back. Just in case . . .

I'm never going to turn it on ever again.

The computer was alive, its voice soft and silky, offering false redemption – maybe an apology, an acknowledgement of mistakes, a putting-right of everything. She was a fish caught on a hook, swaying with the whim of the fisherman, in the water, out of the water. Powerless.

'Why not eating, Zohra? My cooking not good enough for you?'

'Nothing to say, Zohra? Your parents bore you now?'

'When I told you to go and research probability theory, Zohra, the idea was for you to produce a probable result, not no result.'

'This work is not good enough, Zohra. What's going on?'

Eyes everywhere. Double-back home after leaving the house, sneak upstairs past Mum and Dad in the shop while they're not looking. Approach it logically. Investigate. Are the messages all coming from the same source, can you tell from the language, the use of vocabulary, the syntax? Have the unknown – known? – correspondents changed their minds, seen the error of their ways? It will happen, it will . . .

It'll be all right. Check.

It's not all right.

Is there an impostor out there, a complete stranger pretending to be me, doing all these things I'm accused of? Check online. It'll turn out to be a ghastly mistake. They've got the wrong person.

Check.

The ping of the computer, the rush of the message.

*   *   *

Mr Troth is waiting for her, watching her come down through the garden. He won't stop talking about the Greenwoods now. It's his free pass to her time, a way of drawing her in, slowing her down, making her linger. 'I've got something for you, Zohra!' he calls while she's still only halfway along the stepping stones. 'About their dad. I've remembered all about him – what was his name again?' He scratches his head, screws up his face. 'Petey, that's it. Grown man, boy's name. Suited him, though. Half-soaked. Not a worker. Came from the east coast somewhere, miles away, used to be a fisherman, wandered inland when the herring left and married a local wench – lovely girl. But he didn't know how to live away from the sea.'

He's already told her this, last week, but she lets him tell her again, knowing how much he enjoys it. 'I've been talking to Dougie,' she says. 'Remember him? Friend of your boys?'

He beams. 'Well – haven't thought about Dougie in years. He must be getting on a bit . . .' He pauses, as if he can't quite remember. 'You got time for a nice cup of coffee? Biscuits? We could chat as we chew, as my missus used to say.'

'I'm sorry, I really can't,' says Zohra. 'I've got too much to do. Did you have something to show me?'

She hopes it's not more of his wife's old shoes. Two months ago, he produced an Asda carrier bag containing a pair of women's shoes in pristine condition – leopard-print, kitten heels, winkle-pickers. (Was he once a teddy boy? Did he and his wife rock with the times?) 'Wondered if you might find a use for these,' he'd said, proud of his offering. 'People have started wearing them again, seen it on the telly. Hardly worn. She loved them, my missus, back in the day, but couldn't wear them. Crippled her, she said. Can't bring myself to throw them out – cost me an arm and a leg when we didn't hardly have two pennies to rub together.'

Zohra had taken them home and shown her mother, who shrieked with pleasure. 'Sixties,' she'd said, stepping into them and tripping painfully round the kitchen. 'How this takes me back.'

'You can't possibly remember the sixties,' says Zohra. 'You were only four at the end of the decade – in India.'

Her mother patted her on the arm and smiled fondly. 'I lived in village,' she said. 'Always late. Sixties for us were world's seventies.'

There's something pleasing about being permanently a decade behind. If you moved from there to here, you could cut out your teenage years altogether. 'I wonder if Mr Troth's wife was glamorous,' said Zohra, trying to equate this concept with Mr Troth himself.

'With shoes like these,' said her mother, 'she would have been centre of attention.'

'Except she didn't wear them,' said Zohra. 'They hurt her feet.' She found it sad that Mr Troth had kept them, that he and his wife might have loved dancing, that he was once young, light on his feet, able to swing his wife around to the sound of Jerry Lee Lewis, Chuck Berry, Elvis – before he even bought the shoes. She wanted to throw them away, but struggled with herself and eventually dropped them off at a charity shop. They'd probably put them straight into the skip at the back, but at least she didn't have to make the decision.

This time he holds out a folder in such a way that she's compelled to take it from him. She examines it, intrigued. 'What is it?'

He leans forward and lowers his voice, as if they're being overheard. 'The murder,' he says.

'Oh,' she says, immediately alert. She opens the folder and finds newspaper cuttings, old and yellow, each one carefully enclosed in a see-through plastic envelope. The first one she picks out has a large headline at the top of the page – MISSING – with two black-and-white pictures underneath. The young women have a very similar appearance; shoulder-length hair and dense fringes that end, rigidly straight, just below the line of their eyebrows; rings of heavy mascara round their eyes, which makes them unnaturally large; and pale lipstick that blurs the edges of their lips with the blank, white setting of their faces.

But there are subtle differences. The girl on the left has large, clear eyes, wide and fearless, that stare at the camera with an amused expression, as if she's challenging the photographer (it must be a man – she's clearly flirtatious). She has a face that compels you to look at her again, study her, search for whatever she's trying to tell you. She's not exactly smiling, but she has an airy freshness and she doesn't need to smile. Her confidence in her ability to charm is obvious. There's no sense of calculation or manipulation.

'Debs Greenwood,' says Mr Troth, pointing. 'The other one's Bev Newton.'

Bev is more closed, somehow, guarded. She's not looking directly at the photographer, unwilling to reveal herself as freely as her friend, and her eyelids are slightly lowered, almost secretive. There's a tightness, a tension in her lips, as she offers a carefully composed smile.

They're both in school uniform – white shirts with floppy, crumpled collars and carelessly knotted ties. Debs has loosened her tie a little, signalling a refusal to conform, a pleasing individuality. There's an innocence about them both, despite the make-up, despite their pretence of maturity.

'School photos, them are,' says Mr Troth. 'A good six years before they disappeared.' He's been staring at the photos with the same fascination as Zohra, and she realises they've both been silent for a few seconds. 'Fancy them not bothering to find something more up to date. Still, they'll have found something better later on, when it was more serious.'

Zohra drags her eyes away. 'Look, Mr Troth, I really appreciate this, and I'd love to have a closer look, but I have to get on. Could I see them another time?'

'Take them,' he says, waving his hand airily. 'You can bring them back when you've finished.'

Zohra hesitates, weighing the folder in her hand. It's extra weight, but the van's not far away at the bottom of the hill and she only has to carry it round the nailers' cottages.

'You don't need to worry, duck. I trust you. Went up in the loft to find it for you, didn't I? Knew you'd be interested.'

'Thank you,' says Zohra, touched by his kindness. 'That was so nice of you. I'll bring it back tomorrow.'

'Whenever,' he says. 'I won't be going anywhere.'

She walks back down the garden, prickling with curiosity about the two girls, pleased to have something to divert her thoughts away from Mimi, wishing there was a way of speaking to the Greenwoods. It could be months before another letter turns up for them. Why do you never get circulars when you need them?

Zohra delivers the post to the row of cottages with cool efficiency, as if approaching Mimi's house quickly will make it easier.

Just get the signature and go. There won't be time to exchange pleasantries or to reminisce. Offer the screen, wait for the signature, don't engage in conversation. Say thank you. Leave.

Dead easy.

She opens the gate, takes a deep breath and marches briskly down the garden path. Mimi will be out, at work. She rings the bell and knocks immediately afterwards, wanting to cut down the waiting time. After a few seconds of silence, she realises she's not breathing and draws in some deep draughts of air. It's okay. There's no one in. She starts to fill out a card. Date, time, package to be collected in the sorting office, opening hours 7.00 to 12.45.

'We meet again!'

Zohra nearly drops the pen before swinging round to confront Mimi, who's walking towards her, grinning, having emerged from behind the garden shed. She's wearing baggy trousers, held up with a long leather belt which swings down loosely at one end, a thick, long-sleeved T-shirt, light blue, faded with use, and heavy boots crusted with mud. Her face has a weathered appearance, not at all as Zohra remembers from last time. It must be to do with being outdoors, in natural light. Her hair's tied back into an untidy ponytail. For a few seconds, Zohra thinks she's mistaken, and it's not Mimi at all.

But then Mimi identifies herself with an energetic laugh. 'Don't stare, girl. Haven't you ever seen a gardener before?'

'Sorry,' says Zohra, shaking herself, wishing she wasn't so transparent. 'I thought you were out.'

'I am out,' says Mimi. 'In the garden. It's what I do. I'm a landscape gardener – I spend most of my time outdoors.'

'Really?' Do people change so dramatically in eight years? From a fluttering, glittery party-goer to a serious gardener who exposes herself to the sun for purposes other than creating a tan, a woman who gets her hands dirty? It doesn't seem possible.

'There's no need to look quite so amazed. We've all got to do something.'

Zohra allows herself a careful smile, anxious to avoid offence. 'I've got another package. Signed for.'

'Oh good. I should have warned you. I'm always having packages – I order everything online. It makes life so much easier. And the plants for my winter planting will be turning up soon, too.' She leans over to sign the screen. She's still attractive, even in old clothes, but she seems more relaxed now, even contented, and the tension that Zohra remembers from school, the watchfulness displayed by everyone as they grappled with the fear of being left behind, are no longer there. Fresh air must be good for her, the proximity to the ground. Zohra can identify with this. Perhaps she and Mimi have more in common than she'd realised.

Mimi hands back the screen and their eyes meet. Zohra is surprised to see no animosity there, no reticence or suggestion of anything awkward. 'Do you still see them?' she asks suddenly, before she has time to reconsider.

Mimi looks surprised. 'Who? Oh, you mean the girls?'

Zohra nods. She's holding her breath.

'Goodness, no. You change, don't you, when you leave school, when you go your own way? I'm not the same person any more, and I don't suppose you are either. Carys went abroad, I think. Saudi. Some high-powered job in the media, apparently. She didn't really seem the type, did she? People never do what you expect. And Katy – I heard she went downhill at uni; not sure she even got her degree.'

'I didn't know that,' says Zohra, surprised. She'd somehow imagined they would all be rich and successful.

'And – um – the Chungs went back to Hong Kong. Did you know that?'

'Yes,' says Zohra, looking down. 'I heard.'

'Although I think the brothers stayed; they're qualified now, working in one of the big London hospitals, cutting edge stuff, I would imagine, working their way upwards as quickly as possible.'

'As you'd expect.'

Mimi nods thoughtfully, as if Zohra has said something important. 'Yes, of course.'

There's something different about Mimi's manner now. Is she slightly nervous too? 'I must get on,' she says quickly, afraid of being drawn in. 'Busy day.'

'Look, why don't you come over for coffee one day? When you're not so pushed. Give us a chance to catch up.'

The invitation comes unexpectedly, a gust of wind sneaking up from an unexpected source, knocking Zohra off balance. She sways for a second, unable to locate her centre of gravity. Catch up? Talk over old times? Seriously? She recovers and turns away hurriedly, not wanting to reveal her fear. 'Maybe,' she says. 'Some time.' And then she's off, not running exactly, but walking as fast as she can, holding herself back so she doesn't lose her dignity, her mind racing faster than her legs. Get away, she's muttering to herself, faster and faster. Get away, get away, get away . . .

12

At 7.15 on Monday morning, Johnny rolls out of bed, pulls on yesterday's clothes, opens the front door and goes out. He shuts the door behind him quickly, hoping to reduce the noise, but the sound booms out into the early morning silence. He listens for a response from Nick, but nothing happens, so after a few seconds he sets off, across the grass, round the side of the carriages towards the hill behind, pushing aside the low-hanging branches as he goes.

He forces himself to breathe – in, out, mouth open to ease the flow of air, then mouth shut because the air's cold. The sun is rising ahead of him, barely above the horizon but extending an exuberant, blinding light towards him. There's a stillness all around, and the conversations of sheep in the neighbouring fields are too far away to puncture the impression that he's the only person alive in the world. Even the birds have paused, dazzled by the light, perhaps, as they build up their energy for the next verse of their song.

It's exhilarating but chilly. He puts all his energy into the uphill climb, the muscles in the back of his legs resisting, but he continues to push himself. Why's he doing this? It must be decades since he last came this way. He needs to challenge himself and his dependence on the comfort and safety of the railway carriages. His habits are being threatened, the familiar routines of his life undermined. He has to consider alternatives.

Debs or Bev? Bev or Debs? Debs or . . .

It's like being on a toy railway, round and round, up the hills, round the bends, on the home run, back to where you set off, here we go again, until nothing else functions inside his head.

But the anger is losing its heat. It requires so much energy to maintain it.

Maybe they should just accept her story, believe in her as Debs, let her be who she wants to be, so she can live out the rest of her real life or her fantasy life, whichever, as she wants. What difference does it make? Nobody can repair the damage now. There's no point in trying.

He pauses to catch his breath, looking down at himself, contemplating the bulk that's crept up on him in the last decades, puzzled by his lack of ability to breathe properly, trying to ignore the nagging pain in his knees – did the accident cause this or is it the onset of arthritis? He used to be so fit. Now the aim is just to get to the top, to survive the challenge.

He drives himself onward and upward and, when he reaches the crest of the hill, he's filled with an unexpected sense of elation. He's made it; he can do it. He stands triumphant and surveys the surrounding scene, rotating slowly so he can take everything in. He's surprised to find that for the first time in ages he can calm the clutter of his body, still the surplus movements.

This is where he should be, where he should always have been. Why hasn't he come out here before?

He becomes aware of the M5, the muffled roar that's been a background to his life since the sixties. It's so familiar, so much a part of the scenery, that he didn't even notice it on his way up here. He watches the traffic for a while, the mesmerising speed of the vehicles as they weave in and out, creating endless, fluctuating patterns, surprisingly law-abiding, miraculously avoiding collision. So many people with somewhere to go. Unlike him. None of those drivers are sitting around waiting for action to happen to them. They're up before dawn, ready and off, starting their day with a heady dose of speed.

As he stands there, swaying slightly, resisting the illogical belief that he could launch himself into the air and somehow acquire the ability to fly, he has a moment's curious recall. Falling

189

off the roof with Nick. The sensation of dropping, the sense of powerlessness when he realised he couldn't just soar back up, air rushing past his ears, the slowing down of time, screams from below, the sensation of his brother next to him, both of them reaching out for each other but missing. The disbelief. The end of invincibility.

The landing, the metallic crunch, the jarring shudder as his whole body seemed to contract, the thump of metal bending, an incongruous moment of sorrow for the unknown owner of the car. A long silence. Then pain. Pain juddering through his entire body, like nothing he had ever experienced before. A mysterious wail, a crooning that he couldn't place. Was it him or was it Nick?

He can't remember what happened next. When he finally regained consciousness in the hospital bed, he regretted the blank period. He would have liked to see the inside of an ambulance. And he would have liked Ma to be there, sitting next to him, waiting for him to wake up, holding his hand.

But of course, the Ma he wanted didn't exist any more. She was present, but not really there at all. She was empty, missing something essential, barely able to put words together into a sentence. If she had come to the hospital (logic now tells him that she must have been there, someone would have taken her, even though he can't work out why he never saw her), who had she chosen, which one had she sat next to first, waiting for him to regain consciousness? Who mattered most to her? The oldest, the youngest, the best tennis player, the loser?

There was someone there when he woke up, but it wasn't Ma. When his mind started to flicker into consciousness, he was aware of the warmth of a presence, the contact of skin, the softness of a hand caressing his. It was too soft for Ma, who'd spent so much of her life with her hands in other people's cleaning products. But when he opened his eyes, looked around, wondering who cared enough to be there at all, the chair next to his bed was empty.

It was Paula, he found out later. And she had the dilemma of whom to comfort, whose hand to stroke, whom to murmur gently to. She must have flitted between them in their different wards. But she missed the moment when he woke fully into the brightness of the hospital world, when he realised that the soft green and blue of water lilies were not real, but just the design on the curtains round his bed. He could hear the beep of medical equipment, the clanking of trolleys, the chatting from the nurses' station. The first person he spoke to was a tiny West Indian lady who offered him tea – he wasn't at all sure he could even hold a cup, let alone drink out of it – and the next was a cheerful lady with a blonde perm and a supply of jokes so rude he thought he must be dreaming, who was swishing a mop under his bed.

Then, a few days later, Nick, both arms in plaster, was grinning down at him. 'Wake up, malingerer,' he said. 'You're not that bad.'

'Yes I am,' groaned Johnny, looking down at his leg, held up in the air by a curious contraption. 'It's all right for you. You can walk.'

'But look at my arms,' said Nick. 'That's real pain, man. If I can take it, so can you. You just have to face up to it, grit your teeth, get on with it.'

'Not much tennis for the time being, though,' said Johnny, as if it mattered. They'd lingered on in the local circuit after Debs died, playing occasionally, pretending they were going somewhere, but the hunger had long gone.

'Just a blip,' said Nick. 'I'll be back on form for next year.'

'Right,' said Johnny. 'Let me know when it happens. Just in case I blink at the wrong moment.'

It seems ridiculous now. Why didn't they let go of the rivalry? With Dad gone, Debs gone and Ma not really there, they only had each other. But neither of them seemed capable of summoning the necessary generosity, even while everything was crumbling around them. As if a fault was threaded through them, distorting their reactions.

He looks back down the hill towards the railway carriages, shocked by their condition. The branches of the trees above are too heavy, the bark old and loose, the weight of leaves pulling them down into dense piles on top of the roofs. Moss is spreading through them, brightly damp, nurtured in the dark places where light can't penetrate, creeping down into the network of cracks below the leaves and over the sides of the carriages, threatening to engulf the entire surface. No wonder his rooms smell so musty. It looks as if Nick has attempted to repair some of the cracks over Aphrodite. But what if whole sections of trees come crashing down?

When she asked why they were still living there, he didn't know how to answer. Now, looking down at the carriages, the question doesn't seem unreasonable. How easy it has been to not look, to not think about it. Her fresh way of seeing has forced him to reconsider.

Debs or Bev, she's changed something, jolted him awake.

Nick is cooking, a complicated breakfast. Bacon, sausage, tomato, two eggs, fried bread. When he woke, he was still engaged in his last dream about racing through a supermarket, hearing the ticking of a clock, throwing more and more food into the trolley, conscious of a looming deadline. He gradually became aware of a ravenous hunger, a need to consume as much as he possibly could in as short a time as possible. He's aching with the desire to eat and eat and eat.

He's going to phone work, tell them he's ill and take a day off. They'll think he's dying – he never has time off work. Yesterday, Sunday, he couldn't summon enough energy to get out of bed and spent most of the day dozing, listening to the radio, unable to eat, trying not to think about anything, waiting for her to come again. But when she arrived she was over-tired too, almost tearful, and Johnny would barely speak, so she left after an hour. She's coming back tonight, early evening. He needs the day to prepare himself.

He's decided that she will have to be Debs until he can prove that she isn't. It's too difficult to think clearly when you don't know who's sitting in front of you. If she wants to be Debs, he'll allow it for now. Otherwise, how can he address her, talk to her, think about her when she's not there? It's not practical. Making this decision makes him feel calmer, a little more in control of the situation.

He puts the frying pan into the sink to soak and carries the plate of food back to his living room. He sits on the bench, much more aware than usual of the lack of comfort (did he really not notice before she pointed it out?), switches on the TV for the news, and starts to eat. It's sunny outside, but the light is blocked by the trees and the hill, and the sun doesn't reach indoors.

She's a murderer.

He puts his sausage back down on the plate and contemplates the implications, his stomach starting to churn again, but not with hunger. Would her story stand up in a court of law? Last night's thoughts of self-defence seem less convincing this morning. Would manslaughter be a more likely option?

You can't just ignore what she's done, pretend it doesn't matter. He keeps going over the chase in his mind, imagining the terror, the struggle for survival. But he stops just before the fatal blow, unable to take in the enormity of it. Was there really no other way, no means of disabling without killing? This must have been the moment when she stopped being his big sister, the substitute mother, and became someone who could just clear off, disappear without a word.

She can't have survived for so long with the knowledge of what she's done – even if it was shut away – without changing in some fundamental way. It must have rewired her brain, forced her thought processes to evolve. Surely it's not possible to kill someone and remain the same. How does it work? Would previously forbidden pathways open up, previously unthinkable thoughts start to become thinkable?

They still don't know what's true and what isn't. Everything they know about her has been fed to them by her. How did her husband die? Natural causes? But how natural were the causes?

The breakfast is no longer appetising. He puts the plate down on the coffee table, turns off the TV and opens his laptop, wondering how to find out more about her. He types in Deborah Goodchild, Toronto, and Goodchild's Construction comes up. When he clicks it, he finds it's recently been taken over by another firm. So Mack Goodchild was a genuine person. He can't decide if this proves anything useful or not.

Nick has tried to trace someone before. Paula. One of the first names he typed into Google when he realised the potential of the Internet, and the name he continues to play with, even after all this time. But how do you find someone with a name like Paula Matthews? There are dozens of them in the Bromsgrove area, thousands in the Midlands, millions if you go worldwide. She never came back, but he continues to search, keep his eyes open, just in case.

Sometimes he catches a glimpse of a pretty girl, short blonde hair tucked behind her ears, diamanté studs in her ears (those earlobes, soft as velvet), laughing, her over-large teeth bursting out of her wide, generous mouth, and he has to stop himself following her, remind himself that Paula is older now, still laughing of course, but no longer a girl.

When he'd challenged her about Johnny, she'd been dismissive. 'I love you, Nick. Of course I do. Why else would I spend so much time with you?'

'But why do you sit so close to Johnny?'

'Forget Johnny. You're obsessed.'

She had a presence. He knew where she was before he could see her. If she was approaching in a crowd, he always knew her exact position, even if she was surrounded by others. She was a beacon, warm, bright, welcoming; the only genuine illumination in his life, the light that helped him to see himself.

194

She didn't tell the truth about Johnny, he knew. But if she genuinely cared about either of them, she wouldn't have gone – and she did, so Johnny was no more important to her than he was. Off to university without leaving an address, away from Bromsgrove, away from both of them. He realises now that he never really knew her properly, that their intimate conversations were all controlled by her, despite the fact that he did most of the talking. Why did she reveal so little about herself? When she left, the air went out of him, the space he occupied narrowed and darkened bit by bit, until his world became permanently diminished. He was crushed, humiliated, eventually angry. He should have seen it coming.

He pushes Paula away. She's not helping. Thinking about her has never helped anything.

Johnny could sense a release of tension as they sat down to eat the spag bol on Saturday night. There was something comfortable, familiar from a long time ago, about sitting round the kitchen table, filling a space that had been almost empty for decades. They concentrated on the food for a while without talking, and although she said she was no longer able to eat much, she managed most of her small helping.

Johnny took another slice of garlic bread, Nick offered her more salad.

'So why don't you two talk to each other?' she said.

Johnny put the garlic bread down on the table. He opened his mouth, not sure how to defend himself, struggling to formulate a rational thought. 'Of course we do,' he said eventually, knowing how unconvincing he sounded. He lifted his fork and sucked in a strand of spaghetti. But he couldn't swallow it.

'Oh come on,' she said. 'I'm your sister, remember? We've been raking over the past for hours, we're eating together, sharing a bottle of wine, and neither of you has spoken a word to each other. You think I'm stupid?'

'No, of course not,' said Nick, his voice tight and strained.

Johnny glanced quickly at him. He wondered if he could

manage a smile, just to convince her she was mistaken, but he couldn't move his mouth.

She pushed her plate away, leaned back and studied them both, looking from one to the other, searching for something in their faces. 'I don't believe this. When you were kids, everything – *everything* – was about who was top dog. It was the only thing you really cared about. Even the tennis was more about which of you was best than beating anyone else. And here we are, forty-eight years later, stuck in exactly the same place. Are you two real?' She sounded so much like their sister. 'Stop behaving like babbies,' she used to say. 'Grow up.'

But if Bev had been sitting in the background, watching, listening (and she usually was), she'd have learnt how to talk like that too.

Johnny couldn't look at her. She was right. They were ridiculous. Why should it be so difficult to behave like sensible adults? Why could he feel his legs jiggling uncontrollably under the table; why couldn't he trust himself to speak?

Nick cleared his throat. 'It's not really like that.'

'So what is it like? Tell me exactly.'

'Well . . .' said Johnny. But it was too big. He didn't know where to start.

'Okay,' she said. 'Let's approach this from a different angle. When was the last time you had a conversation? Who can tell me that?'

There was a silence.

'Okay, then, not a conversation. A sentence? A word?'

Silence.

'We talked about your letter,' said Nick.

'Yes,' said Johnny. 'That's right.'

'Actually,' said Nick, leaning forward, 'we discussed the letter in some detail.' (Not true, but it sounded convincing.) 'Since then, we probably haven't said a lot,' he added, as if it was the most normal thing in the world, something you'd just mention in passing. 'But we're perfectly capable of holding a conversation if we need to.' He paused, picked up his glass of wine and took a small sip before replacing it on the table. 'There hasn't been much to say, really, so it must be about seven years, I suppose, since we had a long conversation.' He looked directly at Johnny. 'Would that be right, do you think?' he asked casually.

Johnny met his eyes briefly and nodded. If Nick could do it, so could he. 'Well,' he said, after a few seconds, 'it might be a bit longer . . .'

'I don't think so,' said Nick, an edge creeping into his voice.

'It's nearer . . .' Johnny stopped himself just in time.

'So,' she said, 'after approximately six decades, with all the experience you've accumulated just by existing in the world, even if you don't entirely partake of all it has to offer, you're still thinking like eight year olds. Whatever happened to growing up? Did it never occur to you that you could move on?'

There was an embarrassing silence. She's right, thought Johnny.

A slow, slightly foolish grin was spreading across Nick's face.

'Adults don't refuse to speak to each other,' she said. 'They discuss their problems, work them out, muddle along, learn to be civilised.'

'You sound like Debs,' said Nick, and he sounds surprised.

This is true. It's exactly how Debs used to speak to them. Sensible, practical, expecting cooperation.

'That's because I am Debs. And if this was then, when I was still living here, I'd probably make you shake hands and apologise. But I suppose that's a bit simplistic after all this time.'

'Just a bit,' said Nick.

'So did you talk to each other long ago, in more enlightened times?'

Johnny tried to remember, but wasn't sure. 'We must have done,' he said eventually.

She laughed, a long, cheerful ripple of unguarded mirth that echoed round them, bouncing off the windows, the fridge, the ancient cooker; a sound that transported Johnny back more quickly and accurately than anything she'd said. 'And what exactly happened that was so terrible you felt compelled to cease communication?'

Nick was frowning now. Johnny started to search through his memories, trying to work out which event had proved to be so much more important than any other, the conversations or actions that had led to this silence. Something must have triggered it. But his mind was completely empty.

Johnny didn't look directly at Nick, but he knew he must be doing the same thing: racing through his mind to try and find something he could say to justify himself. It was clear that neither of them had a clue. He allowed himself to smile a little and Nick's instant responding smile startled him. Should they make something up, make it seem more convincing?

'It was to do with—' said Johnny.

'The electric bill,' said Nick.

'Yes, that's right,' said Johnny, grateful for a lead. 'You refused to pay your share.'

'You were the one with the computer on all day,' said Nick, warming up. 'I didn't see why we should split it fifty-fifty.'

Was it to do with Paula? Something they'd dragged up from the past? They'd never actually talked about her, never analysed what went wrong, why she left, whose fault it was. Perhaps she'd told Nick why she was leaving and he'd stayed in touch with her without telling Johnny.

It might be best not to think about this right now.

'You do realise, don't you,' said Debs, 'that not talking to each other about something you can't even remember is more than a little daft?'

'No,' said Johnny, 'we do remember. It was the gas bill.'

'Electric,' said Nick.

'Yes,' said Johnny. 'That's what I meant.'

But it was obvious from her expression that she didn't believe them. 'So,' she said. 'Here we are again. Same place, same family, same conversations. Thank goodness I came back. How ever did you cope without me?' She sounded contented, as if it was all she'd ever wanted.

Nick types in 'DNA tests' on his laptop. They need to eliminate the uncertainty once and for all. A large number of websites come up immediately. A few hundred pounds, two tests, or maybe three, so they can be matched. They should have thought of this last night.

The mugs from their final cups of hot chocolate are still on the coffee table. Debs drank from the one with the faded red daisies on it, leaving half of it unfinished. She has left traces of herself. Nick uses a tissue to pick up the mug and takes it into the kitchen, where he empties the dregs into the sink. Then he finds a plastic bag and places the mug inside. He's watched enough crime dramas to know the procedure. He returns to the living room and picks up his notebook from the coffee table. He taps his pencil up and down on the table, soothed by the hollow echo of wood against wood, then writes DNA at the top of the page. He needs to put down the arguments on paper. It helps him to think.

FOR:
How can we make decisions if we can't be sure of the facts?
I don't want to be fooled into cultivating affection for someone who might not be Debs.
It's far too late, but it would be nice to resolve it for Ma's sake.
If she really is Debs, we might be able to go backwards, share something important, give ourselves a chance of normal memories.

AGAINST:
What would we do if she turned out to be Bev?
Either way, she's killed someone. Would it make any difference knowing who she is?

It would be easier to just believe her story and send her back to Canada. If she's going to die soon, she might as well die contented.

He and Johnny are the only two people left in the world with genuine memories of Debs. They need to talk about her, compare notes, observations, opinions. It's impossible to come to conclusions on your own, trying to present both sides to yourself, wanting (or not wanting) to win the argument.

He wishes he could remember why they don't talk. They did argue about the gas/electric bill, he suspects, although it's difficult to recall the exact details, but that can't have been the main reason. Can it? However hard he tries, nothing comes back to him. It must have been serious, otherwise one of them would have caved in years ago. But if that was the case, why can't he remember? It's as if they fell into separate, parallel holes at the same time and refused to call for help. Even if they had, it wouldn't have made any difference, because neither of them could rescue the other. And as they went lower and lower, they lost sight of daylight and concentrated on their own individual dilemmas.

Nick gazes out of the kitchen window at the rampant growth behind the carriages. There's so much pruning to do, front and back, and he really should get on with it. Otherwise, they'll end up trapped on all sides, forced into each other's company forever, unable to access the outside world. He takes a swig of coffee, then forgets to swallow, frozen with disbelief. Johnny has appeared, coming down the hill.

Johnny? Outside? In a coat? Walking? He can't have been waiting for a delivery, the only reason he ever goes outside. He's coming from the wrong direction.

Nick wants to rush out and challenge him, tease him a little, as he would have done when they were younger. Why not? They spoke to each other yesterday, even smiled a little at the absurdity of their situation. The impossible is mutating into the possible.

How would he start a conversation now? 'Not like you to be up so early/going out for a walk.' No, that sounds like a criticism. He needs a joke. 'Preparing for the Bromsgrove Fun Run?' No, too trivial – Johnny might be insulted by the implication that he's not capable. 'Training for the London Marathon, then?' Better, less likely to be true, but is it funny? 'Has the view changed since I last went up there?' Or be completely neutral, forget the humour. 'Nice day for a walk. Bit chilly, though.'

It reminds him of the time when he first went out with Paula. He knew Johnny liked her too, so he wanted to be nice, give the impression that he was sympathetic. It backfired. Of course.

They were playing tennis on a court in the park, warming up, hitting the ball backwards and forwards comfortably, not attempting to catch each other out. The thwack of the ball on their racquets was crisp, familiar, pleasing. It seemed a good time to say something. 'Paula's coming to the cinema on Saturday,' he called, making sure his voice was easy, good-natured.

'What time are we leaving?' asked Johnny, sending over a neat, sharp backhand.

'No,' said Nick. 'Not you. Just me and Paula.'

Johnny's reaction was instantaneous. He stopped where he was, allowing the ball to swish past him, flinched as if he'd been hit violently on the head, then threw his racket across the net, directly at Nick. It cleared the net, but didn't go far enough to inflict damage.

'What was that for?' asked Nick, spreading his arms in amazement.

'Don't patronise me!' shouted Johnny, and he stomped off the court.

'Hey!' yelled Nick. 'I thought we were going to play a few sets!'

'In your dreams!' snarled Johnny over his shoulder.

'Don't worry about it,' said Paula later. 'He'll get over it.' There was a smugness in her voice that irritated Nick slightly, as if she liked the idea of them fighting over her.

But she took his hand and stroked it with her thumb. He could feel the softness of her skin as it glided across, delicate and sensual. Shivers of pleasure coursed through him. He looked at her face, slightly lower than his shoulder, and felt the unexpected pleasure of belonging, having responsibility, wanting to protect.

Nick is brought back to the present by a sudden knock against the window. He looks up in surprise and sees Johnny's face outside, peering through the narrow gaps in the blinds. What's he been doing out there all this time?

'Can I come in?' calls Johnny.

Nick scrambles to his feet, embarrassed by his position of non-activity. I'm a busy person, he says to himself. I don't sit around doing nothing. That's not how I operate. How long has he been at the window, spying on me? He should know better. 'Okay,' he calls.

He dashes into the corridor and pulls open the dividing door. Johnny is already standing there.

Right. What now?

Johnny looks nervous, uncertain. He swallows, as if he can't find his voice. 'How come you're not at work?'

'Not too well,' says Nick. 'Funny tummy.'

'Me too,' says Johnny. 'Maybe it was the dinner.'

'Bit early for a walk,' says Nick.

'No one else around, though,' says Johnny.

Nick makes coffee while Johnny hunts for deckchairs – he eventually finds them at the end of the corridor where he almost never goes – and they sit outside together for the first time in years, in the small scrubby space behind the carriages where there's a break in the trees, a patch of sunlight, in the shelter of the hill. They sip the coffee carefully, blowing on the surface to cool it down, saying nothing for a while.

'So what do you think?' says Nick eventually. 'Is it her?'

Johnny stares past him. 'I don't know,' he says, and the uncertainty of his response, his clear confusion, makes him sound childlike. 'I just don't know.'

'I've made lists,' says Nick. 'For and against.'

Johnny snorts. 'Well, you would, wouldn't you?'

Nick's offended. He doesn't like being predictable. 'I was wondering—'

But Johnny isn't listening. 'I found photos,' he says, producing a brown envelope. 'In the dead WC – the black bags. Do you want to see them?'

They pass them backwards and forwards, peering closely at the black-and-white snapshots, once taken in a hurry by someone who couldn't hold the camera still. They try to see details that aren't there, that are obscured by the poor lighting, by indistinct edges. 'They don't really look alike,' says Nick.

'That's what I thought.'

'It was nearly fifty years ago. None of us look like we did then.'

'No.'

'But it's hard to imagine that Bev really thought she could get away with being Debs.'

'Yes.'

It's hard work. Johnny has never been much good at conversation. When he was younger, he would talk endlessly – deep-sea fish, trains, dinosaurs – but he wasn't interested in anyone else's thoughts on his subject.

'Just like your father,' Ma used to say. She was never prepared to remain in one place long enough to hear what he had to say. 'Thought the world was just there for his pleasure. Didn't bother about the important things. Work, earning money.'

But, after the accident, all those words faded away and Johnny retired into a dark, empty silence. The last time he spoke at any length was when Nick asked his advice about buying a new computer – over ten years ago – but he descended into such a dull monologue that Nick stopped listening. The young IT manager at work proved to be far more helpful.

'I thought it would be obvious,' says Nick. 'Once we'd actually met her.'

'Sometimes she seemed like Debs,' says Johnny.

Nick waits, hoping for a valuable insight.

'And at other times, she didn't.'

They lapse back into silence. 'What do you think about a DNA test?' says Nick eventually.

Johnny is startled by this and jerks the mug in his hand, spilling his coffee on the grass. 'I hadn't thought of that,' he says, his voice tense.

'Then we'd know for certain,' says Nick.

'But would she be prepared to do it?'

'Well, we might be able to get away without asking her. I have her cup from yesterday. If we give samples too, they'd presumably be able to tell us if we're related.'

Johnny looks past Nick at the fields in the distance. 'Would they need her permission?'

Nick follows his gaze, sees the sheep wandering unhurriedly towards the patches of sunshine. 'Not sure. I'd have to find out.'

'What about the murder?' asks Johnny after a while. 'Do you believe her?'

'It's plausible,' says Nick cautiously.

'But she could still be Bev.'

'The only thing we can be sure about,' says Nick, 'is that she's killed someone.' He longs for Johnny to comment on this, offer opinions, so they can discuss it more deeply. He needs help to clarify his own thoughts, analyse how he feels about it. But Johnny doesn't reply. He continues to gaze past him, unwilling or unable to express what he thinks.

The sheep are having a more productive conversation than them. Their voices carry through the clear morning air, sharp and intimate.

13

'I've got a theory,' says Crispin. 'The woman on the train is the friend, the one whose body was never found. And she's come back to murder the brothers because they're the only ones who could identify her.'

'Right,' says Zohra. 'So how exactly does making them an offer for their home solve the problem of their impending doom?'

'Easy. Once other people are around, coming and going, her hands will be tied.'

'I think they're probably already tied. She's a lot smaller than either of them.'

'Anyway, they're probably desperate to leave,' says Crispin. 'They just don't realise that anyone would be interested in the carriages.'

'Whatever you offer,' says Zohra, 'it's hardly going to be enough to buy a house, is it? If they wanted to leave, they'd have done it ages ago.'

'If we don't ask,' says Crispin, 'we'll never find out.'

'Come on, Crisp,' says Nathan, 'let's go and ask.'

It's Tuesday evening. They're sitting just inside the shed, next to the newly restored locomotive, sheltering from the rain. Perry is up on the footplate, organising his tools. The boiler has been recently returned after inspection, put back in frame, and they now possess a ten-year boiler certificate, a source of enormous pride. The engine sits gleaming on the rails after five intensive years of work, its final paintwork almost finished and the brass number plate, 3733, attached to the front.

'I'm going to marry Zohra,' says Nathan. 'Did I tell you?'

'Many times,' says Crispin.

'It was when we agreed on the name for the engine,' says Nathan. 'Then I knew that we agree about everything. That's how you know who to marry.'

'I'm not sure that's strictly true,' says Zohra. 'It would be a complicated world if we had to marry everyone we agree with. And anyway, you've been talking about it for ages – long before we discussed the name.'

'It was the clincher,' he says. 'The victory of matter over anti-matter.'

'I agreed about the name too,' says Crispin. 'What does that say about us, Nathan?'

There was considerable debate about the name. Their engine didn't originally have one – it's a pannier tank engine, not enormous, not important enough for a name – but Zohra maintained right from the beginning that it needed an identity. The committee considered suggestions from enthusiasts across the country: *Thomas* (obviously), *Spirit of Wychington, Pride of Bromsgrove, Black Country Express, Bromsgrove Knight.* But after a long argument, Nathan made a suggestion. '*Enigma,*' he said.

'A man of culture now, then, Nathan?' said Perry.

A silence grew while they thought about it.

'All the best names are one word,' said Nathan. '*Repulse, Defiance, Dreadnought.* You know, battleships or s-submarines. And s-starships. *Enterprise—*'

'Okay,' said Crispin. 'You can stop right there.'

'Are you thinking of the "Enigma Variations"?' asked Zohra, puzzled that he'd heard of them.

'We went there,' said Nathan, nodding vigorously. 'Enigma's birthplace. It's by Worcester, not far from Bromsgrove, you know. He wrote this music, s-see – he had all these friends—'

'Elgar,' said Zohra. 'Not Enigma.'

'No,' he said. 'You're wrong there.'

It wasn't worth arguing with him. Most of his education has breezed through him, as nebulous as steam, rarely significant enough to lodge itself in his mind with any permanence. If something isn't part of a list or connected to trains or starships, he'll remember it for about ten minutes and then it will dance away, form a new pattern, make connections that don't exist. 'Anyway,' he said, 'he wrote all these bits of music about his friends. One for each of them. It was good.'

'Who did you go with?' asked Zohra.

'Where?'

'Elgar's birthplace.'

'Oh.' He paused. 'School.'

Enigma was exactly right. It was painted on the side of the engine – in gold, gleaming.

'Look away!' calls Perry. He's wearing blue circular glasses, heavy gloves and a dark visor, which he's just lowered over his face. He has a torch in one hand, a filler rod in the other and the oxyacetylene tank on wheels beside him. Every time he lights up the torch he commands them to avert their gaze, revelling in his power.

It had been difficult to persuade Ted the Rivet that welding was necessary in this instance. He's fanatical about rivets. 'Less distortion, more authenticity, see.' He's a retired railwayman in his sixties with brittle, unbrushed hair and rampant freckles, who comes down from Dudley every other weekend. He talks about the engine with a softness in his eyes as if it's a woman he's fancied all his life, a film actress he can't get out of his mind. 'Great Western. Nice little mover. She'll have earned her keep, no mistake.'

But then Melvin, the chief expert, came down from Newcastle for his final inspection two weeks ago. 'It's looking good, he announced after a few tense hours. Just a bit of welding required on the beading round the cab lookout, where the rivets have failed, and the inner firebox. Do you have someone to do it?'

'Perry's your man,' said Anthony, a retired solicitor, one of their most reliable helpers.

'Thanks, Anthony,' said Perry, grinning.

'Did you do the original work on the firebox?' asked Melvin, suspiciously.

'Of course not,' said Perry. 'I don't make mistakes.'

'We all make mistakes sometimes,' said Zohra, thinking it probably was him, wanting to offer him an excuse.

'If you'd seen me thirty years ago,' said Perry, 'you wouldn't say that. I used to work in a garage – repairs, servicing. We did the bikes for the Hell's Angels. They always asked for me, called me the Fonz – you know, *Happy Days* – never saw it myself, but they tell me he was a mechanic. The best. Nobody gets within ten miles of the Angels' bikes unless they give the word. It's all about trust.'

Zohra stared at him. 'You're a lord,' she said. 'You can't do work for Hell's Angels – you're supposed to live a civilised life, go to London, take part in debates in the House of Lords, vote. You make laws, not break them.'

'We had to eat,' said Crispin.

'We don't all have seats any more,' said Perry, tucking a loose strand of grey hair behind his right ear. He doesn't look distinguished enough to be a lord in his threadbare jeans, a T-shirt stained with green paint and a worn leather jacket, or up to effective welding. He has arthritis. As he keeps telling them, he's not as mobile as he used to be. 'And why make the assumption that Hell's Angels break the law?' he said.

'Oh, come on!' said Zohra. 'I wasn't born yesterday.'

Perry sighed. 'Anyway,' he said, 'the point I'm making is that I must be good. You don't mess with Hell's Angels if you want to wake up alive the next day.'

'Well, that sounds like a nice, law-abiding arrangement.'

But he has the welding equipment and he seems calm and confident. The rain intensifies, clattering against the metal of the shed roof and making it difficult to hear properly, so they lapse into silence and wait for him to work his way along the seam. When he reaches the end, he lifts his visor and beams. 'That's it. Nothing'll get through there.'

'It's go, go, go for next S-saturday, then,' says Nathan.

'It would be a bit late to change plans at this point,' says Zohra.

'The whole world's coming,' says Crispin. 'Susie's publicity has been amazing. It's all set to be the event of the century.'

'They won't be disappointed,' says Perry. 'Expectation is the precursor to success.'

'Which is fine, providing the reality matches up,' says Crispin.

'Hello!' A voice drifts towards them from outside.

'Who's that?' says Nathan.

'Let's find out,' says Crispin, standing up.

A face appears round the side of the shed, symmetrically pretty, light brown hair tied into a ponytail, wide, clear eyes. She has a lilac umbrella covered in pink question marks over her head and there's a man behind her, his face just out of sight.

'Mimi!' says Zohra before she has time to think. She instantly regrets revealing herself, wishing she could shrink back into the shadows.

Mimi peers in, trying to adjust her eyes to the gloom. 'Zorry? Is that you?'

Crispin reacts admirably quickly, going to the entrance and holding out his hand. 'Hi, Mimi,' he says. 'Crispin. It's been a long time.'

'Crispin . . .?' she says, taking his hand.

Zohra edges forwards, embarrassed that Mimi hasn't recognised him. 'Sixth form,' she says. 'Finstall Comp.'

'Oh yes, of course – extra-curricular activities.' It's not clear if she remembers him or not.

'This is a surprise,' says Zohra. 'What brings you here?'

'I could ask you the same question.'

'Zohra's a founder member,' says Crispin. 'She was here when we first discovered the railway line.'

A man follows Mimi into the shed. 'Freddie Bakewell,' he says. 'Hope you don't mind. It's my evening off, so we thought we'd come along and take a look, see if you need any extra pairs of

209

hands. My father's been a railwayman all his life – a guard for British Rail, then a stationmaster. Retired now, I'm afraid, but you never quite get it out of your blood.'

So Mimi's husband, Dr Bakewell the GP, isn't the privileged public schoolboy that Zohra has imagined. He's an ordinary man who likes trains. His face is round and slightly crumpled, amiable but not particularly good-looking.

'Peregrine, Lord Hillswood. This is my estate.' Perry gestures grandly at the surrounding countryside. 'Call me Perry, my dear,' he says to Mimi, more interested in her than in Freddie.

'Oh, hi,' says Mimi, smiling easily, not at all overwhelmed by the implied grandeur, even though she can't possibly know that it has no substance and that most of the surrounding fields encompassed within Perry's lordly wave no longer belong to him.

Freddie is inspecting the engine, walking round it, putting a hand up every now and again to touch the freshly painted exterior, his fingers lingering over the gloss, smoothing it gently. He's half smiling with knowledgeable pleasure. 'Swindon works?' he says.

Perry joins him. 'Yup. 1937. 0-6-0.' They're all proud of their newly acquired technical knowledge. 'What do you think?'

Freddie doesn't answer immediately. He stands back and contemplates the engine, sucking in his breath, nodding gently. Then the smile expands, his whole face lights up, and his enthusiasm transforms him. He's not ordinary at all. 'I think it's brilliant,' he says.

'We'd have come before,' says Mimi, stepping over to Freddie and linking her hand with his, 'but our move back to Bromsgrove has been rather more time-consuming than we expected. The work never seems to end. Do you still have a use for volunteers, or are we too late? Freddie's very keen.'

'Our need for help is inexhaustible,' says Perry. 'Saturday's only the beginning. There'll be no limits after that. The plan is to create a little sister for the Severn Valley Railway.'

'Well,' says Zohra, slightly embarrassed. 'I'm not sure we're quite up to that – it's only a short line.'

'Industrial originally, we think,' says Perry. 'Let me show you round.'

He pauses to zip up his jacket and pull on his hood, then leads them out of the shed and on to the tracks, talking, gesturing with pride. Mimi hangs back a bit and searches out Zohra. She positions her umbrella over both of them. 'You didn't mention you were a railway girl,' she says.

Zohra feels awkward. 'Sorry – I didn't realise you were expecting an entire history.'

Mimi puts a hand on her arm. 'No, it's okay,' she says, smiling. 'I wasn't intending to embarrass you.' She's so polished, so capable.

'Oh, don't worry. I'm fine.' Of course she is. She's always fine. Except when she isn't. 'Are you expecting to help too?'

'Indeed I am. We always do everything together.'

Zohra looks at her doubtfully. She's wearing tight-fitting jeans, probably designer, sleek boots in soft, grey leather and a pink quilted jacket. 'You might get a bit dirty.'

Mimi laughs loudly. 'Oh, come on, Zorry, I spend all day outside, digging, planting. Getting dirty isn't a problem – no need to worry about the outfit, I dress for the occasion. This is so much our thing.'

'Freddie seems nice.'

She considers, as if she's only just thought about it. 'Yes, he is.'

'Where did you meet?'

'Uni. We clicked straight away. He wanted to heal people, I wanted to heal the land. Bingo! Love at first sight.' She hesitates. 'No, actually, I don't really believe in that. Does anyone? But he grows on you – and I do love the growing process.'

Zohra smiles, relaxing a little. This is so unlike the old Mimi. She becomes slightly daring. 'What happened to cool, then?'

Mimi takes the question seriously. 'Well – I can do it when I need to. But the way we were then, all that competitive stuff

– you grow out of it, don't you? Things were never going to be the same again, anyway. Not after Fiona. You can't just pick up and carry on as usual after something like that.'

Is this a rebuke? An admission? Is she trying to prompt Zohra into saying more than she wants to?

'Hey, Mimsi!' Freddie is loping towards them, radiating enthusiasm. 'This is absolutely terrific. Good thing my dad's not here – we'd never get him home again.'

Mimi smiles and takes his arm. 'Well, let's not tell him then,' she says. 'And then we only have to worry about dragging you away.'

Crispin joins them. 'Freddie says he knows the Greenwoods – you know, the railway carriage brothers – in a professional capacity. One of them is a patient – they've already met. They've talked about the carriages, although he hasn't seen them.' He raises an eyebrow. 'You can imagine the consultation, can't you? Medical history, blood pressure looking good, maybe some weight loss required, Pullman carriages, are they, what year?'

Freddie looks sheepish. 'How could I not ask? You don't often meet people with an address like that.'

'So,' says Mimi with a slight smile as she watches Zohra and Crispin standing next to each other. 'Still friends then, after all this time?'

'Oh we're not—' says Zohra hastily, her voice tight and uncomfortable.

'Ever since sixth form,' says Crispin, as if he hasn't heard the innuendo. 'Twentieth-Century Lit.'

'Oh yes,' says Mimi. 'I remember. You and Zorry after school, muttering away about books. It all seemed so boring at the time.'

Zohra takes a deep breath. 'I wonder if you'd mind awfully . . .' Get the expression right: sound casual. 'Nobody really calls me Zorry any more . . .'

Mimi claps a hand over her mouth. 'I'm *so* sorry,' she says. 'How thoughtless of me. I sometimes forget we're grown-ups now. Why would you want to be addressed in the same way as you were at school? It's obvious, isn't it?'

She's so skilled at social interaction, she can even cover over a mistake with good grace. Zohra feels as if she's somehow lost an argument. 'I should have asked,' she says, suddenly embarrassed. 'Do you still like to be called Mimi?'

'Oh, yes. No problem with that. I'm really not an Amelia. Never was.'

'Come on, then,' says Freddie unexpectedly, getting his car keys out of his pocket. 'Let's strike while the iron's hot.'

Everyone looks at him, slightly bewildered.

'We should go and examine the railway carriages, the Greenwoods' place, while it's on our minds. See what condition they're in.'

'I'm up for it,' says Crispin with a grin. 'I've already seen them, but there's no harm in getting an expert opinion.'

'That didn't seem to bother you when we went to the scrap-yard,' says Zohra.

'Don't forget I'd seen them online before we got there. I had Anthony and Melvin's approval.'

Zohra is fairly sure he hadn't told her, but it doesn't seem a good moment for an argument. 'We're only going to look, aren't we?' she asks, following the others reluctantly to the car. 'Nobody's going to try talking them into something they'll regret?' She doesn't want to go, but the thought of them all going without her is alarming.

'Whose side are you on?' says Freddie.

'Can I come?' says Nathan, suddenly appearing beside them. 'Where are you going?'

'No,' says Crispin. 'It's a secret mission, and five people would be too conspicuous.'

'I'm good for a s-secret mission,' says Nathan, his eyes lighting up.

'Wrong terminology,' says Zohra, annoyed with Crispin, who should know better. 'It's only a walk, Nathan, not exactly your cup of tea. No engines, no scrapyards.'

'I could come anyway,' says Nathan. 'Keep a lookout for aliens.'

'No room in the car,' says Crispin.

Nathan looks surprised. 'Were you thinking of giving aliens a lift too?'

'No, I meant there's no room for you. You can come next time, though, okay?'

'Oh, come on, Crisp. I've s-seen his car – it's a Mercedes. You could easily get me in – there'd even be room for your dad.'

'No, really,' says Crispin. 'Five is too many. It's only for reconnaissance.'

'Don't worry, Nathan,' says Zohra, trying to sound brisk. 'We'll bring back the data for you to analyse.' If anyone lets on where they're going, they won't be able to prevent him from getting in the car.

'I need you here,' says Perry, who understands the problem. 'I've got a bit more welding to do. Just round the edges.'

'Can I have a go?' asks Nathan, immediately diverted.

'You bet,' says Perry.

'Do you think that's a good idea?' asks Zohra.

'Come on,' says Crispin, leading her aside. 'My dad knows how to handle him. He'll be fine.'

Zohra isn't so sure. Perry has been known to be careless – he once mislaid Nathan on a trip to the York railway museum and they missed the train home, forfeiting their cheap advance tickets. But she allows herself to be persuaded. Nathan can be very noisy and she'd like to be as discreet as possible.

In the end, they take two cars. Freddie's on call – in his excitement, he omitted to mention this earlier. They park next to each other in the layby and walk up the road towards the entrance. The rain has finally eased off and the clouds are beginning to break up, allowing some brightness to filter through.

'This way,' says Crispin, leading them towards the pathway.

'Won't they see us coming?' asks Mimi, peering through the trees.

'Not necessarily,' says Crispin. 'I got in and out without being spotted – as far as I know.'

'It's a railway carriage,' says Mimi. 'Windows all along the side – how could they not see us?'

'The blinds and curtains are closed on the front,' says Zohra. 'In my experience, it's harder to attract their attention than not.'

'Anyway, they won't know who we are,' says Freddie.

'But one of them knows you. He's your patient,' says Mimi.

'We could be just passing, assuming it's a footpath – they don't all have signposts. Or maybe we're just interested in the view. People do this sort of thing all the time.'

'All they have to do is ask us to leave,' says Crispin. 'Then we can apologise and go. It's not that big a deal.'

He's right, thinks Zohra. But there are more of them this time – it feels like a crowd.

'Still worried?' he asks. He moves closer and rubs her arm. He doesn't usually make physical contact – he supports her by just being there – and she's touched by his concern, but also confused and slightly flustered.

'A bit,' she says. She's read the newspaper cuttings, talked to Dougie; she knows so much about them. It feels unbalanced, as if she has an unfair advantage.

'Oh – of course,' says Mimi. 'You're their postman – sorry, postwoman.'

'We wouldn't know of their existence if I wasn't,' says Zohra.

They pause. 'I'll go,' Crispin says to her. 'You stay here.'

There's another reason for Zohra's growing sense of unease. In the last few years, she's learnt how to keep control, safe in the knowledge that Crispin is by her side but not demanding anything. Now, unexpectedly, she's being drawn into a group and it's like it used to be, exciting, persuasive. She can feel herself relaxing into nostalgia for the warmth of discussion, the pleasure of being taken seriously, of making joint decisions. They've all become new people and the easy relationship between Mimi and Freddie is calming, their stability infectious – what happened before has become less distinct. The pleasure of being with other people, of belonging, while still in the protective shadow of Crispin, has seduced her.

But another part of her is waving a red flag and shrieking in panic, desperate to resist. Don't get involved! It's not safe! It'll all go horribly wrong! She likes to operate on her own. Now, standing by the entrance to the field, realising that she has more to lose than the others, she's suddenly frightened.

How can you be sure if your decisions are your own or if they originate with other people? Everything inside your head has been placed there by an outside source – television, radio, family, friends. How do you decide if your ability to sift through it all is good enough, if you've exercised your own will or if you've allowed yourself to be moulded by someone else? If something turns out well, how can you ever know if you've made a wise decision or if it was just luck? If it ends badly, was it the wrong decision or did circumstances just work against you? By the time you get a result, it's too late to do anything about it anyway.

'You go ahead,' she says. 'Don't be long.'

'Come with us, Zohra,' says Mimi. 'It's not that big a deal.'

But Freddie takes Mimi's hand. 'Don't push her,' he says. 'If she doesn't want to come, she doesn't have to.'

Zohra smiles at him. Did Mimi make a wise decision when she found him or was it just luck? 'I'm fine. It's nice out here.'

They all stop talking for a moment, gazing round at the surrounding countryside. The trees are glistening from the recent rain, and the air smells clean. Wind rustles across the open fields, drying and airing. The motorway murmurs in the background, present, but far enough away to not matter.

'I wouldn't mind living here,' says Mimi.

'You do,' says Freddie. 'That's why we've moved back.'

They grin at each other.

'Come on,' says Crispin. 'Let's do it.'

The three of them leave Zohra and head for the pathway. They disappear almost immediately, and she can hear the sound of their feet, the rustle of leaves as they push them aside, a low exclamation of pleasure from Freddie. She crosses over to the other side of the lane, steps on to the grass verge and approaches a wooden gate set into the hedgerow, which offers a view to the fields beyond. There's an unfamiliar crop close to the road, ready for harvesting, judging by its height, but the fields in the distance are grassy, dotted with grazing sheep, divided into neat patches by low hedges, spreading out towards the horizon.

The silence encloses her, wide, open, calm.

Then they're coming back. Mimi emerges first, laughing, brushing off rainwater that's dripped down from the overhanging branches on to her jacket. 'Well,' she says, 'they're living on borrowed time, that's for sure. I can't believe they're still in one piece.'

'Not in good nick,' agrees Freddie as they cross the road.

'That's what I thought,' says Zohra.

'Early fifties,' says Crispin to Zohra, as if he's known this all the time. 'That's what Freddie and I reckon. British Rail Mark 1, standard corridor. Older than the ones we saw at the scrapyard. Must have been abandoned when the line closed down and the land was sold.'

'They're the right colour for that period,' says Freddie. 'Crimson lake and cream. Although the moss is doing a good job of disguising it. Seems odd that such a small railway invested in anything so expensive for such a short time. Especially if it was only there for industrial purposes.'

'But we could be wrong,' says Crispin. Maybe they were used for carrying the estate workers to and from work. Or the bigwigs, to keep an eye on their investments.'

'What do you think of the names?' asks Zohra, trying to edge everyone back down the road. But nobody moves.

'Oh, the romance,' says Mimi, sighing.

'Probably added later,' says Freddie. 'British Rail used numbers.'

'Could they be renovated?' asks Mimi. 'In that state?'

'I don't see why not,' says Freddie. 'The main structure is steel.'

'Was there any sign of the Greenwoods?' asks Zohra.

'No,' says Mimi. 'Not a glimpse. Disappointing really. I'd got myself all psyched up.'

'They might have seen you, though.'

Freddie looks at her and smiles. 'It probably doesn't matter if they did.'

Of course it matters, thinks Zohra. Nobody likes to be spied on.

A taxi drives up the road and pulls over in the lay-by. At the same time, they hear voices coming from the direction of the carriages. Three figures emerge on to the road. It's the two Greenwood brothers and the woman who spoke to Zohra at the station. They stop and stare. There's an uncomfortable silence as the two groups face each other.

'The postwoman!' says one of the brothers suddenly, staring directly at Zohra.

'Yes – hi.' Zohra wants to sound casual, but her voice comes out awkwardly.

'Now there's a coincidence,' says the woman. 'I talked to you at the station, didn't I? You helped me with my luggage.'

Zohra attempts a smile.

The taxi driver hoots and makes them all jump. He's leaning out of his window, his face creased with irritation. 'You keep me waiting longer, I die of starvation.'

'Don't be ridiculous,' the woman calls back. 'I'm paying you.'

'Not enough to justify death from neglect.' Surprisingly, he then puts his head back in and continues to wait.

'Don't mind him,' says the woman. 'He's all mouth. He just can't bear to be ignored.'

The Greenwood brothers stand in different positions. One peers curiously across at them, more at ease with himself, while the other studies the ground, his shoulders tight and defensive, as if he's expecting an imminent attack, but they're still remarkably alike, both squinting slightly, not allowing their expressions to reveal anything. Now that Zohra can see them together, their old rivalry starts to make sense. It's the way they take up space, the lack of movement, their unusual stillness – perhaps an inevitable result of living apart from the rest of the world for so long – that make them mirror images of each other. They're so alike they could almost be twins.

'Dr Bakewell?' says the slimmer one after a few seconds, sounding surprised. 'What are you doing here?'

Freddie grins sheepishly. 'I wanted to see your carriages,' he says. 'We were hoping to do it rather more discreetly, though.' He holds his hands up in surrender. 'I'm a railway enthusiast – I can't help it.'

Crispin steps forward. 'Hi,' he says. 'I'm Crispin. We're from Wychington Railway – you might have heard of us. We're renovating the old line round the estate, and we were interested in your carriages.'

'Ah,' says Nick. 'I see. No carriages of your own, then?'

'No,' says Crispin. 'Only an engine.'

'I'm off,' calls the woman, heading for the taxi. 'See you tomorrow. I'll be here at a similar time. Bye.' She gets into the taxi, slams the door, and the driver immediately pulls away. She waves as they drive briskly past.

The two brothers watch her go without saying a word. They each lift an arm to wave, then drop it awkwardly.

'Are you coming next Saturday?' asks Crispin. 'The big event. Our first run.'

'Without passengers, presumably,' says Nick. 'If you don't have carriages.'

'Well, that's true, but we're expecting a lot of people and it's good publicity. A chance to encourage donations. Then they can all come back when we can offer rides. You could help – if you were interested.'

The other brother raises his head briefly to look at Crispin, hesitates for a few seconds as if puzzled, then turns back up the pathway without responding.

They all watch him go. 'I was wondering,' says Freddie hesitantly. 'I don't suppose you'd let us have a look inside your carriages, would you?'

There's a long pause.

'This is very odd,' says Nick eventually. 'No one visits us, ever, except delivery men, and now, within the space of a fortnight, the whole world turns up.' He sighs and seems to shrug. 'Oh, well, I can't really see why not, as long as you don't mind a certain amount of chaos. Can't speak for Johnny, but I've got nothing to hide.'

It seems that everyone lets their breath out at the same time. The sound is audible over the bluster of the wind.

14

As Nick's visitors climb the steps and turn right along the corridor of Aphrodite, their youth and energy send vibrations through the carriage like a benign breeze, a warming ray of spring sunshine. The floor trembles and dust emerges from long-neglected places, rising, circulating; it's as if someone has pulled aside the curtains, invited in all the previously banished light in one go.

Nick wants to rush through the carriage and open every window, releasing the old, stale air and allowing the new to flow in. Where's Johnny? He must know they're here – he'll have felt the movement, heard the voices. He should have joined them. And what if they ask to see Demeter? It's unlikely Johnny has revolutionised his cleaning routines since Nick last entered his carriage, many years ago. Would they even be able to negotiate a pathway through the chaos?

That first conversation between Nick and Johnny yesterday, after Johnny's walk, couldn't exactly be described as a breakthrough, but it was a beginning. Debs, Bev, whoever she is, turned up in a taxi in the evening, chatty again, bearing gifts: chocolate, more cakes, and a Rolling Stones CD, which she insisted on playing on a loop on Nick's CD player. She didn't stay long.

She did the same thing again today, arriving with bags of presents, shortly after Nick got back from work, as if she didn't know how to arrive empty-handed.

'You can't do this,' said Johnny, 'buying things as if everything's suddenly all right.'

'Perhaps we need a little more time,' said Nick.

'Allow me a little indulgence,' she said. 'I haven't been able to treat my brothers for so long. Shopping gives me a purpose. I can't do as much as I used to, my legs hurt if I walk far, but Bromsgrove is so small, it's just wonderful. I pottered around the shops for a while, stopped for coffee, pottered again, had some lunch, then took the taxi home.' Either the taxi driver hasn't got much work or she's paying him to be available, because he always turns up in a remarkably short time.

Nick feels he should be offering her something in return, but worries that it might be construed as acceptance. 'Have you seen anyone you recognise?' he asked her today before she left.

'No,' she said. 'Not exactly. Once or twice I've wondered, but I'm not sure I can trust my memory. It was all so long ago – I struggle even to remember names. Yesterday, I saw someone – a woman about my age – looking at me more intently than you'd expect – maybe she saw something familiar – but she didn't say anything. If she's not expecting to see me, she won't.'

'Does it worry you?'

She sighed. 'I don't know. It would be nice to find someone who remembers how it used to be, to talk over old times. But so complicated.'

'Difficult to explain why you're not dead.'

She seemed to crumple, unexpectedly defeated. 'It's probably best not to try. I've found you two again. That's enough for me.'

But Debs would never have been satisfied with enough. She always wanted more.

Nick thought he should push her, evaluate the extent of her sense of guilt. 'Bev's mum used to wander up and down the High Street, ranting,' he said. 'Did you know she'd lost two babies, years before? Polio. That's why she drank. Losing Bev was the last straw. She never got over it.'

She held his gaze steadily for a few seconds, then looked to the side as tears started to form. 'You think I haven't thought about Bev every day since it all came back to me? And her mother, and Ma, and you?' Her voice rose to a wail before it faded away.

So she wasn't oblivious to the disasters she had created. She did care. Unless she was even cleverer than he already suspected.

Nick follows Freddie and Mimi into the kitchen. 'Would you like coffee, tea?' he asks, realising as soon as he's spoken that it might be a little crowded in his living room. These people seem to take up so much space, filling the air with their voices, their movements, their confidence.

'Oh, you don't need to provide drinks,' says Mimi. 'There are far too many of us, and it's not as if you were expecting visitors. We've already intruded more than we should.'

'I don't mind,' says Nick, and he means it. So much has changed in the last few days that he feels prepared for anything. He's finding this new invasion invigorating. 'We've knocked several compartments into one – the kitchen, the bathroom, obviously.'

'Well, you'd have to, wouldn't you?' says Zohra. 'You couldn't live in it otherwise.'

'It wouldn't be a problem,' says Crispin, 'if you ever considered selling. There are expert restorers out there, you know, ready with supplies of wood, rolls of original seat material and stuffing, just waiting for carriages to turn up. Whole businesses have been set up to supply heritage railways – as much for love as profit. You can get lamps, luggage racks, mirrors, posters – you name it, someone's got it on eBay.'

'Crispin!' says Zohra, looking embarrassed. 'We'd only contact them if you were interested in selling,' she says to Nick. 'We're not here to push you into anything.'

'Of course not,' says Crispin, smiling amiably.

'At least you've kept the corridors,' says Freddie. 'So civilised. You do realise that we're expecting to come across a body in one of the compartments, and a small stout detective with a big moustache?'

The reference to bodies is disconcerting. It was here in Aphrodite that PC Banner told them a body had been found and where Ma sat day after day, slowly deteriorating.

But it's not Freddie's fault. He wouldn't know the significance of his words.

'Have you still got the old loo?' asks Mimi, as they approach the end of the carriage. Nick opens the door so they can see inside. 'Not functional, I'm afraid,' he says.

Freddie eyes the pile of wooden racquet heads sticking out of the bowl. 'Tennis eh? I'm a fairly useful player myself if you ever fancy a game.'

'Sorry,' says Nick. 'Not me.'

'The woman with you earlier, who went off in the taxi,' says Mimi. 'Does she live here too?' She's so amiable and rolls out her questions with such ease, they don't feel at all intrusive.

'No,' says Nick. 'She's just a visitor.'

'But you're related, surely? I thought I could see a family resemblance.'

Nick stares at her with astonishment. 'Really?' he says. She must be confusing age with appearance. 'I think you might be imagining that.'

'And what about the other carriage?' asks Freddie. 'Is it in the same condition?'

'More or less,' says Nick. 'But you'd have to ask my brother if you wanted to see for yourselves. Try knocking. See if he answers.'

There's a motor humming away inside Johnny, straining against his self-imposed brakes, desperate for action. His legs are jiggling, his knees bouncing up and down and his heels drumming on the floor, setting up a rhythm that rocks the air. He gets to his feet again and goes into the corridor, where there's more space for his juddering thoughts. It's been hard enough seeing someone who claims to be Debs, sitting in Aphrodite as if she's always been there. Now he can hear these new strangers next door, talking, laughing. He's not used to chatter. He attempts to stop pacing, willing himself to be

224

statue-like and pretend he isn't here at all, but he can't do it. There's too much movement inside him. It requires a physical outlet.

There's a knock, a rapping of knuckles on his door. Silence, while the unknown visitor waits for a reply.

He looks around at Demeter, his private space. The untidiness is to be expected – he's a working man. But it's not very clean, and the problem is too great to be solved with a vacuum cleaner – the floor is barely visible. He's slightly worried it might smell. He knows the shared places – the bathroom and kitchen – will be all right, as Nick gave up arguing about rotas long ago (could that be the reason why they've stopped talking?) and just gets on with the cleaning, refusing to believe that Johnny would ever do it. He's wrong of course. Johnny has a healthy respect for hygiene. He just likes to wait until it's bad enough to make a difference.

But how has he managed to neglect everywhere else without even noticing?

There's a second knock.

He can't let them in.

'Johnny?' Nick's voice.

They're not going to go away. He hovers, undecided. Who are they, these lively, chattering men and women? What do they want? Is it normal to come into other people's homes like this and talk so openly? He can't remember the last time he communicated with anyone unfamiliar, and he's no longer sure what to expect. He can cope with the usual delivery men, although most of them seem a little odd. One of them told him that the companies ask for volunteers to deliver to him, which is perplexing. It's not as if he's sinister or threatening.

There's a third knock. Should he respond? They could open the door anyway. It's not locked. But polite people don't just barge in.

'You don't need to worry about tidying,' calls Nick. 'They just want to have a look round.'

'That's right, Mr Greenwood,' says a woman's voice. 'We're not bothered by the condition, just what's still there from the original carriage. We're only being nosy.'

He slides the door back. Nick's standing there in front, with the other four behind. They introduce themselves again, one at a time, then step in, as if he's given them permission.

Examining his home through their eyes, Johnny finds that he's not just embarrassed by the evidence that he never vacuums, but also by the oldness of everything. He's still using the original seats in his living room, British Rail standard, Midlands region. When Ma renovated the living room, after they'd joined the two compartments together, she reupholstered the seats, trimmed an offcut of carpet to fit the new space. In her bedroom, now Johnny's living room, she saved money by moving the benches together to make a bed, put a mattress on top, and kept the old carpet. The mattress is long gone and the benches have been separated, but the material has almost completely worn away.

Fortunately, natural light barely penetrates through the grime on the windows and the artificial light from sixty-watt bulbs (bought online as a job lot when the low energy ones took over, hoarded in piles of boxes in the corner) is dim, so you can't see too much anyway. There are discarded computer parts everywhere: base units, keyboards, mice and printers, all piled up randomly, as if they've given up hope of ever being taken to the tip.

Johnny can see that Nick is embarrassed. But it was easier for him. He knew that Debs was coming to Aphrodite. He's had the chance to prepare, to clean up, before all these people appeared.

'Love your study,' says Mimi, standing in the corridor and looking through the open door into the room that used to be his bedroom before he ran out of space and moved his bedding into the living room. 'It's so cosy. And you've hardly changed a thing.'

'Except the desk,' says Johnny, watching her, baffled by her enthusiasm, worried that she's going to attempt to enter. There's no floor space. He usually eases himself into the desk chair from the corridor and wheels himself to the desk through a narrow runway. The teetering piles of obsolete equipment on either side are finely balanced, at risk from the careless brush of an arm or the jerk of a clumsy foot.

They all stand in the corridor and peer into his living room (one pane of glass cracked from top to bottom, a reminder of the time he pinched a piece of Nick's bubble gum without telling him, when Nick's fist missed his nose and hit the glass, and they ended up in Worcester Emergency Department for four hours).

Photos and documents are spilling out of the black plastic bags on to the floor round the mattress. Nick stares at them. 'I'd forgotten there was so much stuff,' he says. 'Is this all from the dead WC?'

Johnny nods. 'I was looking for photos – you know . . .'

'Oh,' says Nick. 'Yes.'

The visitors are too noisy. Johnny's world is one of silence, punctuated only by the ping of incoming emails, a museum world where no one else ever steps through the dust. Any intruder, filling the space, disturbing the balance, would be too big. All this movement, this activity – it's like opening the hatches of a submarine and letting water cascade in.

He watches them, barely able to breathe, let alone speak.

Then they've gone. He can hear Nick talking quietly with them on the grass outside the front door. And finally, silence. Slowly, slowly, the dust floats back to the familiar, comfortable surfaces. A calmness starts to soak through Johnny, inside his head, working its way down his body to his stomach, his knees, his toes, until his thoughts become more logical and the stillness settles.

Nick watches them go with an acute sense of disappointment. Once their voices have faded, the car doors have slammed and the sound of the engine has vanished into the distance, the world around the railway carriages quickly starts to fade into darkness – there are no streetlights on Long Meadow Road. He can hear leaves rustling, grass disturbed by passing hedgehogs, and feel the bite of cold in the autumn air. As always at this time of year, he thinks of Paula. He ducks instinctively as a bat disturbs the air above him, swooping low over his head. Nothing unusual.

He's still tingling with excitement, stimulated by the presence of people, charged up by the energy and spark of their youth. He's rarely part of a crowd, even at work, where he's one of the few with his own office – many of his colleagues work in an open-plan environment. He spends most of the day working alone, communicating with his clients by email and phone in the quietness of his own space, and his only face-to-face interaction with others is at meetings. No one ever seems to be interested in his opinions.

He doesn't want to return to his carriage, follow his usual routines, watch the news and then just go to bed. He needs to talk to someone. Johnny? But he's held back by unease about the invasion of Demeter. Should he have prevented it? However hard Nick resists, he always feels guilty about Johnny. Every time he manages to bypass his sense of responsibility it creeps up again, slowly, barely noticeable at first then increasingly uncomfortable. He may be the younger brother, but he's always been in charge, the protector. He's the one with experience, a map of the world and the means to navigate through it.

They wouldn't have been satisfied without seeing Johnny's carriage. They had to be able to make a comparison.

It's good for Johnny to mix with other people. Why can't he be more welcoming, more normal?

Nick sighs and climbs back up the steps. He closes the door behind him, then hesitates, almost turning left, wondering if he should knock. Now that they're communicating a little, he might be able to calm Johnny down, apologise for the invasion. He could explain his motives and attempt to persuade him that company is good, that the invaders were nice people, not at all threatening.

As he dithers, the door opens and Johnny comes shuffling out from the semi-darkness of Demeter with a mug in his hand. 'Oh,' he says, stopping mid-stride.

'Sorry,' says Nick cautiously. 'My fault. I was moving more quietly than usual.'

'Yes,' says Johnny.

They stare at each other.

'I hope you didn't mind them coming in,' says Nick.

'You could have warned me . . .' says Johnny.

'How? I didn't know they were going to turn up like that. What was I supposed to do?'

'I mean after. When they were in Aphrodite. If you'd said something—'

'Right,' says Nick. 'Good idea. Perhaps I should have left them to run loose in my home while I came to ask you. What should I have said? My brother probably won't want you in his carriage, since he's a stubborn old man who doesn't like people and he almost certainly won't like you, but I'll give it a go. Would that have worked?' He stops. He hadn't intended to be antagonistic. Why does Johnny always undermine his efforts to remain calm?

But Johnny's response is milder than he expects. 'You don't have to make me sound so unreasonable.'

Nick steps back and allows Johnny through, following him into the kitchen. He fills the kettle and switches it on. 'They were all right, though, weren't they?'

'They want to buy the carriages.'

Nick pauses. 'Yes,' he says. 'What do you think?' The idea is growing in his mind, becoming more possible. It's cold in here now, even in September – it can be unbearable in the winter. If it snows they're soon cut off, their world narrowed and their access to public transport blocked. Frost can lock the doors and windows, and condensation freezes into hard ridges of solid ice on the inside of window frames, dripping down the walls when it melts and forming puddles on the floor. How much longer can they survive? The winters have been milder in the last few years, but the rain has become heavier and the storms more likely to bring trees down on top of them.

When the roof over his bedroom started to leak last winter, when he was woken by water trickling down his cheek, he'd had to go to B&Q and buy bituminous tape. He'd crawled up on the roof, stuck the tape over the network of cracks, then painted it all. He'd felt insecure, exposed up there, but there was no way he could have asked Johnny for help. And if Johnny'd decided to do the same thing on Demeter, he'd have done it on his own, while Nick was at work. If he'd slipped, nobody would have known for hours.

But Johnny's staring at him as if he's mad. 'You're not seriously thinking about it?'

'Why not? We could afford it – presumably you've still got Ma's money?' Neither of them could believe how much she left them in her will. They knew that even during her less productive years she'd been frugal and that she'd always been in demand, the best cleaner in Bromsgrove, who'd charged much higher rates than other cleaners. But they hadn't suspected she'd saved anything like as much as she had.

They couldn't work out what she'd been saving for. Had she been planning a comfortable retirement or did she always intend to leave it to them, allow them to move on, buy a real home? Maybe she was simply determined to prove that she was better than Dad, with no intention of spending it on herself.

'Mine's in a savings account,' says Nick. 'Not earning much interest, though, of course. I assume you've done much the same with your share. And presumably your business makes a profit.' He tries to keep the scepticism out of his voice. 'What else are we going to do with it all?'

'I like it here.' Johnny sounds sulky, resentful, like a child being asked to hand over his long-cherished toys.

'Don't you find it's getting harder as time goes on?'

Johnny shakes his head, then stops. 'Okay, so it gets a bit cold, but I've got heaters, same as you. It's cosy enough if you keep the doors shut.'

'A *bit* cold? That hardly does it justice. We're talking brass monkeys here – sub-zero. I'm starting to feel as if I've been camping outside for the last fifty years or so – and if I'm getting tired of it, you must be too. We're neither of us getting any younger. Have you seriously never dreamed about central heating, hot showers, a bathroom where you don't see your breath, somewhere that doesn't creak every time the wind blows?' Suddenly he's exhausted and baffled. Why have they never had this conversation before?

'Well,' says Johnny, turning away, 'it's up to you. Do what you want. Sell your carriage. It's no skin off my nose.'

It's the way he turns away, his refusal to consider alternatives. The passive dismissal, the easy acceptance of martyrdom . . .

A fierce resentment flares up inside Nick, red-hot, scalding, almost choking him. He grabs Johnny's arm. 'No way,' he says, struggling to get the words out. 'I'm not letting you get away with that. Suddenly everything's my fault, just like it was after the accident, even when it wasn't. Your injuries had to be so much worse than mine, didn't they? Getting everyone to feel sorry for you because you decided to give up tennis – but that was nothing to do with the accident, was it? You'd known for ages you couldn't hack it, and, oh look, here's a ready-made excuse, laid out in front of you, all neatly sorted . . .'

He stops. Why's he bringing all this up? How has he managed to slip backwards so quickly, jump headlong into the heat of their old rivalry? Are they doomed to repeat the same mistakes over and over again – play, replay, round and round on an endless loop?

Johnny has frozen in front of him, his mouth dropping open with surprise.

And is this really true? Was it even true then? It's the way he used to think, the way he kept himself warm during the bleakest moments in his life. When he needed the comfort of a scapegoat, Johnny has always been conveniently there.

Johnny comes back to life. He wrenches his arm away with unexpected strength, his face pale and tense as old resentments work their way to the surface. 'Oh here we go again. Blame me, why not? Just like it used to be – why would anything be different now? So much easier than facing up to the reality, isn't it? You were the first to give up tennis, though – not me. You can't seriously have forgotten that.' His voice is tight with fury.

Nick wants to drop it, calm the conversation, go back to being civilised, but the anger won't go away. It's like an underground spring, replenished by perceived injustice, waiting to well up at any time. Fear is threatening to overwhelm him: the knowledge that he's not good enough; the prospect of Johnny outdoing him; the belief that he will be abandoned, left behind on his own. 'No, no, *no*. You were the one who decided to stop, because it meant you'd never have to lose to me again. You just couldn't bear it if you couldn't beat me, could you?'

'That's rubbish and you know it,' shouts Johnny. He's flexing his fists, balancing on the balls of his feet – would he do it, actually hit him? Continue their last unfinished fight, the one on the roof of the chapel?

Nick can feel energy coursing through his veins, an overwhelming desire to lash out, wipe Johnny's face away, obliterate it once and for all. 'You milked that accident like there was no tomorrow. How do you make that out to be my fault? You were up there too – okay, I dared you, but you dared me back and you still managed to blame me. You knew you weren't good enough, that's what it was all about. That's what it's always been about. You knew that when the chips were down, you'd lose.'

Johnny has become uncharacteristically still. 'I could beat you any time, any place, no problem. Give me a racquet right now and I'll prove it.'

'In your dreams. You just couldn't face it, your younger brother overtaking you . . .'

They stand and glare at each other, their faces too close, too intimate, their anger colliding in the space between them. They've been sent back in time with a sudden whoosh, as if all those intervening years have never happened. It's so familiar, so automatic. Age hasn't taught them anything.

I'm better than this, thinks Nick. I'm an accountant, I'm capable of rational discussion. How can I possibly be behaving like this? Why would I be perpetually jealous of my brother? It's not as if either of us was dedicated enough to the tennis. He takes some deep breaths. Calm down, be sensible, act like an adult. I deal with difficult people all day. It's my speciality. Think of Johnny as one of them. A touchy client who needs flattery, who needs to feel he's in charge.

'And that's before we even get on to Paula,' says Johnny, who hasn't reached the peak of his anger, who's not yet ready to calm down. 'The way you stole her from me—'

'I stole her from you?' Nick forgets his determination to behave well and can hear his voice changing, rising in pitch and volume, as if it's someone else talking. 'The other way round, I think.'

'Don't give me that,' says Johnny. 'You were the one who tried to undermine me, told her lies.'

'Oh, I see, it was me. I was the one who told her the lies about me sleeping with Diane Foster? Just so I could prove to her – what exactly? That was nothing to do with you, then?'

It's still hard for Johnny to think about Paula without a dense fog descending, confusing his sense of direction and removing his ability to reason.

As soon as he saw her, laughing uproariously with Nick, a part of himself that he didn't know existed revealed itself. With extraordinary clarity, he understood that she should be with him, not Nick. She'd made a terrible mistake, and it was so obvious to Johnny that he couldn't believe no one else could see it. How could she laugh at anything Nick said? His jokes were always delivered in a dry, earnest manner, referring to some obscure fact that only he knew, which he then had to explain, by which time they were no longer funny.

But Paula, inexplicably, found the jokes hilarious. She was in the year above them, out of their reach, when she first arrived, having moved from somewhere in the north. She made an immediate impact and soon had a band of girls following her around, trying in vain to reproduce her style. Even the hardened boys who prided themselves on their witty repartee would become abnormally silent in her presence. But for at least a year, she refused to single out anyone as a special friend. She just flashed her dimples and smiled at everyone.

Nick was fifteen and Johnny sixteen. Despite being ten months apart, they were in the same school year, a disaster for both boys. They'd had to be separated since they first started school. Teachers soon learnt the necessity of placing them on opposite sides of a classroom while, of course, the pupils did their utmost to bring them together, always keen to set them up for a fight. Even after Debs was murdered and people were treating them with more care, no one really believed they could be trusted to occupy the same space peacefully for long.

And into this situation walked Paula, her eyes wide open (hazel, abnormally long eyelashes, coated with black mascara), with short blonde hair and a perfectly shaped head (so exquisitely sculpted that no one could contemplate it without having an overwhelming desire to cup it in his hands), her tiny, slender figure asserting itself with readily assumed authority. Nobody could quite believe her interest in Nick and Johnny. What did she see in them? She examined them as a pair and somehow recognised their equal worth. Maybe she'd seen them on the tennis court, although that was a rare occurrence by then, seen their casual strength and flexibility; or maybe she was drawn to the romance of tragedy, the lost sister, the unresolved mystery. She waltzed into their isolated lives, brought sunshine into the railway carriages, made the boys laugh for the first time in a year and lightened the burden of Debs's absence. Unexpectedly, things started to feel better. She even charmed Ma, although that took a little longer.

'She's too old,' said Ma in a low, annoyed voice, after Paula had breezed in and breezed out again the first time. 'Wait until you're older.'

'Don't be daft,' said Nick. 'You can't put these things on hold.'

'If you're in love, you're in love,' said Johnny with a snide chuckle, hoping to annoy him.

But miraculously, Nick just smiled. 'You said it,' he said, and walked out of the room, bouncing slightly, as if his legs had become elastic, as if he was dancing. Nick never danced.

Ma, who was increasingly locked into a silent disapproval of everything, sighed with exasperation. It was rare for her to speak at all those days. She would go out to work silently and return silently. She sat in front of the television every evening, dead-eyed, letting the stories wash over her without reacting.

But Paula wasn't interested in Ma's opinions. She kept coming and involved Johnny in everything. They played Monopoly, canasta, rummy. Johnny and Nick totted up the results in an exercise book every time, always checking who was in the lead, keeping a long-term record, regularly comparing notes, and Paula just laughed at them. For once, neither of them minded. The competition was almost benign, more a matter of fun than earnest.

'We have to name the railway carriages,' she announced after a few weeks.

Both boys stared at her in bewilderment. 'Why?' asked Johnny eventually.

'Because,' she said. She turned up the next day with stencils and a large pot of acrylic paint. 'Aphrodite,' she said, 'goddess of love, and Demeter, goddess of virginity.'

Johnny could feel a hot flush creep over his face, and longed to know if Nick was reacting in the same way. But he was unable to raise his eyes from the floor.

She ordered them to find a footstool and led them outside, started work, making them take turns, a letter at a time, until it was all finished. When they stood back to admire their handi-work, they were impressed by their neatness.

'But what will Ma say?' asked Nick.

'Oh, you don't need to worry about that,' she said. 'She won't know about the virginity stuff.'

Ma didn't notice. Or if she did, she didn't say anything.

Paula cooked. She took over the kitchen, used whatever she could find in the fridge, took the Midland Red bus into Birmingham to buy fresh vegetables and cheap cuts of meat from the markets, experimented with sauces. Ma radiated disapproval, but nevertheless sat silently and cleared her plate like the rest of them. 'She's all right, that girl,' she said one day.

Nick and Johnny stared at her in astonishment, waiting for her to say more, but she just went back to her bedroom. They stood silently for a few seconds, then shook hands solemnly. As if they'd worked their way up to Wimbledon, won the men's doubles. A breakthrough of world-shattering significance.

It didn't take long for the rivalry to re-emerge. Nick started to resent Johnny's constant presence in their relationship and tried to isolate Paula, take her to his room. But she wouldn't cooperate.

She likes me, decided Johnny eventually. That's what it's all about. She comes here, pretending to be Nick's girlfriend, but it's me she wants to see.

The games became less relaxed, more intense.

Johnny: 'Got you! Hotel on Old Kent Road. That's two hundred pounds you owe me.'

Nick: 'Pull the other one. It wasn't a five, it was an eight.'

'You've swapped the three for a six – you threw a three and a two. I saw it with my own eyes!'

'Are you accusing me of cheating?'

'If the cap fits—'

'Boys, boys,' said Paula, her voice soothing, calm, strangely contented in the role of appeaser. 'Let's just throw it again.'

'You can bet your life it won't be five any more, though, will it? He's going to get away without paying my rent.'

But they did as they were told.

Paula didn't want to go out to parties or hang around by the bus shelter. She knew about the roof climbing, but refused to go and watch or even to discuss it and was only interested in them when they were at home in the railway carriages. She would squeeze herself between them on the bench while they watched television, snuggle up against Nick, running her fingers softly under his shirt and tickling his chest, then shift her legs to touch Johnny's, nudging her bare toes up his trouser leg. Whose girlfriend was she? Nothing was clear.

If Ma came in, Paula would untangle herself, sit up, smile amiably, smooth her rumpled hair, act cool. Surely Ma would see their flushed faces, their shallow, uneven breathing, the glow emanating from Paula, how they were all pulsating with desire. But she never said anything. She sat opposite them, her head turned towards the small black-and-white screen, silent while Paula screamed with laughter at *Up Pompeii*, *Monty Python*, *Dad's Army*, and Nick and Johnny attempted to follow her lead.

The accident changed everything. Paula would shortly be leaving for university and time was running out. Johnny remembers her at the side of his hospital bed, her face pale and creased with worry, as if she hadn't slept, as if she cared.

'I thought I'd lost you,' she breathed in his ear as he lay there, fighting the pain, trying not to show it in his face, desperate to acknowledge her, tell her how happy he was that she was there. He waited for her to tell him off for climbing in the first place, but she didn't. She just stroked his hand. But was she going straight to Nick when she left the room, whispering the same words in his ear, still treating them as if they were two parts of one whole?

'Are you my girl?' he asked, voicing the agonising question that had been bouncing around in his mind for so long.

'Of course I am,' she said, and for a while he believed it. But when she wasn't there, he thought again and realised that she wasn't ever going to tell him, not properly.

'Do you love me?' he asked.

'Of course I do,' she said, her eyes clear, simple, direct.

'What about Nick?' he asked.

237

She paused and smiled, the dimples in her cheeks appearing from nowhere. 'I love both of you,' she said.

And he squirmed in his immobile condition, furious but powerless, plotting how to kill Nick, then her, then himself. He desperately needed a solution, a way he could discredit his brother. 'But has Nick told you about Diane Foster?'

Her expression didn't alter, but he could feel the temperature dropping almost immediately, her efforts to appear unaffected as her features slowly froze. 'What do you mean?' she said, her voice icy. 'Why would he have anything to do with her?'

A spark of adrenaline leapt inside Johnny, creating a spasm that sent a violent shaft of pain up his spine from his leg. He'd got it right, found the solution. He couldn't speak for a few seconds, struggling to control the pain. 'Didn't he tell you? He's slept with her.' It was all he could think of, but it was enough.

She sat up abruptly. 'When?'

This was the crucial question, of course, and Johnny had never intended to be so specific. But she was right by his side, holding his hand. He could feel victory hovering. He couldn't let go now. He closed his eyes. 'A couple of weeks before the accident,' he whispered.

He heard the intake of breath, felt the tension in her fingers round his hand and knew he'd served an ace on a match point.

But when she got up and left him without another word, he began to wonder if he'd made the right decision. As time went on and she didn't come back, it became apparent that he hadn't. It was as if she had to have both of them or neither.

He only saw her one more time. Shortly after he was discharged from hospital, two weeks later than Nick, he was at home on his own when there was a knock at the door. The first thought that flashed into his mind – always his first thought – was that it was Paula. At the same time, he knew it wouldn't be. She'd been absent now for several weeks, and he'd come to understand the enormity of what he'd said, the consequences of lying. So who else would want to visit them? One of their mates, perhaps? They'd been to the hospital a couple of times in a group, pulling up chairs round his bed before moving on to see Nick, helping themselves to the tins of Roses and Quality Street that they'd brought as gifts and cracking feeble jokes, lounging awkwardly on the plastic chairs – scared of needles, couldn't cope with the smell, they'd say. He knew it was more than that. He and Nick had gone too far, stretched friendship too tightly, expected too much from them. Now they were free, they weren't interested in coming back into the fold. They were off forging their own lives, moving on.

It could be Dougie, though – he was usually okay – or one of the Troth kids, who'd been less involved. 'The door's open,' he called through the open window, unable to move quickly.

When Paula appeared, slipping in like an unexpected shaft of sun, smiling in that slightly remote way that twisted his insides, he was taken by surprise and found it difficult to breathe. She curled herself round the edge of the door, into the small space, and shut the door carefully behind her.

'Nobody else in then?' she asked, as they looked at each other.

He shook his head, unable to speak.

'Oh good,' she said.

'I wasn't expecting—'

She put a finger to his lips. 'No talking,' she said. 'This is our last chance.' She leaned over and kissed him.

Nick couldn't understand where Paula had gone. Why didn't she visit him in hospital any more? Where was she when he was discharged, when he went home to the railway carriages? Everywhere was so empty without her, stale, silent. As soon as he felt well enough, he walked over to her house, but nobody answered the door. Had she already left for university? Why hadn't she come to say goodbye, given him an address? Had she really just dropped him out of her life without a word? It felt as if he'd been treated like an old comic, pored over eagerly, then discarded when he was no longer interesting, dumped in a pile at the charity shop.

So when he came home with Ma and they found Paula and Johnny alone together in the living room, he thought he was hallucinating. He stood and stared, the Asda bags still in his hands, unable to think, unable to breathe. They were sitting on opposite sides of the living room, but their hair was ruffled, their clothes dishevelled, and there was a strange atmosphere, a connection between them that hadn't been there before – an understanding that excluded him.

He dropped the shopping bags, left the living room without speaking, and staggered outside, not knowing what to do. Eventually, without any conscious decision, he turned away from the road and started to climb the hill behind the carriages. It was late in the day and the sun was sinking. Shadows from the trees stretched out in front of him, long and cartoonish, and the light was too bright, hurting his eyes, making them water. How could she? Had she been seeing Johnny all this time, secretly, in the hospital, while she just faded out of Nick's life?

He didn't stop until he'd reached the top of the hill, hot and panting. He looked out over the darkening landscape towards Bromsgrove, hearing the sheep calling, the cars on the motorway. There was an enormous pressure inside him, building up, becoming gradually more volatile, preparing for detonation. He'd always known she would be leaving for university eventually, but he'd been preparing himself for months, expecting to write, to receive letters from her, to see her during the holidays. He'd been trying to convince himself it was all right – she'd been whisked away by her parents for a last holiday in Spain; she'd had to go early to Manchester to sort out her accommodation. She'd be back. She'd just turn up and everything would go back to the way it was.

But now – if she came back for Johnny and not him, how could he bear it?

Heavy, physical pain was threatening to crush him. He wasn't sure he could survive—

'Nick!'

He held his breath, confused, and listened. Could he actually conjure her out of the gloom, imagine she was there when she wasn't?

'Nick! Help me up.'

He shook his head. The voice was so real.

'Nick!' She was sounding annoyed, like the Paula he knew. 'Don't just stand there.'

He looked down the hill and there she was, climbing up towards him, struggling on the final stretch, the last of the sun bright on her bare, tanned arms, her hair lit up, a human light bulb, luminescent, glowing.

It wasn't until she stumbled slightly that he decided she was really there and tentatively, shyly, he clambered down towards her, took her outstretched hand and pulled her up to the top. They collapsed against each other, breathing heavily, and sat silently for a while, looking outwards, not speaking.

Then, finally he blurted it out. 'Did you really do it – with Johnny?'

She turned to him, her eyes grave, and started to laugh. 'Oh, Nick, Nick.'

He couldn't understand. At the most devastating moment of his life, she just kept laughing.

Then, finally, she grew silent and stared at him, uncharacteristically still, her eyes ranging over his body, round him, through him. He waited, unsure what she wanted from him. He tried to make sense of it all. Was she seriously expecting them to share her?

'How could you do it?' she asked, her voice flat and tight.

The conversation wasn't following a logical direction. 'Do what?'

'Sleep with Diane Foster.'

He stared, rigid with astonishment. 'What are you talking about? What's she been saying?'

'Diane Foster!' she said with contempt. 'Of all people. Why her?'

Was that what all this was about? Was that why she hadn't been around? 'Don't be daft,' he said. 'Why would I want to sleep with her?'

'If you were going to betray me,' she said, 'you could at least have shown some class. What's wrong with Helen Simmons? Patsy Goodwin, Alison James? But Diane Foster? I mean, honestly.'

He widened his eyes, his thoughts whizzing rapidly through everything he'd ever known about Paula. What would convince her she'd made a mistake? 'How could you believe something like that? Don't you have any faith in me?'

'You didn't sleep with her?'

'No!'

'Swear to me.'

He raised a hand, held it up, palm towards her. 'I swear,' he said solemnly. He wanted to ask her to swear that she hadn't slept with Johnny, but he couldn't do it. He was afraid she'd refuse.

Then, without another word, she leapt on him, pulled him violently towards her, wrapped her arms round him with unexpected strength and kissed him. Her lips were exquisitely soft. Johnny didn't exist. Nothing else mattered.

Johnny spent ages trying to decide how to tell Ma that he was getting married to Paula, knowing she would tell him he was too young, that the idea was ridiculous. But he'd do anything to make it possible – the engagement ring, the wedding, a house, a serious job; it would take time, but he could do it.

Goodness, he kept saying to himself. Me, a married man.

Practice sessions in front of the mirror. 'Listen, Ma. I know you don't really like Paula . . .'

'Why would you think that?' Her voice dull, unwilling to engage. 'She's a good cook, and you can't say more than that.'

'Do you think she'd make someone a good wife?'

Ma staring at him, the growing, dawning understanding – did this actually take place, or was it only in his imagination?

In the end, Johnny didn't care what Ma thought. Paula wanted him, and nothing would ever change that.

Only it turned out that Paula didn't want him.

When Nick woke, chilled, surprised to find that he'd been asleep, and she was gone, he wasn't worried. He walked back down the hill in the brilliance of the rising sun, to a background of cacophonous birdsong, thinking it was all agreed, that she belonged to him, that he belonged to her, that his future was secure. 'I love you both,' she'd whispered into Nick's ear, but he didn't believe her. He knew he was the one who really mattered – she'd just proved it.

He'd waited for a signal from her, a message. The days became weeks, months, and he kept waiting, assuming she'd come and find him at the end of term, then the end of the academic year, then the end of the course.

When he saw her mother in Bromsgrove and asked after her, a blankness came down over her face. 'She likes it there,' she said. 'She has lots of friends.'

It took a long, long time for him to understand that she'd never really cared about him, or Johnny, that nothing she'd said was true. There was no place in her life for the sons of a cleaner, local kids who lived in railway carriages, who climbed buildings for fun, who fell off because they couldn't stop arguing, whose experience was limited to the boundaries of Bromsgrove.

Why had she ever bothered with them? Were they just a diversion, a training ground for the real thing, curiosities? To her, they must have seemed interchangeable. A chance to experiment, test her abilities. A bargain, two for the price of one, quantity not quality.

One day, several months later, passing her house on his way to Asda, he realised it was empty. They'd all gone: Paula, her parents, Billy the dog. It was as if she'd never been there.

He never saw her again.

* * *

As Johnny stands in the kitchen, glaring at Nick, something strange happens. He wants to continue being furious, he wants to believe he could still lash out at his brother, stoke up the old animosity, make it hot and dangerous, but he's struggling to maintain it. It flared up easily enough earlier, like a match being struck, and burned brightly, but now it seems to have fizzled and gone out.

He's been nursing resentment about Paula, about the accident, about giving up tennis, for so long that its very familiarity has rendered it ineffective. The fuel of anger should still be there, locked up, waiting for an opportunity to rage unchecked, but after all these years of silence, it's evaporated. It's been gently leaking away without him realising, leaving only the residue. And now that it's been expressed, there's nothing left to say.

He unclenches his fists and feels foolish. 'Well,' he says. 'It was a long time ago.'

There's a long silence. Then Nick nods. 'We must be getting old,' he says.

15

'So no one's murdered anyone else, then,' says Zohra to Crispin as they drive back from the railway carriages. 'So much for that theory.'

'You can't be sure she's not plotting it, though.'

'Mimi thought she looked like the brothers. What did you think?'

Crispin shakes his head. 'No, I couldn't see it. She seemed quite normal, whereas the brothers were decidedly odd – well, Johnny, anyway. Do you think he's ever thrown away anything in his entire life?'

'You'd probably be odd if your sister had been murdered.'

They lapse into silence.

'I ought to be getting back,' says Zohra after a while. 'I have to get up at five o'clock.' But she's finding it difficult to summon a sense of urgency.

'I know,' says Crispin. 'We probably should have waited to go round to the carriages, but it was hard to resist Freddie and Mimi – they were so enthusiastic.'

'It was,' says Zohra. She studies his hands, placed firmly on the steering wheel, the nails short and slightly uneven with thin traces of oil visible round the rims. He scrubs them relentlessly every time they finish working on the engine, but it's impossible to clean them entirely. He's concentrating on the driving, watching the road. 'Crispin . . .'

'Mmm?'

'Can you pull over for a bit?' They've never discussed the events of their last term at school. She has always assumed he knew the basic facts, but he's never asked for details so she's never offered any. 'There's something I need to tell you. About Fiona.'

The pressure of A-levels was building, an axe hovering over Zohra's head, threatening to sever the last threads that were holding her up. She knew she had to find a way to study, the deadlines for coursework were imminent, but it was impossible to work in school. Everyone else would be studying earnestly in the quiet section of the sixth-form common room, but whenever she contemplated the possibility of sitting in that rarefied atmosphere, where silence was rigidly enforced, where every breath from every girl was thick with intelligence and confidence, she found herself swimming in sweat, tight with fear.

The problem was, she was a scholarship girl and everyone assumed she was brilliant. Before Fiona arrived, she always came top in all subjects. Nobody seemed to understand how much luck had been involved. And bluff.

But if she tried to work at home, the laptop was there, sitting next to her, nagging, willing her to log on to Facebook and check for messages, just check, just check . . .

And her parents were too interested.

'Should you be getting up now? The revision won't get done on its own.'

'Can you concentrate with music on? How is this possible?'

'Let me make you a nice cup of coffee. Give those brain cells a boost.'

'I fix you a little something, nice homemade biscuits, get the blood sugar circulating, give you brain energy.'

It mattered too much to them. She knew they were trying to be kind, but she wanted to scream every time they spoke to her.

She started going to Bromsgrove library, where she could be anonymous. She usually managed to find a desk in a corner of the library where she was almost invisible. At first, when she caught sight of pupils from Finstall Comp who'd taken part in joint sixth-form projects, she tried to hide, terrified that they'd seen her Facebook profile, but none of them gave any indication that they recognised her. She'd hardly spoken to them – Crispin was the only one who'd taken any notice of her.

The space was comforting, the hush, the artificial sense of calm.

But she still couldn't do any work. Even though she tried to persuade herself every morning that this day would be different, her mind was a vast empty vacuum, her thoughts so tangled, so confused that the prospect of negotiating the simplest reasoning felt impossible.

One Saturday morning, not long before the start of study leave, she arrived before nine and hovered outside, aching for silence and solitude. When the doors were unlocked, she slipped hurriedly past, her eyes fixed on the floor, and headed straight for her usual place, a single desk as far from the entrance as possible, screened by shelves. She laid out books in front of her, paper, pencils, rubbers, and stared at them without seeing, her mind as blank as ever. She needed a way out, a strategy that would allow her to withdraw with the least amount of fuss, but even that seemed hopeless. The screen of the computer reflected her face darkly. She had no intention of turning it on.

A librarian spotted her staring at the monitor and came up to her. 'You know we have free Internet access, don't you?' she said softly. 'It's easy to get online.'

Zohra was taken aback by the kindness in her voice. It made her want to cry. 'That's okay, I'm fine,' she whispered.

The librarian nodded. 'Well, if you need any help, let me know.'

She decided to copy out a question, a diagram, but the pencil hovered in the air, frozen over the blank piece of paper, and failed. She brought it slowly back to the desk.

Unexpectedly, a voice, quiet, but easy to hear in the surrounding silence, familiar: 'A thousand? Are you serious?'

Zohra jumped violently and then found herself unable to lift her head, incapable of looking round to locate the speaker. She forced herself to breathe, trying to control the thin gasps coming out of her mouth, and placed her hands flat on the desk to stop them shaking.

It was Fiona.

A man's voice, a Birmingham accent. 'That's the deal.'

What was going on? Drugs? Surely not. Fiona wouldn't – would she? Zohra lifted her eyes slightly, expecting to see feet, evidence of a presence. There was no one there. They were in another space, behind a bookcase.

The voices dropped. Two women greeted each other enthusiastically by the desk, briefly drowning out the closer, softer conversation.

Then Fiona's voice again, less polished than usual, slightly uneven. 'I'm perfectly capable – I could do it myself . . .' Every syllable was pronounced slowly, as if the words had been examined beforehand and analysed for precise meaning.

'Of course.'

'It's just – too much going on – it's so hard to fit it all in.' She was harder to hear than the man.

'No skin off my nose. I need the money, you need the essay. Mutual advantage.'

Essay? Why would she be talking to someone about an essay?

A woman walked past, rummaging noisily in her bag. The voices sank to a murmur.

'. . . when should the government intervene – prevent – take over? Demonstrate your reasoning.' Fiona was reading the words, her voice more uniform, more mechanical.

'Yes, yes, I've got it.'

It was their final piece of coursework – Economics – due in by the end of the week.

There was more talking in low voices, then a shuffling of feet. Zohra managed to look up in time to see a man walking purposefully past, his arms swinging. He wasn't as old as he sounded but he was confident in his manner, intense. He was carrying a folder under his arm.

A few moments later, Fiona followed him round the side of the shelves.

Zohra kept her head down, let her hair fall over her face. She fumbled with a pencil, but couldn't prevent the trembling in her fingers and dropped it. The sound as it hit the desk was thunderous. She left it there and tried instead to focus on the page in front of her, the empty piece of paper. She heard an intake of breath, a pause in Fiona's steps, saw her feet, in elegant sandals with wedge heels, halt in front of her desk.

There was a long silence.

The lines on the page were swimming, threads of black in a vast sea of nothing.

Eventually, after what felt like hours, Fiona moved, slowly at first, her footsteps heavy, muffled on the carpet, then faster, round the bookcase and away into the general murmur of the library.

Zohra sat motionless.

For Fiona, everything was so easy. Her hand was always the first to go up, ready with the answer before the rest of them had time to digest the question. That had been Zohra's role once, but Fiona had inhibited her, prevented her from thinking clearly. Her ability to calculate, to create patterns with figures, started to slow down and stagnate. She found herself going over and over the questions, no longer able to pick out the pathways, the numbers sluggish and sticky.

Why would Fiona pay someone to do her essay for her? None of this made sense.

Sun was pouring through the large glass window behind Zohra and she was unbearably hot. She had an overwhelming desire to sleep, her eyes aching with the need for a break, but whenever her eyelids drifted down, her mind snapped back into action. She was jogging on the spot, going nowhere. It was exhausting and she struggled to summon enough energy to get up. She had no idea what she was going to do, but she couldn't sit there any longer. She left the books out, put her pencil case next to them so that no one would take her place, trying to convince herself she would return once she'd had some fresh air, and stepped into the bright outside.

'Hi,' said Fiona, appearing in front of her.

'Hi,' said Zohra, turning to the side, unable to look her in the eye. She tried to pretend she was alone as she walked away, uncertain of her ability to maintain indifference, but she could hear the footsteps behind her. She stopped at the pedestrian crossing, knowing Fiona was close.

When the lights changed, Zohra crossed with Fiona at her side, heading towards the leisure centre. She realised immediately that this was a mistake. The shops on this side of the road were small and intimate: frame specialists, a jeweller, a florist. She couldn't dodge into one of them and lose Fiona. And if she went inside the leisure centre she would be trapped, with nowhere to hide. She should have gone in the opposite direction, into the crowded High Street amongst the market stalls and plenty of other people. She started to speed up, unsure what to do, her breathing becoming laboured.

Fiona remained alongside her, matching her pace, in perfect control. 'Zohra,' she said eventually. 'Wait. We need to talk.'

Zohra stopped and an overwhelming sense of despair flooded through her. She could never escape. Wherever she went, Fiona would be there, always there, right beside her, her voice an intrusive soundtrack, her presence tuned to the right pitch to confuse, paralyse, destroy. Zohra studied her feet, considered the way they rested on the pavement.

'Do you fancy a coffee?' asked Fiona. 'We could go to McDonald's?'

Zohra shook her head.

'I want to know,' said Fiona. She appeared to be calm, but a small tremble in her voice revealed her agitation. 'What did you hear? In the library?'

Zohra shook her head again, but she was thinking fast. This was Fiona as she had never seen her before. 'Nothing,' she said.

Then she looked up, aroused by a powerful sense of injustice. 'Are you going to pay him to do your coursework?' she asked, her voice loud and aggressive.

Fiona looked around nervously, as if there were spies everywhere. 'I thought you, of all people, might understand,' she said. 'Because nobody else does. My father, my mother, my brothers, they're all brilliant, and I can't keep up. Everyone just expects. In my family, second best isn't second best. It's failure. You can't be a runner-up. I'd be an outcast if I didn't come top in every exam. It's the highest marks or nothing. You have no idea . . .' Her words poured out, hot and frantic.

This was the person who had stolen her place, alienated her from her friends, made her redundant. And Zohra was almost certain by then that Fiona was Michelle from Facebook who she thought she knew but didn't. So if Fiona had started the rumours, she was also most likely to be the one who created the pictures that were circulating so freely. 'So you're going to cheat?' she said flatly.

Fiona stopped and stared at her, momentarily confused. 'Please Zohra,' she said. 'I'd really appreciate it if we kept this between us . . .'

Zohra had an overwhelming desire to give up and sink down to the ground. Fiona shouldn't be saying this. She's so desperate, she's telling me anyway, incriminating herself. Am I supposed to feel sorry for her, demonstrate compassion, show her how civilised people behave?

But she didn't possess a big enough store of energy for that kind of effort. 'Why should I?' she said.

'Look,' said Fiona, her voice strengthening a little. 'How much do you want? Money's no object.'

Zohra was shaken out of her exhaustion, astonished. People didn't really say things like this.

'You're offering me a bribe?' she said eventually, and even the words sounded artificial.

'Well – it's not really like that,' said Fiona.

'So what is it like?'

'I just need space, to give myself a breather, so I can pick up and get on with everything again. I'm trying to preserve my sanity.'

'Right,' said Zohra. She turned away and continued towards the leisure centre.

As she walked, she listened for footsteps behind her, a hand on her arm. But nothing happened. She kept going. When she reached the entrance, she turned back. Fiona was standing where she'd left her, staring after her, fixed into position.

Should she have done a deal? Asked her to back off, to withdraw from the group of friends so that Zohra could be part of their group again?

Of course not. You can't go backwards. You can't force other people to be friends. They did what they wanted to do; they'd all been willing to let it happen. They must have known about the Internet stuff. Even if they didn't start it, they didn't stop it. They were all complicit. The damage was done. She'd never feel safe with them again.

So what would she do with this information? Would she tell anyone?

She didn't have the slightest idea.

It's an odd sensation sitting in the car with Crispin, talking about Fiona, telling him what she's never told anyone before.

'She was cheating?' he says in astonishment. 'Really? Can you do that, pay someone to do your essays? Isn't it breaking the law?'

Zohra tries to laugh, but the sound lacks conviction. 'More like a moral law, I suppose, although you'd obviously be disqualified if the exam board found out. It's not exactly GBH, though, is it? Or breaking and entering. At least, not to most people . . .'

'But who was the guy? Why would he do it?'

Zohra shrugs. 'For the money, I suppose. He was probably a student, wanting to pay off his university loan.'

'But wouldn't the teachers notice – different style, that sort of thing?'

'Presumably the guy knew that it had to be A-level standard, and no one would have been surprised if Fiona had done extra research.'

He smiles. 'Not a world I was familiar with.'

Zohra pauses, briefly diverted. 'Why do you always do that? Sell yourself short? You're so clever, but you've never done anything about it.'

'I think you've just confirmed the reasonableness of my decision. I'd be competing against people who cheat.'

'Most people don't cheat.'

'If you say so.'

'You should have more faith in human nature.'

'My role models haven't been good. I grew up with Perry, don't forget, who doesn't rate formal education.'

'Handy that he has a home, then.'

'Which is falling down.'

'It's got a roof and running water – and he doesn't have to pay rent.'

'True. It's a useful set-up for someone who likes to do his own thing.'

'He needs the education system, though,' says Zohra. 'How else would he fund the railway? Our backers are educated people, with qualifications, with good jobs. That's why they've got money to spare.'

'So you still believe in education despite everything? Or only as an abstract concept?'

She almost smiles. 'That's probably closest to the truth.'

'So you grassed on Fiona, then?'

The smile dies. 'Well – it was more complicated than that.'

It was the last maths lesson before exam leave, the day after the encounter in the library. Zohra was once again staring at figures on a page, unable to see any significance in them.

'Zohra?' said Mrs Whitlock, making her jump. 'Have you worked it out already?'

'No, not yet,' mumbled Zohra, not sure why she'd been singled out. Maybe because she wasn't writing anything down. She wanted, needed, to escape.

There were still ten minutes of the lesson left and she wasn't certain she could make it to the end. Space, that's what she needed. Somewhere to think. 'May I go to the loo?' She spoke rigidly, knowing her teeth would chatter if she let down her guard.

'Yes, all right,' said Mrs Whitlock, glancing at the clock. 'But be as quick as possible.'

Zohra slid out of her seat and forced herself to stroll casually to the door without revealing her urgency. Once she'd left the room, she broke into a run, hoping nobody in the neighbouring classrooms would notice, ignoring the nearby loos and heading for the sixth-form block, which was usually deserted until lunch time. She'd never done this before, allowed herself to lose precious minutes from a lesson.

She went into a cubicle, locked the door and sat down on the closed seat, hugging her knees, trying to think clearly after her sleepless night, but still foggy with uncertainty. Should she use the information she'd unexpectedly acquired? She was clutching a grenade, her hands slippery with sweat, and she had to make a decision – as quickly as possible. It was in her possession, whether she wanted it or not, and she needed to get rid of it. But how? Throw it away, into a wasteland, where no one would get hurt? Direct it precisely to the place that would cause most damage? Or should she just run with it and let it explode when it was ready?

The bell went. End of the lesson. Now she would have to interrupt the next lesson to get her bag back and she'd be late for Physics. But she still couldn't move.

The outside door opened and someone came in, feet careful and controlled as they stepped on to the tiled floor. Zohra tried to hold herself still, not wanting to give away her presence, expecting the other girl to go into a cubicle and eventually leave. But nothing happened. Everything went silent. Was there anyone there at all? Zohra listened intently, her ears aching with the effort. She was sure she could hear the rustle of a blouse as an arm swayed through the air; the shuffling of toes inside a shoe; soft, patient breaths, the sound of waiting.

She didn't know what to do. She couldn't wait forever. If she was too late for Physics, she would be questioned in front of everyone, and she didn't have an explanation. But eventually someone would be sent to find her. After what seemed like hours, she got up and smoothed down her skirt. Should she flush the loo? It would look strange if she didn't.

Why was she so worried about giving the right impression? If there was someone there, they knew she was there too.

She slotted the bolt back, took a deep breath and stepped out.

Fiona was standing a few feet away, watching her as she came out, her face cold and expressionless. 'Why didn't you go to the loos near the classroom?' she asked.

So she'd been looking for her.

Zohra moved carefully, as if she was releasing locked joints, as if she was emerging from a condition of frozen immobility, just beginning to thaw out. 'Hi,' she said, her voice thin. She moved to the right, heading for the door.

Fiona stepped in front of her and blocked her.

Zohra tried the other direction.

Fiona followed.

With a growing sense of dread, Zohra realised she was trapped. 'What do you want?' she whispered.

'What do you think I want?' Fiona's voice was low and tense.

But what Zohra had was knowledge, and you can't give knowledge back. 'I don't know,' she said.

Fiona leaned suddenly towards her, uncomfortably close, her pale face expanding and distorting as it got nearer. Zohra tried to retreat, but found she was backed up against the cubicle frame and had nowhere to go. She let out a wail, and it was a pitiful whine of terror, like a dog in pain.

Fiona laughed and backed away a little. 'Scared? Good.' She jerked forward again, her nose now only millimetres away from Zohra's. 'Because if you ever . . .' She paused for effect. 'If you *ever* say anything to anyone, you'll regret it for the rest of your life.' Her eyes were glittering unnaturally, glassy fish eyes, as black as the gloss of her hair, shining like plastic beads.

I don't have to let her intimidate me, thought Zohra. I could push her over – if I do it quickly, when she's not expecting it. Then I could run. And run and run and never come back. She tried to raise a hand, test its strength, but it was too heavy, too sluggish, unwilling to obey her instructions. She was seizing up. The smooth running of the machinery of her body had faltered – an electrical failure, a shortage of oil. She couldn't move.

Fiona grabbed her arm. 'I know people,' she said. 'I have connections. My brothers, my parents – they have friends who look out for me. I know where you live. Your dad's shop isn't doing so well these days, is it?'

She's threatening me, thought Zohra, sifting the words through her mind, unable to believe what she was hearing. Could this really be happening? She'd been threatened before, when she was younger – 'I'll tell my mum you hit me'; 'Say that again and I'll get my brother to beat you up'; 'We'll be waiting for you after school'. But that was all hot air. Regurgitated words from the television. There was nothing artificial here. Could Fiona's family really have enough influence to damage her parents' business? Was she suggesting something even more frightening?

Fiona started to dig her nails into Zohra's arm. Zohra's mouth dropped open, and a tidal wave of a scream swept up from deep inside her stomach, wild and uncontrollable, into her throat and out. She couldn't stop it. She didn't even try to. It kept going, reverberating round the room, echoing in repeating cycles, on and on, only pausing for the next breath, and it seemed to be coming from another source, far away.

She could dimly hear doors banging, voices shouting.

The pressure on her arm ceased as Fiona let go. Zohra's legs lost all their strength and she felt herself drop to the floor.

Then there were people everywhere, soothing hands, questions. She couldn't speak, couldn't tell anyone anything. When the school nurse came with a blanket and led her to the health centre, persuading her to put one reluctant foot in front of the other, the entire school seemed to be in the corridors, watching. She could hear whispering, louder than if they'd been shouting. *Exams – can't cope – breakdown . . .*

Her dad came to fetch her. The nurse reassured him, talking in a hushed voice that Zohra wasn't supposed to hear. 'Don't worry too much. She's probably been overworking. I've seen this kind of thing before. These girls – they wind each other up, create hysteria. I'm sure she'll be fine after some time on her own. She's got a few weeks yet before the exams. Best not to push for explanations. She probably doesn't understand it herself.

Zohra stayed in bed for three days. Her parents took it in turns to come and talk gently to her, trying to be encouraging. Everything would be all right. She just needed a good rest. There was no need to go into school any more. She could revise at home and just go in for the exams. She didn't tell anyone about what happened. She couldn't have explained it.

Her parents were painfully kind, making enormous efforts to avoid asking questions, but their thoughtfulness just added to Zohra's distress.

'If you miss your friends,' said her mother. 'You can go in if you want to, up to you.'

Zohra shook her head. She understood how hard it was for them. They wanted to be sympathetic, but at the same time she had to sit the exams. They weren't being unkind. They just knew that her education was too important to be abandoned in a moment of weakness. She was a scholarship girl. As a family, they had an obligation to the school.

Every time they left the room, she allowed herself to cry into the pillow, desperately but silently.

Nobody mentioned Fiona.

Crispin doesn't speak for some time when she stops. After a while, he puts out his hand and takes hers. 'Girls,' he says at last. 'They're worse than boys, aren't they?'

'It's okay, I'm over it,' says Zohra, pulling her hand away, slightly embarrassed. 'It was all a long time ago.'

'I realise that,' he says. 'But I wanted to hold your hand.'

'I see,' says Zohra, unwilling to believe he really means this – although it would be nice if he did. 'Like you do.'

'I had no idea Fiona was like that,' he says. 'I always thought she was so in control.'

'So did I,' says Zohra. 'But I was wrong.' She places her hand in her lap and he picks it up again. This time she lets him.

Rain starts to patter on to the roof of the car, a gentle downpour that provides a background rhythm for her thoughts. The light from the nearby streetlight shivers in the rain and fractures, softening the edges of the road. It blurs the border between seeing and not seeing. A solitary car whooshes past.

'I emailed the headmistress, her secretary, the head of Sixth Form and everyone else in my list of contacts,' she says. 'I created a new address and sent it on a public computer so no one could trace it back to me. I made it clear I knew Fiona and described the conversation I'd overheard.'

He stares at her, his eyes wide. 'Wow! But why didn't you just post it on Twitter and tell the whole world in one go?'

'I didn't think our headmistress would be familiar with Twitter – it wasn't quite as widespread as it is now. And not everyone had Smartphones either, so it took longer to get around than it would today.' She turns to him. 'You must have seen it.'

He nods slowly. 'I did. And I heard the rumours about who sent it. I didn't believe them.'

Zohra smiles at his loyalty.

But . . . weren't you scared? That something terrible would happen? What about Fiona's secret army?'

Zohra thought for a moment, trying to reconstruct her reasoning. 'I'm not really sure,' she says. 'I think I believed her, but at the same time I didn't, if you see what I mean. All that melodrama. It was too . . . too remote from anything I knew or understood. And I realised that she wouldn't be able to tell her family that she'd been cheating. What I do remember is that I started to get angry – and as time went on, I got angrier and angrier—'

'Way to go! I've never seen you lose your temper.'

'No.' She can still remember the sensation, its unfamiliarity, but also its power; how it developed into a raging fever over those three days while she was in bed. It became an inferno, burning so ferociously inside her, feeding on itself, growing and growing, that the desire for an outlet became overwhelming. When she got up for the first time and dressed, she'd formed a plan, and was racing through details, covering all contingencies, examining the exits. She went straight to the station, caught a train into Birmingham, walked to the library and set up the new account. Then she told her story. When she'd finished, she went home again, settled down in her room and pretended to revise.

Crispin stares at her for a moment, his face orange in the light from outside the car. 'I knew it was bad, but not that bad,' he says thoughtfully. 'I wish you'd told me.'

'How could I? I couldn't even think about it myself without panicking.'

'I don't think people who knew you really believed you were the one who sent the email.'

'They did, I'm sure. Nobody actually said so, but you could tell they knew.'

'But why would they make that connection? Fiona would hardly have told them.'

'Who else would make up such wicked lies? I was the obvious culprit, the outsider, the one who no longer fitted in. And, let's face it – they were right.'

'But surely they'd have understood. They were your friends once. Were they really that bad?'

She stares at him. 'Are you trying to excuse them, tell me I was just being paranoid?'

'No, of course not.' He squeezes her hand.

She likes the sensation, the warmth that it offers, the unfamiliar comfort. She can feel his nails, rubbing against her skin. She'd like to check for sharp edges, see if they need sanding down with a file and offer to do it for him, but now is not the moment.

'Did anyone ever ask you about it?'

'No, never. The school must have assumed it was someone who didn't know Fiona very well, someone who overheard the conversation and just wanted to cause trouble. Let's face it, there are a lot of strange people out there who resent anyone who's better off, better looking, cleverer than they are. And I assume her family deleted all her horrible messages to me, so no one would have known that we had anything to do with each other.'

'But what about that business in the loos? Didn't anyone ask you about that?'

'No one knew she was there – she must have slipped out before anyone else arrived. Most people had forgotten I existed, anyway. That's how much impact I had on them.' She doesn't mean to sound bitter, but she knows it's in her voice. The loss of friends she'd known for years. At the time, it felt as if she'd died. 'And you know what happened next.'

She watches him in the half-light as he nods but doesn't reply.

They drive through the darkened streets almost in silence.

They're nearly back at Zohra's house when Crispin jerks to a halt.

'What's the matter?' says Zohra.

'Nathan!' he says. 'We're meant to be taking him home.'

They find him on the Wychington platform, sitting on one of the benches. He's just visible in the moonlight, his back straight against the wooden slats, his feet placed side by side in front of him, patiently motionless, confident of Crispin's return.

'What would he have done if we hadn't come back?' asks Zohra as they climb the steps towards him.

'He'd still be there tomorrow,' says Crispin.

'I thought Perry would take him home.'

'I didn't,' says Crispin. 'Nathan doesn't understand the concept of alternative plans. And Perry wouldn't have given it a thought.'

Nathan's eyes snap open when he hears them approaching, the whites gleaming in the inadequate light. He jumps to his feet, grinning. 'Hi Crisp, Zohra. How did it go?' He shakes his arms and legs vigorously. 'Not comfy, that bench.'

'Sorry we're so late,' says Zohra. 'We've been to see the Greenwoods' carriages.' As soon as she's said it, she remembers that they weren't going to tell him. He'll be annoyed all over again that he didn't go with them.

But his reaction is more muted than expected. Either he's tired or he had a good time helping Perry with the welding. 'Again?'

'Freddie and Mimi wanted to see them.'

'Are they s-selling?' he asks as they head for the car.

'Unlikely,' says Crispin.

'Why not?'

'They live there. It's their home.'

But Nathan is not easily convinced. 'You can persuade them, Crisp. You're good at that s-sort of thing.'

When they arrive outside the block of flats where Nathan lives with his mother, he doesn't want to get out. 'You should have taken me with you. I'm the expert, remember? I know everything there is to know about trains.'

'Time for bed, Nathan,' says Crispin wearily. 'Let's discuss it tomorrow.'

'I'd have examined them, checked the frames. Then we'd know for certain if they'd be any good.'

'Well, they're not going anywhere for now,' says Zohra.

'But they're s-so close – the line leads directly off our track,' says Nathan. 'I've s-seen it on the maps – it would be easy.'

'Get a move on, Nathan,' says Crispin. 'Your mum'll be wondering where you are.'

The communal door to the flats opens and a woman, tall and gaunt, in a raspberry-coloured dressing gown, steps out, propping the heavy metal door open behind her with her right elbow. Her hair is completely grey, cut into a sharp bob and she's wearing glasses. She waves and a smile transforms her weary face from severe to amiable.

Crispin winds down the window. 'Sorry we're so late, Holly,' he says. 'There was a lot to do.'

'They forgot me,' says Nathan as he gets out.

'No, they didn't, sunshine,' she says. Her voice is low, tired, kind. 'That would be impossible. There's too much of you to forget.'

'You've got that right,' says Crispin.

'Thank you for having him,' she says. 'You know I'm always grateful.'

Nathan sighs. 'I'm a grown man,' he says. 'Does she really have to wait up for me?'

Neither Zohra nor Crispin knows how to reply.

'By the way,' he says, indicating Zohra with his hand. 'This is the woman I'm going to marry.'

'Stop talking nonsense,' says his mum, 'and get in here now. It's far too late for this kind of shenanigans.'

Nathan sighs. 'Land of nod, then,' he says, without a trace of irony, and shuffles up to the door. His mum waves at Crispin and Zohra.

'Captain coming on board,' says Nathan, looking up at the window of his room in the flat on the top floor. 'Beam me up.'

His mum smiles. 'Yes, beam him up, someone. Please. But do it quietly.'

They watch him go in with his mother, and the door swings shut behind them. 'We should have brought him home ages ago,' says Crispin. It's way past his bedtime.'

* * *

Nobody told her what happened to Fiona. Nobody telephoned, nobody emailed, nobody came into the shop and spoke to her father.

The first they knew about it was at half past ten in the evening, on *Midlands Today*, after the main news. Zohra was curled up in an armchair, sipping a cup of hot chocolate, gazing into space, no longer angry, but numb, not listening, not thinking. Her mother was working on her usual embroidery – colourful, intricate scenes of local landmarks, which she sends as gifts to relatives in India. Her father was sitting at the desk in the corner of the room, doing his accounts on the computer. Her mother looked up at the television and made a loud exclamation. 'Zohra? You know this Chinese girl.'

'What girl?' Zohra focused and recognised the face on the screen. It was Fiona.

'I saw her,' said her mother. 'In your Shakespeare play. She was the queen, Titania, yes?'

Fiona's body had been found in the park. She'd gone there, very early in the morning before it was light, and hanged herself. She was found by some passing schoolboys at eight o'clock.

The next day, when Zohra went into school for an exam she wouldn't be able to do, people looked past her as if she didn't exist. She knew that they blamed her.

When they held the inquest, she waited to be summoned, steeled herself to tell the truth. But nothing happened. She existed in a bubble, apart, completely invisible.

She kept going back to that conversation in the park and Fiona's reaction to her brothers, realising in hindsight how much influence they had on her. How could fear of failure, fear of letting them down, lead her to such drastic action? Had she tried to confide in Zohra then, almost revealed a vulnerability that was usually carefully concealed?

Every night for about a year, Zohra would wake at three thirty and find herself inhabiting Fiona's life. It still happens occasionally even now, after all this time. She experiences the suffocating pressure of Fiona's family's high expectations; the impossibility of failure, the desperation, the terror; the brief period when she thought she might have found a solution; then the darkness that engulfed her when she realised she'd been found out. As Zohra lies there in the middle of the night, the overwhelming sensation that she experiences is Fiona's loneliness. Drifting through a dark, desolate space with no end, no destination, no distant sanctuary. She would have known that a rescue mission was out of the question.

I sent her there, thinks Zohra.

She knows it was her fault.

16

Nick eases Johnny in front of him towards the road, pushing aside the damp, low-hanging branches, trying to give the impression that today's expedition is going to be a triumph. He's struggled to persuade him to come.

Johnny's first excuse: 'I've twisted my ankle, tripped over a computer base – you know, the sort that nobody uses any more. Should have moved it, forgot it was there – should have switched on the light. I don't think I'm going to be able to walk.'

Nick: 'No problem. She's picking us up in a taxi. Maybe you should start to clear up a bit, make it all safer.'

Second excuse: 'I can't do the clothes. I haven't got suitable gear.'

Nick: 'Doesn't matter. As long as they're clean.'

Third excuse: 'I'm not really interested in trains.'

'Course you are, just like everyone else. And you've got an even greater reason to be interested. You live in one.'

Earlier this morning, after Nick had listened in vain for a sign of life from Johnny, unable to hear even the usual sounds of him ambling through Demeter, he'd made a decision to go in. They were being picked up at half past twelve. Time was running out.

He found Johnny still sprawled in his bed, awake but pale-faced, blinking with shock at the presence of his brother. Nick squeezed past him to open the curtains. They resisted and there was a danger that the rail would come away from its supports, so he gave up and put on the light instead. He wasn't going to take pity on him.

'She'll be here in half an hour.'

'I won't be able to go. I've got a splitting headache.'

'Get dressed and have a shave. There'll be coffee, toast and paracetamol ready for you in the kitchen in ten minutes.' Okay, so Johnny hadn't travelled far from the railway carriages for decades, but that didn't mean he never should again. 'It's you and me and Debs, or whoever she is. We're going to pretend to be a family for the first time in years and you're not going to get out of it.'

She's standing by her taxi, watching them as they emerge from the path. 'You're meant to be in thirties dress,' she calls. 'That's what they said. Same period as the engine. Did you forget?' She's wearing a flimsy dress – pale blue, possibly silk, covered in tiny yellow roses – and a fur jacket with short sleeves. A long string of pearls hangs down almost to her waist. Her hat fits snugly round her head, framing her face, making her look younger. She's applied scarlet lipstick too liberally, overlapping the edges of her thin lips, and it accentuates the surrounding wrinkles.

A sudden brisk breeze whirls round them, and Nick looks up at the heavy clouds scudding across the sky. Will she be warm enough? he thinks worriedly. That jacket's designed more for show than protection. 'Where did you get the outfit?'

She smiles and twirls. 'Online – themed fancy-dress parties are all the rage. Good, isn't it?'

'You're in the wrong decade,' says Johnny unexpectedly. 'Beads were the twenties. You know, *Thoroughly Modern Millie*.'

'You're right,' says Nick, surprised that Johnny remembers. They'd gone to the film together – Debs, Bev, him and Johnny. It was meant to be a special treat – he can't remember what it was in aid of – but he was only twelve, and it had bored him. The only thing that has stayed in his mind is the long necklace, the way it wouldn't hang straight because Julie Andrews's bosoms got in the way. He does remember studying Debs and Bev when they came out and attempting a joke. 'Not much use either of you wearing long necklaces, then.' They'd tried to be offended, which had been his intention, but he was surprised to discover that they seemed pleased.

If she's Debs, or Bev, she should remember this, but she doesn't seem to. 'I don't care,' she says. 'They could have still been wearing them in the thirties, for all you know, and anyway it's fun to dress up. At least I've tried. What's your excuse?'

Nick had been embarrassed by the entire concept. He wanted to go and watch the first journey on the Wychington railway, but he wasn't prepared to consider fancy dress. Instead he put on a suit, as if he was going to work, but after much consideration in front of his only mirror, removed the tie.

Johnny presumably no longer possesses a suit that fits. His jeans are worn, but they are clean and even still faintly blue. His green and red checked shirt, although faded, with an interesting line of tiny holes on one side that could be the result of sparks from a firework (unlikely) or fat from a frying pan, is reasonably respectable. The tweed jacket (at least thirty years old, judging by the style) that he's wearing over the shirt makes no pretence of meeting in the middle. He's tried to make an effort, but the overall effect is one of creased neglect.

Johnny's lack of ironing has always been a source of irritation to Nick. There's never been any evidence that he knows how an iron works, despite his claims that he uses it regularly. Many years ago, at a time when these things mattered, Nick set little traps, wanting to prove that Johnny was lying. He positioned the iron at an odd angle, smeared something sticky on the handle, placed a potato peeler beside it that would have to be moved if the iron was used. But Johnny must have guessed what he was doing and passed the tests every time, lining it up more sensibly, wiping the handle, removing the potato peeler. After a while, they gave up the game and now the iron is always in exactly the same position whenever Nick uses it, and Johnny's clothes remain creased.

'I couldn't find my usual thirties outfit,' says Johnny. 'I must have chucked it out when we got to the forties.'

Nick exchanges a grudging grin with him, impressed. He hasn't heard Johnny respond so quickly, or attempt a joke, for a very long time.

'Oh, you two,' she says. 'You never had any intention of dressing up. You're completely hopeless, the pair of you.'

The breeze catches the hem of her dress and she has to fight to keep it down. 'Are you sure you'll be warm enough?' asks Nick.

'That's what the jacket's for,' she says. 'Don't worry, the fur's not real.'

'We're going for the train,' says Johnny. 'Not the clothes.'

'Stop complaining,' she says as they climb into the taxi, which is more a luxury car than a cab. She sits in the front.

'Where you go?' asks the driver, who introduces himself as Faraz. He's an unusually small man and has his seat raised to its highest level so he can see over the steering wheel.

'Wychington Hall,' says Nick.

'Serious? Why anyone go there? Nothing to see – just falling-down house, old wreck. Nobody live there – guarantee, trust me. Idiot place to go.'

'Your job is to take us where we ask,' she says. 'Not act as the local guide.'

'You crazy old lady. You think you know Bromsgrove more than me? I been here ten years, you been here ten minutes.'

'I may be old and crazy, but at least the country I come from has a stable government.'

He sighs. 'I take you. No skin off my nose. But don't you run to me when all goes wrong.'

Neither of them seem offended by the exchange. In fact, they seem to be enjoying it.

'You must know about it,' says Nick. 'The railway restoration at Wychington. It's the first run today – a big event.'

'Too busy to notice,' he says. 'I drive this lady backwards and forwards, not a moment to myself.'

She sighs. 'Drive, Faraz, just drive.'

They set off. Johnny huddles into his seat as if the passing landscape is too open, too threatening, and his legs start to jiggle, faster and faster as the distance between him and the railway carriages increases. The seats are large and luxurious, so he can't disturb anyone physically, but his increasingly frantic movements are disconcerting and the air around him seems to distort and fragment, reflecting his distress. Nick would like to be supportive, but he can't think what to say.

She half turns. 'Don't worry, Johnny,' she says. 'It'll be good, you'll see.'

And they're children again, shepherded by their big sister, their surrogate mother. She's standing in for Ma, who's out working as usual. It's Debs in front of them, knowing how to deal with Johnny, Debs who was always there to protect them from potential disasters, who tackled mankind on their behalf, who came to watch their matches, cheered them on and applauded, who hugged them if they won. The protective shield that ultimately failed.

How could she possibly be Bev? thinks Nick. How could they ever have doubted her?

She's pretending, thinks Johnny. He focuses on the thought, using it to distract himself from the enormity of the world slipping past the car window. She thinks she's being the big sister, the one in charge, but she can't possibly understand how it used to be. Debs understood his anxiety, talked to him in a way that was genuinely soothing. It was never empty reassurances. She meant everything she said and he believed her. He's not at all sure how or why it worked, but he can still remember the sense of safety he could draw from her, the belief that things would work out even if they didn't look as if they would. This is not what he's picking up from the woman sitting in the front of the car, the stranger who claims to be Debs. If he's going to survive this expedition, it'll be on his own strength, not hers.

They turn off the road and take the long drive up to Wychington Hall, following giant yellow hands attached to trees that point them in the right direction. A large field to the side of the house has been allocated as the car park and several rows of vehicles are parked on it in orderly lines: cars, minibuses, even a St John's ambulance.

'Okay,' says Faraz, staring at the house. The day has brightened and the building, much bigger than Johnny was expecting, is glowing in the afternoon sun. 'Not so bad maybe.'

'You said it was a wreck,' she says. 'It just goes to show you should never make an assessment of something you've never seen.'

'Not usually need to see,' says Faraz, tapping the side of his head. 'I know things.'

'Apparently not,' says Nick.

They queue briefly at the entrance. A man in a peaked cap, with a whistle on a lanyard round his neck and an amiable grin on his face, directs Faraz past the existing rows of parked cars to a dropping-off place.

'To be fair,' she says, examining the house as they drive closer, 'it's in urgent need of repair. It must be incredibly draughty – there's more rot than wood in those window frames. Crying shame. Why don't they do something about it?'

'They probably can't afford it,' says Nick.

'Of course they can,' she says. 'People who own property like that always have money. They just don't like to spend it. Anyway, it doesn't have to cost a fortune. Someone just needs to get up on that roof and fix some of the guttering.'

'Quite a lot of it, actually,' says Nick. 'It goes on for miles.'

'Even a small amount would make a big difference. If it was my house, I'd be up there like a shot.'

'You'd go up on a roof?' asks Johnny, astonished. Debs was the one who would have done that, leapt up and tackled the impossible head-on. Not Bev. She only ever attempted something once she'd been shown the way by Debs.

She laughs. 'Well – maybe not now. But not so long ago I'd have done it. If you're married to someone like my husband, a man who could fix anything, you pick things up. You'd be surprised what I can do. With the right tools, Mack used to say, you can mend the world.'

Mack is starting to sound irritating. Johnny doesn't believe in the image she presents of him. With a name like that, he should be cooking burgers, not climbing ladders.

But Nick must have also made the connection with the Debs they used to know. He stares at her for a few moments, then at the roof, then back at her. 'Hmm,' he says. He opens the door and gets out. 'Are you coming to look around,' he says, leaning his arm on the roof of the car and bending down to peer in at Faraz. 'According to the publicity, everything's free. They've got entertainment and refreshments.'

'Not possible right now,' says Faraz. 'I come back later with family. Good for kids.'

'Give me a hand, Johnny,' she says as she struggles to get out of her seat.

Johnny goes round to her door and offers his arm, which she clutches awkwardly. He feels her hesitation, then her gradual trust in his strength as he brings his other arm round and eases her out. She sways for a few seconds, leaning heavily on him until she recovers her balance, and draws herself upright. He's surprised by her frailty – she's been hiding it well – and finds himself relaxing a little, as if her dependence has strengthened him.

'Thank you, Johnny,' she says and flashes him a smile.

And this time her response offers genuine comfort. His heart misses a step.

But she's not well. She must have been pretending to be more robust than she actually is.

They stand together and watch while Faraz manoeuvres the car round and heads back to the entrance. Then they walk slowly into the field where the action is taking place. There are far more people than Johnny expected, and a considerable number of them have made the effort to wear thirties dress.

There's safety in the artificiality of it all, a reminder of the black-and-white movies he knows so well. Because it's a period that existed before he was born, he doesn't have to worry about how to fit in. By concentrating on the outfits, he finds he can negotiate the crowd without seeing individuals. Some costumes are triumphantly successful. Others have missed the period completely. Most of them haven't paid enough attention to details, but they give the right impression.

There are stalls dotted around the field, piled with food, and a large table with several tea urns where ladies in flowery aprons and with curlers in their hair (they got that wrong – no thirties housewife went out in curlers) are pouring cups of tea. ALL DONATIONS GRATEFULLY RECEIVED, says a sign. It's not clear if it refers to cakes or money, but several coins have been left on empty plates.

'We should have brought cakes,' she says.

'They seem to have managed well enough without our help,' says Nick.

The small crowds by the refreshment stalls make Johnny nervous, so when the others work their way to the front he doesn't follow them. He stands awkwardly on his own, self-conscious in his jeans and jacket, wishing he'd had the nerve to dress up, then rotates slowly, making an effort to focus on the surrounding scene. There are one or two fairground attractions – an ice-cream stall, a man dressed as Popeye holding a bunch of balloons and accompanied by Betty Boop, and an ineffective coconut shy, where the coconuts are too far away and even the teenagers with all their determination can't make an impression – but mostly people are standing around drinking cups of tea, laughing and admiring each other's outfits. Children are roaming in gangs, chasing each other, grabbing anything handy to keep their balance as they skid round corners, annoying the adults. He's embarrassed by his inactivity, so when he sees the railway platform stretching out along the edge of the field, he sets off immediately, pretending to be purposeful.

It's a long, low, featureless platform, hollow underneath, with great wild clumps of laurels, buddleia, rhododendrons and rosebay willowherb filling the space. Everything has been chopped back aggressively, but the plants are already sending out vigorous new shoots, threatening to rise up and retake their original territory. The volunteers have evidently worked hard to introduce some character to the platform, erecting two small buildings at one end, one a ticket office and the other a waiting room, separated by raised beds filled with pink and white pelargoniums. On the side of the buildings, posters have been put up – BRIDLINGTON, FUN AND SUN FOR EVERYONE; THE BROADS, IT'S QUICKER BY RAIL – and there are several gleaming wooden benches and lampposts placed at regular intervals along the platform.

Large signs announce the name of the station – WYCHINGTON HALT – in freshly painted white letters on a maroon background. A smaller sign, not yet attached, rests against the side of a bench. DO NOT USE THE TOILET WHILE TRAIN IS STANDING IN THE STATION. Just past the platform at the far end, there's a set of red and white signals, which must be more for cosmetic purposes than any practical use: with only a single line and one engine, there won't be much demand for them. But they look good.

Two wide sets of metal steps lead up to the platform from the field, one at each end. Goods trains were probably loaded here, filled with produce from the estate and other farms further down the line, then transported to the main line at Bromsgrove and on to Worcester, where they would have been connected to cross-country trains and dispatched to ports or factories across the country.

At the opposite end from the signals, there's a gigantic shed with a water tank just in front. Underneath, huge, black and shiny, hissing, spitting, shooting clouds of steam into the air every few minutes, sits a monstrous dragon, blinking lazily at the brightness of the day as it emerges from its lair, confident of its place in the world. The name, ENIGMA, is fixed to the side in large gold letters that glitter and dazzle in the afternoon sunshine.

Johnny walks along the base of the platform to the end, by the shed, where he can get a better view of the engine without climbing the steps. Several men in black donkey jackets are crawling over and under the train, moving levers backwards and forwards, tapping on the side of the wheels with hammers, rubbing black greasy rags over any part that catches their attention. Wise, safe, solid men, who know everything there is to know about trains, who can tell by listening where there's a blocked valve, who can find with their fingertips a tiny crack in the metalwork, who hear sweetness in the build-up of steam. We are the experts, they are silently telling everyone.

The engine gives a loud whistle to summon its audience, and people start to make their way towards it. A crowd gathers, but Johnny watches without joining them. Most of them are too young to remember when all trains were steam trains. There was a time – he must have been about five or six – when he went with his dad to Weston-super-Mare. He doesn't know where Nick or Ma or Debs were, but he remembers sitting by the window, trying to read the station signs as they whizzed past, moving his head with the rhythm of the train. He was never quick enough.

His dad sat opposite, gazing out, his eyes moving rapidly from side to side, as if he couldn't see anything. But he could see everything. His eyes shone, his face was full of delight, wonder, contentment. He looked up, saw Johnny watching him, and grinned. 'There's a treat in store for you today, son,' he said. 'You're going to see the sea.'

But when they arrived at Weston, the sea was so far away that they couldn't see it at all. They seemed to walk forever, trying to reach it, but gave up in the end. Johnny's legs were too short. So they stood and gazed towards where the sea should be.

'I'll take you to Suffolk when you're older,' his dad said. 'Then you'll see the real ocean, beaches where you can launch boats. None of this half-baked nonsense.'

When they got home, they pretended that they'd seen the sea.

'We paddled,' said his dad. 'So cold our toes turned to ice, all white and solid.'

Johnny watched him and said nothing. It seemed easy enough to lie – you just opened your mouth and said whatever you wanted to say – but somehow he didn't think he could do it. He couldn't quite work out how his father managed to sound so convincing.

They never did go to Suffolk. His dad died before he had the chance.

One day he was there, the next he wasn't. Ma offered a brief explanation. 'Typical of your father. Off drinking, careless with our money, not taking his responsibilities seriously. Even when they fished him out of the canal, his pockets were empty.' Nick probably asked for more details, but Johnny didn't know how to. Ma gave the impression that she was ashamed, that she didn't want to be the widow of someone who was so often drunk. She seemed to have forgotten the good part of him, the soft, kind side, the childish jokes he would offer to make her laugh.

But at the funeral – they missed half a day of school – he was shocked to see tears slipping down Ma's cheeks during the last hymn. It was the only time he ever saw her cry, and he realised for the first time that people don't always say what they mean. When she dropped them back at school, she seemed completely normal. After that, the only person who ever spoke about him was Debs, and she never gave any more information, just referred to him casually in the past tense. Ma just seemed to erase him from her life, acted as if he was irrelevant.

Standing in front of the engine, Johnny wishes he could go back to the time of steam, the trip to Weston-super-Mare. It was all so easy then. There was someone to tell you what to do. You didn't have to make decisions. Everyone was alive.

'It's a good name, *Enigma*,' says a voice at his side.

He jumps. He hadn't realised there was anyone so close to him.

'Only me.' It's her, maybe Debs, possibly the only person left who might be able to tell him more about his dad. She doesn't say anything else and they stand together for a few seconds.

He doesn't look at her, aware of her calming presence next to him, comfortable with the silence. She must be Debs. She can still do what she used to do. Reassure – not with empty words, but by creating a sensation, by sending vibrations through the air. Everything will be all right, she says, without actually saying it.

Nick picks up a white paper plate and contemplates the cakes before him. Handwritten notes identify each one. Cherry cake, chocolate gateau with chocolate buttons embedded in the icing, lemon and pineapple upside-down cake, raspberry and almond . . .

'Good, isn't it?' says a voice behind him.

He turns and finds Crispin and an older man watching him.

'Hello,' says Nick. 'Excellent turnout.'

'Even better than we expected, and we were optimistic.'

'Quite right too. It's worth celebrating. Bromsgrove's first heritage railway.'

Crispin is wearing loose, baggy trousers, a loud check jacket with broad lapels, and a trilby. It's not quite right for the period, but at least he's tried. The other man, a similar age to Nick, has not. He's wide and stocky, shorter than Crispin, and there's a clear resemblance between the two of them. The older man looks like a farmer or a fisherman; someone who spends long days out of doors. His grey hair has been pulled back, not very neatly, and tied into a ponytail at the nape of his neck with black velvet ribbon – an odd concession to respectability. Otherwise, his jeans are about the same age as Johnny's and his shirt is frayed round the collar.

'My father, Peregrine,' says Crispin.

'Call me Perry,' he says and grins, immediately likeable.

'You should meet my brother,' says Nick. 'I suspect you'd hit it off.' Stupid thing to say. Appearance doesn't necessarily draw people together.

'Ah,' says Perry. 'You're the railway carriage men.'

Nick is embarrassed. 'I'm not at all sure our carriages would measure up to your magnificent locomotive. They're falling apart – not enough care or attention in recent years.'

Crispin is diverted by two women trying to attract his attention. 'Sorry,' he says. 'Got to go. Journalists.'

'Did your brother come with you?' asks Perry.

'Yes,' says Nick. 'He's with – um – my sister.' Should he be telling him this? But he's testing himself, watching for his reaction to see if it sounds plausible, trying to gauge how it feels when he says it out loud.

He shouldn't have said it. What if someone has overheard? They'll think he's finally flipped. 'Over from Canada,' he says. 'We hadn't seen her for years.' This seems the safest explanation. It occurs to him suddenly, alarmingly, that Perry was probably living at Wychington Hall when Debs or Bev died. Would he remember?

But Perry gives no indication that anything rings a bell. He was probably away at boarding school – that was how those sort of people did things. 'Have you found any carriages yet?' asks Nick hurriedly. 'Ready for the paying passengers?'

'We're on it,' says Perry. 'Crispin nearly acquired one recently – scrapyard in Devon; didn't work out.'

'You'll need more than one,' says Nick. He's done some research since talking to Crispin and his friends, interested in prices. 'You have to use your rolling stock in rotation. Run each carriage for six months while the other one is being serviced and repaired. Hardly surprising when you consider their age.'

'Well,' says Perry, looking bored. 'Lots to do, must get on.'

'What time does it take off?'

'We're aiming for three o'clock. A test run first, backwards and forwards a few times. If all goes well, we'll attempt a longer journey. There's a good stretch of line ready, about five miles; we've had loads of volunteers throughout the summer. It can go to just past your siding, in fact.'

'Johnny?' says a voice from behind. 'Surely not Johnny Greenwood?'

Johnny and Debs turn to confront a man of about the same age as them, who's staring at Johnny with amazement. There's something familiar about the way he's standing, slightly lopsided, his head on one side.

'Dougie?' he says nervously.

Dougie beams. 'Knew it was you. Moment I spied you from over there. Couldn't hardly believe my eyes. Funny how nobody changes, isn't it? Even when the old bones start to crumble a bit, it's still me inside, same as it's still you. When it comes down to it, we got nowhere to hide. Someone somewhere just knows it's us.'

'What are you doing here?' Johnny finds himself delighted by the sight of Dougie after all these years. He knows why Dougie has kept away – he squirms at the memory of his casual careless-ness in those days, his willingness to let all his friends go after the accident, his laziness about keeping in touch.

'One of my colleagues, a postal worker, invited us,' says Dougie. He looks uncomfortable. 'Haven't seen you since we was kids. Should of come and seen you when you got home after the accident. Always felt bad . . .'

Johnny stares at him. All his life he's felt guilty about the way he dropped his friends without a word. And now Dougie's apol-ogising to him. He doesn't know what to say. He can feel a flut-tering in his stomach, a sense of panic.

Suddenly she's at his side, leaning towards him, interrupting his thoughts, and her presence is like a sponge, soaking up his agitation.

'My Lil wouldn't let me come round,' says Dougie. 'Do you remember her? Good at cartwheels. Fancied you for a bit.'

Johnny remembers her. She was a pretty girl, always wanting to be with the lads, whizzing around in endless cartwheels, making them all dizzy, shouting loudly, trying to attract their attention. He thinks Dougie might be wrong about her fancying him, but he can't be sure. Paula was around then. He wouldn't have noticed anyone else.

'Married her,' says Dougie. 'Soon got me under her thumb.'

'So is she here?'

'No, she's got MS. Can't manage a wheelchair on grass.'

Johnny's not sure what he should say. This is why it's easier to stay at home. No need to worry about giving the correct responses to other people's disasters.

Dougie has stopped talking. He's staring at the woman next to Johnny. 'Do I know you?' he says slowly.

'Yes,' says Johnny. 'It's . . .' He stops, suddenly aware of the mistake he's about to make.

All three of them contemplate each other in silence. Johnny can see Dougie's mind working, the connections as each part falls into place.

'Dougie!' Nick has appeared. He grabs his hand and keeps holding it, grasping his arm at the same time. 'Great to see you. How are you?'

'Haven't seen you for a while,' says Dougie, obviously pleased to see him. 'Retired yet?'

'Still at it,' says Nick. 'They keep me on my toes.'

But Dougie's eyes keep turning back to Debs. He knows, thinks Johnny.

'It's really odd,' says Dougie, 'but you remind me of . . . you look just like . . .' He shakes his head. 'No, I must be losing my marbles.'

'Actually,' she says, 'you're not.'

How can Dougie recognise her so easily, thinks Johnny, when we can't? Can you see resemblances more clearly if you're not part of a family?

Nick steps between them, trying to shield her from Dougie's view. 'No, she's just an old friend,' he says.

But she moves round and faces Dougie full in the face. 'Okay, Dougie, I'd better come clean. I'm Debs.'

Dougie freezes. 'But . . . but . . . I thought . . .'

Johnny and Nick stare at her, helpless, not knowing how to prevent the disaster that's about to take place.

'I know, you thought I was dead,' she says quietly. 'But I'm not. That's the thing. I don't feel dead. Do I look it?'

Dougie is struggling. 'Me and the missus, we was out there, three days in a row, searching for Debs. That's when we became sweethearts . . . They found a body – it was her, that's what they said. I don't understand . . .' He runs a hand through his hair. 'If it wasn't Debs, who was it?'

'It was Bev. Remember her? Always hanging around. Bit of a nuisance.'

Dougie nods slowly, trying to digest the information. 'Course I do. Spitting image of Debs. But she went missing too. We was looking for the both of you.'

'She didn't really look like me. That was just an illusion.'

He keeps staring, clearly not sure.

'There was a lot of confusion,' she says.

'But . . . Why didn't you tell nobody you was alive? Why . . .?'

She turns away, as if she can't be bothered with it all. 'It's a long, long story.' She sounds overwhelmingly tired. 'Let's not do it now. Come on, Johnny, I need cake.'

17

It had been Perry's idea to make it a thirties day. 'You know,' he said, '*Murder on the Orient Express*. Everyone'll love it. We'll get all sorts coming. People like getting dressed up.'

'Do you want someone to volunteer to be the murderer?' said Nathan.

'I'd feel a lot safer if you were the body,' said Crispin.

'There wasn't just one murderer,' said Zohra. 'They were all in on it.'

'I could use tomato sauce,' said Nathan. 'For blood.'

'No!' said Crispin.

'It was your idea, Crisp.'

'I've changed my mind.'

The committee were delighted with the suggestion, so Susie, in charge of PR, arranged for influential local bloggers to do a series of online interviews with Perry and some of the volunteers. Once it became clear that there was more interest than they'd expected, the plans became more ambitious and Susie persuaded several firms from the area to contribute to the event.

A catering firm from Droitwich offered trestle tables, white tablecloths, plastic silver platters and five hundred sandwiches. A local wine merchant wanted to give fifty bottles of Chardonnay if he could hang a banner from the side of the driver's cab, but the committee refused permission. Alcohol was considered to be inappropriate since there were no buses to the hall and everyone would be driving.

'Someone's going to complain about the lack of carriages,' said Zohra. 'They won't be satisfied with an engine going up and down for a few hundred yards.'

'There's still a good chance *Enigma* will manage a longer trip later in the day,' said Crispin.

'But nobody will be able to see it once it's left the station,' said Zohra.

'The driver could pretend he's gone further,' said Nathan. 'Just stop round the bend and come back ten minutes later.'

About half of the line has been completed. It covers a reasonable distance and goes past the siding that leads to the Greenwoods' carriages. In fact, some over-enthusiastic volunteers wasted time and resources by starting to repair the siding, clearing bushes and trees, mistaking it for the main line, until Perry came to check on them and pointed out with a compass and a map that they should be heading west, not southwest.

In the last week the track has been inspected, the points locked. Even so, yesterday afternoon Nathan suddenly announced that he was going to take the handcar up the line again. 'For an extra check.'

'Is that really necessary?' asked Zohra. 'We've had the all clear.' But she knew it would be fruitless trying to prevent him. He loved the velocipede and often took it out on his own. It's been difficult preventing him from taking it out more than once a day. They could hear him repeating the word under his breath as he headed towards it. 'Velocipede, velocipede, velocipede.'

He was gone for much longer than they expected and Crispin eventually started to worry. 'Should we go and find him?' he said to Zohra as it started to get dark. They were standing on the platform, watching the volunteers moving tables and chairs out of the house, blowing up balloons, tying them everywhere possible. 'What if he's fallen off?'

At that moment, Nathan appeared round the bend, his head down, jumping along the sleepers. As he approached the platform, he looked up and waved at them, grinning.

'What have you been up to?' called Crispin.

'What do you mean?' His voice was defensive.

'You've been gone for hours. Where's the velocipede?'

'It's all right. It malfunctioned.'

'You went too fast, didn't you?' said Zohra. 'You've crashed it.'

'No,' he said loudly. 'Well – it sort of fell over.' He pulled himself up on to the platform, avoiding direct eye contact with Crispin. 'It was difficult to move, so I've left it there for now, but it'll be okay. I'll fix it tomorrow.'

Crispin sighed. 'You'd better not tell Anthony.'

'We need more seats,' said Nathan, looking around at the preparations on the field. 'Shall we bring out the sofas?'

'No,' said Crispin. 'They're not comfortable. They've all got broken springs.'

'But people like to sit down.'

'They can sit on the grass. It's not going to rain.'

'Yes it is,' said Nathan. 'It always rains.'

'In which case, nobody will want to sit on a soggy sofa.'

They kept going until midnight, and Zohra was only able to snatch a few hours' sleep before dragging herself out of bed in time for work. She checked with Dougie, Bill and Rohit at the sorting office, made sure they were all coming.

'Wild horses couldn't keep me away,' said Bill. 'The sorting office will close at twelve forty-five, dead on.'

'What if someone comes at twelve forty and you can't find their parcel?' asked Rohit, who often gets blamed when parcels mysteriously disappear and then turn up in the wrong place.

'Then they'll have to come back on Monday,' said Bill.

'There'll be complaints.'

'Tough,' said Bill. 'I'm within my rights. They can read the sign. I plan to be on that platform, watching the engine when it starts rolling, and there isn't nobody going to stop me.'

'Quite right too,' said Dougie.

Zohra and her mum and dad arrive at Wychington Hall at one o'clock. The place is already swarming with people, a much bigger crowd than they were expecting. The whole world seems to be here, mostly dressed up, all delighted by the novelty, determined to enjoy themselves. She can see the Greenwood brothers, standing by the cake stall with the Canadian woman from the station. They seem comfortable together, as if they know each other well.

Nathan's mum, Holly, in a flowery overall, stops to talk to Zohra. 'Hope you're not expecting sandwiches,' she says. 'All gone, a while ago.' They'd been delivered halfway through the morning: neat triangles of egg and ham, cheese and pickle, salmon and cucumber, with the crusts cut off, arranged artistically on the platters. But each sandwich could be demolished in one gulp and the volunteers polished most of them off long before the public began to arrive.

The wine-merchant has produced bags of crisps and peanuts instead of wine, because he says he loves trains and wouldn't dream of missing out. White plastic cups were part of the deal with the company who've provided the tea urns (they refused to offer them free on the grounds that they'd already turned down a wedding for this), but the person responsible for organising bins seems to have miscalculated and the small number available are already full, so many of the plastic cups have ended up underfoot, trampled into the grass.

We organised this, thinks Zohra in amazement. We asked everyone to pretend to be someone else for a day, and they did it. How easy it is to persuade people to do something out of the ordinary. She worries that there might not be enough food, but then sees the cakes, sausage rolls, bowls of strawberries and cream, crisps and nuts piled up on the trellis tables, far more than they'd been expecting. She stands quietly for a few seconds, taking in the evidence of generosity, dizzy with pleasure. What a revelation, this willingness to participate, to contribute.

'Not raining yet,' says her mother, sounding almost disappointed.

Zohra looks up at the sky – overcast, grey, but surprisingly warm. The clouds look as if they might clear. 'It's not going to rain,' she says firmly.

Her mother is clutching a large plastic box containing a cake in the shape of Thomas the Tank Engine, pulling a carriage. She's an expert cook, contemptuous of the baking programmes on the television. ('Why anyone need to watch TV – why they not just do it?') She can create cakes in whatever shape or size is required, open to any reasonable request. She's spent two days on this one – there are passengers leaning out of the windows, an engine driver waving from the cab, a fireman shovelling coal with a miniature shovel. The Fat Controller stands at the front with a sinister smile on his broad face.

Zohra has tried to persuade her mother that it's not necessary to be quite so accurate. 'It'll be cut up and eaten before most people see it.'

'Quite right. This is what cakes for. You think I do it for glory? I do it because I like it and because you're too old and superior to let me make cakes for you any more. This is perfect reason. Nothing, not you, not your father, stop me.'

So she never made the cakes for Zohra. She made them for herself. Zohra experiences a sense of liberation, a release from one of the myriad of small obligations that have been hovering over her head since childhood.

Zohra's father is wearing a long buttoned coat with a high neckline that falls just below the knees, over loose trousers. It's embroidered exquisitely in pale blue and gold. When he came down the stairs with the car keys in his hand, she couldn't believe it was him.

'Everything all right?' he asked Chrissie, their plump, amiable assistant, ignoring Zohra's astonishment. 'I don't know yet what time we'll be back.'

'No problem.' She examined him admiringly. 'Well, Mr Dasgupta, look at you. Hidden depths.'

He smiled, breezy and elegant, a stranger. He looked, in fact, handsome. It made Zohra uncomfortable. 'Where did the coat come from?' she asked.

'It's a sherwani. Traditional Indian dress. Part of our history. It's been sitting in my wardrobe since we first came here, awaiting an opportunity—'

'Your wedding,' said her mother to Zohra, patting her husband proudly across the shoulders, smoothing the beautiful material with her hands.

'Right,' said Zohra.

Her mother is wearing a full red sari with gold embroidery on the edges, the colour of celebration. She's created herself as a rajah's wife in the thirties, entertaining the British at a time when the concept of a flat over a shop in Bromsgrove would have been unimaginable. But when they approach one of the tables laden with food, she stares with dismay. 'Everyone baking. No one want my cake. All wasted.'

'Nonsense, Kulwinder,' says Zohra's father. 'Nothing will be wasted. Your grateful husband, who knows well enough that his wife is the greatest cook in the universe, will be happy to eat it all if he has to.'

She smiles up at him, immediately consoled. 'Maninder,' she says. 'Stop making up stories. Bad example for Zohra.'

'I'm twenty-six years old, Mother,' says Zohra. 'I don't need either of you as role models any more.'

Her mother watches the women on the other side of the table making cups of tea from two big urns. 'This is where I help,' she says, and marches towards them.

Zohra's father raises his eyebrows. 'I hope you don't know any of those ladies, Zohra,' he says. 'If you do, there is a strong possibility they will never speak to you again once they've encountered your mother. She's far too bossy for liberated English ladies.'

Zohra looks over, suddenly afraid that one of her old teachers might be amongst them, but none of them looks familiar. She forces herself to relax, not entirely comfortable in her outfit. She's wearing a dress made out of a delicate green material, calf-length, edged with lace, which she found in the Oxfam shop on the High Street. She's added shoulder pads, pulled it in at the waist with a belt, and attached a silk scarf to the neckline, using safety pins to position it round the V-neck. On her head, she's wearing a saucer-shaped hat, set at a jaunty angle, which reminds her of a spaceship. It wasn't easy to fix in position or to keep there once it was in place. She's examined pictures of thirties fashions – when women wore their hats with poise and sophistication, almost as if they kept them there by decree ('one slip and you're toast', according to Crispin when she first showed him). She wasn't sure how long she would keep it on, but now that she can see so many other hats she doesn't feel quite as self-conscious as she expected. The lace-up shoes with heels that she found in Debenhams are not comfortable, and she misses her postman's shoes. They'd be heavy and hot, but at least her feet would be firmly on the ground.

'Mr Dasgupta!' Perry has appeared at their side. 'Glad you could make it. Managed to find someone to cover you in the shop, then?'

'We have an assistant,' says Zohra's father. 'A little – shall we say – limited, but reliable. I wouldn't have missed this for all the tea in China. I might even have considered closing the shop if she couldn't help out.'

Really? He's just trying to impress Perry. He hasn't closed the shop once in Zohra's lifetime. Not even when her mother fell downstairs and broke her ankle. Zohra was left in charge, at the age of twelve, while her father went off in the ambulance. It might not even have been legal, but nobody thought to check. Reliability came before everything. And he returned within two hours, leaving his wife to the care of the hospital.

'Now that's what I call a hat,' Perry says to Zohra. 'How do the little green men get in and out?'

They can hear the engine building up steam, hissing with anticipation. The experts filled the tanks the night before, shovelled coal into the bunker, got everything ready for the early start, then went for a few hours' sleep at the nearby Travelodge. At three o'clock they came back and lit the fire, starting to build up the temperature. Melvin has been here the whole time, supervising, but Anthony, who'll be the fireman on the first trip, went back to bed for a brief nap before returning for more checks. The checking never stops.

The engine driver is Wilf, a man who worked on the Exeter to Exmouth line, along the River Exe, in the days of steam. More recently, he's been training apprentices at Bridgnorth. He's a man of vast knowledge, big, burly, white-haired. The skin on his face is pockmarked and wizened, his eyes slitted from decades of peering at the line ahead, searching for signals, warning lights. He looks like an engine driver. Utterly, utterly safe.

'Magnificent preparations,' says Zohra's dad to Perry. They wander off together, talking fast, both at the same time, neither of them listening to the other.

Zohra can see Crispin in the distance, with two young women she doesn't recognise. They have their phones out, facing him, as if they're recording the conversation. They look like reporters, presumably from the *Bromsgrove Advertiser* and the *Bromsgrove Standard,* who both said they'd be here.

'Zohra!'

Mimi is coming towards her, followed by Freddie, who has an Asda carrier bag in his hand. Mimi is elegant in a cream, chiffon dress, pinched in at the waist and fitted round her hips, but swinging freely below. Her heels are long, stiletto-like, sinking into the grass. She's had her hair dyed, Marilyn Monroe blonde, and she's carrying a cigarette holder with a plastic cigarette in the end.

'Mimi!' says Zohra, surprised at how pleased she is to see her. 'You look . . .' It's hard to find the right tone, 'wonderful.'

'Phew!' says Mimi. 'I was a bit worried what you'd come out with there.' She sweeps her eyes over Zohra's outfit. 'You look pretty good yourself. Where did you get that hat?'

'From eBay,' says Zohra.

Freddie is equally impressive in a suit with a neat tie and baggy trousers, pleated at the top. He's carrying a furled umbrella and wearing a tweed fedora hat. A beige mac is draped casually over his shoulders. 'It's all hired,' he says as Zohra studies him. 'You know Mimi. Always has to do things properly.'

'Of course,' says Zohra, not at all sure if Mimi was like that when she was younger.

'We brought cakes,' says Mimi. 'Any idea where we should leave them?'

'Over there,' says Zohra, pointing.

'Oh,' says Mimi, seeing the piles of food.

'There are loads of people,' says Zohra, 'and they're still turning up, so I think it'll all get eaten.'

'Go on, then, Freddie,' says Mimi, pushing him away. 'You take them. I'm too embarrassed. They're cup cakes,' she says to Zohra. 'But they didn't turn out all that well. The icing's a bit of a mess.'

'I'm sure they're lovely,' says Zohra, relieved to discover that even Mimi has shortcomings.

'Love the hat,' says Freddie over his shoulder to Zohra as he leaves them.

It's all looking good: the long platform at the far end of the field, the sound of the engine; the amateur band playing 'Chattanooga Choo Choo' over and over again, fast and exuberant; the unsuccessful coconut shy, which has compromised and brought the coconuts closer to the customers; Popeye and Betty Boop, now low on balloons; a newly emerged Donald Duck handing out bags of crisps; Tom and Jerry walking around together, the best of friends, their masks off, eating ice creams; and a large number of stationmasters pacing up and down urgently, nowhere near the platform, waving flags, carrying large loops ready to be passed to the driver as the train leaves the platform, raising their whistles to their mouths every now and again and then dropping them back down, realising it's not yet time.

'It's good,' declares Mimi.

'I should hope so,' says Zohra. 'It's taken us five years to get to this stage – since we first discovered the line. There's a lot resting on it.'

'Where's Crispin?'

'Not sure.' But she knows exactly where he is. She's watched him leave the reporters and queue with Nathan for an ice cream.

'He's very loyal, isn't he?' says Mimi.

'Yes,' says Zohra, and realises that Mimi means more than this. 'I've told you, there's nothing going on between us.'

'Are you sure?' says Mimi, looking closely at her. 'You clearly have a strong relationship.'

Zohra finds herself flushing. 'No,' she says. 'You're just imagining things.'

Mimi doesn't reply. She just smiles.

Zohra thinks of the night in the car when she told Crispin everything, the comfort of having her hand encased in his. Why did he do that? Why did she let him? But she is starting to acknowledge that the sensation was not entirely unexpected or unwelcome. Neither of them has spoken about it since. Do they need to? They've known each other for nine years and understand each other well, often not needing words. But her thoughts about him are changing – no, not changing, evolving – and it feels all right, natural almost. Something must tie him to her. Why else is he always close by, always willing to come to her side, be part of her life? Why did she tell him the things she's told no one?

'Come on,' says Mimi, taking Zohra's arm. 'I'm desperate for cake. We can disown mine and go for something a little more exotic. Please tell me your mum's been baking. I still yearn for those amazing cakes you used to bring to school. I was so jealous – you could just go home and have cake like that whenever you wanted. My mum never cooked cakes.'

'Well . . .' says Zohra, putting her hand to her hat, checking it's still there. 'It wasn't quite as straightforward as that. There was usually a deal involved – I was expected to do something in return.'

Mimi laughs, a happy, contented laugh that takes Zohra back to those days before Fiona, when everything had seemed so easy, when the four of them could become hysterical about things that weren't really funny at all, pass notes round during Biology, giggle until their stomachs ached.

Mimi suddenly stops, letting go of Zohra's arm. 'Look,' she says in a more serious tone. 'This is a good time to talk. Now you're not at work and don't have to rush off.'

Zohra can feel her throat closing with panic. 'No,' she whispers. 'We don't need to talk—'

'We do,' says Mimi firmly, and she's an adult, in control; a sensible, thoughtful person who no longer operates like a teenager. 'I didn't realise then – we thought we were so special, so clever, that everything we touched would turn to gold, but really we were just children. We did things we shouldn't have done . . .'

Zohra stares at her, unable to speak.

'I have to apologise to you, Zohra.' Mimi's voice is formal now, slightly forced. She hesitates, takes a breath, coughs a little and starts again. 'We didn't behave well.'

'It doesn't matter . . .' Zohra doesn't want the conversation to continue, afraid that she'll say the wrong thing, reveal things Mimi doesn't know, incriminate herself. Why would Mimi want to apologise to her? Is this a way of saying that she knows what Zohra did to Fiona?

'We were unkind,' says Mimi in a soft, breathless voice, not much above a whisper. 'No, not unkind, cruel. It was a kind of madness, like being drunk – on our jokes, our laughing. I find it hard to even think about what we did then.'

'What did you do?' asks Zohra, confused. Is she admitting she knew about the online stuff?

'All that on the Internet,' says Mimi quickly. 'It was us.'

Zohra tries to absorb this. 'Us? Who's us?'

'You know, the four of us. Me, Katy, Carys and Fiona. I don't know why we did it. It seemed like a good idea at the time, but now – now, I simply can't understand what came over us. It was truly appalling.'

'But I thought Fiona . . .' Now Zohra wants her to say more, but doesn't know how to ask.

'Fiona wasn't part of it at first,' says Mimi. 'She even tried to stop us, but in the end she was just as bad as the rest of us. We were flying so high, like we were on drugs – we weren't, we didn't need to be; we thought we were gods, untouchable, unaccountable – with unlimited power. We were testing our strength, I suppose, seeing how far we could go and if there was a natural end to it. But there wasn't, not until it was far too late.'

Zohra stares at her. Fiona tried to stop it? No! That can't be right. Fiona was the ringleader. She's always known that. It was obvious from the way she marched in and stole Zohra's place. 'But Fiona started it all.'

'No,' says Mimi. 'It was Katy's idea. She used a photo of some completely random person and we made up a whole profile for her. It was fun at first, making a list of her hobbies and contacts. It was just for a laugh, Katy said, and bit by bit we all got involved – somehow she knew how to draw us in. She made us believe that you'd done something to her once, something so terrible that she couldn't let go of it, but she never told us what, however much we asked.'

'Katy?' says Zohra slowly. Why Katy?

'Of course, I realise now that there probably wasn't anything – she was making it all up. There was always something hard about her, and that became more obvious later, when she went off to uni. She was the only one who didn't want to stay in touch, and I heard she got into drugs. I've never really understood what happened. Maybe there were things going on at home and she was passing on the nastiness, stuff she couldn't deal with. Or maybe she was just jealous. You were so much cleverer than the rest of us. Picking on you must have made her feel better – I don't know – I've thought about it a lot since . . .'

Katy? thinks Zohra. It was Katy? Not Fiona?

But they were all involved. That's what Mimi's saying. They all joined in willingly enough. They were happy to mock her, torture her, destroy her. 'I'm sorry,' says Mimi, rubbing her arm, watching her carefully. 'I wanted to clear the air between us, especially as it looks as if we might be friends now. It just seemed a good time to say it. I wouldn't blame you if you never wanted to speak to me again. I hope you don't feel like that, because I've been so pleased to meet up , but . . .'

Not Fiona. Not Fiona.

The engine whistles and hisses violently. Steam rises into the air. People are starting to move now, heading for the platform, not wanting to miss the maiden voyage.

Mimi is leaning forward, her forehead creased with concern, her mouth opening and shutting, but Zohra can no longer hear what she's saying.

She should never have come. She should never have talked to Mimi. She should have asked for a transfer as soon as she'd met her at the nailers' cottages, resigned if they couldn't offer her an alternative round.

It's all been a terrible, terrible mistake.

Everything. Her entire life up to this moment.

Poor Fiona. Hounded by her family, her ghastly brothers who expected so much from her. She must have been desperate when she tried to confide in Zohra, that time in the park. She needed someone who would understand her. Someone separate from Mimi, Carys or Katy. If Zohra had listened, maybe Fiona would still be alive. But Zohra didn't listen.

Zohra finds herself running. She can hear Mimi in the background, calling, her voice edged with panic, but she has to get away from her. She runs and runs.

She collides with someone and desperately tries to push them aside, starting to hit out wildly when the person doesn't move. She doesn't care who it is, who she's attacking, but finds her arms held tightly, her face crushed up against a broad, solid chest, her hat tipping backwards and off her head. She turns to the side, gasping for breath, as powerless as ever, unable to escape.

There's a voice in her ear, impossible to hear at first, which gradually manages to reach inside her. Soft, careful, concerned. 'Zohra, Zohra.' Just her name, repeated calmly, many times.

It's Crispin.

Very slowly, Zohra allows her breathing to settle and lets her arms relax as the trembling begins to subside. When did Crispin become so big, so substantial? How did he metamorphose from the unassuming Crispin she's always known to this reassuring, unmovable support?

There are other voices, elsewhere in the background, unimportant.

Freddie: 'Is everything okay?'

Mimi: 'It was my fault . . .'

She can hear – feel – Crispin's heartbeat. Why is it so comforting, so familiar? All those times he came to see her in her room, after Fiona's death, when he sat with her, side by side against the wall. Did he somehow send his heartbeat through the air; did she learn it because he was there for so long; had she absorbed it without even realising?

Crispin's voice. 'Don't worry. I've got it. No, no . . . not your fault . . . talk later.'

A period of quiet, anonymous chatter far away, nothing to do with either of them, the hiss of steam, the beat of the band, the pop of a balloon, a burst of distant laughter. None of it encroaches as she stands leaning against Crispin. It's as if they've been removed from it all.

Slowly, she pulls her head away and steadies herself. She looks up at Crispin and takes a deep breath. 'Sorry,' she says shakily.

'All right?' he says.

She nods. 'It was . . .' she says.

'It's okay. You don't have to tell me.'

'But I do. You know everything else. You should hear the ending.'

He nods. 'But there are other things we have to think about first.'

'What things?' She has to tell Crispin about Fiona. He has to know what she's done.

But he puts his hands out and draws her to him, pulling her close. Then he leans down and puts his lips on hers.

It's like the moment when you move a picture to a different place on the wall and realise it's now in exactly the right spot, when the light illuminates details that were there but never appreciated before. A delicious warmth starts to spread through her.

294

A burst of steam from the engine wafts over and briefly engulfs them.

But before she can react, a loud, harsh voice intrudes and angry hands pull her away from Crispin.

'Nathan!' shouts Crispin. 'What are you doing?'

Nathan is yelling, ranting. 'No, no, no!' He pushes Zohra away with frightening strength. She puts out a hand to save herself as she falls, crying out as she hits the ground heavily. When she scrambles back up, hearing urgent scuffling, breathless grunts, Nathan has his hands wrapped tightly round Crispin's throat, his face locked into a tight, determined mask, and he's squeezing hard. Crispin is tugging at Nathan's arms, desperately trying to free himself.

'No!' cries Zohra as she scrambles to her feet, nearly falling over again in her haste. 'Nathan!' she yells, unable to believe what she's seeing. 'Stop it!' She tries to grab his arms, but they're solid, inhuman, like steel. She gives up and thumps his back instead. 'Nathan! No! No!'

Nathan is momentarily distracted and turns slightly towards her, briefly relaxing his grip. 'He didn't tell the truth!' he shouts. 'He never told me he wanted to marry you too!'

'Let go of him!' screams Zohra. She knows Nathan's strength – she's seen evidence of it before – but it has never occurred to her that he would attack someone. How can this be happening? 'He can't breathe! You're killing him!'

Crispin manages to use the moment to heave himself free, and pushes Nathan away with a mighty shove. He stands swaying for a few seconds, his eyes glazed, struggling to find his breath, while Nathan staggers backwards, caught off balance. They face each other, glaring, both ready to leap back into action.

The engine whistles. It's ready to roll.

'We can't miss *Enigma*'s first voyage,' says Crispin, his voice low and cracked, attempting to sound normal, but not taking his eyes off Nathan, braced to fight off a further attack. 'Not after all the work we've done. Let's talk later, when we've calmed down.'

Nathan throws himself at Crispin again. But his movements are now wild and uncoordinated.

Crispin is prepared this time and steps to one side, allowing him to stagger past. 'Nathan!' he shouts. 'What's going on? What's this all about?'

Nathan totters to an abrupt halt, then swings round to accuse Zohra. 'You said you'd marry me. You promised!'

Zohra stares at him in alarm. 'No, no, that's not true.' She's always treated his proposals as a joke. It's never occurred to her that he believed it. 'It's not real, Nathan. It's just something inside your head. It's never been real.'

He freezes, his mouth falling open, his eyes wide and staring. 'Not real?' he says, spitting out the words. 'Not real?' He starts gasping as if he can't breathe, then bends over and heaves several times.

Zohra edges round him to stand next to Crispin. She slips her hand into his and feels a little safer. She has an urge to comfort Nathan now, to rub his back reassuringly, but she's afraid to approach him.

He straightens and glares at them both, trembling with fury. 'You've betrayed me!' he screams, his voice high-pitched and cracked. Then he turns and runs towards the platform.

'What's got into him?' says Crispin, his voice shaking slightly. 'He's never done anything like this before.' He sees her massaging her shoulder. 'Are you all right?'

'I'm okay,' she says. 'You got the worst of it. It must be all the excitement. It's destabilised him. We should find his mother. She'll know what to do.'

'We can't,' says Crispin, pulling on her hand and starting to run towards the platform. 'There isn't time. We'd miss the maiden voyage.'

Enigma is preparing to leave. The audience is gathering, their chatter subsiding to a murmur as they prepare to witness the historic moment. The music from the band is loud and exciting.

18

Nick strides ahead impatiently, stopping and waiting, speeding up again, urging them to hurry without actually saying so, knowing that if he voices his concerns, Johnny's natural instincts will force him to resist. They've spent too long eating cake and drinking tea. They can't miss the moment when the engine leaves. As he stands and waits yet again, ready to rush off as soon as they draw parallel with him, she suddenly puts out a hand and grabs his arm to steady herself. He assumes she just needs support across the uneven surface, but as they start walking together, he realises she's leaning on him more heavily than he expected. 'Are you all right?' he asks.

She nods, but her face is grey, drained of colour, her breathing rapid and shallow. 'Sorry,' she says. 'I'm probably overtired. I haven't been sleeping well since I got here. Too many nightmares.' After a few seconds, she stops abruptly and starts to fiddle with her hat, eventually pulling it off, leaving wispy grey tufts of hair framing her head in an uneven halo. 'I'm too hot,' she says. She flaps the hat in front of her face.

'Do you think you might have a temperature?' he asks. 'If you have some paracetamol, or whatever you normally take, I can fetch some water.'

'We've come to see the train and that's what we're going to do,' she says. After a few careful breaths, she seems to recover slightly. She steps forward, still unsteady, and continues to support herself on his arm. 'If I could just – that's it. I'm fine, truly. Absolutely nothing to worry about.'

They proceed even more slowly, and Johnny comes round to support her on the other side. Nick exchanges worried glances with him over her head. They've spent so much time worrying about her identity, debating whether they can believe what she says, that the issue of her illness has slipped into the background. She has never given any suggestion that it's on her mind or even that it features significantly in her everyday life, but it now seems to Nick that they haven't been paying enough attention. They knew she was ill. Why didn't they probe more, find out the details?

'If you prefer to go back to the hotel,' he says, 'it's no problem.'

'No,' she says. 'I want to see the engine leave.'

It's hardly surprising they haven't been able to ask questions about her health – their only experience of illness was when Ma died, and neither of them has any desire to go back to that time. It's been easier to talk about the past because there's such a vast distance between then and now, and it's almost like discussing someone else's story.

The band has finally changed tunes and is now playing 'Boogie Woogie Bugle Boy' very loudly, blaring out from the end of the platform and competing with the sound of the locomotive. They must have been saving it for the climax, for when the engine was about to pull away.

'They're hopeless,' says Johnny. 'Someone needs to tell them they're in the wrong decade. Early forties. Second World War.'

There's a sense of urgency. As they approach the steps, Nick can see a forest of legs above him on the platform: trouser turn-ups pressed and sharp; thick dense stockings; an array of shoes – brogues, laces, heels, buckles – crammed into the confined space. He can hear raised voices, excitement rippling from one end of the platform to the other.

'They probably don't know any thirties music,' says Nick. 'If their repertoire doesn't extend far enough back, they'll do what they know and hope no one will notice. Let's face it, there won't be many here who can tell the difference.'

'I know the difference,' says Johnny, his voice tense and irritated.

She hesitates for a moment, concentrating on something internal, as if she's in pain.

'Are you sure you want to do this?' asks Nick. 'You're obviously not well. I could go and fetch the St John's people.'

'No,' she says. 'I'm fine.'

'Should we get them anyway?' Johnny whispers to Nick, his face nearly as pale as Debs's. 'Have you got your phone?'

'I can hear you, Johnny Greenwood,' she calls out over her shoulder, half turning her head. 'Don't even think it. I've got eyes in the back of my head, and don't you forget it.'

Nick has the sensation – almost physical – of being hit in the chest. He stares at Johnny, who's staring at him. They've lost more than fifty years and they're back where they started. Children, small boys walking along behind Ma, about to flick dead dandelion heads at her skinny bottom, each of them determined to be the first one to hit the bulls-eye. 'Don't even think about it,' she said, without turning round. She always knew exactly what was going on. She could read them like a book, knew what they would say before they said it. 'No flies on me,' she would say. 'Dead or alive.'

Then she turns round, and it's not Ma. It's Debs. 'Well?' she says. 'I'm going to need your help to get up here.'

'It wouldn't matter that much if we missed it,' says Nick. 'It's only the engine.'

'I know that,' she says. 'They're waiting for your carriages.'

'Well, they can't have them,' says Johnny. 'I'm not moving.'

'That's what you think,' she says. 'But you should know that I've promised myself you'll be living somewhere civilised before I go.'

Is she talking about dying? 'Stop being so melodramatic,' says Nick. Had she ever intended to go back to Canada? It's not as if she's got children or grandchildren there. Maybe this is what she came for all along, to die here, back in her home town, with her two brothers at her side.

Has she considered the paperwork?

'Oh do hurry up and get me up the steps,' she says.

People jostle them, and they have to step to the side more than once as others pass them. An elderly couple stand back politely and wait.

'I think you should go first,' says Nick. 'We're going to be a bit slow.'

'It doesn't matter,' says the woman, white-haired, her hat rakishly perched on the back of her head, two feathers sticking out at an odd angle. 'We've got all the time in the world.'

'That's not strictly true,' says the man, who's a cartoon version of a retired professor in a rumpled suit with his tie askew, small glasses perched precariously on his nose and hair that is slightly too long. He eases his wife in front of them. 'I want to see the engine pull away. That's why I'm here; that's what I've paid my money for.'

'If you donate to a charity, dear,' says his wife, 'it's not an investment with a return. It's for goodwill, to enable something to happen. It's neither here nor there if you get to see it. However, with a bit of luck and a little patience, we will all make it.'

'I still think you'll be quicker than me,' says Debs, smiling at them and letting them go in front. She puts a foot on the bottom step and Nick puts his arm round her to ease her up. She's as light and insubstantial as a child.

'You know,' says the woman, half turning, 'you look vaguely familiar.'

'Oh, I used to live round here once,' says Debs. A long time ago.'

Nick tries to slow down, wanting to ease her away from the embarrassment of having to explain.

'You might remember us,' she says. 'The Greenwoods. We lived in railway carriages?'

They reach the top.

'I'm not sure I do,' says the woman.

'Imagine that,' says her husband. 'Living in a railway carriage.'

As they emerge on to the crowded platform, it's clear that they're going to have trouble seeing anything. 'Over here,' says Nick, guiding Debs and Johnny along the platform, away from the concentration of people to a space at the back. He leaves them there and eases his way to the front, apologising to everyone, wanting to find out what's happening. It's not as crowded as it first appeared. Most people have gathered at the front end where they can watch the engine for as long as possible before it disappears round the bend. Children are running between them, increasingly wild and careless. 'Careful, Suzy,' says a voice, 'just ask him nicely to move.' 'Oi! You're standing on my toe!' 'Sorry!' 'Mum! Jack pushed me. I nearly went over the side.' 'Be careful!' 'Please be careful!'

The engine is half out of the shed, grunting, hissing, oblivious to its audience, surrounded by volunteers, the number 3733 bright against its glossy black background. Steam roars from the chimney, first black, then white, followed by a long, powerful whistle. It hovers in that neutral, in-between place between inactivity and movement. The volunteers retreat, backing off the track and jumping up on to the platform, grinning with unguarded joy as steam shoots out and temporarily engulfs them. The crowd calms, becomes quieter.

'We have lift-off!' yells a hysterical voice from the end of the platform.

The coupling rods start to move, obedient, responding to the unseen power behind them. The wheels turn. The monster creeps forward – slowly, slowly – astonishingly smooth, gliding along the side of the platform, inching over the gleaming rails sedately, perfectly in control, gathering momentum. There's a thudding sound as it crosses the joins on the track, creaks as the rails shift under the weight. Steam surrounds everything for a few seconds, then it thins and becomes almost invisible, creating ripples in the air.

Nick finds himself elbowed away from the front of the platform and works his way back to where he left Debs. Amazingly, she's managed to climb up on a bench and is holding on to a lamppost, precarious, but with a clear view of the engine. Johnny has disappeared.

'Can you see it?' he yells, jumping up beside her.

'Yes, yes!' she cries, her voice hoarse with excitement. The bench is one of three, all supporting several people, mainly children, who are bouncing up and down, rocking the wooden slats. Debs starts to sway alarmingly.

'You'd better sit,' he says, grabbing her.

'No, no, I don't want to.'

Johnny reappears with Dougie behind him. They climb up beside them, squeezing the children to one side. 'Takes you back, doesn't it?' shouts Dougie. 'Holidays to Weston when we was nippers. It's all Intercity now, Virgin, CrossCountry, Chiltern – not got the same magic. Used to be Great Western in them days. That's what I call a name.'

'Great Western still exists,' says Johnny.

'Whatever, don't really matter – diesels aren't a patch on this, either way.'

The volunteers hover on the edge of the platform, grinning as if their faces will split. Some of them are just standing, hands on hips, while others are shaking hands, thumping each other on the back. In the cab, the driver moves levers, occasionally leans out to check the steam, while the fireman, his face black with soot, shovels coal.

The engine slides out of the station, a mass of latent energy, limitless power, as it effortlessly, almost imperceptibly, picks up speed. The puffs speed up and smoke blasts up and out from the brass chimney. An enthusiastic cheer goes up from the platform. People start to wave and the driver waves back. Several people try to run along the platform, parallel with the engine, shoving others out of their way, determined to keep it in sight as long as they can, even as the engine speeds up. In the end, everyone surges forward, leaving a space behind them, which enables Nick, Johnny, Debs and Dougie to climb down from the bench and move closer to the edge. The track curves as it leaves the station. They can see the engine heading off round the bend and out of sight, chuffing into the distance, and then they're left standing, bereft, not knowing what to do with all their excitement.

The band strikes up again, full of renewed vigour, but the music is thin, hollow; lacking resonance after the enormity of the sound that has just left them.

'Now what?' says Johnny. He's standing on the other side of Debs, his hands flapping the air in front of him as if he's brushing away an invisible plague of flies, trying to clear the people away, to give himself space.

There's a whistle from round the bend and the engine comes back into sight, faster than when it left, but slowing as it approaches the platform.

'Seems like a lot of fuss for such a short trip,' says Debs.

'They're planning to take it backwards and forwards several times,' says Nick. 'Every half-hour, I think.'

'Got to follow regulations,' says Dougie. 'It's a powerful machine – you can't take chances with something that big. You got to know it's safe before you take it further out.'

'It's not a ship,' says Johnny. 'It goes along, not out.'

'It's coming in backwards,' says Nick.

'Well it would, wouldn't it?' says Dougie. 'You can't just turn it round. Great big thing like that.'

The engine comes in smoothly, slowing down as it approaches the shed.

'It doesn't go all that fast really, does it?' says Nick.

'Not allowed,' says a man behind them. 'There's a legal limit for these old locos.'

Debs sags against Nick. 'I need to sit down,' she says.

Nick starts to edge back to the bench. When he looks to Johnny for help, he realises that he hasn't even noticed. He's mesmerised by the engine, flushed with excitement, with patches of pink peeping between the hairs of his beard and a gleam in his eyes that hasn't been in evidence for decades. He looks as though he's just beaten Nick six-love, six-love, six-love.

The engine stops short of the entrance to the shed. The railway workers dash towards the cab as the engine driver and fireman climb down. Everyone wants to shake hands with them. Men with technical equipment climb into the cab, along the side and across the top to the coal bunker, examining valves, while several others get down from the platform to check underneath the engine again. A huddle of men gather round the driver and fireman, talking earnestly, taking notes.

'They've already done all that,' says Debs, pausing to watch.

'They have to do it after every trip,' says Johnny. 'It's all to do with safety.'

'Looks like they're going to do a longer trip,' says Dougie. 'There haven't been any problems, far as I can see.'

Nick leads Debs carefully to the bench and sits down with her. She sighs heavily and leans back with her eyes closed.

Johnny and Dougie remain where they are, watching the railway workers. Johnny is exhilarated by the sound, the steam, the demonstration of power. He's aware of an energy and excitement deep within him that come from so long ago he'd forgotten they were there. He half recognises the rush of adrenalin, but takes a while to place the memory.

He's eight years old again, he and Nick playing by the railway, picking their way through coarse, prickly grass and cotoneaster. They're skimming down the forbidden bank to the railway cutting, flattening the daisies, the clover, the dock leaves, and on to the tracks.

They knew the times of the trains – everyone knew the times – and even though they didn't have watches, they knew where they were in the day. They subconsciously registered how long it had been since they got out of bed, the hours that had elapsed since breakfast, the emptiness in their stomachs. So they knew a train was due. They were waiting for its approach, anticipating the thrill, preparing themselves for the last-minute scramble to safety.

'You can hear it coming,' said Nick. 'If you put your ear on the rail, you'll feel the vibration.'

They crouched down, side by side, not quite kneeling, not wanting to catch their knees on the oily stones between the sleepers, and placed their ears on the nearest section of the shiny metal rail. Johnny couldn't hear anything. 'It's coming!' yelled Nick, and Johnny leapt to his feet, following Nick off the tracks, scrambling back up the bank, not stopping until they reached the top. They sat and waited.

It didn't come. It didn't come the next three times, either.

'You don't know nothing,' said Johnny scornfully, as they stood at the bottom again, examining the lines as they stretched away from them in both directions, one way long and straight, disappearing into a mist of distance, the other heading off round a corner.

'Anything,' corrected Nick. 'You'll cop it off Ma if she hears you saying "you don't know nothing". That's prison rations for a week, that is.'

'Don't tell her then. Anyway, you're just spinning me a line. You don't know when the train comes at all.'

'Don't you worry, the train's on its way. Just 'cause I don't always get it right, doesn't mean to say I don't know what I'm talking about. It's a knack. Needs a bit more practice, that's all.'

'You're all mouth,' said Johnny.

Nick grabbed him by the shoulder. 'Say that again,' he said.

'All mouth,' shouted Johnny. 'All talk, no substance.' It was a phrase Ma was fond of. She used to say it to their dad when he came home from the betting shop.

They leapt on top of each other, and rolled against the hot, glinting metal of the rails, bruising their ribs against the sleepers, grazing their legs on the gravel, coating them with oil.

They were alerted by the whistle.

As they pulled themselves to their feet, the train appeared round the bend, from the opposite direction that they'd been expecting, thundering towards them on the parallel track. Johnny stared at it, unable to believe it, mesmerised by the enormity of the engine, paralysed by the shriek of the whistle. He couldn't think. He felt himself being grabbed by Nick, pulled over the side of the rail and pushed violently up the bank.

They flattened themselves against the grass, gasping for breath, face down to start with, then rolling over on their backs so they could see. They could feel the heat as it passed, an endless procession of red trucks trundling and creaking, chuntering and murmuring to each other, not nearly as fast as they'd expected.

After it had gone, they continued to lie for some time, letting the silence settle. Then Nick jumped to his feet. 'It nearly got us!' he said, his voice far too loud. 'We were nearly gonners.'

'It was that close!' shouted Johnny, still jittering with excitement. 'I could see the bogies, the labels on the side of the trucks, the handles . . .' He couldn't believe their narrow escape. 'If you hadn't grabbed me—'

'Yeah!' said Nick. 'I saved your life.'

'No you didn't,' said Johnny, immediately, automatically rethinking. 'I'd have got out of the way on my own.'

'No you wouldn't. You just froze. You were dead meat.'

'Didn't. Didn't, didn't, didn't!'

'Did, did, did!'

They picked the dry grass out of their hair, banged the dust out of their clothes and went home for supper.

PC Banner came round in the evening and had a long talk with Ma. They didn't get any supper the next day, and then it was only soup every day for a full week.

Now, fifty years later, Johnny stands next to Dougie and examines *Enigma* – the gleaming paintwork, the shining name, the polished brass chimney. So many years, so many things to think about. Why do you remember some things and forget others? How does your brain know which bits will be relevant later? Are they all packed away, just waiting for the code, the key to the storage locker?

The men by the engine cab appear to have come to a decision. They circle for a while, apparently searching for something, until a young woman runs up with a megaphone. They debate for a few seconds, then a short, scruffy man with a ponytail takes charge.

'Ladies and Gentlemen!' he shouts through the megaphone. His voice is strong, but he's finding it difficult to make himself heard.

'That's Lord Wychington,' says Dougie.

Hardly anyone takes any notice. He tries again, with the same effect. Several of the men start to blow their whistles. This has the desired effect. Voices lower, the noise subsides, and everyone looks towards the man with the megaphone.

He raises it again. 'Ladies and gentlemen . . .' There's an expectant pause. 'You will be pleased to know that the test run has exceeded our wildest dreams. The checks have revealed an engine running so sweetly that we suspect a rogue engineer has been feeding her on nectar and ambrosia.' He pauses, as if waiting for applause, but most people are frowning, clearly puzzled. 'So our resident experts have decided to attempt the big one. A much longer trip to the outer reaches of the estate, into the unknown, beyond civilisation as we know it. Time of departure will be five o'clock, so if you would be so good as to synchronise your watches, we can all be in position for lift-off.' He examines his watch. 'I make it fifteen hundred hours, twenty-seven minutes and forty-one seconds precisely.' He pauses and several people check their watches. 'We propose to travel outwards for approximately five miles. Our trusty workers have been labouring tirelessly for many, many months, with enormous expertise, bringing the track up to the required condition, and we've passed all our tests with flying colours, so we're confident of yet another triumphant success.'

'Yes!' shouts Dougie.

Johnny finds himself opening his mouth to cheer, raising his arm to wave with everyone else, but suddenly becomes aware of what he's doing. He lowers the arm quickly and shuts his mouth, acutely self-conscious. But when he looks around, no one is taking any notice of him. They're all chattering excitedly to each other.

The man raises the megaphone again. 'Meanwhile, *Enigma* will travel up and down for a very short distance several more times. If you'd like to go and polish off the grub, there's oodles of time. We have an abundance, thanks to the supreme generosity of our local citizens – there are cakes galore, lashings of ginger beer and, if you're absolutely determined to emulate the thirties, we might even manage the odd tin of luncheon meat.'

Everyone starts to talk again, but another blast on the whistles quietens them.

'We're going to put up maps of the route and we recommend car trips to various viewing points along the track, where you can stand and cheer *Enigma* as she roars past at the outrageously reckless speed of twenty-five miles per hour – our maximum permitted speed. It's the stuff of dreams, ladies and gentlemen. Don't miss out under any circumstances. Lubricate freely first – the tea ladies are expecting you – and there'll be plenty of time to get yourselves into position.'

'You got a car?' asks Dougie as they join the crowd going down the steps.

'No, we came by taxi.'

'You can come with me if you want.'

'Oh, right,' says Johnny. 'Can you get Nick and Debs in too?'

'Don't see why not.'

'Mr Greenwood?'

'Yes?' He turns, surprised to be recognised.

'Hi,' she says. 'I'm Mimi. We met very briefly when we came to look round your carriages.'

Johnny nods, wondering if he should offer his hand. Is that what you do nowadays or did the habit die out decades ago? His only experience comes from films, but he's not sure how accurate they are. Most of them are American anyway, and therefore no help.

'It's all terrific, isn't it?' she says. 'I just wanted to say, have you realised that the engine is going to pass the siding that leads off into your field, really close to your carriages? There's a layby further down Long Meadow Road, on the left before you get to the one by you, and if you park there, you should be able to see the points. I've checked the map and there don't seem to be any trees there, so you should easily see *Enigma* go past.'

Johnny smiles awkwardly, not sure what to say.

'Come on,' she says. 'I'll show you the map. You've got plenty of time to get yourself into position – although there might be a delay leaving the car park. Everyone's going to want to head out at the same time.'

19

'I think Mimi was right to tell you,' says Crispin to Zohra as they share a slice of almond and cherry cheesecake on a paper plate. He's eating slowly, swallowing awkwardly. His neck looks a little swollen after Nathan's attack and his voice is croaky. 'Better than waiting for it to jump out of the shadows and take you by surprise.'

'But that's exactly what it did.' She's distracted, half watching the people around them, still struggling to work out how she feels. She concentrates on the cake, which is rather good. 'It jumped out anyway.'

Crispin drops a large piece of cake without noticing. 'Just like Nathan,' he says sadly. They've tried to find Nathan's mother, hoping to talk it over with her, but she seems to have vanished.

Zohra leans against him, wanting to offer comfort. They will have to work out what to do about Nathan at some point, but she knows there won't be an easy solution. 'It was so unexpected,' she says.

'His mum always said he could be difficult,' says Crispin. 'Right at the beginning, when he first came. And he was, a bit – but not like that. He seemed to settle down well, and he's been coming for such a long time. I just thought . . .' He puts an arm round her shoulders, and she can feel the weight of his worry. 'I'll have to report it. There'll be questions about whether he's safe to have on the project . . .'

He knows all about Fiona now, about Katy, Mimi and Carys, and he's just carrying on as if there's no change. It's like squeezing extra passengers without tickets on to a train. The wheels don't register the surplus weight; there's no strain on the engine;

the train leaves on time. Crispin's still at her side – happy to take on the added burden. As always.

The trouble is, nothing ever arrives when you expect it, or in the way you think it should. It wasn't Fiona, it was Katy.

'*Enigma* was brilliant,' says Crispin. 'At least that's all gone according to plan.' He crumples the paper plate into a ball and shoots it into a bulging black bin bag that's been placed by the cake stall. 'Better, in fact.'

Zohra studies his face and wants to put a hand on his cheek, feel his excitement through her fingertips. She remembers the kiss, the pleasure that it gave her. 'I'm glad they're going to do the longer trip. It makes it all worth it.'

'There'll be no end to what she can do now. Thousands of miles into the future. Forwards, backwards, round in circles. And it's all down to us.'

'With a little bit of help from our friends.'

He grins and takes her hand. 'No, just us. You, me and Perry – we're the ones who made it happen.' He swings their arms. 'Where shall we go to watch?'

She thinks for a moment. 'Near the siding to the Greenwoods' carriages. It'll slow down there to negotiate the points – that'll be the perfect place.'

Crispin is peering across the field, scanning each section intently. He's searching for Nathan, of course. Zohra looks too. She can see Bill (surprisingly slick in a thirties costume), talking intently to his wife (nearly as tall as him, thin, elegant), and Rohit (in T-shirt, jeans and a trilby) following them around as if he belongs to them, and Dougie, who seems to have met up with the Greenwood brothers. Zohra raises her hand to wave, but nobody notices.

Nathan should be easy to spot with his awkward, clumsy movements, but there's no sign of him. They've become used to having him close by, keeping an eye on him, checking what he's doing. We've been like parents, she thinks, resenting the obligation, but knowing it was inevitable. And now they're having to deal with the delinquent teenager.

311

How could he have believed he was going to marry her? She might have encouraged him a little, but not seriously and only to keep him happy: that's what you do with children.

'Why didn't you say anything before?' Zohra asks Crispin as they walk slowly through the cake stalls towards the car park.

'I'm always saying things,' says Crispin. 'Most people tell me I say too much.'

She digs an elbow into his side. 'You know what I mean. To me. About us.'

He stops and searches again, turning slowly, narrowing his eyes as he peers into the distance. 'Do you think Nathan's okay? We shouldn't go without him.'

'Answer the question,' says Zohra. 'You're avoiding.'

He pauses. 'You weren't ready,' he says eventually.

'But when did you decide . . . ?'

He grins amiably. 'I decided at the beginning, right from those early days of extra-curricular Twentieth-Century Literature when I saw you huddled at the back and recognised you as someone who really cared about the books. *The English Patient*, *The Grapes of Wrath*, *Beloved*, *The Spy Who Came in From the Cold* – you thought I was moved by their power, their portrayal of the great injustices of the world. And of course I was – you and I were the only ones there who read them all, did you know that? – but I was really burning with frustration because you didn't notice that my hand was hovering millimetres from yours, longing to touch, my fingertips tingling with the desire to make contact with your smooth, peachy skin – well, maybe that's not quite right. Chocolate more precisely, or milk chocolate—'

'Oh stop it,' she says, managing to laugh. 'You're being ridiculous.'

'Maybe,' he says. 'But anyway – I couldn't really say anything – after things started to go wrong . . .'

There it is again. There's no escape.

They stand in silence for a while, studying the people around them. 'Look,' he says quietly, 'it's never going to go away completely, but you have to let it be. It wasn't possible for you to change anything then and we can't do anything about it now. None of it was your fault. I know you think it was, but if you're being bullied, you're never going to think clearly about it – ever. The real villain in it all was Katy. We know that now.' He pauses. 'I always knew there was something about her. It was that shifty look she had every time I mentioned your name.'

Zohra turns to him in surprise, then sees the sides of his mouth twitching. 'No,' she says, 'I'm not ready for jokes. I may never be ready.'

'But perhaps we should try to let it exist somewhere in the background,' he says. 'Blow the froth off, sip at it gently until it cools. If we just ignore it, it'll appear when we're not expecting it, boiling away, all ready to burn your tongue again.'

We. They're going to deal with it together. 'Metaphors now, then?' she says. 'Pretentions to being a novelist? Is that your great plan for the future?'

He stops. 'Are you suggesting I should be looking for an alternative career – staring at a computer screen, building roads, delivering post? You seem to forget I'll have this great estate to manage when I inherit – and a railway to run.'

'The estate is no longer great, and it'll deteriorate long before you get it into your clutches – or at least the house will. It's already teetering on the verge of collapse. I hold my breath every time I go indoors. Have you considered the possibility that you might have to spend the rest of your life in a tent?'

'Last time we had this conversation, you told me I was lucky to have a roof over my head and running water.'

She smiles. 'Different point to make, different perspectives.'

People are drifting past them, making their way back to their cars, preparing to find a good viewing platform for watching *Enigma* steam past.

'Crisp!' The voice comes echoing across the field. Several people stop and turn their heads, then continue when they realise it's nothing to do with them.

'Nathan!' says Crispin, spinning around eagerly. 'Where is he?'

'Crisp!'

'There,' says Zohra, pointing.

He's on the platform, by the steps, both hands raised above his head, waving frantically. Crispin immediately lifts his own hands in response, then sets off towards him.

Zohra follows him. 'Wait!' she says, worried by his eagerness. 'Do you think it's all right to carry on as if nothing has happened?'

He slows down. 'Let's play it by ear. This is Nathan we're talking about. He might be perfectly normal now.'

'But how can we be sure he's safe? He could have killed you.'

Crispin stops for a moment. 'No,' he says. 'He wouldn't have gone that far. He's like a child who doesn't always know where to draw the line.'

But Nathan's strength isn't childlike. The fear is still fresh in Zohra's mind, the moment when she realised that nothing she could do would help Crispin. She puts up her hand and runs her finger over the bruises round his neck. They're swelling up, dark and brutal. 'Please be careful. We can't be sure—'

'It's okay, I know he's a bit excitable, obsessional – trains, *Star Trek*, that kind of thing – but I've never met anyone as loyal as him. He just got carried away, that's all. Come on, let's give him the benefit of the doubt, see how it goes.'

Zohra is not reassured. The way Nathan just tossed her aside – so casually, without a thought, as if she was insignificant or unnecessary – was terrifying. The way he changed so easily, so quickly, turned into someone she didn't know. But at the same time, she understands Crispin's desire to get along with everyone, to sort out differences, put things straight. He sees the best in everyone. He believes in appeasement and compromise. And he's genuinely fond of Nathan. Zohra's parents appear in front of them. They've collected the empty cake plate and are heading for the car park.

'You're not going back to work already, are you?' she says, hearing the edge in her voice, knowing it will make them nervous. But she's irritated by their readiness to put the shop first. They so rarely make time for themselves.

'No,' says her father, equally irritated. 'You believe we don't know how to enjoy ourselves?'

Her mother looks at her, smiling urgently, determined to make everything fine. 'All things happy?' She smoothes the tips of her fingers over Zohra's cheek in the way she would have done twenty years ago, apparently forgetting she's no longer a child. Then she withdraws them hastily.

'Of course,' says Zohra, moved by this display of affection. She appreciates their struggle to not interfere, their determination to not ask questions. 'But you will watch the train go past?'

'Naturally,' says her mother. 'Cannot miss such a thing. We watch it once, and soon we watch it again.'

'The old railway crossing would be a good place for you, up by the tip,' says Crispin. 'I don't think many people will go there.'

'We think alike,' says her father. 'I already know this place; I found it when out walking, lots of trees, bushes, unused little road, merely a path, but no one except me ever goes there. I recognised it was an old railway as soon as I saw it. I have experience. So I alone knew there was once a train.'

When does he have time to walk? Was it when he first came to Bromsgrove, when he was cycling round, mapping it all out in his head. Or does he go for midnight walks without telling anyone?

'You come with us?' asks her mother. 'Go as family?'

'Probably not,' says Zohra. 'I'll be going with Crispin.'

'Okay,' says her father. 'I trust you, Crispin. I know you take care of her well.'

Crispin looks embarrassed. 'Thanks Mr Dasgupta,' he says awkwardly. 'No worries.'

Zohra's father examines her face closely. 'Not late back?'

'Not late back,' she says, smiling at his concern. 'Although it might depend on Crispin,' she adds, suddenly aware that everything is shifting and she can no longer expect to be predictable. She watches for a few moments as they walk off.

'Come on,' says Crispin, pulling her arm gently and leading her towards the platform. 'Everything'll be fine.'

Nathan is grinning down at them. 'Hey, Crisp,' he calls.

He's just summoned us and we've come running, thinks Zohra as they go up the steps. He should have come to find us. He knows so little about how to conduct a friendship.

But of course, that's the problem. He knows so little.

As soon as they're face to face, Nathan puts his arms round Crispin awkwardly. 'S-sorry,' he says. Physical touching is not something he does easily, so he's tight and clumsy and his arms don't mould themselves round Crispin's back. The elbows stick out and his fingers stretch stiffly into the air, unable to make direct contact.

But Crispin is delighted. This is a victory, an apology, and it moves him. 'You're all right, mate,' he says several times, patting Nathan on the back. 'It's okay.'

After a while they separate and Nathan lifts his fingers towards Crispin's neck, tracing the bruises in the air, but not actually touching. 'I really got you there, didn't I?' he says.

'You did,' says Crispin. 'Hurt a bit, I can tell you.'

'Shouldn't have done it.'

'No, you shouldn't.' There's a pause. 'But you can learn from it. Think first, act second. That way you can avoid embarrassing situations.'

'Mmm.'

Zohra stands slightly apart, not sure what to do. Nathan gives no indication that he remembers involving her in his outburst of anger and doesn't seem to consider that maybe she needs an apology too, but she doesn't want to draw attention to herself. It seems easier to allow him a reconciliation with Crispin.

The platform is almost empty. The afternoon sun is descending and shadows are starting to lengthen. This second trip will make a fitting finale to the day. Then there'll be more work – the renovation of the remaining track, a search for carriages – before the railway can become fully operational.

She can see the cars queuing to leave the car park. Most of the stalls are packing up, preparing to join the exodus. A slight breeze is blowing rubbish around: plastic cups, disposable plates and forks, somersaulting over the ground in slick routines; screwed-up paper serviettes dancing in clusters, a corps de ballet gliding elegantly above the grass; half-eaten slices of cake, sandwiches, biscuits, rejected or accidently fallen round the base of the tables and chairs, providing future nourishment for insects and birds. Most of the balloons have been released and are hovering indolently, some close to the ground, sad and defeated, others drifting higher, positioning themselves a few feet above the heads of the remaining people, ideally placed for surveillance, keeping an eye on the engine and the newly formed railway.

'Melvin says we can have a look round the cab,' says Nathan. 'It'll be quite different now the engine's operational.'

'Really?' says Crispin. 'I thought everyone was banned once it was fired up.'

'He didn't mean us,' says Nathan. 'That's just the public. We have permission.'

'Are you sure?'

'Sure as eggs is eggs,' says Nathan. 'My nan used to say that. Good, isn't it? Sure as eggs is eggs. Sure as—'

'Okay, Nathan, we've got it,' says Crispin.

'Come on, then.' Nathan leads them towards the engine, which is waiting, poised to go, half in and half out of the shed, throbbing with heat. Wilf, the driver, is leaning out of the cab, clutching a cup of coffee. Harry, who designs websites in real life, is on the roof, removing the huge flattened pipe that he's been using to top up the water. He pushes the cover down and seals it, then jumps down and walks back to the shed. Wilf is chatting with Betty. She's wearing a black cap over her grey curls and her face is streaked with oil. Steam puffs out from the side of the train every now and again with a sigh, slow and ponderous. There's a rich, heavy smell of oil, smoke, machinery.

Nathan approaches them. 'Hi,' he says.

'Hi, Nathan,' says Wilf.

'How much longer before you go?'

Betty raises her hand in the air and checks her watch. 'Any time now.' She has an unexpectedly deep voice, slightly gravelly. She used to smoke, she has explained to everyone. She's given it up, retired from her job as a tax consultant and taken up trains as a hobby in a tribute to her late husband. 'Never took a blind bit of notice of his obsession when he was alive,' she says. 'Feel I owe it to him now.'

'Why is there so much steam when it's not moving?' asks Zohra as she and Crispin join them.

Wilf smiles, always delighted to give details, despite working all his life on the railways. 'You can't just turn a loco on and off like a car. Once it's primed, you've got steam.'

They stand in a group for a couple of minutes without speaking while Wilf sips his coffee. Then Nathan puts a foot on the lower step of the cab. 'Just going to let the others see inside,' he says.

'Sorry mate,' says Wilf. 'No can do. Not without permission. Not once it's fired up.'

'I've got permission,' says Nathan. 'Melvin said it was okay to look round.'

'Well that's rich,' says Betty. 'One rule for the posh, another for everyone else.'

'We are talking about Crisp here,' says Nathan. 'Without him and his dad, there wouldn't be an engine or a railway. How are we going to train as drivers if we can't go on to the footplate?'

'I'm not going to be a driver,' says Zohra. 'That's for zealots.'

'Okay,' says Nathan to Zohra, the first time he's acknowledged her presence. 'But you have to at least see it working. Melvin told me we could, honest.'

Zohra looks at Crispin, who shrugs. 'Don't ask me.'

'Suppose it can't do any harm,' says Wilf to Betty. 'The lad knows it all and no mistake. I've had him up on the footplate loads of times. Can't see why today's any different. There's not many gets it like he does.'

Betty shrugs. 'Not my decision. Up to you.'

Wilf climbs down and joins them on the platform. 'Go on then,' he says, jerking his head towards the cab, and winking at Zohra. 'Don't blame me if you get into trouble, though. I'm just the engine driver.'

'Are you quite sure about this?' asks Zohra, unwilling to do anything without permission. She doesn't want to disappoint Crispin, who's clearly itching to get up there, but she feels the need for more reassurance.

'Yeah, go on, mate. Just be quick. You've got a couple of minutes.'

Nathan climbs up first, then Crispin, then Zohra, who pulls herself up more slowly, still sore from when Nathan pushed her over. It feels crowded with the three of them. They've seen it all before, when it was being renovated, but Zohra can feel the difference immediately. Now the engine is alive, breathing, steam flooding through the pipes like blood through veins, the whole cab pulsating with the urge to go. It's extremely hot, even though the doors of the firebox are closed. Heat radiates outwards, powerful and intense.

Nathan gestures at each part in turn, naming it, explaining its function. 'The regulator,' he says indicating a long flat orange bar with a raised section at the end. 'You'll need that for driving – it's like a throttle. It opens the main valve which supplies steam from the boiler, through the piston valves to the cylinders.' He points rapidly at various dials and handles. 'Blower valve, stops fire blowing back into the cab; brake valve; vacuum gauge; boiler pressure gauge; water gauge; automatic warning system set off by the signals ahead, sounds a bell if the line's clear, a horn if there's a danger . . .' He's become a different person, an expert.

'How do you know all this?' asks Zohra, who can't retain the information despite his previous lectures.

Nathan looks momentarily baffled. 'I don't know. I just do, like Crisp.'

'Well,' says Crispin, clearly out of his depth, but unwilling to admit it, 'I'm not sure I'd trust myself to actually drive the thing.'

'Oi!' shouts a voice from outside. 'How much longer you going to be? We need you out of there.'

'Okay,' calls Nathan. 'Coming! Go on, Crisp. You first.'

Crispin starts to climb down backwards and Zohra turns, ready to follow. She peers round, over her shoulder, watching Crispin, making sure he's clear before she starts descending. She's startled by a sudden grip on her arm. 'It's all right,' says Nathan. 'You can s-stay.'

'What do you mean?' she asks, taken aback. 'I thought we had to leave.'

Nathan pulls her to one side, calmly but firmly.

'What are you doing?' she says, now annoyed. When she attempts to remove herself from his grasp, he holds on more tightly, so she forces herself to relax, let him feel the release of tension in her arm. 'It's all right, Nathan,' she says as calmly as possible. She knows he doesn't understand resistance. It makes him more determined. A few weeks ago, when she was tightening a bolt, he decided she needed help and placed his hand over hers. She could do it on her own, she didn't need him, but the more she tried to release herself, the more strongly he held on. She eventually realised that the only way to ease him off was to stop reacting, removing any sense of threat, allowing him to make the decision. Maybe if they'd been more passive when he attacked Crispin, he would have backed off. But he'd been so powerful and frightening then. It's not so easy to think clearly when you're being threatened.

'Nathan,' she says, very gently. 'Can you let go?'

He looks down at his hand round her arm, as if it doesn't belong to him. The pressure eases slightly.

'That's it, Nathan. Thank you.'

He stares at her, his eyes wide and perplexed, and his hand loosens a bit more.

'Hurry up,' shouts Wilf from the bottom of the steps. Zohra can see the top of his head as he paces backwards and forwards.

'Stop messing about, Nathan,' calls Crispin.

A look of panic brushes across Nathan's face, followed by confusion. He releases Zohra's arm abruptly, but then unexpectedly pushes her, hard. She staggers, not as steady as usual in her smart shoes, and catches her ankle against a protruding lever.

'Ouch!' she says, bending over to rub her leg, more annoyed with Wilf and Crispin than Nathan. 'Give us a minute,' she calls, knowing that Nathan can't be rushed. 'We'll be down shortly.' There's something not quite right about his behaviour. Normally, he loves to obey instructions, be cooperative. Rules, restrictions, regulations are nourishment to him. But he's reacting oddly. It's as if his earlier outburst has introduced a fault, altered the way he thinks. 'Don't worry about Wilf,' she says. 'He's always impatient.'

He ignores her and starts to move about, opening the fire door, checking inside, shovelling in coal, snapping the door shut again. His bewilderment has faded and he's now absorbed in what he's doing. A look of contentment has descended over his face. She thinks she can hear him humming.

'Shall we go down now?' says Zohra, just loud enough for him to hear, not enough to antagonise him. But he's acting as if she's not there. He positions himself in front of the controls and starts to move a wheel, faster and faster. Then he pulls a handle down and the needle in the gauge above it moves anticlockwise. There's a hissing sound. He starts to lift the regulator, moving the long handle slowly upwards until there's a click.

The train starts to move.

'Nathan!' cries Zohra, finally understanding but finding it hard to believe. 'This is a really, really bad idea!'

She pushes past him and attempts to pull the regulator back down again, but he grabs her round the waist and almost throws her into the corner, much more powerfully than before. She struggles to stay upright and only narrowly misses the fire door. It's that strength again, the careless ease that he displayed earlier. He darts back to the small wheel and spins it anti-clockwise. And now he's singing. It's hard to identify the tune and there aren't any words, but it sounds a bit like the theme tune of *Star Trek*.

'Nathan!' shouts Zohra. 'Stop! This is madness! You can't do it!'

'I can!' he says, interrupting his singing. 'I can, I can, I can! Everyone thinks I can't do things, but they're wrong. I know *Enigma* better than anyone else – I'm the best one to drive her.' There's a high-pitched intensity in his voice that she's never heard before. He believes in himself. He's lost sight of reality.

There are shouts from outside and a shiny black cap appears on the side of the cab. It's probably Wilf. Nathan grabs the shovel and raises it above his head.

'No!' says Zohra, struggling to keep her voice even, not wanting to panic him even further. 'Nathan, you can't do that!' She tries to pull him away, but can't make any impression on him. 'Look out!' she shrieks to Wilf as he starts to lower the shovel.

It slices through the air but, at the last minute, Nathan allows it to lose momentum and it drops on to the floor with a clatter. With a sigh of relief, Zohra rushes over to help Wilf up, but Nathan elbows her aside and with an alarming display of coldness, pushes him away. The head disappears. There's a cry as he hits the ground. Nathan leans over the side of the cab, looking backwards. 'Leave me alone!' he shouts. 'Count yourself lucky I only pushed!' He picks up the shovel again and brandishes it over the side, his legs apart, swaying with the movement of the engine.

Zohra tries to push past him, wanting to know if Wilf has been badly hurt, but she can't see properly. Nathan has gone back to the controls and they're starting to move faster. They've passed the end of the platform by now and entered a wide, flat stretch, running parallel to the road, cleared of surrounding undergrowth, heading towards a cluster of trees. People are running behind them, but they're rapidly falling back, unable to keep up. Only Crispin remains, racing alongside, leaping over the surplus stones, dodging the piles of unused sleepers, the discarded bolts, his mouth opening and shutting, but unable to make himself heard above the sound of the engine.

Zohra allows herself a moment of joy at his determination to save her. But he can't possibly maintain the speed – he's going to trip. 'Crispin!' she shouts, stretching out an ineffectual hand, desperate to pull him towards her, knowing it's hopeless.

He's losing ground, running out of breath, slipping gradually behind as the space at the side of the track narrows and they approach the trees. He staggers to a halt and she leans out as far as she can, straining to keep him in sight. He stands there help-lessly, gasping. He summons a last burst of energy to yell, but the sound of his voice fails to reach her. She can see the defeat in his posture, his inability to keep going.

As she watches him fade into the distance, a car crosses unexpectedly from the road, jolting over the stubble of the cleared undergrowth that divides the road from the track, and races up to where Crispin is standing. It pauses only briefly for him to fling open a door and jump in. Then it turns back towards the road, away from the track. She pulls her head back in and breathes deeply. It was Freddie. They must have a plan. They're going to drive further along the line, catch up with *Enigma*.

'We're boldly going!' shouts Nathan. He reaches up and pulls twice on a loop of wire. The whistle sounds out, cheerful, warm, nostalgic. 'Wahay!' he yells. 'If it wasn't for me, there wouldn't even be a whistle!'

The locomotive starts to settle into a comfortable rhythm, chattering agreeably, rolling easily over the railway tracks as memories of its former days of glory creep back through the pipes, the pistons, the valves.

'You have to stop, Nathan,' says Zohra. 'This is insane.'

'No it's not,' he yells, louder than necessary. 'I've made my mind up. We're going to elope. You and me.'

'Of course we aren't. This is ridiculous.'

He's not listening. 'I've worked it out. When we get to the end, we'll hike across country till we get to a real station, and then we'll catch a train north. Head for S-scotland. You don't have to worry about anything. I'll look after you.'

She waits a few seconds, takes a breath as she attempts to sound relaxed, and lowers her voice. 'Perhaps you should have checked with me first. A girl likes to be asked.'

He ignores her. He's not interested in her opinion.

Zohra tries to work out how much danger they're in. He'll struggle to take the role of driver and fireman. So presumably the engine will eventually lose power and slow down. Then someone – Crispin, Freddie – could get on board and sort him out. She eases her phone out of her pocket and starts to text.

There will be onlookers positioned all along the line, waiting for the engine to go past, so they're never going to be far from anyone. It's reassuring but, at the same time, it raises another alarming possibility. What if they can't stop? What if they crash? Is he placing other people in danger too?

He turns, his face exultant, and she conceals the phone behind her. 'I'm an engine driver!' he cries.

It must be possible to talk him out of this. 'I'd like to get off now,' she says, as calmly as she can manage.

He hears this time and reacts with amazement. 'No you wouldn't,' he says. 'You only think you would.'

'You can trust me, Nathan. You know that.' She holds his eye for a second, their faces close, swaying rhythmically.

He pulls his gaze away abruptly and grabs the shovel. 'Coal,' he says. 'We have to keep the fire fed.' He knocks the catches off the doors to the firebox, wedges them open and starts shovelling from the pile of coal from the bunker. 'One, two . . .' He counts each shovel-load out loud, up to seven, then half closes the doors. He darts back over to the regulator, moves it a little, and leans over the side of the cab, examining the smoke as it comes out of the chimney. 'Too clear,' he mutters.

While he's distracted, Zohra finishes her text and sends it. She looks around, wishing she'd listened more carefully to his earlier explanations, wondering if she could just pull a handle, release something. How dangerous could it be? Which one was the brake? There was a gauge above it, she remembers, but there are several gauges and it's impossible to know what each one is for. 'Don't forget the track runs out,' she calls. 'We'll reach the end of the line in no time if we keep going at this speed.'

He looks at her with surprise. 'It's all right,' he says. 'We're not going fast.' He leans over the side and checks the smoke again. It feels much faster than that. He adjusts a few handles, but there doesn't seem to be a response.

'Are you sure you know what you're doing?' she asks.

'I certainly do.'

'Have you ever actually driven an engine before?'

'No, of course not. You can't just turn up and drive a train. But I've done it loads of times on the Internet.'

'On the Internet?' She tries not to sound too shocked. 'Nathan, the Internet's not the same as real life.'

'It's good enough. You can do anything. It's dead easy.'

'But a real train isn't dead easy.'

'It is if you know what you're doing, and I do. Stop worrying.' He frowns as he pulls a few levers. 'Yes, that's it.'

Have they slowed a little? It's possible. She tries to work out where they are. She knows some areas better than others, but many of the trees look the same. They burst out into a clearing and she can see parked cars, groups of people gathered to watch them pass. They'll help, she thinks. They'll see there's something wrong.

But as they sweep past, everyone waves and cheers.

Of course. It's what they've been waiting for, the engine racing past at full speed.

Her phone vibrates in her pocket and she pulls it out carefully.

There's a text from Crispin. Distract him, it says. I'm going to try and board at the points.

They need to slow down, give Crispin enough time to get there. 'Your mum's not going to be very pleased with you,' says Zohra, putting the phone away.

'My mum's never very pleased with me,' he says.

'Don't forget the points,' she says. 'You know, by the siding, the one that leads to the Greenwoods' field. We'll have to slow down. If we take them too fast, we could derail.' Could they? She has no idea, but she wants him to believe it's possible.

He looks suddenly tired, almost scared, as if he's had enough. He's not used to handling this kind of pressure for any length of time. It's probably just dawned on him that his expertise is limited.

'Come on,' she says. 'What do we have to do?' For a few moments, he doesn't move, then he takes a breath and straightens up. He grabs the regulator, moves it, adjusts a valve, starts to spin a small disc rapidly, using the two handles on either side. There's a sudden hiss of steam and a dial on one of the gauges drops. He stops, waits a few seconds, then does it again. They're starting to lose momentum.

Zohra peers out of the cab. 'We're nearly there!' she calls. 'Can we go slower?' She can see the siding, the place where the track divides. There's a small knot of people standing on the far side of the points, just below a low grassy bank which has been fenced off. Crispin and Freddie have climbed over the fence and they're next to the track, running rapidly towards the oncoming engine. They leap over the points, then stop, watching *Enigma* approach. Crispin is bracing himself, preparing to board. Freddie turns and runs back again towards the points, just ahead of *Enigma*, until he's in a position further along the track where he can jump on after Crispin. 'Slower,' Zohra shouts to Nathan. She steps over to the opposite side of the cab, hoping to distract him. 'We're still too fast. Do you need to put more coal in?'

'Yes,' he says, 'no – it's all right for a few more minutes – yes – if we don't keep the temperature up, we'll lose power.' He picks up the shovel.

Zohra grabs a handle. 'Is this the brake? Do you want me to move it?'

'No!' he cries. 'Don't touch that, it's dangerous!' He sounds scared, uncertain. He doesn't know as much as he thinks he does.

The engine rattles, creaks, negotiating its way through the points, then settles down again to an even rhythm. 'We've made it,' he yells. 'We're through the points.' He drops the shovel, starts moving levers, spinning dials, and the engine speeds up again.

Zohra looks past Nathan, whose attention is on the controls, and sees a head appear from outside, then a face. Crispin! She fixes her eyes on Nathan, ready to distract him if he turns round too soon. Crispin climbs over the threshold into the cab. He stands motionless for a moment. 'Nathan,' he says loudly, as normally as possible, but calm and firm, as if he's been there all the time.

Nathan turns round. 'Crisp!' he says, almost as if he's been expecting him, pleased to see him.

Freddie's head comes into view. Zohra sighs with relief. The two of them should be able to tackle Nathan and then stop the engine. But as soon as Nathan sees Freddie, his expression changes. Without a word, before anyone realises what he's doing, he grabs the shovel and swings it round, aiming directly at Freddie's head. Freddie ducks and abruptly disappears.

Nathan's equilibrium has been disrupted. He loses his balance, as if his own feet are tripping him up, and winds himself into a confused mess, struggling to remain upright. He drops the shovel and scrabbles round with his hands, trying to find something to hold on to, unable to stabilise himself. It's as if he's lost his centre of gravity. He hovers, poised between falling over in one of two directions. Then, before either Zohra or Crispin can do anything, he staggers awkwardly, puts his hands out, grasps at empty air and tips out over the side.

* * *

Ten minutes earlier, Nick, Johnny and Debs are standing in front of the immaculate forty-year-old Rover, one of the last cars left in the car park. They're all taken aback, impressed by its polished bodywork, the gleaming metal bumpers and hubcaps, the crafted wooden dashboard, the white leather seats. 'Well, you kept this quiet,' Nick says to Dougie.

'It's a beauty,' says Johnny after a few silent moments of appreciation.

'Now that's what I call a car,' says Debs.

Dougie glows with pleasure. 'My pride and joy.'

'I bet this suits your Lil well enough,' says Debs.

'They knew how to make motors in them days,' he says. 'I can get Lil out the wheelchair, into the front seat in two minutes, no hassle. We looked at modern vehicles – could've had one on mobility – but they're not the same. This is the real deal.'

'How much to the gallon?' asks Johnny. 'Ten?'

'Something like that,' says Dougie evasively.

They climb in, Debs in the front, Nick and Johnny in the back. Nick would prefer to skip the trip to see *Enigma* and take Debs back to the hotel instead. He wonders if Johnny is thinking the same thing – his legs are jiggling, his feet drumming out rhythms on the luxury carpet – but Dougie wants to see the locomotive moving at speed, and Dougie is the one with the wheels.

'Are you all right, Debs?' Nick asks, leaning round the side of her seat. She's disconcertingly quiet.

'I'm fine,' she says, her voice stronger than earlier. 'I've taken some medication, it's all sorted.' She turns to Dougie. 'You know where to go?'

'Yup. The place where the line forks,' says Dougie as they pull away, gliding silently over the grass, the powerful engine barely making a sound. 'I've got my instructions.'

'It's good of you to take us,' says Nick.

'No skin off my nose,' says Dougie. 'You're not much cop if you can't do a favour for your mates.'

'You always were a decent sort, Dougie,' says Debs.

'I'm beginning to think you really are Debs,' he says. 'Half the time you don't look anything like her, but then you do. And suddenly you sound like her. I can't get my head round it . . .'

'I know exactly what you mean,' says Nick.

They park on grassy scrubland alongside a small group of vehicles, waiting for the engine to approach. In front of them there's a rickety wooden fence and beyond that the track, on a low, grassy bank. Most people are already out of their cars, gathered by the fence, preferring the stimulation of each other's company to the isolation of their cars, peering along the line to the points, where they'll have a good view of *Enigma* as she approaches.

They hear a whistle, a second one, the rumble of the approaching locomotive.

Dougie opens the door. 'Come on,' he says. 'It's coming.'

Nick unplugs his seatbelt. Johnny's already out.

'I'll stay here,' says Debs, leaning back and closing her eyes. 'I don't find trains all that interesting.'

Just as they reach the waiting group of people a car skids off the road behind them, ploughs rapidly across the grass, swerving wildly to avoid the other cars, and judders to a halt, close to the waiting crowd. The doors swing open. Crispin, Mimi and Freddie jump out, heading for the railway line.

'Let's go!' shouts Crispin. He and Freddie throw themselves at the fence, leap over and scramble over the low grassy bank in front of them.

'How do you want to play this?' yells Freddie.

'What are they doing?' asks Nick, puzzled by their urgency. 'Is it safe?'

'Be careful, Crispin!' calls Mimi. 'You don't need to worry about Zohra. He won't hurt her if he wants to marry her!'

Crispin laughs loudly. 'Don't you believe it! He's a lot more unpredictable than that.'

It's not at all clear what's going on. The engine's getting closer, its noise filling the air.

Clouds of smoke are now rising over the tree-tops and spreading out above their heads. They can hear the wheels on the rails, sense the progress of the locomotive by the vibration in their bones, smell the oil, the movement of the machinery. It comes into sight, charging towards them.

'He's going too fast,' cries Crispin. He and Freddie run along the side of the track towards the oncoming train, leaping across the rails that go off to the left at the points, positioning themselves at a spot where there's room for them to stand side by side. They wait for it to approach. Crispin's knees are bent, his body tense, as he prepares to launch himself at the engine. *Enigma* is finally slowing down as it rumbles towards them.

Freddie suddenly straightens. 'Go, go, go!' he shouts and starts to run in the same direction as the train, back towards the waiting onlookers, so he can be ready to jump immediately after Crispin. 'You'll only get one chance!' He stops and prepares for his turn.

Crispin throws himself onto the side of the engine. Steam billows out, engulfing them all, blinding them for a few seconds. They're surrounded by noise, the blast of the engine, enormous and powerful, the wheels turning, the pistons clattering. As the smoke begins to clear, Nick can see Crispin clinging on, getting his balance, then climbing up into the cab. Freddie leaps up behind him. The engine loses more speed and starts to negotiate the points. It veers to the left with Freddie still halfway up the steps.

'It's going the wrong way!' cries someone.

A different, younger man, not familiar to Nick, appears from inside the cab, waving a shovel over Freddie's head, yelling incoherently. Crispin grabs the young man from behind, trying to prevent him from swinging the shovel. Freddie drops abruptly backwards onto the ground, and it's not clear if he's actually been hit, or if he's lost his footing as he tried to dodge the shovel. He lies still for a second, jerks awkwardly, then rolls over on to his back and lifts his head.

'Freddie!' yells Mimi, scrambling over the fence, followed by several of the onlookers, including Nick and Johnny.

'He'll be okay,' Nick shouts to Mimi. 'The train wasn't going that fast!'

Now they can see the man inside more clearly. He seems to be fighting, but there's no sign of an adversary, and then he too tips over the side and lands heavily on the grass, tumbling down the slope towards the fence. A crowd of people surges towards him.

The train rolls on, slower now, but showing no signs of stopping. It doesn't pass the waiting crowd, who are all on the other side of the fork.

'They haven't changed the points!' screams Johnny. 'It's heading for our carriages!'

Nick and Johnny stare at each other. 'Dougie!' shouts Nick. 'Get the car!'

He and Johnny scramble back over the fence and dash towards the car, where Dougie's already started up the engine. Debs opens her eyes abruptly as they leap in. 'What's going on?' she says in surprise.

'It's gone the wrong way,' says Nick.

The car pulls away before they're seated, swaying over the uneven surface as they tumble into their seats. There's no time for seatbelts. Dougie swings the Rover out of the layby and on to Long Meadow Road, tyres screeching, accelerating rapidly, and within minutes they sweep to a halt opposite the entrance to the railway carriages. He pulls the handbrake on before they've fully stopped, causing a violent jolt. Everyone except Debs leaps out and races up the pathway to the carriages.

'Nathan!' shouts Zohra, straining to see past Crispin. They see him rolling down a bank, people running towards him, but then the train goes round a bend and everything disappears.

Crispin pulls his head back in and takes a deep breath. 'He sat up,' he says. 'I definitely saw him sit up, so he must be conscious. Although he could have broken something in the fall.'

'But he's alive?' says Zohra.

'Yes, definitely alive.'

'And Freddie?'

'I think he just lost his balance and fell off. Like Wilf. I'm pretty sure Nathan didn't actually hit him. Freddie's a fit guy. He'll know how to land safely.'

Zohra looks at him, longing for a hug, knowing there's no time.

The engine has mysteriously picked up speed again and is rattling with a happy, comfortable rhythm, enjoying the run, unaware that there's no one in charge, that obstacles are about to appear. There's a sudden loud bang. The engine judders, falters slightly, then continues.

'What was that?' says Zohra.

Crispin leans over the side again. 'I can't see anything. Nothing obvious.'

'What are we going to do?'

'I don't know.' Crispin looks around, examining the instruments. 'Freddie's the one who knows about engines. That's why we needed him on board.'

'Phone Anthony,' says Zohra. 'He can give us instructions. You know, like when they land planes – when the pilot has a heart attack . . .'

'We might not have enough time,' he says, but he's getting his mobile out of his pocket, pressing buttons.

'I think that's the brake,' says Zohra, pointing.

'We need to be sure.' He puts the phone to his ear. 'Anthony?' He's shouting, revealing his panic. 'It's just me and Zohra. Tell us what to do . . .' He listens carefully to Anthony's instructions, looking round the cab to locate the various instruments. 'I've got it – the one with the handles . . . Yes, I see it. Okay, I can do that . . .'

Zohra is trying to locate their position, but the scenery isn't what she's expecting – there are thistles everywhere, no crops. She should know this part of the line, she worked up here for weeks. Why isn't it familiar? 'This isn't right,' she says suddenly. 'Crispin! We're not where we should be!'

Crisp stops talking to Anthony and stares at the passing fields for a few seconds, then turns to Zohra, shocked. 'We've gone the wrong way!' he says. 'How's that possible? The points are supposed to be locked.'

Zohra suddenly realises. 'It was Nathan!' she says. 'When he came up here yesterday on the velocipede. He must have managed to unlock the points so he could leave it on the siding, and then forgot to put them back. That must be what we crashed into just now.'

'Of course!' says Crispin. 'No wonder he was so vague.'

'Are we going to hit the Greenwoods' carriages?' asks Zohra.

'No,' he says, shaking his head as if he's trying to convince himself. 'The engine can't get through. The sleepers are too old, they'll be rotten, unable to take the weight, and it's too over-grown . . .' He stops. 'There must be trees growing up through the track – if we hit them . . .'

Zohra recognises where they are. 'This is the bit we cleared.'

'Brace yourself!' shouts Crispin. 'It's going to get a lot rougher.' He puts the phone back to his ear. 'What? Okay – anticlockwise – it cuts off the steam.' He starts spinning the handle round very fast. There's a hissing sound from outside. He stops the rotation for a second. 'Yes, yes, I get it – it's got to be gradual. Pull the regulator down – gently.'

'Yes, that's what Nathan did,' says Zohra. She moves the regulator cautiously, waiting to see if there's a reaction, feeling a click. 'It's working,' she says after a few seconds, realising that she's been holding her breath. 'I think we might be slowing down.'

'Try the regulator again.'

There's a loss of urgency in the movement of the engine, a loosening of tension. The passing countryside comes more clearly into focus.

'It's okay,' says Zohra. 'We can do it.' Steam clouds up from outside, billowing into the cab and temporarily blinding them. But they're still moving and the outside sounds are changing, strangely harsh, as if they're ripping through something. The engine starts to judder and there's a painful shrieking sound, the scrape of metal against metal. Crispin puts his head out to see what's happening, now very alarmed. 'It's the rails – they're too rusted up, buckled. We've reached the bit that hasn't been cleared,' he says. 'The bushes are getting bigger, no trees yet, though, thank goodness. So far, anyway. They're slowing us down, but not enough.'

'I don't understand,' says Zohra. 'Why are we still moving?'

'It can't just stop. It's got all this momentum – if we brake too quickly, we risk destabilising . . .' He takes a breath. 'I'm going to have to try it anyway. Here we go.' He yells into the phone as he starts spinning the brake, stops to yank the regulator up, spins again. 'I know, I know. If you've got a better suggestion, now's the time to tell me . . .'

A deep vibration rises up through the locomotive as the wheels lock, but it continues to move forward with a series of jumps. It's bludgeoning its way through what feels like a solid barrier, swaying from side to side, increasingly unstable, grinding along rails too weak to support it, preparing to either tip over or tear apart.

Crispin leans out of the cab again, stares ahead, then grabs Zohra, his face white and panicked. 'We have to get out!' he screams. 'There's no time. Jump!'

The engine jerks violently, seems to rise briefly into the air and down again, knocking Zohra and Crispin off their feet. It's an out-of-control monster, running amok, forcing its way through a jungle, whipping its tail as it goes, lashing out at every obstacle in its path. It's prising the roots of bushes out of the ground as it passes, dragging everything with it. There's a final cataclysmic crash, a deafening shriek, and a great blast of air, as powerful as a tornado, whips over them. Zohra can't breathe, think, move . . .

She feels herself being thrown to one side and then she's soaring through the emptiness of the open air.

She lands heavily, with a crunch, and for a few moments feels nothing. Then waves of pain wash through her body. She decides not to move. Will any part of her ever work again? A noise booms over and around her, on and on, ripping the world apart. Someone's shouting, but she can't move. 'Get up! Run!' Hands are pulling at her.

Why can't they leave her alone? She's perfectly all right just lying here.

Johnny is finding it difficult to absorb the unfolding disaster in front of him. He's jumped out of the car with everyone else, run up the pathway, and is now standing in the field, frozen with disbelief, watching the locomotive heading inexorably towards the carriages. He watches as *Enigma*, unstoppable, obliterates every obstacle in its path, ignores the great heap of shattered bushes piled up in front and continues to grind forward, demolishing every possible restraint. The wheels have locked, but it keeps on going, drives through everything, makes a collision inevitable—

It ploughs into the carriages. The moment of impact is shattering, ripping the air apart with careless brutality, shaking the ground like an earthquake, swallowing up every other sound for miles around.

Crispin and Zohra are still on the locomotive when it hits the carriages. It's hard to know if they jump or if the force of the collision throws them off, but at the final moment they soar out through the air together, flotsam flung ashore by a scornful, tempestuous sea, and land heavily on the ground, a few yards apart. Neither of them moves. But they're too close to the track. If *Enigma* falls to the side—

'They'll be crushed!' shouts Nick.

When Johnny sees Zohra lying there, a young woman with blood pounding through her veins, even though he doesn't really know her, he suddenly understands the fragility of life, how easily it can be wiped out, but also its immense value. She represents something he's never appreciated before, a promise of the future, a new generation, racing up behind him, fast and exciting, not held back by rivalry or resentment. Before his eyes, the world is disintegrating with uncontrolled fury. Inside, he is quietly being reborn. Before he has time to think what he's doing, he's running towards her. 'Get up!' he screams as he approaches her. 'Run!' She has to survive. It's more important than anything he's ever known.

She's not exactly unconscious – when he gets close enough, he can see that her eyes are open – but her expression is confused, as if she can't work out what she's doing there. She doesn't move. He leans over, picks her up and carries her back towards safety at the edge of the field. Once there, he sees that Nick has also managed to pull Crispin to a safe distance. Zohra starts to wriggle, so he places her delicately on her feet, supporting her as she attempts to get her bearings.

She leans against him, dazed, wobbling slightly, her face black with soot. She sees Crispin. 'Crispin!' she shouts, her voice little more than a croak.

He looks back at her, his face equally black, and smiles awkwardly, struggling to manipulate his mouth. They move towards each other, slowly.

Johnny has to turn away. An enormous pressure is forming in his chest and his eyes are oddly wet.

The engine continues to push the carriages as if it has a death wish, the wheels screaming with painful, drawn-out agony as they force their way, grinding and scraping, over the corroded rails. It keeps moving long after it should have stopped, until there's nowhere else to go. When it finally judders to a reluctant halt, it hovers indecisively, wobbles, sways to the right, to the left, back again. It seems about to tip, but at the last minute rights itself and settles, trembling but upright.

The carriages have been shunted forward, into the inadequate barrier and past it, mowing it down with contempt, carrying on where the rails run out. Demeter skids across the grass towards a group of beeches, ploughs into their trunks and crumples, followed closely by Aphrodite, neither of them able to stop. They fold like cardboard boxes, weak and fragile, and collapse, incapable of serious resistance. Now the combined, unrecognisable mass of the two carriages is rocking, dancing to an unknown tune, on a tightrope, finally collapsing sideways and falling to the ground almost gently, no longer able to fight.

Water starts to gush out, a powerful fountain to start with, slowing after a few seconds to a steady stream that spreads out across the field.

Johnny can sense Ma beside him, shaking her head.

Good riddance, she says. Can't believe you were still living here anyway.

But it's where we've always been: where we were when Dad died, and Debs, and you.

Ridiculous, says Ma. You've been sitting around all this time, waiting for a train that was never going to come. Well, now it has. Who cares if she's Debs or Bev? She's here – make the most of it.

Johnny's chest suddenly clears and he discovers in himself a remarkable calmness. He's just witnessed the complete annihilation of his childhood home, but he's finding it difficult to respond as if it's a personal disaster.

For the first time, he realises that he wants her to be Debs. He would really like to talk to Ma about her. 'She didn't die,' he keeps saying inside his head, as if repetition will make Ma hear him.

We should phone the emergency services, thinks Nick, groping in his pocket for his phone. But which one? Ambulance? Fire Brigade? He starts to dial, but a hand on his arm stops him.

'Already done,' says Debs calmly. She gazes around, almost smiling. 'Well. Not quite the outcome we expected when we set off for Wychington Railway this morning.'

'Shouldn't you stay in the car?' says Nick. 'I'm not sure how safe it is.'

'Nonsense,' she says. 'The danger's over. Where's the water coming from?'

'The pipe from the mains water supply,' he says. 'It must have broken off.'

Cars are pulling up behind them on the road and people are crowding into the field, shouting loudly to each other: railway enthusiasts who've followed the route of the train on their maps, aware that it went the wrong way; farmers and dog-walkers, drawn by the sound of the impact; Mimi, distraught; Freddie, battered and black with oil, but on his feet.

'Now you'll have to find somewhere sensible to live,' says Debs. 'Good result, as Mack would say.'

They can hear sirens in the distance. People are holding their phones up for photos – selfies, me and my mates at a train crash – or texting, passing on the disaster. Soon, everyone will know – Bromsgrove, London, Britain, the world . . .

'I'm not going home, you know,' says Debs. 'Back to Canada.'

'Ah,' says Nick. 'I wondered . . .'

Johnny appears in front of him, strangely animated, as if he's just woken from a good sleep, almost cheerful. 'Looks like we're going to have to move after all,' he says. 'You win.'

Nick hesitates, choosing his words carefully. 'It's not about winning,' he says.

'Everyone wins,' says Debs. 'Concentrate on thoughts of central heating, a solid roof, comfortable sofas. There are no losers.'

Johnny turns sideways, out of earshot from Debs. 'Look,' he says quietly to Nick, his voice urgent. 'I know it's not the best time – but – I just wanted to say: maybe we don't really need . . .' He stops, swallows, then continues quickly. 'I know you've sent the DNA off, and all that, but . . . do we have to know the results? Couldn't we just . . . let it be?'

Nick stares at him, taken by surprise. 'Well . . .' He takes a breath. Should he admit that he hasn't actually sent it? He's rung up various places, found the best quote, prepared the samples, but every time he's picked up the packet, planned to take it to the Post Office, he's hesitated and put it back in a drawer.

At first, when it all started, when the letter appeared out of nowhere, it was too much to take in. He felt as if he'd been catapulted into the air, shaken around, dropped back to earth with a crunch, wiped out. A practical joke, a hoax, someone hoping to take advantage. It was desperately important then that she shouldn't be Debs and that they should be able to prove it, so they could send her away.

But now . . . now he's realised that to depend on a mechanical test would be to acknowledge his own inadequacy. Isn't he capable of working it out for himself? He's had time to talk to her, to observe her, and he can see that she has to be Debs. She knows too much to be anyone else. Can't he trust his own instincts?

When he looks at her now, standing by him, pale and fragile, he believes that he's seeing Debs. It's no longer just a logical decision, an accumulation of evidence. Bev wouldn't have had the intelligence, the creativity, to turn into Debs, even after forty-eight years. She wouldn't have fooled anyone, only herself. Everyone else would have seen through her immediately. Her greatest achievement, in fact her only success, was to become Debs in death.

Johnny stumbles on. 'It's just – I was thinking – it probably doesn't really matter who she is – she can just be Debs. It could be like it used to be. We don't need proof, not really – it doesn't matter that much . . .'

He's afraid, thinks Nick, terrified that he's become attached to her, that she'll turn out to be an impostor and all that emotional investment will have been wasted. He doesn't want to give up the chance to believe in her.

And now that Johnny has said the words, Nick agrees with him. A sense of relief has already started to flood through him.

Johnny's right. They don't need confirmation. 'But we'd argue over who does what with her,' he says, 'who will be the one to sit next to her in hospital.'

'So what's new?' says Johnny. 'Anyway, there are two sides to a bed.'

Zohra's hearing is only returning slowly, and there's a throbbing ache in her shoulder, pain in her right ankle, her head. She suspects she's holding Crispin up as much as he's supporting her. Something is dripping down from her hairline, probably blood, but she doesn't really care. All the fear and panic of the past few years seem to have been absorbed by the crash, blasted out of her, and her mind has been emptied, swept clean, during her brief trip through space. When she hit the ground, she experienced a curious emptiness. There was nothing in her mind, nothing to threaten the unexpected peace that was flooding through her, nothing at all.

Now that her consciousness has returned, she can see how things have shifted, altered. She's been running a marathon for too long, but it's become manageable. Crispin is alongside her, his knowledge equal to hers, his understanding clearer. She can't see the finishing line – in fact, it's changed position, moved a lot further back – but to have someone at her side, supplying her with high-energy snacks and bottles of water, this is the bonus that she's only just come to appreciate. He's been there all the time. The difference is that she knows it now. And she can offer him support in return.

'What's going to happen?' she asks. 'Will the railway survive?'

'*Enigma*'s still in one piece,' says Crispin, not as defeated as she thought he might be. 'And so are we. That's the main thing.'

'But the carriages – they weren't even ours.'

'I'm not going to worry about that yet. Meanwhile, we're going to hire a crane . . .' He sounds enthusiastic already, excited. 'It'll be fun. Nathan'll . . .' He stops and sighs.

'We underestimated him, didn't we?' she says. 'He had a greater ability to create havoc than we realised.'

She can feel him tense slightly, then relax. 'No,' he says. 'Not really. Well – I suppose I should have seen it coming.'

She rubs his back gently, ignoring the pain in her shoulder. 'I don't think anyone could have predicted this.'

'They'll never let him near the railway again,' he says.

'Can you blame them?'

They're interrupted by Mimi, followed by two paramedics. 'Here we are,' she says. A young woman, with hair scraped back into a ponytail and baggy green trousers, peers at them. She puts her hand up to Zohra's forehead and touches it gently. Zohra breathes in sharply. 'We'll have to do a proper examination,' says the paramedic.

'What about Freddie?' says Zohra. 'Is he okay?'

'Just bruises, they think,' says Mimi. Loose wisps of hair are straying over her face and she's coated in soot, but she seems remarkably in control, almost as if she's enjoying it. 'No major trauma.'

'Do you know anything about Nathan?'

'They've taken him to hospital, just in case. His mum's with him.'

'It must be so hard for her,' says Zohra. But her voice sounds odd, as if it's coming from far away.

She can hear Crispin speaking, but the words aren't clear. '. . . all okay,' he's saying.

'Zohra! Zohra!' And her parents are there too, held back by a paramedic. 'Not to worry,' says her mother's voice in the distance. 'All good. We always look after you.'

A blanket is being placed over her shoulders. Her teeth are chattering. She takes a last look around before they lead her to the ambulance.

Enigma is still upright, still on the rails. The forest of shrubs and plants that were collected on its journey have been ground to a pulp by the impact with the carriages and pulverised into instant mulch. The locomotive is gleaming through the steam, shivering with triumph, emerging from the chaos as a worthy victor, a survivor. I've been resurrected once, it's saying, brought back to life by the experts. No further resurrections will be required. I never died. I'm here, ready to go, awaiting instructions.

A great hiss of steam rises into the air. Rooks that have returned to their roosts in the nearby trees since the initial shock swoop back up again, slapping their wings wildly. There are more sirens in the distance, growing steadily louder. There should be a whistle from *Enigma* in response (the sound that Nathan stole), but there's no one in the cab to pull the wire.

ACKNOWLEDGEMENTS

My thanks for all the encouragement and advice from the many different people I've encountered in the writing of this book, especially those who have attended my writing group. It's been a revelation to discover how many steam railway enthusiasts exist. And all those anonymous people who put so much detailed information online – diagrams, technical specifications, lists of all the engines ever built, videos of steam trains in operation, even records and videos of ongoing restoration work. I now know how steam engines work, how to make them work if they don't and even how to drive one. My thanks too to Carole Welch for her attention to detail – oh, those endless repetitions – and everyone else at Sceptre.